Out Of The Dark

Marshall Hughes

The Revenge Trilogy

Book 1

Copyright © 2016 Marshall Hughes
All rights reserved.
ISBN-10: 1530077206
ISBN-13: 978-1530077205

DEDICATION

IN MEMORY OF MY FATHER

CONTENTS

	PROLOGUE	1
1	KILLER INSTINCT	3
2	THE SMOKESCREEN	25
3	JUDGE JURY & EXECUTIONER	49
4	THE MISTRESS	75
5	THE INTERROGATION	103
6	NATURE OR NURTURE	133
7	LOST AND FOUND	157
8	SECRETS AND LIES	184
9	THE TRAFFICKER	212
10	THE CONFESSION	237

ACKNOWLEDGMENTS

First, I would like to thank my trusted friends, Liza Tonner and John Bell Thomson, for all the dedication and hard work in reading and commenting on my drafts. In times of despair, both gave me the encouragement to continue, to keep writing and develop the storyline/characters. Also, from the point of view of the proofreader, I would like to say a special thank you to Nicholas Grier as well as the numerous people who crossed my literary path who gave me advice on Police Scotland (Alan Murray) and creative writing techniques (Elaine Thomson), both offering support and encouragement along the way. The book would not be complete without some the images provided on the author's website/social media by ©Scott Jessiman (Front Cover: Foggy Lane), ©Gregory Crawford (3: Glencoe), © John Bell Thomson (7: Kristina Cooper) and ©John Bell Thomson (9: The Trafficker).

There is also a need to thank my gatekeepers (Group Managing Partner and Creative Partner) from *the* best advertising agency in Scotland - not just for the encouragement in completing this work of fiction, but for all the help with my academic thesis. The contemporary context and creative backdrop of the advertising sector has been inspirational in the development of my character's life.

PROLOGUE

Seven years ago

The time had come.

He had no idea what was about to happen. It was two o'clock in the morning. I lurked in the recess of a dilapidated building in a lane that led towards the New Town. I had been stalking him for the last year. He would come soon, returning home after a night with his mistress. It was just one of many extramarital affairs. The fog lingered in the night air, visibility low, apart from the flicker of light emanating from a solitary streetlamp. I heard footsteps as a silhouette appeared from the shadows, his distinguishable overcoat flapping in the wind. I knew it was him. There was no time left to change my mind. I had one chance to get it right.

He passed me oblivious of his fate.

I crept up behind him, reaching for the knife concealed in the sheath around my waist. I put one hand on his shoulder as the other swept across his neck. The blade slit his throat with precision. I clutched hold of his body as he staggered back into my arms. The sudden loss of blood was instantaneous, spilling from the gash in his neck and then, it petered out, sputtering like a dying flame.

The car was parked at the side of the road, the boot prepared with a plastic sheet. Dragging his body away from the pavement, I heaved it into the back of the vehicle. His eyes rolled to the back of his head as he moved in and out of consciousness - desperately trying to cling onto life. As a last feeble attempt his hand reached out towards me. I looked at him in disgust. Unable to speak, he stared at me with familiarity before I slammed the door shut. It was over. I left him there to bleed to death.

I felt a deep sense of sadness. It overpowered me just as much as the burning desire to kill him. At that moment, all the emotions that I felt for this man escaped from the depths of my very soul, evaporating into the night. Looking up at the dense blanket of clouds in the sky, droplets of rain brushed across my face. I saw the blood dilute, then disperse into the water, and watched as it disappeared down a drain at the side of the road.

Composing myself, I took off the overalls, leather gloves and shoes and put them in a plastic bag. I climbed into the car, driving off into the night. There was only one thing left to do: dispose of the body. No corpse, no evidence, no crime scene and no remorse for the termination of a life and my first kill. It was my first, but certainly not my last.

1

KILLER INSTINCT

"We are all evil in some form or another."
(Richard Ramirez)

Present day

Come. Come here. Come closer.

Let me whisper in your ear. Let me tell you my secrets and take you on a journey that will chill your very soul. I want to invite you into the life and mind of a serial killer. My story may fascinate you or it might disgust you but only you can decide. My name is Jayden Edward Scott; a killer with no remorse, no guilt and no fear of retribution. I am too clever to be caught, too meticulous in my method of killing and too smart to care. At thirty years old, I am a self-made millionaire; businessman, entrepreneur and venture capitalist with copious amounts of money to spend on a lavish lifestyle. I observe the London skyline from my apartment, contemplating how an innocent child can turn into a premeditated serial killer. The riverside property overlooks the Houses of Parliament, Big Ben and the River Thames. The lights from the gothic buildings ripple eerily on the soft currents of the water as the clock in the tower bellows out eleven resounding strikes. The noise startles me from my reverie of whom and what I have become. My life has taken me from a sleepy coastal town on the east coast of Scotland, to the cosmopolitan city of Edinburgh and then, towards the capital city of London and beyond.

As a young boy, I lived in a picturesque village built around a functional harbour and fishing port. It was nestled into the rugged coastline overlooking the vast expanse of the North Sea. The winding streets, cobbled pavements, ancient buildings and Presbyterian Church were all part of village life. The local minister, Reverend Charles McIntyre, christened me on the 3rd November, 1986; one and only son to Edward and Carolyn Scott. My mother taught English at the state school in the village. She became an influential member of the small community, organising the annual summer fair situated in the sprawling grounds of the church. Many local dealers came together to sell their arts and crafts - sculpture, glass, jewellery, watercolours, flowers, pottery and furniture. There was also face painting, raffles and cake stalls as well other delicious treats, especially for the children.

On the other hand, my father worked in the city of Edinburgh. I never saw him much in the early years of my life as he was always away on business. My mother explained that he worked hard to pay for our house in the village as well as his properties in Edinburgh, Argyll and London. He was a violent man with an unpredictable temper. When he did return home, there always seemed to be a lot of shouting late at night. Curled up in bed, I listened to the arguments, frightened by her cries of pain, not knowing how to help. Worse still, dark bruises - with angry looking purple blotches - appeared on my mother's arms and legs, but she never complained. He also hit me with his belt and somehow, I managed to detach myself from the reality of the situation, living my twisted childhood with some degree of normality. Despite these dark memories, I remember most of my earliest years with fondness and adventure.

It really was the epitome of village life. I liked exploring the small caves buried into the side of the precipitous cliffs with my childhood friend. I had known Kristina Cooper since nursery school. We became inseparable by the time we were ten years old. She turned out to be my best friend and confidante as well as my crab-hunting soulmate. At school, I looked forward to the end of the day, escaping the confines of the small classroom so we could make our way to the beach.

One particular summer, after returning to school after the holidays, I stopped writing. I peered over at the clock. A smile passed across my face. Just then, the shrill of the bell echoed around the school. The quiet class erupted into chaos. Kristina looked towards me, gathered up her books and dashed towards the door.

"Stop running children," shouted Miss Allen. "And... remember to do your homework." Nobody listened. We barged into each other as everyone tried to squeeze through the narrow door of the classroom. Raising her hands in the air, she said, "I give up. See you all tomorrow."

Kristina was one of the first to reach the other side. "Hurry up, Jayden," she said with a playful look on her face. "I'll race you to the beach."

"Have you brought the crab container with you?" I cried.

"I've got it in my bag. You'll lose the race if you don't hurry up."

I climbed over the school gate, closing in on her from behind. I saw Kristina darting through the narrow streets. She ran passed the pottery shop, then disappeared between the whitewashed cottages near the harbour, clambered down the grassy bank and headed towards the beach. We were both out of breath by the time we reached the shoreline. I stared up at the sky, noticing the reflection of the sun shimmering on the sea. It stretched all the way to the horizon where they both met in perfect unison.

Throwing her arms up in the air in triumph, Kristina interrupted my thoughts. "At last, I've won a race," she said. "Did you let me win? I bet you did. You did, didn't you?"

I shrugged. "Of course not!"

"You're a liar. I know you too well, Jayden Scott."

"I suppose you do!"

"Can we go to our special place? I want to search for animals in the rock pools."

"Good idea."

I stretched out my arm, offering her my hand.

She rejected the proposition. "I'm fine. I'll manage on my own."

I felt a bit deflated. "Watch you don't slip on the seaweed."

The tide was out as we clambered over the rocks and made our way towards the secluded bay. I looked at Kristina with affection, a warm fuzzy feeling developing in the pit of my stomach. The gentle breeze had forced a stray lock of hair onto her face. She twirled it around her thumb and middle finger, tucking it behind her ear. As I searched for crabs under the rocks, my friend started rummaging about in the schoolbag, took out the crab container then burrowed it into the seaweed. She looked across at me, was about to say something, but changed her mind.

"What is it?" I asked.

She turned her head away. "It's just something my mother mentioned. It's nothing. Forget it."

"Tell me… we tell each other everything."

Just then, her hand touched mine as she leaned forward and whispered in my ear. "We must always be the best of friends and never be apart. Promise!"

My mind went blank, my face flush with embarrassment and I felt hot, sweating but not sweating, paralysed with fear, not knowing what to say. *I know she likes me. We spend all of our spare time together. I do enjoy her company. Tell her!* "Always… forever," I said at last.

The awkwardness of the moment passed as we spotted a movement under the seaweed. She lifted the wrack of kelp clinging to the surface of the rock. The speckled brown shell was almost invisible against the colour of the rockweed. It scurried sideways, searching for a new hiding place in a hole in the rock. Its eyes were perched on two thin stalks, twitching at the sudden exposure to daylight. She stretched out her hand to pick it up; placing a thumb on top of the hard shell as her forefinger moved to the underside of its body, the oversized claws snapping in the air, ready to confront its attacker.

I admired her bravery. "Watch out for the pincers. You've made it angry."

"Pass the container. QUICK!" she ordered. "What are you laughing at anyway?"

"You… you're fearless!"

"I'm not scared of anything."

I watched as Kristina handled the enormous crab.

"Ouch!" she cried, as it took hold of a finger.

Droplets of red liquid splashed onto the rock. *Drip, drip, drip…*

Staring down at the blood-spattered stone, the anger I felt at that moment consumed my every thought, my eyes flashing with rage at her assailant, wanting to kill the predator for hurting my friend. Lunging forward, I was just about to snatch the crab from her hand, smash it on the ground and crush its stupid body to pieces with my foot.

She looked at my reaction. "Don't touch it."

I stopped dead in my tracks, those few words saving it from a gruesome fate.

With a look of triumph on her face, she placed the writhing crab in the container and closed the lid. Kristina put the wounded finger into her mouth, sucking the blood from the gash, spitting out red saliva onto the seaweed. I wrapped my handkerchief around the wound, tying a small knot to keep it in place. Sitting down on the sand, we huddled closer together, safe in the knowledge that the sea creature was no longer a threat. I studied the crab in more detail. Its pincers frantically clawed at the sides of the container, desperate to escape the enclosure and then, started to calm down, realising the hopelessness of the situation.

"What a beauty, Jayden."

My anger subsided. "I suppose so. I did tell you to watch out."

"I'm fine… let's put it back. The poor thing looks frightened."

She decided to return the crab back to the rock pool rather than imprison the beast in the container. We watched it scuttle back under the seaweed. Looking up towards the sky, I noticed the setting sun radiated a yellowish-red glow against the fading daylight. In the distance, the volcanic colours of the clouds moulded together like a flow of lava as wisps of black clouds merged into the fiery furnace in the atmosphere. There was an eerie silence just before I felt the warmth of the sea air brushing against my face, the swirling wind increasing in strength with each passing moment. A storm was coming. I watched it approaching as the threatening presence crept over the village.

"It's getting late," I said. "We need to go."

As we climbed over the rocks, claps of thunder rumbled overhead, the noise moving closer and closer. Forked lightning flashed across the molten sky, before meeting the ocean's surface for a few seconds - the outline of the waves rippling in the afterglow of the magnetic current.

"WOW! … look at that," she shouted. "That's spectacular."

At that moment, I grabbed her hand. This time, she had no time to refuse. "It's getting closer. Hurry up!" I cried.

We sprinted along the beach, leaping up the stairs of the stone path - two at a time. High up in the clammy atmosphere, another deafening roar of thunder rumbled overhead. **BBBOOOMMM**… **BBOOMM**… BOOM. Catching our breath for a moment, we ran towards her house.

She rushed up the path to the front door. "See you tomorrow. Hurry home before it starts to pour with rain!"

7

I waved. "I don't think I'm going to make it!"

The heavens opened up, the storm raging through the small town. I ran through the centre of the village, afraid of the electric currents flickering above me, lighting up the village for a split second before turning a deadly shade of black. The rain pelted across my face as the lights from our house came into focus. I dashed through the front door, slamming it shut behind me. *I'm safe now,* I thought to myself, *safe from harm.*

As I changed out of my wet clothes, the comforting smell of food lingered in the air. After dinner, I settled into bed to complete my homework for the following day. My mother snuggled closer, listening to the story. As she stroked my hair with her tender fingers, tiredness overpowered my weary limbs. She tucked me up, shut the book, turned off the light and closed the door. I drifted in and out of sleep, but somewhere in a conscious part of my mind, I heard the waves crashing against the rocks below our house and the wind battering on the shutters. Wrapping the covers tighter around my body, Kristina's words brought me comfort, despite the chaos that engulfed the village. *Jayden, we must always be best friends and never be apart.*

The next morning, my eyes slowly began to open, blinded by the spears of light radiating through the slits in the shutters. I rubbed the back of my hands across my eyes, listening. The storm had passed. Dragging myself out of bed, I made my way down the stairs to the welcome of my mother making breakfast. The bowl she was holding stood at an angle on the wooden surface as she beat the eggs with a whisk.

"Hi there," she said, "did you sleep well?"

"Not really. The weather was pretty bad during the night. What's for breakfast? I'm starving!"

She poured the flour over the eggs. "Pancakes and bacon. It's your favourite."

"Great!"

The tone of her voice changed. "Sit down. I've got something to tell you."

I looked at my mother with suspicion. "What?"

She sat down next to me, placing a reassuring hand over mine. "Your father is coming home this weekend. We've got some news that might upset you."

"What news?"

"We're going to be moving to Edinburgh by the end of the year."

"Why?"

"We just have to."

At that moment, I felt my whole world falling apart around me. Soon, my life here would be over - my friends, our school, the beach, and hunting for crabs with Kristina. I had to fight back the tears welling up in my eyes. "I want to stay here."

"We can't."

My fingers curled up into a ball, nails biting into my flesh as my fists came crashing down on the surface of the table. "This is our home. I don't want to go to a city I've never been to before."

"I understand... but..."

"And, I promised Kristina Cooper that we'd never be apart."

She raised an eyebrow as a faint smile flickered across her face.

What so funny about that? I pushed my chair back from the table then ran towards the kitchen door. "I'm not going. You can't make me!"

"COME BACK!" she shouted.

I ran up the stairs, crumpling into a heap on the bed, unable to control the gut-wrenching sobs from deep within my body. I felt the tears rolling down my cheeks, trickling onto my lips, tasting the salty tears in my mouth. "I hate him!" I cried. "He's the one forcing us to leave. I'm not leaving. I'll tell him that. I'm staying here in the village. Nobody is taking it from me. I'm NOT leaving my best friend."

Gaining some kind of composure, I looked at the disturbing pictures I had drawn of his face in my sketch book. Those expressionless eyes were like the vacant stare of a dead corpse, staring back at me. I threw it onto the bed, stood up and started pacing around the room. I grabbed hold of a rock from the shelf, hurling it at the mirror, cracking the surface - the fractured lines distorting my image as I stared into the shattered glass.

"I HATE HIM... HATE HIM!"

Just then, I saw my mother's broken reflection.

"Jayden... Please, calm down. It's..."

"Get out of my room," I shouted. "OUT!"

She retreated without a word of protest at my disruptive manner, but all I wanted her to do was to take me in her arms. My mother never seemed to be able to comfort me when I needed it the most. I left the house without having any breakfast, the rest of the day passing by in a haze. I avoided Kristina Cooper at school. When the bell rang, I walked home along the clifftop on my own.

Looking out across the sea, a solitary bird hovered in the sky before it dived headfirst into the water. It emerged from the sea clutching a fish in its beak, returning to its nest on a ledge on the rock face. The excitable squawking of the young birds made me think about my own situation. In contrast, I dreaded the return of my father and the decisions that would change my life forever.

As I entered the house, my mother saw me before I had time to bolt up the stairs to my bedroom. "Don't look so sad," she said, looking in my direction with pity in her eyes. "We have to sell the house as your father needs the money for a business investment."

My arms reached out. "I don't care. I don't want to leave the village. Please... can we not just stay here?" I begged.

She took hold of my hand and shook her head. "We can't stay here any longer. We can talk about this later. Your father will be home soon. I need to go and prepare the dinner."

I waited.

He was late.

Crouching against the bannister at the top of the stairs, I heard the key turning in the lock at seven forty-five. Craning my neck to get a better look, I peered at him over the railings as he walked through the front door. He was dressed in a tailored business suit hanging effortlessly against his tall frame. His striking yet most terrifying features were his menacing brown eyes - sinister and dark like his temper. Looking flustered, he paused for a moment, loosened the dimple on his tie and then, unfastened the top button of his shirt before throwing his briefcase against the coat stand.

He made his way straight towards the kitchen.

I listened to the dull tone of voices drifting up the stairs. Suddenly, I heard footsteps on the wooden floor approaching the hallway. They came to an abrupt halt. "Come down for your dinner," shouted my father.

"I'll be there in a minute."

I ran down the stairs, stopping at the bottom, waiting for him to let me past. Our eyes met only for a brief moment. He moved out of the way. I felt his threatening presence as he followed me towards the kitchen.

"Sit down. Eat your dinner."

Sliding the pasta around on my plate, I nibbled away at the meal my mother had taken so much time to prepare.

"Stop doing that," he warned.

"What?"

"Stop playing with your food."

I shuffled about on my chair. "Sorry."

"What's wrong? Do you not like it?"

"I do. I'm just not hungry that's all."

"EAT," he repeated.

"Edward, leave him alone. He's upset that we have to leave the village."

"You've told him?"

"I have…"

With a trite look on his face - devoid of any kind of real emotion - my father explained the situation through what he thought was a meaningful speech. He started his conversation full of confidence and ended it full of anger. "It's for the best. You'll see. It's time that we all lived together as a proper family. I miss you both very much. We need to sell the house for a business investment. It is guaranteed to make us a lot of money. Your new house is just as beautiful as this one in a lovely part of Edinburgh. You'll have your own room. We've already found you a local school. You'll make new friends and move on from this… this *small* village. Living in Edinburgh will bring more opportunities for you in later life. It has excellent universities if you choose to stay and study there."

"I don't care. You can't make me. I'm staying here. I want to be with my friends," I declared.

He stared in my direction, his icy stare stopping me in my tracks, paralysing me for what seemed like an eternity. Out of desperation, I pointed at my mother in need of her support. "She doesn't want to go either." My voice began to get louder and louder. "I'm not going. I hate you! I'm not going," I yelled.

He clenched his fists, banging them on the table just as I had done earlier in the day to my mother. *"NEVER…* speak to me like that again, you spoiled little brat. I know what's best for our family." He leaned forward, his threatening eyes glaring at me for challenging him. It seemed as if all of his anger was focused in that one stare, and if it were a weapon, then that devastating look could easily win an entire world war.

My words tailed off as I looked at him, then at my mother, then back towards my father. "I'm sorry. I didn't mean to upset you. I don't... I didn't... mean to... upset... you."

Now I'm in trouble, I thought to myself. I knew from experience his behaviour was unpredictable. *What have I done?* Glancing at the belt around his waist, I dreaded the consequences of my actions. He stood up and stared at me, his lips pursing together and those brown eyes flashing with rage.

I froze.

She grabbed his arm.

My mother's calm demeanour quickly changed as a look of terror passed across her face, trembling at the possible consequences of my outburst. "Don't you bloody touch him, Edward."

This is bad, I thought, s*he never swears.*

He turned, striking her across the face. She fell to the ground, crying on the floor, curled up like a frightened animal as his foot kicked her in the stomach. "Stop interfering, you stupid bitch."

"Don't, Edward," she gasped, trying to catch a breath. "Our baby..."

He bent down, pressing his forehead against her brow. "How many times do I have to tell you, I don't want another child. Why do you always undermine my authority? You and that boy, you're a pair of fucking idiots."

I looked at him in disbelief. "LEAVE HER ALONE!"

He stood up, focusing his attention on me instead. "Shut the fuck up."

Striding towards the table, he swept his arm over the top if it - the plates and glasses smashing into pieces on the hard tiles.

"I'm sorry," I said, shaking uncontrollably.

In a flash, my father seized my arm. I tried to resist - kicking and screaming - as he dragged me up the stairs and threw me onto the bed. My heart was pounding in my chest as I saw his hands coming towards me. With a powerful grip, he started to shake my body.

"You disrespectful little bastard," I heard him saying under his breath. "We're all leaving by the end of the year whether *you* like it or not. Do you understand? Answer me!"

I whimpered. "I understand. I do… I'm sorry, Daddy."

Looming over me, he unfastened his belt, never taking his gaze away from my eyes. It glided from around his waist with one swipe of his arm. He let it fall to his side, the pin on the buckle at the end of the strap hissing at me like a venomous snake, ready to attack. I watched him as he threaded the end of the belt through the clasp, tightening it around his knuckles to get a firmer grip. He folded it in half to shorten the length before pulling it apart and snapping it shut… CRACK!

I was petrified.

In anticipation, I curled up into a ball, my arms protecting my head, my knees hugging into my chest. *I'm like that frightened crab hiding in the hole of the rock, but for me, there is no escape.* Breathing heavily, he raised the belt above his head and brought it down with such a force, focusing on exposed areas of skin, lashing out at my arms, legs and back, stinging my body, striking me like the lightning hitting the surface of the ocean. I winced in pain, shouting at him to stop, but he ignored me. Unable to bear it anymore, I pleaded with him.

"DON'T HURT ME ANYMORE… STOP, DADDY," I shouted. "HELP ME, MUMMY… *PLEASE* HELP ME."

Despite my desperate pleas, the physical attack was relentless. I saw my mother standing at the door, watching in the shadows. Her motionless silhouette appeared as a ghostly white figure through my tear-stained eyes, almost like an apparition. I received *the* worst beating of my life, beaten into submission into leaving the village by the time I was eleven years old.

****

I mentally return to the recognisable setting of the apartment overlooking the River Thames. Unable to relax, my body refuses to find comfort as I stare out into the murky night. The apartment is familiar, but tonight, it disturbs me. There is only a hint of light from the crescent-shaped moon. It is hiding behind the overcast clouds scattered across the threatening night sky. The darkness usually calms me, but now, I find it menacing. A shiver passes through my body remembering the attack and the relentless beating, anger and physical strength of a mentally unhinged parent like a sinister shadow overpowering a helpless child. I dismiss the thought, refusing to dwell on the gruesome episodes of the past for any length of time. I find a more comfortable position on the sofa, wrap my arms around a cushion, thinking back to the day we left the village and moved to our new home in the city.

The house was in chaos. Rushing around in a panic, my mother was trying to pack up the last minute objects. As I lay sprawled on the couch - trying to watch my favourite television programme - I heard her shouting on me from the hallway.

"Jayden, where are you?"

She must have heard voices coming from the sitting room. I heard footsteps marching towards my destination. Standing in front of me with a box, my mother pointed a finger in my direction. "Stop watching that. Give me a hand. We don't have much time left before the removal van arrives."

"You're in the way."

Shifting my head, I tried to continue watching the programme. She snatched the remote control from my hand, aimed it at the television and switched it off. Looking frustrated, my mother drew in a deep breath and placed a hand on her hip.

"Please help me. We've only got two hours left to finish the packing. Can you get all the things out of your room and put them in this box. Here... take it."

I found myself sneering, the corner of my lip tightening on one side of my face, glaring at her with contempt through the narrow slits in my eyes.

She stood in front of me with an angry look on her face, the course words taking me by surprise. "Don't you dare look at me like that, you rude little boy. Go *now*. I'm not telling you again. Please don't give me any of your bullshit today. I'm not in the mood. We just need to get all this done - do it now!"

"Okay, okay! I'll clear it out." I took the box out of her hand. "I'm sorry. I'll do it."

She let out a sigh of relief. "Thanks, sweetheart. I also have to go to see Reverend McIntyre in an hour, so be finished by the time I get back."

I sat on the edge of the bed, looking around the room. All I had left to pack were my pyjamas, a few favourite books, my sketch pad, some toys and the rock collection. I stared at the different colours of stones inside the glass case. My eyes were drawn to the Blood Stone;

the dark green almost black colour of the smooth stone was speckled with deep red streaks. I liked the Red Jasper rock better as it looked like a crab shell. My favourite was the Emerald Calcite; the colours radiating from the stone like the sun shimmering on the ocean. It reminded me of our crab-hunting adventures. *I really should go to see Kristina before I go, but I'm still angry with her*, I thought to myself.

We had fallen out a few weeks before, when I declared we were leaving the village. She told me that my mother had told her mother and that her mother had told Kristina about it. She was going to reveal the truth to me on the beach - the day the crab nipped her finger - but decided against it. Furious that my best friend had kept it a secret, I said, "Why didn't you tell me?" I never waited for a reply and stormed off in a huff.

Blocking her from my mind, it did not take long to pack everything into the box. I sat on the edge of the bed, wondering what our new life would be like in Edinburgh. Just then, the noise of the door knocker echoed around the house. I presumed that it was one of my mother's friends coming to say goodbye.

"It's Kristina," my mother shouted, "she wants to see you."

"Tell her to go away."

Several moments passed before I heard my mother's footsteps bound up the stairs. "Stop being so childish, you silly boy. Go and speak to her. Kristina is waiting for you." She grabbed the top of my jumper, pulling me out of the bedroom door. "Get going. Don't be too long."

I ran down the stairs and looked around the side of the door. She had gone. The little voice inside my head convinced me to go. *You need to say goodbye. Your mother is right, stop being silly*. Grabbing a pair of trainers, I pushed my feet into them and ran out of the door. I saw her walking across the grassy bank close to the side of the cliff heading towards the harbour.

"Wait for me. Come back," I shouted. "I'm sorry. I didn't mean it."

She turned to view her pursuer then kept on walking.

I caught up. "Please stop…"

Kristina turned to look at me.

"Don't be upset… I'm sorry," I said.

"I don't want you to go. We've been friends for a long time. I don't know what I'll do without you."

"You have lots of other friends. We'll come back and visit you."

"You won't. You'll forget about me once you go away. I know you will."

"I won't," I promised.

Not knowing how to reassure her, we sat down on the grassy embankment. I looked out over the ocean at the seagulls hovering above the water - swirling and screeching in the distance. We talked about our years together at nursery school; the time I cut my hand on a sharp edge on a trike and ended up in hospital, the endless hours we played together in the sand pit and the crazy boy who chewed the sole of his shoe at story time. We burst out laughing. As our sniggering subsided, all that was left was an awkward silence apart from the faint shrill of the birds in the distance.

I took hold of her hand. "I need to go now," I said. "We'll be back to see you."

"I'll miss you."

I felt my face flush with embarrassment. "I'll miss you, too."

I left her sitting on the grassy embankment. Looking back, tears trickled down my cheek as she faded away into the distance. *You should have said goodbye properly, you stupid idiot.* The heart-wrenching ache in my chest was overwhelming. It felt like my whole world had come to an end. I desperately needed my mother to comfort me, to make the pain go away.

As I walked towards the front of the house, the removal truck was parked in the driveway. Two men were loading our possessions into the van. Still feeling tearful, I went to find my mother. Out the corner of my eye, I saw her turning at the top of the street. *She must be away to see Reverend McIntyre.* Running as fast I could, but still some distance away, I watched her leaving Mrs Cameron's shop with a bunch of flowers and then, make the short trip towards the church. Once my mother disappeared inside the sandstone building, I bolted past the old gravestones on either side of the path. Reaching for the metal handle on the wooden door, I turned it and tiptoed into the vestibule. Listening to the voices echoing from within, I pressed my head against the adjoining door, eavesdropping on the conversation through the stained glassed window.

"Carolyn, are you sure you're doing the right thing?" he said. "I've been really worried about both of you. What's been going on? Why has Jayden been off school so much?"

She sounded flustered. "Nothing's going on. He's been ill with tonsillitis."

"Tell me the truth," he shouted. "Did Edward do something to him? I know he hits you. I'm not stupid."

My mother lied. "No!" she exclaimed. "He would never hurt our child. Don't worry. This is a chance for us to be a proper family again. Everything will be fine once we leave."

"Why do you defend him all the time?"

"I don't."

"You do."

"I don't."

He sighed. "I say what I'm going say, not as a man of the church, but as a friend. You must leave him. It's only going to get worse once you go to Edinburgh. At least you have friends here. I've come across men like him before. Please... don't go."

"We have to. The house has already been sold. We need the money."

"No... *he* needs it."

She paused. "I love him."

"You call that love? He would not abuse you in the way he does if he loved you."

"He doesn't. Edward just loses his temper sometimes."

"The reality is that you live in fear from the man you love. He humiliates, dominates and controls you. Listen to what I'm saying to you, Carolyn."

"It's not like that. I deserve it sometimes."

"For heaven's sake," he said, "don't say things like that."

"Don't worry. I'll stay in contact with you and let you know how we're getting on. It will get better."

"I can see that I'm not going to be able to change your mind. Don't ever let him touch the boy... or you, for that matter."

She lied again. "I won't."

"Jayden has a special place in my heart... you both do. We've known each other all our lives, grown up together and shared a lot of our life experiences. I care about what happens to you."

"Thanks."

"Are you sure you're okay?"

My mother started to cry. "Not really."

"What's wrong?"

"The past few weeks have all been a bit much," she said. "I lost the baby. I know it was still in the early stages. It was my own fault."

I wanted to shout out loud. *It's not your fault. It's my father's fault. Tell him, he kicked you in the stomach! Tell him, he killed the baby!*

"I'm so sorry. Don't blame yourself."

There was silence for a few minutes. I turned to leave the vestibule, knocking over a vase of flowers perched upon a stone column. The impact of the breaking glass echoed around the empty church. *Damn, what have I done!*

"Who's there?" bellowed the Reverend.

Before I had time to leave, the door opened. He looked at me in surprise. A fleeting glance and a questioning look passed between him and my mother.

"Jayden," he cried. "How long have you been here?"

"I didn't hear anything… I promise. I've just arrived. I'm sorry… about the flowers."

"Are you okay? Leave that. I'll clear it up later. Come over here, boy."

Why does he speak to me like that? I'm not his boy!

He took my arm, leading me into the church, pointing at the wooden seat. "Sit down. Are you looking forward to moving to your new house?"

"Not really," I said. "I want to stay here."

The Reverend could see I was upset. He wrapped a protective arm around my neck, squeezing my shoulder. "It will take time for you to settle in. Your mother is already making plans to come back and see us."

"It won't be the same. I like living here," I told him.

"You'll be fine, I'm sure you will. It's a whole new adventure for you."

"I suppose so."

My mother went to get her bag and picked up the bunch of flowers lying on the pew at the front of the church. As she stopped at the communion table next to the pulpit, her hand reached out to touch the old bible. She opened the leather-bound cover, flicked through it and stopped to read the sacred text. Looking up at the wooden cross hanging on the stone wall, she whispered something as her fingers touched the pages of the book.

The Reverend said, "Remember I'm always here for you, boy.

Take care of yourself and your mother."

Before I could reply, she walked back up the aisle clutching the bouquet of red roses. "It's time to go. Say goodbye to Reverend McIntyre. I'll meet you back at the house.

I hesitated. "Okay…"

"Off you go then. I'm going to put some flowers on your grandparents' grave. I'll see you back at the house."

"Shall I come with you?"

She was very dismissive. "I need to go on my own."

As a farewell gesture, Reverend McIntyre nodded in my direction. He then stretched out his arms and embraced my mother. She kissed him on the cheek before resting her head on his shoulder. He flicked his hand at me to leave them alone.

"Goodbye," I said.

Kicking the stones on the cobbled driveway, I headed down the path towards the main street. *He knows what's going on. Why doesn't he help us? But she doesn't want his help. I don't understand. It's so confusing. Why did she not tell him the truth about my father?* As I walked past the memorial in the centre of the village, Mrs Cameron was planting some winter pansies in the wooden troughs. Her big bum wiggled up and down as she bent over the tub, digging into the dirt. I sniggered away to myself. It cheered me up as I walked towards the house.

My mother arrived home some time later. I could tell she was upset. Her eyes were bloodshot. "I needed some time alone with my parents."

"I know."

"We're all packed up and ready to go," interrupted the driver.

She was extremely direct and full of confidence when speaking to people other than my father. "Here are the keys to the house in Edinburgh. We'll follow you shortly. See you there. Just start unpacking the boxes as soon as you arrive. Thanks for your help."

"No problem. See you there."

She started rummaging about in her handbag. "Here are the keys. Go to the car. Wait for me there."

I did as I was told.

Rain started falling from the dark clouds hovering over the village, pelting against the windscreen. I sat in the passenger seat and waited. *What's taking her so long?* Ten minutes later, I saw her emerge from the house, lock the door, wipe a tear from her eye and stride towards the car. My mother put the key in the ignition then turned on the wipers. "Right... this is it. Let's go and start our new life."

I dreaded the thought of living with my father on a regular basis. I wondered what was in store for us. I gazed out of the window, refusing to look back as we drove out of the village towards our new life in Edinburgh.

****

Back at the apartment, I get up from the sofa and think to myself, *that young, naïve boy has gone now.* A reflection catches my eye in the mirror above the fireplace. I scrutinise the image looking back. *Does it show in my face that I am a killer?* Standing at six feet tall, my physique is slender yet muscular due to an interest in martial art. My masculine eyes are the deepest shade of brown, shielded by dark, thick eyebrows set against a natural skin tone. My short hair is swept back off my brow, but slightly longer than I prefer. I have high cheekbones with a defined jawline, prominent nose and straight but full lips that slightly curve up at the end. In need of a shave, a short growth has appeared around my upper lip and jawbone.

My mouth twitches.

A victorious but devious smile passes across my face. I think about the celebratory bottle of wine waiting for me in the kitchen. After all, tonight is the night to commemorate the life and death of my father. Earlier in the evening, I received an unexpected phone call. I received the news that I had waited seven, long, anxious years to hear.

I recall the conversation.

"Can I speak to Jayden Edward Scott," said the authoritative voice on the other end of the phone.

"Who's that?"

"It's Mathew... Mathew Fleming, your father's business partner and executor of his estate."

"How are you? Is everything okay?"

"Yes, but I've been in touch with the solicitor dealing with Edward's affairs. She obtained a declarator of death from the High Court. In Scotland, a person who is missing for more than seven years is officially declared dead."

At last! "I see..."

"It means that the death certificate can now be signed. The estate can be divided up between his close family members."

I grinned. "That's fantastic news. Sorry... I don't mean to be disrespectful. At least now, we can expect a bit of closure, especially for my mother."

"I understand."

"Actually, it's been a traumatic time for everyone not knowing exactly what happened to him, Mathew."

"I agree. The sudden disappearance of your father needs some kind of closure for all members of your family," he said with concern.

"Finally... hopefully... we can all move on now."

"I'm sure you will. I've also been in touch with your mother. She's upset by the news. Can you make sure you give her the comfort she deserves? I know you're busy in London at the moment, but she needs your support. Can you call her, please?"

"I'll call her later tonight," I promised.

"Good. I'll be in touch shortly to let you know when the estate has been finalised."

"Thanks very much for all your help, Mathew. It's much appreciated."

"It's my pleasure. Take care of yourself. Goodbye."

As he disconnected the call, the phone remained in my hand, suspended in mid-air. I stared at it in disbelief. Time stood still as the ramifications of his words registered in my mind. I never expected the declarator of death to happen so soon. After his phone call, the rest of the evening has passed by in a haze as I find myself reminiscing about Kristina Cooper, our village, the beating from my father and the family's sudden departure to our new home in Edinburgh.

At this moment in time, having to call my mother preys heavily on my mind. *The celebratory bottle of wine can wait a little while longer. I better phone her now. It's not going to be an easy conversation.*

Despite the late hour, I dial the number.

She answers it without hesitation, her voice tinged with an element of hysteria. "Have you heard the terrible news about your father? This is awful. He's never coming back. What's happened to him?"

"Calm down. Listen to me. We don't know what's happened to him. I suspect we never will."

My mother starts to cry, trying to catch her breath. "I'm... it...

the news is so unpleasant," she stammers. "He's dead, officially dead."

"I know. The torture is finally over. It's been a long seven years and the courts have made the decision. Deep down we've known that is the horrible truth."

"I understand that… it's just all very official. Can you come home soon?" she pleads. "I need you here with me for a while."

"I'm dealing with some very important business at the moment. I'm going to try and make it back to Edinburgh by the beginning of next week."

My mother sighs. "Okay."

"You need some time alone to come to terms with the news. Be strong. Mathew can sort out his will with the solicitor. After that we'll be able to organise a memorial with his colleagues, friends and family. Does that sound reasonable?"

She sounds much calmer. "That would be lovely. You're very considerate."

"Promise me, you'll take care of yourself. Call anytime you need to talk. Agreed?"

"Agreed."

"Now get some rest. It's late. You must be tired."

"You're right. I'm exhausted. Call me tomorrow. Promise…"

"Yes."

"Good night," she says, "I love you."

"I love you, too."

With a sense of relief, the conversation is over. I throw the telephone onto the couch and head towards the kitchen. It is time to draw a line under the whole sordid affair. In an almost ritualistic manner, I prepare myself to celebrate his official death. The expensive bottle of wine stands majestically on the sturdy granite surface, waiting for an expert hand to open it. I lift the bottle, release the sharp blade attached to the corkscrew, ready to encircle the foil cover that protects the ruby red liquid encased inside. The cork is perfectly in line with the bottle lip. I wind the corkscrew down into the stopper without piercing the base to prevent any dust polluting the old vintage. With a strong but steady hand, the extraction is a smooth and effortless transition. I feel myself becoming aroused as the intoxicating smell of the earthy, aromatic tones of the forest releases itself from the depths of its enclosure.

I leave it to breathe and return to the living area. The marble surround of the fireplace dominates the open plan room. I light the fire, watching the flames bursting into life. A change of clothes is necessary. I take off my business suit and put on some casual attire. The comfort of the fabric feels soft against my cold skin. I return to the kitchen to select a crystal engraved wine glass and realise that I have not eaten anything all day. Opening the fridge, I find a solution to satisfy the empty feeling in my stomach deciding on some seaweed cones filled with raw fish, rice and vegetables. I take my meal, as well as the wine glass, placing them on the wooden table positioned in front of the fire. I head back towards the kitchen to get the bottle of wine, careful not to disrupt the sediment at the bottom. The elegant curves of the bottle feel sensual to the touch. I place it on top of the mantelpiece. The smouldering red, yellow and amber flames dance together in the fireplace, providing a warm glow against the sublime skyline. As I collapse onto the seat in front of the fire, my mouth devours the sushi. I take in a deep, exhilarating breath as I pour the wine. The blood red fluid flows into the glass with grace. The taste of the wine is *exquisite*. I turn on the music player. The chilling piano melody is almost ecclesiastical, accompanied by the haunting tone of the vocalist reverberating around the apartment.

The words of the song are a distraction.

"Procedamus in pace in nomine Christi, Amen (Let's go forth in peace in the name of Christ)."

"Dis-mois, qu'est ce que tu vas chercher (Tell me, what is it that you seek)?"

"Closure," I say, to the vocalist.

"Dis-moi, pourquoi l'evangile du mal (Tell me, why the gospel of evil)?"

The words register in my mind, but I ignore it, think about a reply, and then answer. "My father's the evil one, not me."

Standing in front of the window, I raise the glass up in the air. Looking out into the depths of the night sky, water droplets begin to brush against the pane of glass. "This is the ultimate revenge for everything you put us through. Here's to your death, you bastard," I say out loud. "Congratulations from this finest vintage from your very own wine cellar."

"Si tu est contre Dieu, tu es contre l'homme (If you are against God, you are against man)."

"Shut the fuck up!" I shout at the singer.

With a feeling of closure, my final words are full of venom. My glass rises up to acknowledge the rain falling from the tear-filled clouds in the sky. "May your soul *never* find any kind of peace… E*V*ER," I cry out in trembling voice.

I sink to my knees in front of the window, holding my head in my hands.

The relief that engulfs me is overwhelming.

"Es-tu diabolique ou divin (Are you diabolical or divine)?"

I'm certainly not divine, I think to myself.

A few tears trickle down my face, not for the loss of a father, but the relief that he is finally and legally presumed 'DEAD'.

2

THE SMOKESCREEN

"I know who I am and who I may be, if I choose."
(Don Quixote)

Daylight.

A noise, somewhere in the distance, disrupts my sleep. It is the familiar tone of the mobile phone from an unknown hiding place somewhere in the apartment. It is persistent. I ignore it. The pain in my head feels bitter sweet, but my body responds to the warmth of the bed covers. I ignore it. Looking around the room, the clothes from the night before are discarded on the floor and the crystal glass stands empty on the bedside table. A feeling of relief passes over me as I recall the events of the previous evening. For a split second, my thoughts return to the moment the blade slashed across his throat. I ignore it. Today is a day to relax. My business meeting is not until tomorrow, so the day is mine to do what I want. Seeing my wrist watch lying beside the empty glass, I stretch over to check the time. It is eleven thirty already. There is no hurry to get up, but I need the toilet.

Leaving the warmth of the bed, I rush towards the bathroom to empty my bladder. The cold feeling of the tiles permeates through my entire body. I shudder and turn on the tap. *It's bloody freezing in here.* Cupping my hands together, I splash some water over my face. It feels refreshing. Reaching for the bath robe on the back of the door, I wrap it around my naked body in need of some warmth, turn on the fire in the sitting room and go to the kitchen to make some coffee.

I feel a dull pain start to accumulate behind my eyes. The coffee beans smell delicious. The machine grinds the beans ready for brewing, but the noise grates in my head. It is almost unbearable. I turn the knob on the steamer, transforming the liquid into a creamy froth. When the espresso is ready, I transfer the coffee into my favourite cup then add the milk, the cushion of foam settling on the top. The coffee tastes divine: robust, smooth and nutty. I take it into the living area and find the phone down the side of the sofa. I notice that there is one missed call and a text, both from Jacquelyn Hayes.

> Your mother told me you were in London! Call or text back. I can come round tonight if you're not busy. I'll bring dinner. You get the wine. Let me know. Missed you baby. Jacques xx ☺

As I become more wrapped up in my own thoughts, the flat is beginning to stifle me. I need a distraction, so text her back to arrange dinner for seven o'clock. I look forward to some company.

> Hi there. Seven o'clock is fine. Sorry, I've not been in touch. Just been really busy! See you then. I've got a lovely bottle of white chilling in the fridge. Look forward to seeing you x

Sitting in the chair next to the fire, I enjoy the fresh yet bitter aroma of the coffee, the taste sensation bringing some light relief to the heavy feeling in my head. Staring into the light, I lose myself in the serenity of the flames as I recall the latter years of my childhood in Edinburgh.

We left the village behind. It was a typical winter's day as the rain pelted against the car. My mother was quiet for most of the trip. I became fixated by the smooth tone of the wind screen wipers. They brought me some kind of comfort on the lonely journey. Several hours later, we approached the crossing towards the city. I rubbed the condensation from the window, gazing up at the impressive structure suspended across the water. The beacons on top of the two metal towers flashed in unison against the fading daylight and huge pillars supported a line of cables swooping down over the bridge. Attached to the thick wires were hanging ropes of steel, glistening in the dark from the reflection of the headlamps, falling to the ground like spears of light. The road was sandwiched in between the cables, metal ropes and colossal concrete blocks which disappeared into the depths of the flowing river below. My heart started to beat faster as the traffic slowed down, converging at the start of the bridge.

"Is it safe?" I asked.

Her hand reached out and squeezed mine. "Of course it's safe, sweetheart. There's no need to be scared. It's just a bridge. You've been across it before."

"I can't remember that."

"When you were younger," she said, "on our way back from our holiday home."

Apart from the trips to our cottage on the west coast of Scotland, I realised what a sheltered life I had led, focused around the familiar setting of the villages scattered along the coastline. *I'm going to miss it.*

Holding back the tears, I asked, "Are we nearly there?"

"It's not that far now."

"What's it like?"

"What's what like? I need to concentrate on my driving. There's so much traffic. I'm not used to it. There's also a speed restriction because of the bad weather."

"Sorry…"

She passed me a bottle of water. "Do you want a drink?"

"Thanks."

We headed across the bridge, the endless line of cars wedged together nose to tail, crawling along at a slow speed. The further we proceeded across the bridge, the force of the howling air increased as the strength of the crosswinds intensified, battering against the side of the vehicle. Rubbing the glass free of condensation, I peered through the window. I had visions of the car being blown off the bridge and landing in the murky water below. Twitching around on my seat, I noticed the water cascading down the front of the window and at last, I saw the toll booth coming into focus through the windscreen wipers.

"We've made it," I whispered.

"What did you say?"

She took no notice that I had not replied and pointed to the compartment holding the water bottles. "Find me some money in there would you… quick, sweetheart."

"How much do you want?"

"Just give me the change."

My mother rolled down the window to pay the toll charge. Rain leapt through the opening, spraying water across her face. She wiped it away with her sleeve and pressed the button to wind it back up. "It's not long now. We're nearly there."

As we approached the other side of the bridge, the wind subsided.

I let out a huge sigh of relief. *Whew!* "What's it like... our new house?"

"Well... it's part of a village just off the city centre."

My heart skipped a beat. "How can you have a village in a city?"

"You just can! It's a small part of a larger city with its own unique character. Edinburgh is built around a group of extinct volcanoes which is why there are so many different levels. The landscape fluctuates between steep hills, medieval lanes, terraces, street-level walkways and sharp declines into hidden valleys housing smaller villages. These places are Edinburgh's hidden treasure," she said, in a mysterious tone of voice.

"In what way?" I asked. "Is that where we're going to live?"

She nods and explained that it was a secluded area that was once famous for its mill houses. The water wheels for grinding the grain were powered by the river, which at one point, had carved out the shape of the land surrounding the village.

"That's quite exciting!"

She pointed a finger. "Look... just below that arched bridge over there. That's where we're going."

My mother diverted away from the main road - away from the mayhem of chaotic traffic - descending down a steep hill into the heart of the village.

I caught my breath.

She looked over in my direction. "It's beautiful, don't you think?"

I nodded, staring out of the window.

The reflection of the white Christmas lights sparkled like diamonds in the branches of the trees at the side of the road. Festive banners stretched across the buildings with illuminated shapes of reindeer, stars and bells. As we drove through the village, the glow from the streetlamps unearthed a labyrinth of passageways that intertwined though the centre of the town like an animal's lair, revealing an eclectic mix of industrial buildings, converted mill houses, new developments, traditional mews and period houses which all meshed together to give it a distinct identity.

I like it, I thought to myself. "Where's our house?"

"It's just at the other end of this road. It's a tall building over three levels. The back garden leads down to the footpath beside the river. It was your father's parents' house before we bought *your* home in *our* village."

Getting excited, I said, "It sounds great."

"I know you'll like it here."

As we approached the driveway, I saw his stern face speaking to the removal man. *What's he doing here? Why's he not working?* My body stiffened with tension. I glared at him through the window. He waved at my mother as she parked the car. Turning off the engine, she got out and ran towards him. My father slipped his arm around her waist and then, his hand flicked in the air, beckoning me to get out of the vehicle.

"Where do you want all the boxes, Mrs. Scott?"

"What's your problem?" my father said, "just take them into the house and put them in the hallway."

"I just wanted to check with your wife first."

"Well... here she is," he snapped, "you can ask her yourself now."

"Calm down, Edward. They're all labelled. Just take them into the house. I'll be there in a minute," she told the driver.

"Fucking stupid idiot," said my father.

"Remember your language... our son is here."

"Okay, okay. Come on, Jayden," he shouted, "welcome to your new home."

A knot developed in the pit of my stomach, the muscles tightening in my abdomen, twisting and turning like a carnival ride, making me feel nauseous. I walked towards him, fearful of his temper and those dark brown eyes. His hand reached out to touch my shoulder. I flinched, recoiling from the condemned hand that beat me like an animal, forcing me to leave the village. *I HATE YOU!*

He put his hand back down then took my mother's arm instead, leading her into the house. I shuffled behind them, gazing up at *his* home, wondering what it would be like to live there - what *he* would be like now that we were together on a permanent basis.

He interrupted my thoughts. "I'll show you up to your room. You can unpack some of the boxes. Leave me and your mother alone to catch up. Okay?"

I agreed.

My bedroom was on the third floor. On the way up the stairs, we saw the removal man. Leaning against the wall, he allowed us to pass. My father said to him, "Are you finished now? "Sorry about before... it's just been a long day."

"No problem."

As we approached the third floor landing, he stretched out his arm, pushing open the door to reveal not only the contents of the room, but also the sharp smell of paint. It irritated my nose, catching at the back of my throat, making me feel light-headed. Composing myself, I walked over to the bay window. One of them was slightly ajar. I heard the tranquil murmur of the river flowing outside, drifting up through the opening, bringing some kind of comfort, despite the strange feeling of being in a new house.

I turned around.

He watched me, intently.

My eyes focused on the double bed, spacious wardrobe, chest of drawers and wooden bookcase tucked under the eaves of the roof. Boxes were strewn across the carpet, waiting to be unpacked. The removal man had slit open the tape with a knife. It was lying on the floor. I picked it up - hypnotically drawn to the shiny blade - looked at the razor-sharp edge for a few seconds and then, handed it to my father.

"Watch yourself. That's dangerous," he said, slipping it into his pocket. "Do you like your room?"

He looked in my direction for approval.

I avoided his gaze.

"I painted it for you this morning."

"Thanks... it's my favourite colour of blue."

"So you like it?"

I nodded my head.

"Jayden... look at me."

I looked at him out the corner of my eye. "What?"

"The night I lost my temper... I'm sorry. I didn't mean to hurt you like that, but you made me so angry. It won't happen again, as long as you behave yourself."

"Okay." *What else could I say! I don't believe you. You're a liar!*

He took a deep breath. I thought he was going to embark upon a lengthy speech. His eyes rolled upwards, thinking about what to say next. *Here we go*, I thought to myself. "I want us all to have a good Christmas this year. Now that we're all here together, everything is going to change. The money from the house has allowed me to become a partner in the consultancy business. You have the opportunity to go to a prestigious school in Edinburgh. Are we all good?"

"Yes," I told him.

He squeezed my shoulder. "Unpack your boxes. Come down when you're finished. I'll make us some dinner."

Maybe he can change, I thought to myself, *just maybe*.

****

I settled into the house much easier than I imagined. Despite the incident with the removal man, my father appeared to be in an amicable mood. As I sorted out my belongings, I heard the sound of infectious laughter drifting up the stairs, giving me hope about our new life together. When I went downstairs, my mother was unpacking while my father prepared the meal, the upbeat noise of his whistling floating out of the kitchen was a comfort to hear, the melodic sound filling my heart with optimism that he could change.

"Come and help me, sweetheart," said my mother. She was raking about in a cupboard, pulling out bags of Christmas decorations to hang on the tree. "Take this one. Put it over there. We can do it after our meal."

"The dinner is ready," he shouted.

"We're just coming," I replied.

Sitting around the table, we enjoyed the meal my father had prepared. I seemed more at ease in his presence. My mother was also in a good mood. He started to tell me about my new school. "You need to go and do the entrance exam. You'll be doing it after Christmas, just before the term starts."

"Why do I need to do that?"

"It's a private school, so we pay for your education. You have to sit a test to be able to go there. You need to pass it first."

I looked at my mother.

"It's nothing to worry about. You'll do well. You're a bright boy. Most of the children will be boarders, but I'll drop you off in the morning and pick you up when you finish."

"What's it like? Is it like the school at home?"

"It's a lot bigger. It's very different from the village school. I'm sure you'll like it," she said.

"I miss Kristina."

"I know you do. You'll make new friends."

"I hope so."

"You're a silly boy. Of course you will."

Everything in our house was peaceful over the festive period. It was one of the best times of my childhood.

Several weeks later, the time came to do the entrance exam. It was an overcast winter's day. I felt excited as we made our way through the busy traffic in Edinburgh. My mother parked the car in the sprawling grounds that encircled the school. I stared up at the gothic structure with wide eyes. *It looks really scary*, I thought to myself. My fingers slipped into her hand as we walked up the driveway towards the building, my heart pounding in my chest, the fear evident as my grip tightened around her hand.

My mother looked at me with a reassuring smile. "Come on," she said, tugging on my arm. "There's nothing to be afraid of, sweetheart."

"Are you sure?"

She laughed. "Of course."

I remember to this day, the monumental scale of the castle-like-structure, its dark haunting features bearing down on us as we walked along the wide path towards the stairs; giant steps waiting like a mouthful of rotten teeth, ready to devour and swallow me up. A spine-chilling shudder swept through my body. *It's like a haunted castle*, I thought to myself. The school stood sombre yet proud against the murky skyline. Huge windows in the main part of the building dominated the surface of the stone walls as smaller ones nestled into the slate roof, jutting out like bulging eye sockets, peering over the extensive grounds and surrounding woodland. My eyes wandered up towards the conical shaped turrets curved around the end of the building with crow-stepped parapets ascending to the top of the roof and the peak of the tapering spire, pointing up… up… up… into the sky.

Glancing nervously around, I walked up the staircase leading towards the entrance, gargoyles staring out of small crooks hidden in the stone walls, distorted shapes of faces staring at me. I shuffled my body closer into her side. Just then, a figure appeared at the entrance of the grand hallway, walking towards us with an air of authority in his step, confident in his demeanour.

"Welcome to our school, Mrs. Scott." He stretched out his hand.

"I am the Headmaster, Richard Spencer. It's a pleasure to meet you both."

She shook his hand. "Please, call me Carolyn."

Headmaster Spencer was a distinguished looking man, dressed in a smart suit with a kind face and nurturing eyes, his fixed gaze never leaving my worried-looking expression. He put his arm around my shoulder, guiding me into the school. "Let's get you settled in to do the entrance exam. While you are doing that, I can speak to your mother." He led me to a small room just off the hallway. "My assistant will take care of you. We'll come back and get you once you've finished. Are you okay?"

Letting go of her hand, I forced myself to leave my mother's side, and said, "I'm fine."

He had a reassuring look on his face. "See you soon."

I found the exam relatively easy. When I finished, he gave us a tour of the preparatory school - an annex at the side of the main building - where I would spend the next year of my life. The classrooms were part of a single storey pavilion with a similar layout to the one in my school in our village.

"When you're old enough, actually next year, you'll be taught where you did the entrance exam... as long as you pass it," he declared. "But for now, this is where you will study. It's been a pleasure to meet you both. I will be in touch shortly."

A week later, we received confirmation by post that I had done well in the entrance exam. Despite my initial fear due to the appearance of the old structure, I knew that I would settle into my educational life, but my first few weeks were still a lonely experience. Although the teachers attempted to introduce me to other children, I sat on my own in the grounds until I met my new friends; Jacquelyn Hayes, Philip Adamson, Grant Rutherford and Alexander Mathieson. As I wandered outside to get some fresh air after our English class, I spotted a solitary figure sitting on the bench with a sketch pad and pencil.

"Do you mind if I sit here?" I said.

She looked up. "Of course I don't mind."

"What are you drawing? Can I have a look?" She handed me the pad of paper. It was an etching of the school. My new friend had captured the sinister mood of the gothic structure, perfectly. "That's really good. You're very talented."

"I love drawing. I have some paintings displayed in the foyer. I'll show them to you later if you want."

"I'd like that. What's your name? I'm Jayden Scott. I've just started. I don't stay here, so I've not met many people yet."

"Jacquelyn… Jacquelyn Hayes. I'm pleased to meet you, Jayden Scott," she said, with a grin on her face. "Philip, Grant, Alex! Come and meet Jayden."

They stopped playing rugby and ran over in our direction.

"Hi there," they all said in unison.

Jacqueline took over. "This is Philip, Grade A pupil, far too serious and intelligent for an eleven year old and comes from Edinburgh. He's a day pupil like you and wants to be a doctor or surgeon like his father. Oh and Philip loves rugby…"

He interrupted. "Pleased to meet you."

"This is Grant Rutherford who is also a boarder at the school like me. You can tell by his accent he's from Glasgow. This boy is the class clown, causing trouble wherever he goes. He gets away with it because he's *so* charming and never studies for his exams, but always seems to get good grades."

Grant raised an eyebrow then shrugged his shoulders. "What can I say to that," he laughed, "that's me."

"And this is Alexander, but likes to be called Alex. He's from the west coast of Scotland, from a beautiful place called Islay. Alex is a boarder at the school and loves everything about the legal system and wants to be a criminal lawyer like his mother." She pointed a condemned finger at him. "He's the poshest, we're not!"

"Nice to meet you," he said, looking over in my direction. "Well… this is Jacquelyn Hayes who also stays at the school. Her parents live in London. This young lady is creative, beautiful and intelligent… and bossy!"

She got up off the bench, her face full of mischief. "Me? Bossy? Never!"

The boys sniggered. "Of course you're not, Jacques!" declared Alex.

They're all so well-mannered, I thought to myself.

She dismissed his comment, but still had a cheeky smile on her face. "Let's go to the refectory to have some lunch. We can all get to know you better, Jayden."

Grant was the first to reply. "We'll see you there. We're off to get changed. Ten minutes! See you soon."

Getting up from the bench she closed her sketch pad then grabbed my arm. "Don't be late!" she shouted to the boys.

That lunch was just the start of our close friendship. We became inseparable throughout our time at school and even now, meet up on a regular basis. However, although my school-life improved, my home-life deteriorated. Despite a normal family time over the festive period, the abuse continued - especially towards my mother. I lost count of how many times I saw him lift his hand. Not only that, I used to sit at the top of the stairs and listen to her crying over the phone, begging him to come home. He stayed at his flat in London on many occasions, but when my father did return, there was always some kind of argument, followed by a fight which then turned into a sexual reconciliation. I soon learned the difference between her cries of pleasure and her cries of pain.

And to my life - it was the constant panic I felt, not knowing how he would react on a daily basis. The emotional and physical abuse persisted; the digs, prods, slaps and beatings. His threatening presence made me anxious, surrounding my existence with a feeling of despair. I also experienced flashbacks to the numerous times he beat me with his belt. As a result, I found it hard to sleep at night and difficult to concentrate during the day. Despite my new friends at school, I felt isolated and found solace in my own company. But... three years later, my life changed for the better one night, over a dinner with my father's business partner and his family.

"Jayden, are you nearly ready? They'll be arriving soon," shouted my mother.

"Just coming."

The doorbell rang.

I heard my father telling them to come in and went downstairs.

"This is Mathew Fleming, my business partner and his wife Rachel, Emily and Robert."

I replied in a shy voice. "Hello."

Mathew nodded. "Nice to meet you, young man," he said, shaking my hand with a firm grip.

"Children you can go into the sitting room. Jayden, show them where to go. Mathew, Rachel, come with me. I'll get you a drink. It's a great vintage from my wine cellar."

"I want to stay with Mummy," cried Emily, clutching hold of her mother's hand.

"Jayden, you get settled with Robert. We'll give you a shout when the dinner is ready," said my father.

I took him to the sitting room.

There was an awkward silence at first.

"How old are you?" he asked.

"Fourteen... just fourteen. You?"

"Sixteen."

Standing at five foot ten inches tall, Robert had a muscular build for a teenager, exuding a degree of self-confidence despite his young age. He was tall and slim but broad-shouldered, with naturally light brown hair sweeping over his forehead and trim, featherlike eyebrows which blended with the natural colour of his skin tone.

"You look much older than that."

"It's probably due to my interest in martial art. It's a Japanese practice that involves weapons-based fighting using a Hanbo... it's like a staff."

"How exciting," I declared. "What... like they use in Star Wars?"

He laughed. "Don't be silly. The Bo is a six foot long staff made out of wood. The Hanbo is the same, but much shorter." Robert looked around the room and picked up the poker. "I suppose the actions are a bit similar to the fighting in Star Wars," he chuckled. "You grip it like that." Grabbing it with both hands, he lunged forward, sweeping the poker through the air, pointing it down towards the ground as it brushed passed my head. "You use it like this, but you have an opponent."

I looked at him with admiration, nodding my head in approval. "Can I try it?"

"Come over here. I'll show you." Robert placed our hands on the poker, guiding my arms in a sweeping motion as he stood behind me. "Try it yourself now."

Feeling a bit embarrassed, I became aware of my face turning red, the burning sensation surging up my cheeks. He watched with fascination, encouraging me to sweep the poker in the air around my head. "Hey, you're pretty good at that. You should come along to the classes."

"I'd like that. Can you ask my parents over dinner? If I ask they'll probably say no."

"Yeah, of course I will... no problem Obi-Wan Kenobi!"

I chuckled. He was my favourite character in Star Wars. "Where are the classes?"

"They're in a community centre in the city. It's not far from here. My father takes me on a Friday night. You can come along with us if you're allowed."

My mother came into the sitting room, staring at the poker in my hand. "That's dinner ready. What are you both up to?" she said, appearing confused by the situation.

"I was just showing Jayden some martial art moves," said Robert.

We looked at each other and started laughing.

"You can tell us about it over dinner. Go and wash your hands first."

My new friend asked whether I could join the martial arts class. To my surprise - after much deliberation - they both agreed. He became like an older brother, spending a lot of his spare time giving advice on training techniques. As time passed, my interest in the arts turned out to be out of necessity rather than pleasure. I learned it not only as a form of self-defence, but for emotional and spiritual development, strength and stamina as well as skill and coordination. It strengthened my mind and the physical contact helped to release the anger bottled up inside. As a result, I found it much easier to concentrate on my schoolwork, once I started to reap the rewards of the training. It also helped to develop my self-control, surrounding me with an inner peace in order to deal with the erratic behaviour of my father.

By the time I was seventeen years old and started to understand more, I realised there was a pattern to his behaviour. After my father lashed out, he felt a deep sense of guilt, apologising for his conduct, making excuses to avoid taking responsibility for his abnormal behaviour before turning the blame on me or my mother. She was *always* blaming herself and *always* defending his abusive actions, hiding our situation from the outside world. He reverted to his normal behaviour for months on end, giving my mother hope, only for him to create a situation where the cycle of abuse would start again. I knew we were trapped, like frightened animals in a cage - trapped in *his* distorted view of reality.

I returned home from school one weekend. Hearing loud voices coming from the bedroom, I crept up the stairs, listening at the door.

"Why do you always question what I say? Why can't you do what I tell you to do? You're such a stupid bitch."

Why does he speak to her like that?

"Let's not argue. Our son is much better off as a boarder until he finishes school. He's a young man with his own life to lead. It allows him to experience a certain degree of independence staying at the school."

"There's no need," he shouted. "Jayden can stay here during the week. He did for the first five years of his education. It's a waste of money. I asked you to sort it out."

"I'm not changing it with only a year to go. There's no point, Edward. He's settled into the dorm with Alex, Grant and Philip."

In response to her defiance, I heard a commotion. He slapped her, probably across the face, shouting at the top of his voice, "You're such a stupid cow. Why can't you just do what I tell you?"

I found it hard to make out the muffled words. Pressing my ear against the door, the faint tone of her quivering voice pleaded with him, "Please get your hands off my neck… don't hurt me Edward… please."

Right, that's enough, I thought to myself. "Unlock this door."

"Go away," hollered my father.

"Open the door," I repeated, rattling the handle.

Suddenly, the key turned in the lock. My father shouted, "Give me that, you stupid bitch!"

Seizing the opportunity, I pushed on it. He slammed it shut, trapping one side of my body between the door and the frame. I continued to push as he continued to crush me. With one final heave, the door flew open. He staggered back, losing his balance, nearly falling to the ground. My mother stood by the bed, wrapping her arms around her body, those wide eyes darting back and forth between us both, wary of the intensity of the situation.

He looked in my direction.

I glared at him.

His threatening stare studied me with caution, his body positioned in a defensive manner, waiting for a response. In a split second, I fixed my feet to the ground, knees bending into position, fists clenched as one arm twisted back and the other pointed straight out in front of me. Taking a deep breathe, I lunged forward as my right arm pounded into his stomach… **BOOMPH!** I breathed out only when the forceful punch found contact with his body.

Astonished, my father gasped, again and again, unable to catch his breath. Clutching hold of his stomach, the bastard lost his balance and crumpled to his knees. "For fuck sake," he groaned.

All the years of anger I felt for him overwhelmed my thoughts at that moment in time. I repositioned myself, raising my arm in the air, poised, ready to strike him over and over, but somehow managed to restrain myself. I looked at him in disgust. At that moment, I heard the Reverend's words in my mind. *Jayden, take care of yourself and your mother.* I turned towards him and said, "Don't you *ever* touch her again. No more... it stops now."

Startled, he stared up at me with a frightened look in his eyes and then, looked back at the floor like a defeated animal. I left him there on his bended knees. I took my mother into the sitting room. "This has got to stop. He's a fucking lunatic."

She started rubbing her hands together, looking at me in disbelief. "What did you do that for? It was my fault. I should have done what he asked me to do."

"Just stop it... STOP IT NOW!"

"Stop what?"

"Making excuses for his violent behaviour and taking the blame."

"I don't."

"You do. You don't even know you're doing it! You even lied to Reverend McIntyre that day in the church. Why do you put up with it?"

"I love him and he loves me. Your father just gets upset every now and again. He only has me to rely on."

In a grand gesture, my arms stretched up in the air then dropped down to my side. "I... don't... fucking... care. He's been like this all of my life. I give up."

"Stop swearing! I better go and see if he's okay."

"LEAVE HIM... just leave him alone," I shouted. "He better not touch you again. I've had enough."

"I know you have. Just let me go. I need to see if he's okay."

I sighed. "Suit yourself."

She left the room.

Fuck it. Noticing my father's bottle of single malt whisky on the table, I poured out a double measure, the fiery liquid calming me down. I rubbed the side of my arm. Lifting up the shirt, tinges of different coloured hues appeared down the side of my body, moulding together, with nasty purple blotches appearing before my very eyes, changing colour just like a chameleon. I thought to myself, *no more, no more now.*

****

I get up from the sofa, gaze out over the Thames, dismissing the dysfunctional memories about my mother and father. I check the time. *Shit! It's nearly six thirty. Jacquelyn will be here soon.* I take a shower and throw on a pair of jeans and a shirt. I light some candles and make the apartment more comfortable for her arrival. *We can select the wine when she gets here, depending on what food she brings,* I think to myself. I turn on the music player. The chilling piano melody is followed by the same haunting vocals from the previous evening, but the words are more appeasing to my situation at this moment in time.

"The principles of lust are easy to understand, do what you feel, do what you want… do it until you find… love!"

"That's better," I say to the singer, "you're not so judgmental tonight."

I hear the buzzer from the intercom in the hallway just before seven. I press the button to unlock the main door. "Hey baby, it's me. Hurry up and let me in. It's freezing."

"Up you come."

I hear the familiar tone of the lift arriving on the top floor. She looks adorable, dressed in a warm winter coat, pink woollen hat, matching mittens, chunky scarf and leather boots. Wisps of hair cling to the side of her pretty face. With a smile, she stretches out an arm, offering me the bag of food. I take it. She wraps her elegant arms around my neck as her soft lips find mine.

Mumbling between the kisses, I say, "Nice to see you, Miss Hayes."

Taking in a deep breath she whispers, "You smell lovely… I've missed you."

I feel myself becoming aroused. "I've missed you, too. It's been a while."

She raises an eyebrow. "Far too long… it's actually been six months!"

"Sorry, it's been pretty hectic trying to sort out the new business in London."

"I realise you've been busy."

I offer her my hand. "In you come. Let's get you warmed up."

Jacques peels off the layers of winter clothes then stands in front of the fire. She is wearing tight black jeans, knee length boots and a silky cream blouse. Her tousled blonde hair is unusually wild. The makeup is subtle, the gloss on those full lips, just noticeable. Against the light of the fire, I notice the outline of her lacy underwear through the transparent top. *I want you now*, I think to myself.

She stares into the mirror above the fireplace.

"You look gorgeous tonight, Jacques."

She appears startled by my comment. "Thanks. It's not like you to give me a compliment."

Shit! I need to watch what I'm saying. I've known her for a long time, but I know she wants more than I'm willing to give. "I'll just hang these up for you. I'll be back in a minute."

I place her coat on the hook, pick up the food bag, peer inside then head towards the kitchen. There is fish, salad, bread, butter, garlic, salad, tomatoes and red onion. Opening the fridge, I ponder over the choice of wine. "What would you like to drink?" I shout.

"You choose... as long as it's white!" she cries back.

I reach for a bottle of Chablis. Pouring out the wine, I pick up the glasses then make my way into the living area. She is still standing next to the fire as I pass the drink.

Stretching out her arm, she says, "Cheers."

The glasses clink together.

I take a sip. After the mature red wine from the previous evening, it tastes refreshing on my palate. "So... you're on dinner?"

"Yes, I'll make it."

"What kind of fish did you get?"

"Salmon... I know we both like it." Before I have time to reply her hand reaches out to stroke my face. "I really have missed you, Jayden."

"I know you have."

I place the glass of wine on the fireplace. *I can't resist it any longer.* I pull her towards me, my mouth pressing against her lips. She responds. My hands wander over the silky blouse, feeling the contours of her body beneath. She reaches for the belt on my jeans, fumbling with the buckle.

"Are you sure you don't want to wait until later?" I ask.

"I want you now."

Our kisses become more passionate. Raising her arms in the air, I pull off the blouse, discarding it on the floor. She places a hand on the mantelpiece while I take off her boots, unfasten the button on her jeans and attempt to pull them off.

Looking down at me, she says, "They're a bit tight!"

My companion helps me out. Stamping up and down on each of the trouser legs, I watch in amusement as she starts to win the battle. My hands flow up the inside of her legs. I look up, saying in a teasing manner, "Take off your underwear, Miss Hayes."

She complies, unclasping the bra before kneeling down next to me, her greedy lips finding mine while she unbuttons my shirt. Jacques watches me as I stand up and take off the rest of my clothes. I lift her up and position my playmate on the sofa.

For a second, her svelte body awaits my touch.

Unable to contain ourselves any longer, we kiss with an almost animalistic passion. Moving closer, I plant lots of kisses on that beautiful body as my head moves down to the top of her underwear, kissing the inner thighs, excited at the prospect of my tongue giving her pleasure. In anticipation, my fingers part the folds of skin.

She grabs my head, trying to pull me away. "Not just now... later."

Jacques wraps her legs around my back. Losing myself in the moment, I feel myself building towards an orgasm and stop. I sit up and pull her on top. She straddles across my groin, kissing me as she wraps her arms around my neck and then, her body grinds into mine.

"You're such a good lover, Jacques."

"So are you, baby... so are you."

Unable to contain myself any longer, my climax comes to a head. Gasping for air, I wrap my arms around her naked body, my hands wandering over her soft skin. We hold each other, savouring the moment. I whisper through my heavy breathing, "That was *really* good."

"So good," she replies, planting a kiss on my cheek. "Can I go and have a bath... do you mind?"

"Of course not. I'll run it for you."

Grabbing my clothes off the floor, I head towards the bathroom, clean myself up then get dressed. I look at the dishevelled image in the mirror. "You look like you've just been fucked," I say, with a grin on my face. Smiling to myself, I run the bath, search for some foam and pour it in. "It'll be ready soon, Jacques."

A naked body appears at the door. "Thanks."

I eye her up and down.

"What?" she asks.

"You're a sexy lady, Jacquelyn Hayes."

She winks. "I know… Jayden Edward Scott."

What a tease, I think to myself.

I move forward. Her lips find mine. There is still a tinge of hunger in those kisses. She takes my hands, inviting me to caress her body.

I respond.

She relents.

I turn off the tap.

Jacques leans against the wall as I slide down onto my knees. I move forward, grasping her hips with my arms, moving towards the sumptuous folds of skin. Her hands run through my hair, guiding my head towards her slightly parted legs. She tastes divine. I hear that first initial gasp as my tongue makes contact with her genitalia. I gently spread the lips of skin apart with my fingers, teasing with the surface of my tongue, penetrating deeper into the point of pleasure. My lover's breathing increases as she becomes more sexually aroused. I feel the flutter of tiny contractions against my mouth, sensing her building up towards the dizzying heights of pleasure. It is not long before she pushes my head, moaning with pleasure from the sensation of my tongue. Just then, I feel her orgasm, the aftermath of the pulsating bursts of intensity vibrating over my mouth. She lets out a huge sigh of relief as her legs tremble in the aftermath of the climax.

"That was… really intense."

"Good… I'm glad you enjoyed it."

I turn to put the tap back on.

She grabs hold of my arm. "Wait… just hold me."

I wrap my arms around her body. "Are you okay?"

"Yes… just hold me for a minute."

She lets me know when it's safe to let go.

"You okay?"

"I think so."

"Get yourself in the bath."

Checking the temperature, her foot hovers above the water as she dips in a toe. "Bloody hell, it's roasting!"

I turn on the cold water. "You get in and I'll bring your wine through."

Leaving her alone, I pick up my glass then light a cigarette on the candle. I relish the fresh taste of the wine and decide to go outside onto the balcony to finish my cigarette. Opening the doors, the chill in the crisp air takes me by surprise. Featherlike snowflakes fall from the dense white clouds, the breeze from the wind sending waves of cold shivers through my body. *Shit! It's freezing!* Despite the icy conditions, the after-sex-smoke fills my lungs with pleasure.

"Are you bringing my wine?" she shouts.

"I'm just coming. I'll be there in a minute."

Flicking the cigarette into the air, I head back to the warmth of the apartment. Rubbing my hands together to heat them up, I get the wine and make my way towards the bathroom. The bubbles in the water cover her body. She sits up as I pass the glass, exposing her pert breasts. I stare at that body, wanting to make love again, but dismiss the thought. *Later*, I think to myself, *later on tonight.*

"What took you so long," she says, smelling the air. "Have you been smoking?"

"Nope!" I say, jokingly.

She chuckles. "Liar… you have snow on your head!"

I run my hands through my hair to get rid of the evidence. We both start to laugh, but I know deep down that she hates me smoking. "I won't do it anymore tonight, I promise. Do you want me to start making the dinner?"

"If you want… you don't mind?"

"Of course not! Come and give me a hand when you get out."

I leave her to enjoy the bath. Filling up my glass, I take a sip and prepare the salad. Crushing the garlic in the press, I blend it with the butter and slice the bread. I search around the kitchen for a grill pan to cook the fish then pour on the olive oil. *That's it all prepared. She can cook the fish.*

I wonder how she is getting on with the art business. As a freelance artist, her many talents include abstract paintings of landscapes, mainly buildings that have some personal value. Jacques gave me a picture of our old school which is hanging in the hallway, crafted through the use of different textures to produce a detailed and realistic visual of the structure. She has captured the stone archway, turrets, pinnacles, buttresses and gothic spire against the Edinburgh skyline.

With the help of her technology obsessed brother, they set up an online business for up-and-coming artists to display an eclectic mix of art, paintings, photography and sculpture. It has grown in popularity over the last few years. The last time we talked, she told me it was attracting local as well as international artists. *I'll make a point of asking her over dinner*, I think to myself.

I gather up the cutlery, salad and condiments and set the table. "Are you coming out?"

"I'm just putting my clothes back on."

As I lean over the table, I feel a pair of arms wrap around my waist. I turn around and kiss her on the cheek. "You ready to cook, Miss Hayes?"

She nods.

I smell the aroma of the fish while I sit in front of the fire. Feeling relaxed, I think how much we enjoy each other's company. She *is* a lovely person, but not someone I want to spend the rest of my life with. Jacques is high maintenance - talented but very clingy and needy at times. I made it clear that I am not interested in anything serious. However, she insists on seeing me every time I am in London on business. Tonight, she is a distraction from my own reflective thoughts about my past. I also love her body which is an added bonus.

"It's ready, Jayden!"

She places the meal on the table, returning to the kitchen to get the garlic bread. I close my eyes, taking in a deep breath. The salmon smells of the crisp scent of the ocean. My eyes are drawn to the explosion of colours on the plate; the base of the dish covered in green foliage from the salad, with vibrant slices of lemon resting next to the pink salmon and a red onion salsa. I try the fish, dipping it into a bowl of freshly-cut coriander and lime mayonnaise.

"This tastes lovely. How's business? I would have asked earlier, but we seemed to have been distracted."

She smiles. "A nice distraction though!"

"Indeed…"

"It's fantastic. My client base has expanded. We have some exceptional artists. I am reorganising the website, categorising the art into subject area rather than product type. We now have a wide range of styles; oil paintings, watercolours, etchings, prints, acrylics, digital photography and bronze sculptures."

"Well done."

She takes a small mouthful of food and continues. "I have included an editor's choice. I select these on a monthly basis. I have also added a favourites list for potential purchasers."

"That's great news... I knew it would all work out for you. You're a very talented artist."

"Do you think?"

"Of course I do."

"I couldn't have done it without your financial investment."

"That's what friends are for. And remember, I do make a profit out of your hard work!"

"Is that all we are, Jayden? Just friends?"

Oh no, here we go, I think to myself. "Of course we're more than that." I change the subject then take hold of her hand across the table. "Come on... eat your food. Do you want more bread?"

She seems deflated. "No thanks."

I change the subject. "I'm off to view some business premises tomorrow for the new advertising business."

"Where about?"

"Here... in Westminster."

"That'll be expensive?"

"It's worth it. We need a presence in London. The business in Edinburgh is working at full capacity and we've extended our client base."

She perks up. "How exciting! What about your venture capitalist investments? How's that going?"

"You know me. I'm always looking for the next successful idea, just like my father. It's going well, very well actually."

"How do you feel about him? Your mother told me today about the official ruling from the High Court."

"I really don't want to talk about that."

"Why?"

"It just stirs up old memories. All that matters is that we can find some kind of closure now and move on."

"But..."

I interrupt. "I'm not speaking about my father. Are you finished eating? Do you want some coffee?"

"No thanks. I'll just have some more wine. You sure you're okay?"

"I'm fine."

She knows the subject area is off limits. I pour us both another glass and sit in front of the fire, reminiscing about our school days in Edinburgh.

"How are the boys?"

"Not sure. I've not seen anyone. I've just been so busy trying to sort out the plans for the new agency. I want to invite you all to the opening."

"I'll definitely be there. It's so exciting."

"Thanks for the support. I'm hoping to get a colleague of mine who used to work in the agency in Edinburgh to run the one here in Westminster. He was headhunted by a London agency. I felt gutted when he left. I'm not sure he'll agree though."

"Who?"

"Richard McKenzie."

"I remember him. He's good."

"I know… that's why I need him. I'll find out tomorrow! We have an online meeting in the morning."

Jacques puts her glass down on the table. "That's good," she says, cuddling into me.

I check the time. It's getting late. "Right… bedtime Miss Hayes, you're working in the morning. I also have the conference call to make to Richard and a business meeting in the afternoon to view the premises for the new agency."

"Do we have to go bed now?" she says, fluttering her blue eyes. "Can we not have some more wine?"

"We've had enough! Get your pretty ass off to bed. I'll be there in a minute."

With reluctance, she says, "See you soon. I do feel a little bit drunk."

"Just a little?"

"Well…"

You're so adorable at times. "Now go!"

"Don't be too long."

I clear the table and dump the dishes in the kitchen. I want a cigarette, think about it and resist the temptation. Switching everything off, I brush my teeth before heading towards the bedroom, wondering if my playmate is still awake. The room is dark apart from the faint reflection of light coming from the riverside developments dotted along the Thames. I close the blinds, remove my clothes then climb into bed, curling my body into her back.

"Are you still awake?"

She laughs. "No!"

My hands wander over her silky smooth skin. I move her hair out of the way, kissing the nape of her neck, losing myself in the moment. She moans, pushing those pert buttocks into my groin. I tease the outer folds of skin between her legs with my erection and then, I enter from behind, thrusting in and out, enjoying every stroke. I feel a pang of guilt as I hold onto her shoulders, probing faster and faster and faster. My orgasm is quick and functional. I wrap my arms around her body, my fingers drifting between her legs, but she takes hold of my hands.

"Catch me in the morning. I'm too tired."

"Okay… good night."

It is not long before she drops off to sleep. I pull my arm away then roll over onto my back. I need a nicotine fix so decide to get up. Grabbing a pair of jogging trousers, I put them on and head off to find my cigarettes. *There's no way I'm going outside.* I put on the extractor fan in the kitchen, light up and pour another glass of wine. *What a strange couple of days it's been! It's not often that I reminisce about my past; Kristina Cooper, the village, Reverend McIntyre, the abuse and my life in Edinburgh, but the news about my father from Mathew Fleming has released memories that have been hidden away in the deepest recess of my mind.* I refuse to think about it anymore, finish my wine and head back to bed, ready for an early start in the morning.

3

JUDGE JURY & EXECUTIONER

"I believe the only way to reform people is to kill them."
(Carl Panzram)

***D**ark silence.*

What's fucking happening to me? Where am I? Who am I? I feel cold, so very cold. There is a strange metallic taste at the back of my throat. I feel weak. It's dark, almost pitch black. I hear a noise. It's a muted humming sound and it won't go away. My body is crammed into a small confined space. Reaching out into the empty abyss, my hand rests upon something hard. I stroke it with my fingers. It's smooth. I start to claw at the surface with my fingertips. It feels like metal. I push against it, but it doesn't move. I start to feel claustrophobic. Trapped in the small space, I shuffle onto my side and curl up into a foetal position, sensing the life draining from my body. I must be dreaming. When I wake up everything will be okay. It's so confusing. I find it hard to breathe. I try to cry out for help, but can't speak. I see a familiar face looking at me, remembering the feel of her body and the soft caress of her kisses. Who is she? The low grumbling noise stops. I hear a loud bang and then, all is silent. I feel myself drifting off to sleep.

"Edward, wake up, wake up!"

In the distant corner of my mind, I can hear someone calling out a name. It's her voice. It's my lover... Annabel Taylor. Relief overwhelms me. This is just a dream. Opening my eyes, I panic as there is still no light and it is still dark. I'm trapped in the enclosure. I'm Edward? Yes... Edward Scott. I was walking home in the fog to my family home in Edinburgh. It was late. But what am I doing here trapped in this dark void? I feel something trickling down the side of my face. My hand reaches up to feel the warm, sticky fluid around my neck. I realise it is blood. I want to shout out, but still no sound escapes my throat.

HELP ME... SOMEONE PLEASE HELP ME!

My fingers trace the length of the gash across my neck. I know that the darkness is coming to take me. There is no energy left in my lifeless body. Fear engulfs my entire existence. I am aware that I'm dying. I remember now. I remember a hand on my shoulder and the excruciating pain across my neck, I remember being bundled into the boot of a car and I remember his face as he looked at me with hatred in his eyes. *Why Jayden, why?*

****

I am unable to sleep. There is no sound in the bedroom apart from Jacquelyn's soft breathing. Tossing and turning in bed, I keep thinking about the night I killed my own father, knowing from a young age that he would never change. The night I confronted him for hitting my mother, I knew at that moment, that one day I would end his life. I understand now that the mental, emotional and physical abuse that we suffered at the hands of my father has shaped who I have become. My mother is in denial. I am not. *He deserved to die - that's why I killed him.* The events that took place seven years ago on that foggy night in Edinburgh are etched into my mind.

With my father's dying body in the boot of the car, I drove away from the scene of the crime and made the short trip to our family home, avoiding the main roads from the prying eyes of the surveillance cameras. I left the car at the end of the street where it had been parked earlier in the evening. I locked the car and turned to take one last look at the vehicle. All of a sudden, I heard something. I cocked my head, listening in vain to make out the faint noise. *Scratch, scratch, scratch...*
  So he's still alive. Leave him to die! I thought to myself.
  I hesitated for a moment, but something stopped me walking away. I opened up the boot to take one last look at him. I felt my stomach heave at the sight before me. His body was curled up in a ball, the gash at his throat now a blackish slit; the lips of skin where the knife had slit through his thin flesh were covered in congealed blood. Just then, I heard the sound of a ringtone, the deafening noise ringing out into the silent night. Somehow, he had mustered the strength to find his mobile phone. *Switch if off. Quick!* Fumbling in my pocket, I pulled out a pair of leather gloves before wrenching the phone out of his tight grip. I switched it off, throwing it back into the depths of his enclosure.
  My father's dark brown eyes stared at me, begging for help. An evil smirk passed across my face as I just stood and watched the life draining from his body and then, a thought crossed my mind. *Should I finish what I started and end his life, here and now? How easy it would be to*

press my hand over his mouth, silencing his gasps, letting him feel the fear that I had felt all my life and watch him die.

I decided to show no such mercy.

With my eyes locked onto his, I closed the boot of the car.

Creeping along the lane leading to the back of the house, I opened the gate, sneaking in through the back door. With a huge sigh of relief, my shoulders slumped against the wall, my heart thumping in my chest. *I hope nobody heard his fucking mobile phone! It was probably his mistress.* I approached my mother's bedroom, her heavy breathing indicating she was fast asleep. *The sleeping tablets in her drink have worked well.* I felt guilty that I had to do that - to drug her to make sure she did not wake up. *But it had to be done*, I told myself. Dismissing the thought, I tiptoed up the stairs, and once in the safety of my own room, I washed my hands, undressed then climbed into bed, sleep engulfing my whole body, my mind refusing to think about the crime I had just committed.

The following morning, I felt a hand on my arm, shaking me to wake up. "It's time to get up. You've a busy day ahead of you," a voice said. "I had a fantastic sleep. I've not slept that well in ages!" declared my mother.

"Can't you knock before you come bursting into my room? I'm not a child anymore, although you continue to treat me like one."

"*Don't* speak to me like that."

"Like what?" I said, defiantly.

She ignored my comment and opened the curtains. Daylight flooded into the dark confines of the bedroom. "Look! The fog has lifted."

I groaned.

"You need to get up. Remember you're heading off to meet Alex and Grant today at the cottage."

"I know…"

"Do you want me to make you some breakfast?"

"I'm not hungry. Leave me alone to wake up properly." I checked the time. "Bloody hell, it's ten o'clock. Why did you not wake me up earlier?" I shouted.

Leaving the room, she ignored my outburst, probably because I had just given her such a hard time.

Getting out of bed, I grabbed a towel to cover my naked body then dashed across the landing towards the bathroom. The water felt cleansing on my skin, but it failed to wash away the memories from the night before. Dismissing the thoughts, I changed into my clothes, packed a bag and went downstairs to confront my mother; not knowing if I would be able to look her straight in the eye.

My gaze lingered longer than necessary. *She doesn't seem to notice anything different. Why should she?* "I didn't mean to shout at you, but you can't just come barging into my room."

"You're late. It's a long drive. You also need to get the house ready for your friends coming tonight."

She paused… and started twirling a strand of hair around her fingers.

"What's wrong?"

"Your father didn't come home last night. He did say he might be away for a few days on business. I thought he would at least call to let me know."

"He might have planned to go to London for the weekend. That's what he told me."

"I hope there's not another woman involved. I don't think I could cope with that again."

"Stop worrying. He's probably just been delayed. You know what he's like. I'm sure he'll call you soon."

"You might be right. Get going or you'll never get there on time." She picked up the gift lying on the sideboard in the sitting room and placed it in my hand. "Happy birthday."

Making our way to the front door, I kissed her on the side of the cheek. "See you in a few days. Call me later. Thanks for the present," I shouted, running along the road towards the car. I chucked the holdall in the back seat next to the bag of bloodstained clothes, eager to leave Edinburgh behind.

As I made my way towards our holiday home on the west coast, the dead body concealed in the boot weighed heavily on my mind. I felt sick and pulled into a layby just outside the city. Unable to contain any kind of composure for much longer, I began to shake as icy cold shivers passed through my body. Gasping for air, I gripped the steering wheel for a few moments before winding down the window. The force of the cold air brought me back to reality. Rummaging about in the glove compartment, I found a packet of Dunhill. With trembling hands, I lit the cigarette then took a long drag, inhaling the smoke deep into my lungs, finishing it down to the filter before lighting another one.

I climbed out and slumped against the side of the car.

Staring out across the barren fields, lost in thought, I gave myself a quick pep talk. *Get a grip of yourself. This is only the start. You still have to dispose of the body. Your meltdown is better to happen now rather than later, when you're in the company of friends. Get your arse back in the car. Forget about Edward until you're ready to dispose of the body. Now... get going!*

I eventually calmed down and continued on my journey. Several hours later, I decided to stop in the next town to stock up on some supplies, buying enough food and drink to last us over the next few days. I was just about to load it into the boot of the car. *What am I doing?* I stopped myself just in time. *What state would his dead body be in now? Pale, putrefying, bloated, cold and hard, perhaps?* For a fleeting moment, a wave of nausea passed over me, rising and falling like the feeling you get on a stomach-churning descent on a roller coaster ride. My hand reached for my mouth, gagging, waiting for the moment to pass and when I felt it was safe to do so, I packed the groceries onto the back seat of the car.

I somehow managed to lose myself in the scenery rather than concentrate on the dead body that accompanied me on my journey. After several hours, I approached the mouth of the river. The water flowed through the spectacular landscape carved out by the wild forces of nature. It was breathtakingly beautiful. As nightfall crept over the valley, the glow of the sun disappeared under the horizon. My eyes focused on the hostile environment up towards the windswept volcanic remains, formed in the ice age by a huge glacier, the grassy lowlands surrounded by craggy mountains, bearing down over the narrow glen, the low-lying clouds hovering over the peaks of the mountains as water cascaded down the sides of the rock face.

It was just as famous for its bloody history as it was for its wild beauty. Further on, in the heart of the glen, there was an area where a whole clan had been massacred without warning, during the night. Those that remained alive had perished in the cold, wind and rain in one of the harshest winters in Scottish history. I shuddered. *It must have been an awful way to die.* It reminded me of my dead passenger, but *his* death must have been even more horrific, trapped in that small space with no means of escape. I felt a deep sense of satisfaction, knowing he must have experienced a slow, painful death.

Spotting a parking sign, I stopped the car to have another cigarette, to alleviate the gruesome images in my mind. *I really need to stop smoking... soon!* As I stood in front of the mountains, the clouds lifted to reveal a blanket of white dust scattered across the snow-capped hills, my eyes focusing on the stark contrast between the light and shade of the snowfall against the dark treacherous peaks. Steep slopes plummeted to the ground, where marshy bogs surrounded the base of the mountain range, the whin blowing in the breeze as the wind increased in strength. *I love it here. It's so peaceful.*

Just then, the noise of a car interrupted the serenity of the moment. It drove into the layby. A young man in his late teens got out of the vehicle. He swaggered over in my direction. *Fucking great! What the hell does he want?* I thought to myself.

He brushed his hand over the boot of the car. "Hey, mate... ye got a light?"

"Hang on a minute," I said, fumbling in the pocket of my trousers.

The idiot made me nervous. My hand started shaking as he tilted his head to light the cigarette. Breathing out the smoke, he announced, "You awright?"

I wrapped my arms around my body. "It's just a bit cold, that's all."

"Aye, it's freezin'. Thanks for the light, mate. Where ye aff tae?"

"I'm just heading to my house for a party tonight."

He leaned back, sitting on the boot of the car, blowing smoke rings into the air. "A party eh... a love a guid party."

I had visions of the door springing open to reveal the putrefying body concealed inside. "It should be good. I'm looking forward to it."

"Is it far fae here?"

"Black Ridge Cottage, about fifteen miles up the road."

"Yeah a know where that is," he declared. "What's yer party for?"

"It's my birthday today. I'm meeting friends for dinner and some drinks. We're also spending a few days hill climbing."

"Aww... happy birthday, mate. How old are ye?"

"Twenty-three. You?"

"Hey, yer just two years older than me then. I'm headin' to see ma mates as well. I'd better get aff. Am awready late."

"Nice meeting you," I said. "Enjoy your night."

He paused. "What's that smell? Can ya no smell it? It's like shite!"

Sniffing the air, I pointed towards the marshland. "A little bit I suppose. It's probably coming from over there."

"Yeah… ye might be right. See ye around. Hae a guid party!" he shouted, making his way back towards the car.

No you won't see me around. Go on… piss off. That was close!

As I continued along the main road, a white speck emerged in the distance against the dark shadow of the glen, the solitary cottage standing at the base of the mountain. I drove down the dirt track road, breathing out a huge sigh of relief as I parked the car in a remote area at the back of the house. *That was torture. I'm so glad to be here.*

RAT-A-TAT-TAT…

Startled, my head turned towards the noise on the car window.

"Hello there, Squire," he shouted. "What you doing here?"

Winding down the window, I said to the gardener, "Henry, what a fright you gave me. I'm here to meet some friends. What are *you* doing here?"

"I'm just finishing off a few jobs before the winter. I'll be pottering around for a while. That okay?"

"There's no need. Just finish off early this year."

"Are you sure? Your mother said… "

I interrupted him as I got out the car. "I won't say anything if you don't." Reaching into my pocket, I took out my wallet, counting out a hundred pounds. "Here's a bonus for all your hard work. There's no need to come back while I'm here. Take a few days off."

He looked at the wad of money, grinning away to himself. "Thanks, Squire. That's very generous."

"Have a good break," I said. "I need to go and get the cottage ready."

He whistled for his dog. It came scampering towards us, sniffing the air at the rear end of my car. "What's wrong, boy?"

What next? Grabbing his arm, I ushered him towards the narrow path leading to the forest. "You better get going. It's getting dark."

"Come on, Misty," he shouted, "HEEL!"

The dog complied.

I watched them both as they disappeared into the night.

With a sharp intake of breath, I checked the time. I had two hours to prepare the house. Alex and Grant were arriving at seven.

****

I saw the lights of a car passing across the sitting room, the silhouette of the window sweeping across the wall in a circular movement and then, it disappeared. My guests had arrived. I opened the front door as they were both getting out of the car.

"Alex, Grant… glad you could both make it."

"Hey, Birthday Boy," shouted Grant. "It's great to see you." He wrapped his arm around my neck, slapping my back in a manly gesture.

"You too."

I turned towards Alex. "Good to see you."

He shook my hand then ruffled my hair. "Happy birthday, Scottie."

"Come and help us unload the car," said Grant. "We've got enough booze to sink a bloody ship!"

We dumped the luggage at the foot of the stairs. Disposing of the beer, wine and spirits into the fridge, I took the surplus outside to keep it cool. I caught sight of the boot out the corner of my eye. My father's lingering presence made me feel uneasy, the muscles in my neck tightening at the image in my head of his decaying body. I shuddered, putting the thought to the back of my mind. *Don't even think about him over the next few days.*

Alex interrupted my thoughts. "Here… this is for you, Scottie. Happy birthday. It's from both of us."

"Thanks." I opened the present, lifting the lid off the expensive looking gift box, revealing a Black Bottle premium scotch whisky. "Excellent. I can't wait to try it," I said with excitement. "Pass the gift from my mother. It's there on top of the counter."

Alex handed it over. "What is it?"

Ripping off the paper, I said, "It's a hip flask."

Studying it in more detail, my initials had been engraved on the silver plate on the front. "I'm all sorted for our hiking trip tomorrow. What more do I need! A flask and one of the finest blended malts on the market."

We all laughed.

"Let's get the party started. Help yourselves to some drinks. I'll cook the lamb," I declared.

Alex's eyes lit up. "We're starving! Open a nice bottle of red. I'll take the bags upstairs. Come and give me a hand, Grant. I want the double room at the front of the cottage. You can take the single at the back," he chuckled.

"No way, I'm having the double. Let's toss for it."

I heard them arguing about it on the way upstairs. No doubt, Alex would get his own way. He was always the leader of the pack; polite, charming, witty and intelligent. He received a first class law degree from one of the top universities in Scotland. At the age of twenty-two, he started working in a criminal law firm in Glasgow. Grant on the other hand was still working in his father's construction business, but they won lucrative building contracts around Britain. Phil was caught up with his new job as a trainee surgeon and Jacquelyn was out of the country on holiday with her parents. So, it was just the three of us for the next few days. *Once they leave, I'll be able to dispose of my father's body. Then, I'll make my way back to Edinburgh to deal with my mother*, I thought to myself.

I opened a bottle of red wine and prepared the meal. I heard a commotion above me and then, a flurry of laughter. I smiled to myself. I loved it when we got back together. They were like part of my family. I poured a large glass of wine for myself and Alex and took a cold beer out of the fridge for Grant.

"Right you two, come down a get a drink," I shouted. "It's party time!" I checked the old but functional stove to see if it was hot enough to cook on and topped it up with some more charcoal. "Your drinks are ready... come on!"

I heard them bound down the stairs. Grant had a smile on his face, grinning from ear to ear as he entered the kitchen. "I won the toss! He's in the single room," he sniggered.

"You're so childish," I said to him. I looked at Alex's defeated face and we burst out laughing.

"Drink, drink and let's have some more drink. You're only twenty-three once," declared Alex.

"Here, here," said Grant.

All the glasses clinked together at once. "Cheers!"

After finishing the meal, we took our drinks into the sitting room. I topped up the fire with some logs. Grant selected the music, turned the volume up then offered to pour us some more drinks.

"Do you want to open your Black Bottle whisky?" he asked.

"No! I'll keep it for a special occasion. I have a cheaper bottle open somewhere... it's in that cabinet over there," I told him.

As Grant prepared the drinks, I checked my phone. There were two missed calls and a text from my mother.

> Please call me as soon as possible. I can't get in touch with your father. There's no reply from the flat in London. I have no idea where he is. I'm starting to get really worried about him. Call me soon x.

"Sorry guys, I need to go and phone my mother. I'll be back in a minute."

"I see you're still a Mummy's Boy," declared Grant.

I laughed then stuck my middle finger in the air. "Piss off, Rutherford. I think there's a bit of a family crisis at home. I need to find out what's going on."

"It's not anything serious, I hope?" said Alex.

"I don't think so. I'll be back in a minute."

"Don't be too long. I'll pour your drink Mummy's... I mean, Birthday Boy."

I ignored his jibes. "Thanks, I might need it."

He started filling up a glass and looked up at me to tell him when to stop. "Say when."

"That's enough. Stop pouring... it's a big measure. Cheers," I said, taking a large mouthful.

I made my way into the kitchen. Pacing back and forth, I dialled the number, dreading the conversation.

"Jayden, it's so good to hear from you..."

"What's going on?"

"I don't know? I can't get in touch with him. He's not answering his phone. Why is he not answering it? There must be another woman involved."

"I'm sure there's not. Stop worrying. Did you call the flat in London?"

"Yes, but there's no answer there either. What will I do? I'm getting really worried."

I called her bluff. "It's only been a day. I'm sure he'll be in touch soon. Do you want me to come home?"

I waited for her to refuse my offer.

She paused. "No... you stay. Enjoy yourself with your friends."

I let out a sigh of relief. "Are you sure? I don't mind."

"I'm sure."

"Remember, we're going hill walking tomorrow for the next few days. I probably won't get a signal. Are you going to be okay?"

"I don't know?"

"Right... I'm going to make my way home."

"Please don't. You're probably right. He'll be in touch soon."

"As long as you're sure?"

"Just stay."

Changing the subject, I said, "Thanks for the hip flask."

"I thought you'd like it. We both chose it. Your father got your name engraved for you."

I felt a fleeting pang of guilt. "It's perfect."

"How are Alex and Grant?"

"We're having a great night so far."

She ignored my comment. "I hope he gets in touch soon."

"Don't worry. I'll be home on Tuesday evening. I'm sure he'll call you. There will be a logical explanation for it all."

"I hope so."

"You take care. Go and rest. I'll see you soon."

"Thanks... have a good break."

"Good night. Speak to you soon."

That went much better than I expected, but it's only been one day. God knows what she'll be like by the time I get home, I thought to myself.

I returned to the sitting room.

Alex gazed at me with suspicion. "What's going on?"

"It's my father. He's gone missing. My mother thinks it's another woman."

"Well... what a surprise," said Alex. "Edward *is* a bit of a ladies man! Like father, like son," he joked.

"But I'm not bloody married!"

"Calm down, Scottie."

I took in a deep breath. "She seems really worried this time," I declared. "Anyway, let's not let it ruin our time together. We can have a look at the map. I'll show you our route to the Devil's Staircase. I hope the weather holds out for us."

"It's meant to be pretty fair over the next few days. I checked the forecast before we left Glasgow," said Grant.

As we sat on the floor, looking at the map to go over the route for the hill walking trip, a flicker of light just off the main road caught my eye through the sitting room window. I saw the glare of two headlights from of a white car speeding down the driveway. *Bloody hell, it's the police*, I thought to myself. *I've somehow been found out.* The persistent noise from the horn of the car drowned out the sound of the music in the cottage as it sped down the path, screeching to an abrupt halt in front of the cottage.

It was a fight or flight moment.

A sudden sensation of intense anxiety overcame me, fear clinging to my every thought, my mind struggling to find a logical solution to the situation.

"Who the hell is that?" said Grant.

I felt the blood draining from my face, rushing through my body down towards my feet, making me feel light-headed and my voice, it sounded strange, almost like I was saying it in slow motion. "I'm not sure? Nobody ever comes here?"

Alex looked at my reaction. He gripped my shoulder. "Are you okay, Scottie?"

"Yes... I'm fine."

I shook my head back and forward trying to drive the confused thoughts from my mind. I desperately tried to find some kind of coherence. Trying to compose myself, I felt my heartbeat increasing as a rush of adrenalin made me get up off the floor. I headed towards the front door with Alex and Grant behind me. I opened it. It was pitch dark outside apart from the faint light radiating from the sitting room window.

Someone got out of the car.

Grant handed me a torch.

I pointed it at the figure coming towards us.

It took several seconds to register the situation in my mind.

"Hey you! Ye havin' a guid party? Happy birthday, mate."

Relief overwhelmed me at that moment in time as the panic, fear and disorientation subsided. I had never been so delighted to see the little fucker from the layby. "What a fright you gave us!" I declared.

"Sorry mate... a brung along a couple o' friends to join yer party. Ye dinnae mind dae ye," he said, hollering at them to get out of the car.

Fuck sake, I thought to myself.

Grant stood behind me unable to contain his laughter, prodding me in the back. "How do you know him?" he whispered.

"Don't ask," I told him.

Three other people got out of the car, barging passed us into the house.

"Come in, why don't you," I said, muttering under my breath.

Alex stared at me in amazement.

"What? I met him today on my way here in a layby up the road. I never invited him… he's just invited himself."

"It's braw and warm in 'ere. This is Cammy, Gillian and Amanda. They been ma friends since school. I'm Ben. What's yer name again?"

"Jayden… and that's Alex and Grant. I'll go and get you a drink."

I made my way into the kitchen. I got a bottle of wine and a few beers out of the fridge. I turned around. She was standing at the kitchen door. *OH… MY… GOD!* I leered at her, my gaze wandering up and down that beautiful body from head to toe. First, my eyes drifted across her red glossy lips, then over the tight black dress clinging to her feminine curves and finally, her irresistible high-heeled shoes; the light reflecting off the patent leather, creating a rippling effect across the shiny surface. I felt the blood rushing from my head, stirring my groin, lusting after the image standing before me.

"So… is it your birthday today?" she said.

I nodded.

She blew me a kiss from her inviting lips. "Happy birthday. I'm Amanda, by the way."

I calmed down and looked at her in surprise. *She was really quite well-spoken, compared to her Ben friend.* "Pleased to meet you. Is wine okay?"

"Perfect. I'll take the glasses. Where are they?

"Just in that cupboard up there."

She brushed past my body. "In here?"

I felt a bit flustered. "Yes. I'll see you through… there… in a minute."

I took the drink through to the living room.

"Hey hey, the beers are here!" shouted Ben. "You want one, Cammy?"

"Yeah, thanks mate."

"I've got the glasses for the wine," Amanda told her friend who was speaking to Grant.

"Thanks," said Gillian. "Grant's parents have a construction business in Glasgow. We should all meet up some time. We go there a lot, don't we babes?"

"We do," confirmed Amanda.

"All the best tae ye, Jayden!" cried Ben, raising his bottle in the air.

"HAPPY BIRTHDAY!" everyone shouted.

Surprisingly, we all had a good night, drinking into the early hours of the morning. Ben only had one beer as he was driving, but I caught him outside when I went to have a cigarette. He was smoking something suspicious. *Who am I to judge?* I thought. *He smokes weed and I'm a killer. No comparison really!*

"Ye want a toke?"

"No thanks," I said. "It's not my thing."

"Suit yerself. Hey, you seem tae be gettin' on well wi' Amanda. Get in there, mate… she likes ye."

"I'm not sure. She's pretty hot though."

"A know. Wish she eyed me up the way she does wi' you!"

"How old is your friend?" I asked.

"Twenty-two."

I flicked my cigarette into the air. "Let's go in. It's freezing out here."

We all started to settle down. Ben joined Alex and Cammy, Gillian was speaking to Grant while Amanda sat in front of the fire… alone. I gathered up some logs, placing them on top of the hot embers in the grate.

She looked up at me. "Hey," she said.

"Do you want some more wine? I asked.

"That would be lovely."

I'll go and get it from the fridge."

"I'll come with you."

Taking hold of her hands, I pulled Amanda up into a standing position before leading my prize into the kitchen. I closed the door. She invited me in with her eyes. Leaning against the back of the door, I started kissing those luscious lips, my hands wandering over the tight dress then up through her shoulder length hair.

"I want you," I whispered.

I took hold of her hand, dragging her upstairs to my bedroom. She greedily kissed me as we lay down on the bed. Amanda was just about to kick off her shoes, but I insisted she kept them on as my hands pulled the dress over her hips. I unzipped my trousers, sliding them down over my knees as she took off her underwear. In the classic missionary positon, she felt amazing as her legs wrapped around my body, the heels of the shoes digging into my back. It was quick, dirty and fun. We laughed through our heavy breathing when it was all over.

"That was good," I declared.

"We're bad! Pass me up my underwear."

She slipped them on then pulled down the dress. I went to the bathroom to clean up. When I returned, she was sweeping her fingers through her hair. "There," she said, "I'm all sorted."

I winked. "Are you ready?"

"Yes."

I took hold of her hand, leading my birthday girl back to the party. We got the wine from the kitchen then joined everyone else for the remainder of the evening. Ben, Cammy, Amanda and Gillian decided to leave about four o'clock in the morning. By that time we were all drunk, apart from Ben who was driving. I kissed her goodbye. We waved them off and went back into the cottage.

"What a night," said Alex. "All vey unexpected!"

"I know," replied Grant. "You're not going to believe this... I got Gillian's phone number," he boasted.

"I got more than a phone number," I said.

"What?" You're a smarmy bastard, Scottie. How do you do it?"

"It must be my good looks and my irresistible charm."

They both looked at me in disbelief.

"Hey, Grant," said Alex. "Race you upstairs. I'm getting the double bed!"

They both ran off. I left them to fight it out. Alex was right. Despite my initial reservations, it was an unexpected night, but one to remember. "It's time for bed," I said to myself, staggering up the stairs. I tossed my clothes on the ground, got into bed and immediately fell asleep.

The following day, I woke up with a thumping headache. My mouth felt dry. I instinctively reached for my neck, desperately trying to swallow to accumulate some kind of moisture from the limited amount of saliva in my mouth. Looking around the room, it took me a few seconds to familiarise myself with the surroundings. Then it all came flooding back; the body in the car, my birthday, Alex and Grant, the unexpected guests and my opportunistic sexual encounter with Amanda. I groaned as I rolled over in bed. *What time is it?* I got up, pulled on a pair of jogging trousers and made my way towards Alex's bedroom, but Grant was there. *I knew Alex would get his own way.* Grant was sound asleep in the single room. I went downstairs to check the time. It was three o'clock in the afternoon. *Shit! What about our hiking trip to the Devil's Staircase?* It was somehow important to go there before I disposed of my father's body, to look down on his final resting place from above. *Damn! I better go and get them up. We need to change our plans.*

I went to get a glass of water then made my way upstairs. Standing above Grant, I dribbled some of it over his face, waiting for a reaction. His nose twitched. Moaning, he started to open his eyes. "What the bloody hell is going on?"

I laughed. "Come on, Rutherford. Wake up!"

"Piss off. Leave me alone," he muttered.

"Suit yourself. We can just go on a day trip tomorrow across the Devil's Staircase instead."

I left them both to sleep. Besides, it was too late in the day to embark on our walk. I tidied up the house and settled down in front of the fire. My eyes felt heavy, fluttering as they struggled to stay open. I succumbed as sleep engulfed my entire body.

Grant woke me up several hours later. "So much for our two day hiking trip?" he said. "I feel rough."

"Me too. Where's Alex?"

"In the shower."

"Let's just relax for the rest of the evening. We can head off early tomorrow. Anyway, I know a shorter route. It should only take us one day. I suppose we could eat out then make our way back to the cottage. It would save me from cooking."

"Sounds good," said Grant.

"Talking about food… Are you hungry?"

He chortled. "Starving!"

"I'll make us something to eat."

I made a quick stir fry. We settled in for a drink-free night and played some chess. Alex won as usual. We headed off to bed at a decent hour, ready for our trip in the morning.

Getting up early the next day, I felt refreshed after a good night's sleep. We packed the rucksacks with enough food and water to last us through the day.

Are we taking your car?" said Alex.

I paused. *The three of us and my dead father, I don't think so!* "I've not got much petrol. It's a clapped out heap anyway. I need to get a new one. We're better off taking your car, Alex."

As we bundled the hill walking gear into the back of the car, I found it hard to contain my excitement. "We make our way back towards the start of the glen, setting off from Altnafeadh. It's a twelve mile round trip across the Devil's Staircase to Kinlochleven."

"Now that I feel better, I'm in the mood for a good hike," said Alex.

"Let's get going. It'll be a long day," declared Grant, as he ran out the house towards the car. "I'm in the front! You can go in the back, Jayden."

He's so childish, I thought to myself. "Whatever, Rutherford."

We approached the layby at Altnafeadh. Looking up towards the path leading across the Staircase, I noted the weather was favourable, feeling relatively mild for November. The ground mist hovered over the path as the light shimmered on the morning dew. Shielding my eyes from the glare of the sun, I looked up towards higher ground. It was free of low-lying clouds. *Great,* I thought to myself, we *should get a clear view of the entire glen.*

We changed into our hill walking clothes then made our way towards the summit. At the highest peak, we stopped to admire the view. It was mystical, almost enchanting in a sinister way; wisps of clouds clinging to the peaks of the jagged mountain tops. Scattered throughout the glen, waterfalls tumbled over vertical drops, swirling in the river below, winding through the landscape like a slithering snake.

Where's the cottage? "Pass the binoculars, Alex," I said, excitedly. *This is it. This is the moment.*

"Here you go. What are you looking at?"

"Just admiring the view," I told him.

Spinning around, I looked through the binoculars down towards the glen. In the distance was a faint white speck. The cottage was nuzzled into the Aonach Eagach mountain range hovering over the valley. Zooming in on the house, my eyes wandered behind the cottage to the forest, up towards my father's fate. I felt a sense of omnipotence looking down over his burial spot from the Devil's Staircase. *Right now Edward, who is the evil one? Is it me or is it you?* There was no doubt in my mind that my father was more evil - even although he had never killed anyone. I passed the binoculars to Alex. "You can see the cottage from here." I pointed in the general direction. "Just over there."

"So you can," he said. "The panoramic view of the glen is just amazing, Scottie."

"Let me look," said Grant. Taking the binoculars, he spread his arms and shouted, "I've bloody died and gone to heaven!"

"Silly bastard," chortled Alex.

I agreed. *But you're very much still alive, Grant Rutherford. Unlike my dead father awaiting his burial!*

We stopped to admire the view then had a light lunch. I lit a cigarette, savouring the moment, eager to carry out my plan. *Tomorrow*, I thought to myself. *It's not much longer now.*

"You seem very pensive. You okay, Scottie?"

"I'm fine, Alex. I think we should head down to the reservoir, double back over the Staircase then make our way to the hotel at the start of the glen and get something to eat for dinner. It will take us three or four hours. What do you think?"

"That sounds good," said Grant. "Let's get going then."

By the time it took us to circle back on ourselves, the daylight was starting to fade as we descended down the path towards the layby. We drove to the hotel, ate a hearty meal and had a few beers, apart from Alex who was driving back to the cottage. Feeling exhausted, we turned in early, getting up the next day at noon. The rest of the day dragged on until it was time for them to leave. I felt myself becoming more and more agitated - excited yet disturbed at the thought of disposing of my father's body. I made them something to eat before they left to go back to Glasgow and finally, helped them pack up the car just before seven o'clock.

****

Standing alone at the front of the cottage, I waved goodbye to my guests. *Thank fuck they've gone. Now I can get on with what I need to do - the real reason for me being here.* I went back into the house to go over my plan. First, I needed to text my mother.

> I've not heard from you. Alex and Grant have just left. I'm exhausted. I was just going to stay here tonight and head off in the morning. Is everything okay?

Pacing back and forth in the sitting room, I lit a cigarette, waiting for her reply. I contemplated my next move, knowing I had to open the boot of the car. The thought made my stomach churn. *I need a drink.* Pouring out a strong measure of whisky, I tilted my head back, gulping down the contents of the glass. I lit another cigarette, gazed into the fire and had another whisky. My phone received an incoming text... *beep, beep, beep.*

> That's fine. Please don't worry. Have a good rest. I'll see you tomorrow x

What's going on? I was sure she'd be hysterical by now, I thought to myself. *How strange... very odd indeed.* I did not have time to dwell on it. I looked into the mirror above the fireplace, my reflection staring back at me. "I can't fucking do this... I can't," I said, with fear in my eyes. *You can! It's only a dead body! Go and get changed!*

Feeling light-headed, I went upstairs to put on some hill walking clothes; waterproof jacket, trousers, winter hat and gloves. I sat on the stairs and tied the laces on my boots. *Right, I'm ready.*

It was a moonless night. Darkness engulfed the entire valley. The sky was painfully dark, as black as death itself. Shaking, I grabbed the torch lying under the stairs then made my way out to the front of the cottage. Double checking that I was alone, I pointed it out in front of me, giving my eyes time to adjust to the light. Like a thief in the night, I crept around the side of the cottage. My eyes focused on the car as it waited to reveal its secrets. For several minutes, the ray of light from the torch rested on the boot of the vehicle. *Open it!* My hand reached out towards the lock. I turned the key, slowly easing it open. I drew in a deep breath, my legs trembling in an uncontrollable manner. *Holy shit!* The putrid, sickly smell of rotten decaying flesh escaped from the enclosure, attacking my senses, showing me no mercy.

Gagging, I pulled back.

Dropping to my knees, the convulsions in my stomach forced the contents of my gut over the gravel path. The uncontrollable spasms continued, my mouth watering as I spat out the green bile from my mouth. *For fuck sake, this is not good.* Catching my breath, I sat on the path for a while as I thought about what to do next. *Go and look! Do it you coward!* Placing my hands on the ground, I got up off my knees, shining the torch over the dead body. My stomach wrenched… again. *Jesus Christ!* Despite the gruesome sight, I felt an inner strength manifest from deep within my being. I felt nothing for him. He deserved to die. His lifeless body was an empty shell. I found comfort in the fact that he had died alone, trapped in the dark space, with no means of escape.

Studying him closer, he was lying on his side in a foetal position, his bloated hands curled around his throat. His eyes were wide open, staring into nowhere, giving him a zombie-like appearance. The whole side of his face, the side that he was lying on, had turned a deep shade of red - like the Blood Stone in my childhood rock collection. The rest of his body had drained of colour as his skin radiated a greyish/blue tinge. Taking off the gloves, my hand trembled as I reached out to touch his flesh, the waxy texture of his skin feeling cold and hard against my warm touch. I looked down at him with pity, but had no regrets about taking his life.

I left the boot of the car open, trying to get rid of the foul stench. I made my way to the shed that contained the gardening equipment. I had thought this through time and time again. The main road leading towards the forest was far too exposed. And, the path leading from the back of the cottage was not wide enough for a vehicle to drive through. The only way to transport him to his final resting place was to dump his body in the wheelbarrow and take him there on foot. Laughing out loud, I realised how ludicrous it all seemed. It was like a comedy but this was real: real life with a dead body to get rid of.

Shining the torch over his mode of transport, I noticed the shadow of the spade out the corner of my eye hanging from a hook on the ceiling. I lifted it over the catch, placing it on the ground. Double-checking the size of the wheelbarrow, I thought to myself, *it's just big enough.* It had two sturdy wheels at the front making it easier to steer towards the car. Resting the spade against the bumper, I thought about my next move. I forced the layers of sturdy plastic sheeting into a point, twisting it over the top of his putrefying body so I had something to grip onto in order to drag it closer to the front of the boot. I placed the wheelbarrow as close as I could get to the back of the car. Gripping the knotted plastic, I lifted his heavy frame over the top of the bumper. With a thumping noise, it fell down into the base of the wheelbarrow… **BOOMPH!** The sudden movement released the foul-smelling gases trapped in his body. *For fuck sake, not again… please.* A hand jerked up towards my nose, protecting my senses from the rancid fumes. A wave of nausea overpowered me, my gut wrenching from the unpleasant odour, but there was nothing left in the pit of my stomach.

I left him there and went back into the cottage.

The inside of my stomach felt raw. I poured another whisky. Lifting it to my lips, I savoured the honey tones of the sweet liquid despite it burning the back of my throat. I sat in front of the fire thinking about the long night ahead. The journey to the isolated area at the base of the mountain range was over two miles from the cottage. *It's not going to be an easy journey.* The path was surrounded by overgrown foliage. The track might also be muddy at this time of the year. *If this is the case then I'm fucked*, I thought to myself. Filling up my hip flask with whisky, I tucked it into my pocket, picked up my cigarettes as well as the torch and left through the back door. I made my way back to the car, checking the contents of the wheelbarrow. His body lay exactly where I had left it. *Of course he's still there*, I thought to myself, *it's not as if he can go anywhere. He's dead!*

I took the bag of bloodstained clothes out of the car. Placing it in the wheelbarrow, I lifted it up and set off on my journey to the edge of the forest. The start of the track was not far from the back of the cottage. I unclasped the metal lock on the gate. With a loud creaking noise, I stretched out my arm, forcing it open to its furthest point. I managed to maneuver the wheelbarrow to the other side. Closing the gate behind me, my finger searched for the switch on the torch. I pressed the button, the beam of the light streaming across the pathway. I checked the rigidity of the grassy terrain. Stamping my foot on the hard ground, the slight frost in the November air made the path more passable. *Good*, I thought to myself, *at least it's not muddy.*

The moon appeared through the clouds offering a glimmer of light across the grassy terrain. The pathway led across the flat land to the start of the wood, the thicket of trees looming in the distance. Like keepers of the forest, a row of birch trees protected the woodland inside, holding the secret to his final resting place. His burial site was situated on slightly higher ground at the other side.

On the first part of the journey, the overgrown grass, ferns and nettles made it almost impossible to steer the barrow, but I forced the wheels over the unkempt path. The tangled web from the limbs of the overgrown shrubs also blocked the track; the spiky fingers of the gorse bushes snagging at the fabric of my clothes. I pushed them aside to allow a safe passage through the twisted mess, sweat covering my entire body as I battered it with the spade before finally heaving the wheelbarrow into a clearing at the start of the forest.

"At last," I said to myself, as I let out a huge sigh of relief.

Falling to the ground, I lay on my back, wiped the sweat off my face and looked up into the atmosphere. In the distance, the flickering, but faint light of the stars littered the night sky. The dark silhouette of the colossal mountain range stretched as far as the eye could see. Above me, the moon disappeared behind a thick blanket of cloud as darkness engulfed the valley once more. Switching on the torch, I rolled over, flashing it over the ground until I found a more suitable resting place. As I sat on top of a grassy verge, I lit a cigarette, indulged in a little more whisky, my fingers caressing the engraving of my initials on the flask. My head started to spin. I thought to myself, *I better not drink anymore. I have a long night ahead.* Placing the flask back in my pocket, I stood up with a sense of purpose and continued on my journey.

To gain access to the forest, the clearing led towards the trail bridge perched across the flowing river below. The wheels glided across the wooden surface. I reached the other end and then, stopped. I heard a faint noise in the distance. A beam of light flickered through the trees. *What the fuck!* I checked the time. It was just after nine o'clock. *Who is out here at this time of night?* The noise grew louder. It was the sound of a dog barking. Treading backwards across the bridge, I reached the other side, pushing the wheelbarrow across the clearing towards the path covered in gorse bushes. I huddled into the bony arms of the shrub and waited.

I heard the owner calling out the dog's name as he moved closer to my hiding place. "Misty! Where the hell are you, you stupid mutt," he shouted.

Henry, I thought to myself. *Our bloody gardener!* The old man stood on the bridge, shining the torch across the clearing, unaware of my prying eyes. I saw him swinging the light in the other direction and heard the dog barking as it bounded up to his master.

"There you are... sit!" he ordered.

He clipped the leash to its collar. The dog, perhaps sensing something amiss, pulled on it, sniffing the air in my direction. Henry tugged on the lead, but his dog was persistent. At the top of his voice, he shouted, "Who's there?" Swirling around in a circle, I saw him peering around the forest for several minutes, as if waiting for a reply, then shook his head. "Let's go, Misty. There's nobody here."

It reluctantly complied.

When it was safe, I emerged from my hiding place. High on adrenalin, my manic almost hysterical laugh echoed around the empty forest. "Now that would have been funny to be caught by a fucking dog!" I said to myself.

Despite the heavy feeling in my arms and the dull aching pain across the base of my back, I grabbed hold of the wheelbarrow then made my way back across the bridge. I switched on the torch before heading into the pitch black forest. It seemed different at night, my heightened senses wary of every sight, sound, taste, smell and touch. The torch only allowed a slither of light to appear in front of me as my eyes strained to focus on the path. The smell of the forest was overpowering; damp yet acrid from the musky odour of the clammy earth and moist leaves. To make matters worse, the reeking scent of death - clinging to the back of my throat - made it hard to control the waves of nausea permeating through my body. I stopped on numerous occasions, my hand reaching for my mouth as the muscles in my stomach battled to stop the retching.

As I continued on my journey, stray branches crunched under my feet like the sound of cracking bones and just then, I heard another noise, a more subtle sound... *scrape, scrape, scrape*. My eyes darted around the forest, my heart beating in my ears. I realised it was the sound of an animal foraging in the undergrowth and let out a huge sigh of relief. Straining my eyes, the evil-looking trees loomed overhead, casting unearthly shadows from the twisted branches emerging from the limbs of the trees. *Just concentrate on the path*, I told myself, *stay focused*.

Trying to avoid the surrounding forest, I concentrated my efforts on the strenuous journey ahead. The load became heavier and heavier as I travelled further into the depths of the woods, my limbs straining under the weight of the wheelbarrow. I had to stop and rest. *It can't be much further now*, I thought to myself. I lifted my arms up into the air, stretching my body, trying to release the tension in my muscles. *This is painful.* I lit a cigarette and pointed the torch out in front of me. All I could see was the dense thicket of bushes and trees lining the side of the path. Just then, the light started to fade. Banging the torch on my hand, I tried to get it to work. *Oh no!... it must be the batteries.* Staring out into the pitch black forest, a darker more sinister fear passed through my body – fully aware of the severity of the situation. I started to tremble. *Get a bloody grip of yourself!*

Searching for the handles of the wheelbarrow, I grabbed hold of them, finding comfort in the solid structure in my hands. *Straight ahead*, I told myself. Taking small steps, I slowly stretched out each leg in front of me, feeling the ground below my feet before moving forward, but felt disorientated as the dark night enveloped the forest. I forced the wheels of the barrow over the debris on the track. On several occasions, I felt it tilting as I veered off the path but somehow managed to stop the body from falling out of the wheelbarrow. Sweating profusely, I made my way towards our destination.

Looking above me, desperate for some kind of lifeline, I peered through the canopy of trees and saw a glimmer of light from the moon. The clouds parted and there, right there when I needed it the most, the full light of the moon appeared, shining down on me.

"Thank you, thank you, thank you," I said to myself, over and over again.

Finally, I had a better view. I found an inner strength. Deviating from the path, I made my way towards a clearing, forcing the wheelbarrow over the undergrowth before falling to the ground. I lay on my back and closed my eyes and felt myself drifting off to sleep. My body jerked. *Get up! What the fuck are you doing?* I sat bolt upright. I had another swig of whisky then lit a cigarette to keep me awake. The thought of digging his grave filled me with dread. I had no strength left in my weary limbs.

"Well you can't leave him like this, so start digging," I told myself.

The moon was still shining over the forest. I passed my lighter closer to the ground, trying to find a suitable spot to bury him. Out of reach from tree roots, nestled between some bushes, the plot was perfect. Reaching for the spade, I cleared away the debris and started to dig. *How deep? This is going to take me hours!* I decided on a depth of four feet. *Shallow graves can easily be disturbed by animals.* The earth was moist, but it still took a lot of effort to dig it out. Hours passed and I got into a rhythm. At nearly three feet, I stopped to rest. I heard the snap of a branch. I froze. Slowly peering over the top of the grave, I spotted two hind legs underneath the wheelbarrow. I heard the animal scratching at the plastic sheet. I threw some earth at it and the fox scuttled away. *Death… it smells the scent of death.* Becoming paranoid, I started to dig deeper in an almost delirious manner, ignoring the exhaustion and pain in my body. When the hole was up to my chest, I knew I had finished. I dragged myself out of the grave, chuckling at the amount of earth on the ground. *How did I manage that?*

With a feeling of euphoria, I stood beside the wheelbarrow looking down over his dead body. *This is it, Edward. You're final resting place.* Out of curiosity, I reached into his pockets to retrieve his belongings and found his wallet, car keys and wedding ring. *Leave them. Take nothing. Bury everything with him.* I pondered over my thoughts. *I suppose if I take them then I'll need to dispose of them. That's risky. If he's ever found then he'll be identified straight away.* After much deliberation, I decided to leave his wallet and keys, but stared at the gold band, his name inscribed on the inside of the ring. *Cheating bastard. I bet he did that with all his dirty whores, taking it off to ignore the fact that he was in fact a married man.* I tucked it into my pocket, stared down at his bloated face and said, "Rot in hell, you bastard."

Positioning the wheelbarrow at the side of the grave, I tipped it over - watching his body, the bag of bloodstained clothes and the plastic sheet tumbling into the grave. I started to shovel the muck into the hole, watching his face disappearing under the clumps of earth. After two feet, I jumped on it to flatten it down, lessening the likelihood that it would sink into the ground after I left. Shovelling the final mounds of earth on top of him, I stamped on it again then spread the debris back across the grave. Totally exhausted, I sat down near the bush next to his grave and lit a cigarette. Wiping the muddy sweat from my brow, I lay down on my back, thanking the moon for its assistance.

All of a sudden, I heard a noise.

Without moving a muscle, my eyes shifted towards the burial spot. The fox had returned. It was frantically scratching at the ground. Unaware of my presence, I reached for the spade lying at the side of me, gripped the handle, sat up, raised it above my head and then, it came crashing down on its skull. Dazed and stunned it tried to get up.

"Get the hell away from my grave," I cried.

By this time, I was on my feet as the spade lunged down upon the terrified animal, the cries of pain echoing around the forest. In an almost hysterical manner, I battered its body to death. As the night faded and daylight emerged, I tossed it into the wheelbarrow then made my way back through the forest towards the cottage.

4

THE MISTRESS

"I wish I would have known from the beginning how far this would have gone."
(David Berkowitz)

Rigid with fear.

I'm lying on my back in a shallow grave, my arms and legs are taped together. I can't move. There is something above me, peering down with huge staring eyes. It starts to laugh. "Now it's your turn, but for you... I'm going to bury you alive." My eyes are wide with fear. "Don't hurt me, please don't hurt me" I say in a childlike voice. The enormous hands are holding a spade. The first mound of earth lands near my face... THUD! I take in a deep breath, the gritty muck entering my mouth. I shake my head back and forth then spit it out. Another clump hits my chest, then another and another; crushing my body, smothering me as I gasp for air. The looming figure bends down, stares into my frightened eyes and reaches out with its elongated fingers...

"Hey baby, it's time to wake up," says a voice.

Half asleep, half awake and not knowing what is real anymore, my eyes open in fear of what awaits me. She comes into focus, straddling across my body, touching my face.

"Jacques! What a fright you gave me."

"What are you talking about?"

I let out a huge sigh of relief. "I've not slept very well. I was having a bad dream. There were fingers... on my face."

"That was me, silly. Are you okay? You look awful."

"Thanks!"

"I didn't mean it like that. You just look tired. What were you dreaming about?"

"It's nothing... it was just a nightmare."

Jacques wraps her arms around my neck. I feel her naked body on top of mine and start to feel aroused. She says, seductively, "Well... you're not too tired to want me, Jayden."

"It's getting late. We need to get up. Can we leave it for another time?"

Ignoring me, she teases my mouth with her tongue.

"Stop. I feel so tired. I really didn't sleep well."

"It was okay last night when I was feeling tired. Are you sure?"

"Yes! Remember, I need to make a conference call. You have to get to work."

I drag myself out of bed and have a shower. Feeling a bit more refreshed, I put on my clothes and hear the grinder of the coffee machine in the kitchen.

"Here," she says handing me a cup, "this will wake you up."

"Thanks. Sorry, about this morning."

"Whatever. Do you want me to come over tonight?"

"I'm flying back to Edinburgh."

She looks upset. "You should've let me know you were in London as soon as you arrived. When are you coming back?"

"I'm not sure. I've not made any definite plans. I also have to deal with my mother when I get home. She's upset by the official ruling about my father's death."

"I'm going to go. I need to get to work. Take care," she says, walking past me towards the front door.

"Don't be like that. Come here."

I wrap my arms around her neck. Taking this as a sign that I have changed my mind, she kisses my lips as those wandering hands reach for my groin. I respond. This pretty lady is starting to win the battle between my mind and body, but not quite. "Jacques… don't. Please."

She ignores my words.

"Stop it!"

"Why? We don't see very much of each other. We need to make the most of it."

I take hold of her hands, bringing them to an abrupt halt. "I'll be back next month. We can meet up then."

"You really are a bastard at times."

"Sorry…"

Jacques turns to leave the apartment.

Go after her! She reluctantly lets me kiss her goodbye. "See you soon, Miss Hayes."

"Sure, Jayden."

She gets into the lift, the doors close and then, she is gone.

I go back into the apartment. It is nine-thirty. I'm late for the video conference. *Just as well we didn't end up back in bed together.* I dash into the spare room to check the equipment. Opening up the option on my screen, I search the contacts list then click on the icon to call Richard McKenzie.

It rings.

He answers.

"Sorry, I'm a bit late. I've had a busy morning." *In actual fact I've been up all night thinking about the time I killed my own father, dreaming about being buried alive and dealing with a neurotic girlfriend!*

"No problem. How are you?"

"Good. Can you see me okay on the screen?"

"I've got you. Can you see me?"

"Crystal clear. Right... the reason I want to speak to you is that I'm setting up a new advertising business in Westminster. I want you to take on the role as the Managing Partner."

He pauses. "I'm flattered. Why me?"

"You know my business. You know our values, culture and clients. I wouldn't have been able to make the agency so profitable."

"I'm not sure about that. You did a good job on your own building up the business after I left. You also have Jessica ... what's her last name?"

"Jessica Logan. She runs the Edinburgh agency when I'm not there."

"It would have been successful with or without me. You have a good head for business."

"That's true," I say, knowing he can see the boyish grin on my face. "I realise you're settled where you are in London, but I need you. It's a lucrative package, better than the one you're getting at the moment."

"I need to think about it."

"I want someone that I can trust to run this one in London. It's important to have you on board... you're like a father to me."

I see him pondering over my request.

"Look... can you meet me today? I'm going to finalise the contract to take over some premises in Westminster. Then it's full steam ahead from there. My client base in Edinburgh is operating at full capacity."

"What time?" he asks.

"Four o'clock."

"Shall I meet you at the flat?"

"Yes, but come a bit earlier so we can catch up. About three-thirty?"

"That's fine," he says. "See you then."

I end the call.

Punching the air in anticipation, I make my way into the kitchen to finish my coffee, feeling positive about the advertising business. I have worked at the agency in Edinburgh since leaving school, first as a weekend job then as the owner after finishing my degree. Through a contact from my father, an opportunity came up to be an Account Executive, managing the advertising accounts between the clients and the agency. The proprietor at the time was a creative genius. He won many lucrative contracts in a diverse range of industry sectors. The agency also focused on taking underdog brands by finding a strong position in the marketplace through highly creative advertisements. However, it was making a loss due to the owner's lack of business acumen and his inability to manage profit margins.

Seeing it as a business opportunity, the knowledge from my degree gave me the courage to put together a solid business plan. I raised most of the money from the bank to buy it. With reluctance, my father provided the remainder of the investment, seeing it only as a business opportunity. He had accumulated a small fortune from his consultancy business. As a keen venture capitalist, he was always looking for a lucrative investment, but he made it clear that he had reservations about my leadership capabilities. *Fucking arsehole*, I think to myself.

In contrast, Richard always had faith in me. As an Account Director, he took me under his wing when I bought it, helping to turn the agency around. We trimmed down the workforce, placed a bigger emphasis on client relationships, reassessed the workflow and reigned in the creatives who came up with the original ideas for the advertisements. We also assessed our client portfolio - getting rid of smaller accounts with low margins. Within two years, I paid off the debt. It started to make a sizeable profit and five years later, I am ready to invest in some new business premises in Westminster.

"I need you, Richard McKenzie," I say to myself. "I hope you take up my offer."

To be able to function throughout the rest of the day, I decide to go back to sleep. As I climb into bed, my dream still clings to the forefront of my mind. I know it is a mix of my conscious and subconscious mind, creating a vile scenario about my father burying me alive, just to frighten me. I dismiss the thought. *I'll get through this. There's no doubt about that. I've managed for the last seven years.* I wrap the duvet around my body, wishing that Jacques was still here. *Next time*, I think to myself.

I drift off to sleep on a positive note.

Several hours later, I wake up feeling refreshed. I hear the buzzer at three-thirty. I see he's still extremely punctual. I wait outside the front door for the lift to arrive on the fifth floor. As the doors open, he stretches out an arm, walking towards me with a smile on his face. He places one hand on my shoulder as the other brushes across my back.

"Jayden, it's good to see you again."

I stare at him, thinking how well he has aged for a man in his mid-fifties. Richard has an air of sophistication; the just-trimmed smoothness of his grey hair giving him a distinguished look. He stands tall and straight, wears gold-rimmed glasses and carries a leather briefcase. The classic cut of his tailored business suit is well executed, smooth yet simple and the angular precision of his striped tie with an impeccable dimple contrasts perfectly against a white shirt, revealing a blue-faced wristwatch just visible below the cuff. To finish off the outfit, he wears a pair of dark-tanned brogues.

Feeling relieved that he is here, I shake his hand with both of mine, holding onto them for longer than necessary. "Good to see you, too." I let out a deep breath. "Really good."

"Let's go inside. You can let me know more about your business idea."

I go over the plan again, telling him about the premises in Westminster. "It's everything I want for a new agency. We better go. It's impressive. It was made for you."

We make our way there on foot. Approaching the front of the glass-infused building, the angle of the sun reflects off the dark surface, shimmering in the daylight. At street level, retail outlets dominate the first floor and then, it stretches up over another five floors of business premises.

"Which one do we have?" he asks.

We? This is looking good. "Third and fourth," I tell him. "I'm going to sign the lease today. I saw it a few months ago. I've been negotiating the price and recruited most of the new staff… apart from you! It's impressive, don't you think?"

He smiles. "You've done well."

I press the third floor buzzer and the doors open to invite us in. The estate agent is waiting at the top of the stairs as we get out of the lift. "Mr. Scott, it's good to see you again," he says, shaking my hand. "Are you ready to finalise the lease?"

"Just about. We're going to take a quick look around. This is my new business partner."

"Pleased to meet you," says the estate agent.

Richard raises an eyebrow.

I grin at him. *Well… you'll be my business partner by the end of the day*, I think to myself.

The vast space is flexible with small enclosed offices dotted around the perimeter on both floors. I go over the departmental layout. "I want the Reception, Account Management and Planning on this floor and Finance, Creatives and Studio/Production on the fourth floor. The offices will provide breakout areas for our client meetings."

He ponders over the information. "That sounds like a good plan."

I continue. "I've ordered the furniture and technology. It's ready to be delivered over the next month. Your job would be to coordinate everything for the opening as well as manage the agency. Our client base in London can use this agency rather than the one in Edinburgh. I have a few lucrative brands we're pitching for at the moment. They can deal with you, here in London, if we win them."

"Sounds good."

I tell him about his financial package. "What do you think? Do we have a deal?"

He pauses. "How can I refuse. I need to hand in my notice, but I'll work in both places until then."

I embrace him then go and seek out the estate agent. "I'm ready to sign the lease."

He hands me the keys. "Good luck with your business, Mr. Scott."

"Thank you."

I give them to Richard. "It's all yours. I'll never be off the phone. Remember, I'm only a plane ride away if you need me."

We say goodbye outside the agency.

I make the short trip back to the apartment with a grin on my face. "Right... get the hell out of here," I say to myself. My flight is leaving at seven-thirty. I pack, lock up the flat and make my way to Westminster station. I board the tube and change at Piccadilly. It takes me straight to Terminal 1 at Heathrow Airport. I check in, but still have an hour to spare, so order something to eat in the business lounge. *I better not drink too much as I need to deal with my mother when I get home. At least Mathew has told her the news about the court's decision. That's one good thing at least.*

I check the screen. The plane is ready to board. As I head towards the gate, the flight attendant says, "Good evening, Mr. Scott. Can I have your boarding card?" I give it to her, avoiding that flashing smile and fixed gaze. There is also someone to greet me at the other end. I follow the hostess to the Business Class area. "Get settled. I'll come back and take your drink's order." She stretches out her arm. "Here are today's papers if you want them?"

I take them. Actually... can I just have a large whisky just now?"

"I need to wait until we take off. I'll bring it to you just after that."

"Thanks. I understand."

I gaze out of the window. As the plane takes off, London becomes a speck of light in the distance. It climbs higher into the night sky then starts shaking from the turbulence, stabilising as the aircraft emerges through the dense clouds.

I unclasp the seatbelt.

The flight attendant brings me a drink.

I put on my glasses, open up the Edinburgh-based newspaper and scan the headlines. One catches my eye:

"Dead Body Remains Found On Corstorphine Hill"

I read it with interest. A cyclist has found the skeletal remains of a human body from a shallow grave, the bones, scattered across a remote area of woodland. *Animals*, I think to myself. *That's why I killed that fox. And that's why I tortured myself to dig such a deep grave.* The victim is believed to be a woman. The prime suspect is the son. Not dissimilar to my own situation. Taking a large drink of whisky, I flick through the paper, trying to dismiss the thought from my mind. Just then, my eyes focus on a small headline in the bottom right hand corner of the broadsheet:

"Sociopaths In The Corporate World"

I read it in more detail. The news report states that a criminologist is to attend a conference in Edinburgh to provide a unique insight into sociopathic leaders in the corporate world. That's interesting. I read on. "Dr. Kristina Cooper..." I stop reading. What? Who? My Kristina? I scan the article. It outlines her credentials and there, right there it states: "Brought up in a small village on the east coast of Scotland..." My heart skips a beat. I jump up off my seat and start pacing around the cabin. I remember we went back to the village two years after I left, but she had gone. Reverend McIntyre told us that her father found a new job in England and no one had heard from them since they left. *When is the conference?* I grab the newspaper to find out when it takes place. I check the date on my phone. Two weeks on Friday. After all this time, she's going to be in Edinburgh.

I press the button to summon the flight attendant. It is the lady from the boarding gate. She eyes me up and down and then, with a subtle lick of her painted lips, asks how she can help. Ignoring her flirtatious behaviour, I order a double measure of whisky. I start to calm down, drinking the fiery liquid in one mouthful.

"Are you okay?" she asks. "Do you want another one?"

"Just leave me alone."

She looks upset.

"Sorry... no thank you. I've had a pretty stressful couple of days. I think I'll just have a sleep for the rest of the journey."

The hostess has stern look on her face and says, "Okay, Mr. Scott. No offence taken."

I close my eyes and think about Kristina. The last time I saw her, she was sitting alone on the top of the cliff. I must attend the conference. I try not to dwell on it any longer. Instead, I stare out of the window, my mind wandering back to the day I returned to the cottage after the hiking trip with my friends over the Devil's Staircase - after burying my father in a remote grave in Argyll.

****

It was the morning after the night before. I heard something in the deepest corner of my subconscious mind. *It's the door. Someone's banging on the door*, I told myself. It was persistent and became louder as I started to wake up. I rolled over in bed, every muscle in my body aching from head to toe.

The noise stopped.

I just managed to get up. Staggering over to the bedroom window, I rubbed it free of condensation, struggling to see through the film of water clinging to the surface of the glass and wiped it again, my eyes scanning the area at the front of the cottage, but there was no one there. I crossed the landing, made my way towards the back of the house and peered through the window. Just then, I caught sight of someone approaching my car. *Fucking hell! The boot is wide open. The smell will still be lingering around.* I banged on the glass. A figure of a woman turned around, shielding her eyes with her hand, searching for the source of the noise.

I opened the window. "What do you want?"

"Jayden, it's me."

I eventually worked out it was Amanda. She looked different dressed in casual clothes with her hair tied back off her face. I groaned. *What does she want?* "Come back round to the front of the house. I'll let you in."

"The boot of your car is open. Do you want me to close it?"

"No! Just leave it. I need to air it out. Stinking hiking clothes smell."

She hesitated, looked at the car, stopped and headed back towards the front of the cottage. "See you in a minute."

This is all I need. Why today? My aching body did not respond well to the climb down the stairs. Amanda must have wondered what was taking me so long. An agonising pain seared through my muscles as I held on to the bannister, hobbling down the steps one at a time. I opened the door. The daylight hurt my eyes. Shielding them from the unwelcome glare of the sun, she was waiting patiently at the front of the house.

"Hey you! I was just passing and came down to see if you were still here. We didn't swap numbers… I just wanted to give you it. That's if you want to keep in touch?"

"Of course I do."

She looked at me, tapping her foot on the gravel.

"Come in."

"Are you okay? You don't look very well. Were you drinking last night?"

I lied. "No… not a drop. I think I might be coming down with something. My body aches. I feel shivery. I need to go and lie down."

She took my arm, helping me back up the stairs.

Feeling utterly exhausted, my head started spinning. I flopped down onto the bed, the taste of death still clinging to the back of my throat. Stabbing pains seared through my stomach. My mouth started to water. I tried to force the bile back down into my gut as my body jerked in unison to the involuntary spasms.

"I feel so ill," I groaned.

"Do you want me to get a doctor?"

I felt intoxicated, slurring my words. "I'll be fine once I have a sleep."

Cuddling into Amanda, I closed my eyes and felt myself tumbling down into the depths of a bottomless pit, the darkness engulfing my entire existence, my mind slipping into an unconscious world free of pain and discomfort.

Several hours later, I woke up feeling disorientated. I forgot about her until I heard someone coming up the stairs.

She gave me a glass of water. "Hey… you're awake. You've been asleep for three hours. Here take these. It might help."

I sat up, tilted my head back and swallowed the tablets. I drank the whole glass of water. After a few minutes, I started to feel a bit more coherent. The dizziness had subsided, but my body still felt agonisingly stiff. I stretched out in bed, twisting it one way then another, trying to loosen the tight muscles.

"Better?" she asked.

"A little bit. What time is it?"

"Just after one o'clock."

"Bloody hell. I told my mother I'd be leaving early in the morning. I need to text her. Can you get my phone? I think it's in the kitchen."

She brought it up.

I sent the text.

Sorry I've just woken up. I'm leaving in about an hour. I'll be with you just after seven. See you then x

I chucked it across the bed. "I need to leave soon. Come over here."

She lay down on the bed, not sure how to react and then, kissed me on the forehead. The temptation was too much to bear. *What man wouldn't be tempted by that beautiful body,* I thought to myself. My hands wandered over Amanda's curves, kissing her in a desperate manner. *I need this as a release - to escape from the events of the previous night, from the torturous experience of burying my father's body.*

"Stop it. You're not well!"

"I don't care. It's over to you."

She wriggled out of her clothes while I struggled to take off my jogging trousers. Straddling across my body, Amanda placed her hands above my head and then, kissed my mouth with a lingering kiss. "Are you sure?" she asked.

"More than sure," I replied.

She was gentle, but the excruciating pain in my body enhanced the pleasure of our lovemaking and somehow, I managed to lose myself in the rhythm of our bodies.

"Come up here."

She giggled. "Where?"

I pointed to my face. "Here."

"What for?"

"I have a surprise for you."

"Jayden, that's a bit too intimate."

"Don't be shy..."

I grabbed hold of Amanda, pulling her towards my head. *I love the taste of a woman almost as much as the sexual act itself.* She took hold of the headboard, straddling across me, relaxed, opened up and appeared to enjoy the sensation of my tongue before climaxing over my face. Shuffling back down, she found my erection, guiding it to the opening between her legs. Amanda was the one in control as she leaned back and placed both hands on my thighs, grinding on top, those pert breasts moving up and down to the rhythm of our lovemaking. The discomfort seared through my body, but I found my own fine line between pleasure and pain, trying to delay the inevitable, the pressure rising like the swell of a wave in the ocean, building up to the point of no return, before unleashing myself inside her body. It felt like nothing I had ever experienced before. She cuddled into me as we revelled in our after-sex-glow.

"Fantastic," I finally said.

She chuckled. "I know, but I've still to get your number!"

"Pass my phone." *I wonder if we'll see each other again*, I thought to myself. *I doubt it. I'll give it to her anyway.*

"I need to get up now and make my way home soon."

"Pity we don't have any more time together. Next time, perhaps?"

"Definitely," I declared. "Right... let's see if I can get up out of bed." I stretched my weary limbs. It took all of my effort to stand up. She stared at me as a strange look passed across her face. "What is it?" I asked.

She hid her face in the pillow and let out a cry of pleasure. "Your body is just..."

I laughed. "Martial art. It keeps me toned. Can you help me pack?"

"No problem. Let's get you organised. I put all your clothes from the washing machine in the laundry cupboard along with the hiking boots when you were asleep."

"Thanks, Amanda."

"My pleasure."

As I struggled to put on my trousers, I looked at her with a puzzled look on my face. Just then, I remembered taking them off at the back door, loading the muddy clothes as well as my boots into the machine before I had a shower and passed out in bed.

My phone went off as we made our way downstairs.

Okay Jayden. See you later tonight x

"What the hell is going on? Why is my mother so calm?" I mumbled.

"I'll get off now and leave you to get ready. Text or call me soon, Jayden... what's your last name anyway?" she giggled.

"Jayden Edward Scott. And you are?"

"Amanda Kennedy."

I kissed her hand as she left the cottage. "I hope to see you again, Miss Kennedy." *Alex is right, I am a smarmy bastard.*

Despite the pain in my limbs, I raced into the kitchen to check the laundry cupboard. Just at that moment, I remembered about the ring. Pulling the garments off the clotheshorse, I found the hiking trousers and started rummaging about in the pockets for the gold band, but there was nothing there. I grabbed hold of them, turning the item of clothing upside down, flicking the trousers out in front of me, waiting for the goddamn thing to fall from its hiding place.

Nothing.

Panicking, I grabbed hold of the damp clothes, shaking each in turn... nothing. *Where the hell is it?* Crawling about on my hands and knees, my fingers swept over the hard tiles on the cupboard floor. As a last desperate attempt, I checked the washing machine. I spun it around, hearing the whirring noise of the drum, waiting for the clinking noise of metal inside. There was nothing but a deadly silence. Not knowing what to do, my eyes frantically searched the ground, desperately trying to find where it could be. Just then, I decided to pull back the seal in the machine and there, right there in the crevice in the rubber, the gold band was lodged under the flap. Covered in a nervous sweat, I dropped to my knees, retrieving the ring from its hiding place. *Thank God! It's such a vital piece of evidence. I should've buried it along with my father.*

It took several minutes for the panic to subside. With a feeling of relief, I pulled out a handkerchief from my pocket, wrapping the ring into the folds of the fabric and placed it in my pocket. Finally, I stuffed the damp clothes and boots into a plastic bag - ready for disposal. Looking around the kitchen, everything appeared to be normal. I opened the back door to check the step. It was a bit muddy, but not any more than usual.

Racing towards the shed, I spotted the wheelbarrow and looked inside and there, lying on its side, the battered body of the dead fox stared out at me with a glazed look, its head positioned at a peculiar angle, the chestnut fur matted with clumps of dried blood with stiff black paws stretched out in front of its body. *I probably broke its neck*, I thought to myself, *poor bastard.* I went into the kitchen, found a large sack and concealed it inside. Checking the car, the smell had almost gone. However, I could still taste the stench of death clinging to the back of my throat, making me feel nauseous every now and again. I threw the body of the fox in the back then slammed the boot shut. Heading back into the house, I picked up the bags, locked up the cottage and drove back to Edinburgh.

I stopped in the layby, lighting a cigarette before taking the sack out the boot. With a sense of purpose in my stride - marching across to the marshland - I hurled the body of the dead animal into the swampy mass surrounding the base of the mountain range. Stubbing out the cigarette, I thought to myself, *Right… it's time to go home.*

The journey passed by in a haze.

By the time I parked the car at the end of our street, my body had almost given up on me. I felt exhausted. I wound down the window and lit a cigarette, gearing myself up for the reunion with my mother. *This is going to be a nightmare!* As I walked up to the front door, I took a deep breath and pushed it open. The house was deserted. *What's going on?* The quiet tones of classical music drifted in the air from the kitchen. *That's not my mother's taste in music?*

"Who's here?" I shouted.

The kitchen door opened. "Jayden, my boy," bellowed out a familiar voice.

Reverend bloody McIntyre! No wonder she's been so calm. "Charles, what are you doing here?" *As if I didn't know…*

"I've been here since Sunday. You better come and sit down."

I tried to put on a convincing act even although I felt worn out. "What's happened… where are my mother and father?"

"Your mother is asleep. Your father hasn't been seen since last week."

"Is he not back yet? Where is he? Why did my mother not text or phone to let me know?"

"I advised her not to. We didn't want to worry you and disrupt the break with your friends."

That's a convenient excuse for me in the future when the police get involved. "He's not been in touch at all?"

"No… nothing. He just seems to have disappeared."

"Where the hell is he? Have you called the police?"

"Someone's coming here tomorrow morning."

"I wonder what's happened. Did you check at his work?"

"I spoke to his business partner, Mathew Fleming. He's not seen him since he left his work last Friday."

"How's my mother?"

"She's distraught. I'm just going to leave her to sleep. I had to give her some sleeping tablets. She'll be annoyed with me because she wanted to see you, but was just *so* exhausted."

I know how she feels, I thought to myself.

"I'll make us some dinner. You go and get settled. I'll give you a shout when it's ready."

I went back outside to check the smell in the boot of the car. *It's not too bad.* Noticing the bag of condemned clothes, I pondered over what to do. *Don't take them inside. Get rid of it all.* Making the decision to leave the evidence, I picked up the holdall and returned to the house, looking in on my mother before heading off to bed. She was fast asleep. My aching limbs struggled to climb the stairs. I flopped down onto the bed and then… nothing. Feeling utterly exhausted, I passed out.

Sometime later, I heard his loud voice, "Jayden, its ready, my boy."

Joining him at the table, I dreaded having to spend too much time in his company without my mother. Much to my relief, Charles avoided any conversation about my missing father. Instead, he asked about the advertising agency.

"It's going well. I managed to secure a loan from the bank to buy it last year. I know I've not had it long, but we should break even over the next few years. I'm ploughing most of the profit back into paying off the debt."

He beamed at me with pride. "You've done well. You're only twenty-three and already running your own business. I'm so proud of you."

"Thanks, Charles."

He squeezed my arm. "I think we should let your mother rest tonight. I need to go out for a while. I'll catch up with you later if you're still up."

What a relief. I need some sleep. "Okay," I said, clearing away the plates. "Thanks for dinner."

"No problem. See you later… keep an eye on your mother." He made his way to the front door. "And… don't worry about anything."

"I'll try not to," I replied, closing it behind him.

I slid down the wall, sat on the floor and held my head in my hands, relief overpowering me at that moment, grateful to be left on my own. The pressure was all too much. My nose started to bleed - profusely. Taking the handkerchief from my pocket, I just sat there dazed and confused, enthralled by the droplets of blood splashing onto the floor, waiting for it to stop. *Once I get a good night's sleep, I'm sure I'll feel better. I need to get a grip!* I dabbed my nose, the circular globules of blood dispersing and soaking into the white fabric.

Pushing myself up off the floor, I pinched my nose with the tips of my fingers then walked towards the kitchen, leaned over the sink and spat out the clots of red liquid. Throwing away the handkerchief in the bin, I found a box of tissues, holding one to my nose until it stopped bleeding. I cleaned up the mess in the hallway, hobbled up to the bedroom, threw my clothes onto the chair and fell asleep.

In the morning, my head felt heavy after a sleepless night. I kept waking up, tossing and turning in bed, aware of my aching body. Despite the extreme fatigue, it felt good to be home - away from the torturous experience of disposing of his dead body. I got up, washed away the remnants of blood on my face then wandered down to the kitchen.

"Jayden!" cried my mother.

She ran towards me, wrapping her arms around my neck, clinging onto my body.

I flinched in pain.

Eventually... she let go. "I left you to sleep. You must have been tired after your trip. I've missed you *so* much."

"You should've told me what was going on!"

"I know, but we thought he would turn up. I didn't want to ruin your holiday."

"Where's Charles?"

"He's in the sitting room making a phone call to organise an Elder to look after the church. I'm so worried about your father."

"I'm not sure what to say... it's all a bit of a shock."

"I'm tired of thinking about it. You don't have to say anything. Hopefully the police can help. They'll be here in an hour. Do you want something to eat first?"

"No thanks. I'll just get ready for the visit. I hope they find him."

"Jayden..."

"What?"

"I'm glad you're home."

I smiled, giving her a reassuring look.

I decided to have a bath instead of a shower, relishing the thought of soaking in the hot water - soothing my battered body. Finding some bath salts, I settled into the comforting water, dreading the police visit. *I'm not sure I can handle this?* "Of course you can," I said to myself. *Just stay composed!* I rubbed the aching muscles with my hands and started to relax, relying on my martial art techniques, inhaling and exhaling, stretching and releasing the tension in my neck until I found a consistent rhythm with my breathing. Eventually, I felt an inner peace. *Right... I think I'm ready. Just stay calm.* I heard the doorbell just as I finished putting on my clothes.

"Jayden, can you come down."

"I'll be there in a minute."

I took a deep breath then walked into the sitting room.

"This is Inspector Canmore," said the Reverend.

Don't say too much! I shook his hand. "It's a pleasure to meet you."

His look lingered in my direction for longer than necessary.

I avoided his gaze, sat down next to my mother and took her hand.

"You reported a missing person. I have the details from the initial phone call you made to let me see... Constable Peters. I take it he's your husband, Mrs. Scott?"

"Yes, we've not seen or heard from him since Friday morning."

"Go back to the day you last saw him. Did he seem normal? Has he been under any stress lately?"

"My husband seemed fine. We all had breakfast together. Edward left for work and so did my son."

"Did he say anything? Anything at all that might explain his disappearance?"

"No... nothing."

Inspector Canmore scratched his head.

What's he thinking? I thought to myself. "My father did say that he might have to go to London for the weekend."

"Is this a regular occurrence?"

"If he has a business meeting." *Or a mistress to see!*

My mother interrupted. "He normally lets me know," she said, fiddling with the gold band on her finger.

"When did you start to become concerned, Mrs. Scott?"

"On Saturday morning when I woke up and realised he'd not been home. I've been calling him persistently since then. There's been no reply on his mobile phone."

"Where were you on Friday, Mr. Scott?"

"I went to work at the agency. It's my advertising business. I left about six and attended my martial arts class. Got back here about... what time was it?"

"Nine o'clock. Yes, it was just after nine," said my mother.

"And what did you do after you got home?"

I kept my composure. "We had dinner, watched a bit of TV then went to bed. The following morning my mother told me he'd not come home. I left the same day to meet with friends for my birthday on the west coast."

"The west coast?"

"We have a holiday cottage there. That's where I've been since I got back last night."

"So... you left on Saturday and you got back on Wednesday. Were you not worried? Why did you not come back home?"

"Wait a minute," bellowed the Reverend. "*We* decided not to tell Jayden anything and ruin his birthday with his friends. He insisted on coming home on Sunday. We didn't want to worry him."

"I have to ask. It's my job, Mr. McIntyre."

"I'm Reverend McIntyre to you, Inspector Canmore. I don't like your line of questioning. You need to find out what happened to Edward. He disappeared sometime between now and last weekend. God knows where? Your job is to find him... dead or alive." He looked at my mother. "Sorry, Carolyn... it's not looking good."

The Reverend appeared to be in control of the situation. Looking at him with admiration, I was glad he was here. *He's so loyal to our family... well to me and my mother*, I thought to myself.

"I agree," said the Inspector. "Well the best I can do is to file a report with the information that you've given me and share it with the Missing Persons Bureau. Do you have a recent photograph of him so we can circulate it? I'll review his bank records to see if any transactions have been made. We can also check with his work."

Reaching out for the Reverend, she started to cry. "We've already done that. He's not been seen since he left work on Friday evening."

The inspector looked at her with pity. "Mrs. Scott... we'll do everything we can to find him."

"Thank you so much," she sniffed. "This has all been too much."

Charles held onto my mother. "Come with me, Carolyn... you need to lie down," said the Reverend. "Jayden will see out, Inspector Canmore."

"I can see my own way out," he replied.

"Get in touch if you hear anything," I said. "Thanks for all your help, Inspector."

"I'll be in touch soon. I need to check out the all the information you gave me first."

Fucking arsehole, I thought to myself.

On that note, he left the sitting room.

Engrossed in my own thoughts, it did not register in my mind that he had not left until I heard the front door slam, several minutes later. *What's he been doing - text or phone call perhaps? So... he wants a photo of my father to circulate. What about his mistress? Once Annabel Taylor finds out what's happened she'll come forward. This is not good. Not good at all! I have to decide what to do about this and decide soon.*

****

I woke up early the next day and got ready to go to work. Taking a clean handkerchief from the drawer, I folded it up, putting it into my suit pocket. *The ring! Bloody hell, I forgot all about it.* The clothes from the day before were lying on the chair. I reached into my trousers, but it was not there. Just then, I remembered about the nose bleed. *I threw that handkerchief in the bucket. Shit!*

Racing down the stairs, I approached the kitchen, hearing the sound of classical music. The sorrowful almost painful tones of the female soprano blended to perfection with the Reverend's deep voice. He stopped singing as I entered the kitchen.

"Come and sit down. I'll make you some breakfast."

He seemed so keen that I did not have the heart to refuse. *I'll check the bin once he leaves.* "Thanks, Charles."

"I'm making some poached eggs. Here... put the bread in the toaster."

I gazed at him out of the corner of my eye.

The Reverend always dressed in his matching grey trousers, tunic and collar. He was not much older than my father, but his appearance and demeanour were very different. There was an air of authority about him - someone you could trust with your life. Charles was a handsome man with blue eyes, broad shoulders and strong protective arms. He devoted his life to the Presbyterian Church, perhaps to the detriment of his own personal happiness. Living alone, he served his community with such loyalty. *He deserves to be happy*, I thought to myself. *I know he's happy here with my mother despite the circumstances surrounding my father's disappearance.*

I listened to the Latin music, interpreting the lyrics of the song. "Leave me to languish alone with sorrow, weeping and yearning for freedom, dear." *Freedom*, I thought to myself. *We're now free from him, but there is no languish or weeping and there is no sorrow... well not from me anyway.*

He interrupted my thoughts. "Do you like it?"

"What?"

"The music? It's Handel's *Lascio Ch'io Pianga*. It's very sad yet so beautiful."

"I do like it. You sing well," I said, trying to lighten the conversation.

His laughter bellowed out from deep within his heartfelt soul. "Pass me the toast." He buttered it, placed the eggs on the bread and handed me the plate. "Sit down, Jayden."

"Thanks, Charles."

He got his breakfast then sat at the other side of the table. "You must realise that I'm here for you and your mother, not for Edward. I have no idea what's happened to him. I'm not lying when I say I hope he never comes back. I don't wish him any harm. He's never been good for Carolyn. You must know that more than anyone else. He's an evil man... not that I would say that to anyone else."

His words took me by surprise. "I understand." *Do you think he deserved to die? What does your bible say about mental and physical abuse, adultery and murder?*

"I should never have let you both leave the village," he declared.

"I heard what you said to her in the church the day we left. It was so confusing at the time. He did abuse me Charles, as well as my mother, all through my childhood until I confronted him about his behaviour when I was seventeen. Not only that, he kicked and punched her in the stomach. I think that's why she lost the baby."

His eyes filled with tears. "That must have been awful for both of you. I'm so sorry I let you down. In God's name, why did she not tell me?"

"It's not your fault. My mother... she's the one who..."

"I'm here now. I'll take care of her."

"I know you will, Charles. I'm glad you came. We both need you."

He squeezed my hand.

"I have to go to work. Who knows what's been happening while

I've been away. I'll catch up with you both after my martial arts class... just after nine."

"See you then. I'm off to catch up with a few friends today."

"Have a good day, Charles."

He got up and left, leaving me alone in the kitchen. I dashed towards the bin, pressing my foot on the pedal, to reveal nothing but the empty interior. *The black bag must be outside in the main bucket.* As I opened the front door, the noise of the tail lift on the bin lorry clanked into position as the contents of our waste tipped into the bowels of the container, crushing it to a pulp. "Well... at least that's one way to dispose of it," I said, chuckling away to myself.

I arrived at the agency by public transport just before ten. *There's no way I'm taking that stinking car.* Looking up at the tall but lean building, it was situated in the heart of a regeneration area bordering the city centre on the Shores of Leith. It overlooked the waterfront. The same river that flowed past the back of our house, albeit over two miles from there. Spanning over three floors, I employed over sixty people, all committed to making the agency a success.

"Good morning, Mr. Scott," said our receptionist.

I nodded in her direction and smiled.

I gave him a fright as I approached his office and shouted, "Richard McKenzie... it's good to see you."

Startled, he looked up from his computer. "Jayden! It's great to have you back. Did you have a good hiking trip?"

"I had a great time. We need to catch up. You can let me know what I've missed. I'll go and get us a coffee."

He updated me on the client contracts, telling me the agency had just won a pitch for a major grocery retailer as well as a government contract for knife crime.

"Richard... that's fantastic. That's great the agency won the contract for the retailer. We worked hard on that one. That's also an interesting concept on knife crime. *How ironic!* I thought to myself. We should be able to come up with some creative ideas and take it viral perhaps?"

"The government contracts could be a major boost to enhance our client portfolio. We have another one we're going to pitch for as the Local Council want to tackle the issue of raising awareness about mental health issues. It's a hard message to get across. I know we're up for the challenge, Jayden."

"That sounds great. Thanks for running things while I've been away. Catch up with you later. I need to go and check my backlog of emails."

"No problem."

It took a while to catch up with my employees as well as answer the numerous amounts of correspondence. When I finished, I grabbed some lunch and shut the office door. Sitting alone, I contemplated the issue related to my father's mistress. She was the last person to see him alive on the morning he left her flat. *Once she knows something is seriously wrong, she could go to the police. I don't want any evidence of him being in Edinburgh on that fateful morning. What shall I do?* A plan started to hatch in my mind. *Later*, I thought to myself, *later tonight*.

I left the agency to go to my martial arts class just after six. Changing out of my business clothes into a tracksuit, I packed them into the rucksack in the locker. There at the back, I saw the shiny blade concealed in its sheath. *Your name is on that knife, Annabel Taylor.* Dismissing the thought, I locked the door and looked forward to the class. *This will be good for my aching body.*

I pushed myself to the limit. It felt good to be back in control. When I finished, there was not any time left to take a shower. I grabbed the bag from the locker, strapped the sheath around my waist and put on an old baseball cap. With this mistress, they met outside a certain bar at the same time every Friday night after work and then, walked the short distance to her flat. There was a chance she would turn up. I had fifteen minutes to get there. I jumped on a tram for the ten minute ride then settled myself into a small yet busy coffee shop across the road from the pub. Feeling nervous, I scanned the shop for any prying cameras. There were none. However, I noticed several on the main street. *There must be a way out the back of this café to the safety of the side road which she takes to get to her flat.* I turned around, noticing the fire exit sign next to the toilets. *Perfect.* I waited, peering out of the window from beneath my baseball cap.

I spotted her ten minutes later standing outside the pub. His mistress was tall like my mother, but much younger - alluring in a sultry way with an air of mystery in those smouldering come-to-bed eyes. Dressed in a tailored suit, the classic lines of the simple yet elegant skirt complemented the design of the lapelled jacket, nipping in at the waist. She looked sensual with her hair tied back, emphasising her sharp cheekbones and full lips. My groin stirred. *I can see the appeal Edward… very nice. Unfortunately this mistress must die.* It was a waiting game until she left to return home. Annabel Taylor came out of the bar with her drink, sat outside and lit a cigarette. I watched as she crossed her legs, searching for him up and down the street. Half an hour later she gave up, crossing over to the other side of the road. I looked at my watch. It was eight-forty. I put on a pair of leather gloves, leaving the coffee shop by the back entrance and waited.

From the shadows of the recess, I saw his mistress turn the corner off the main road, making her way along the side street that led to the flat. She stopped then stood at the bottom of the stairs leading up to the front door. With her back to me, she started to rake in her bag - probably for the keys. I looked behind me. There was no one else in the street apart from several people who disappeared round the corner at the end of the road. As I passed, I already had the blade concealed in my hand. With a light touch, I placed one hand on her shoulder as other swept across her neck, slitting his slut's throat with precision. It was over within a split second. She fell to the ground as the contents of the bag rolled over the pavement. I had no hesitation in picking up her purse and mobile phone. I stopped and looked at her hand before prising the ring from her finger. Crossing the road, I made my way to the end of the street and then, I turned to take one last look at the figure lying on the pavement. On bended knees, someone was looming over the body, frantically trying to stop the flow of blood from her neck.

Just then, I heard a spine-chilling scream followed by a piercing voice, "HELP! SOMEONE PLEASE HELP ME," cried the woman. "HELP ME, PLEASE."

At that moment, a cold empty feeling passed over me. I emotionally disconnected myself from the situation. *You're disgusting. You must have known he was married, you fucking bitch.* I turned the corner, feeling nothing but exhilaration as I made my way through the backstreets of the city towards our house.

For the remainder of the journey, I deviated up a path that led onto the canal. I crouched down, rinsing the knife in the river, watching a trail of red blood disperse through the clear water. Placing it back in the sheath, I sat on a wooden bench, listening to the soothing noise of the current. I lit a cigarette, savouring the after-kill-smoke in my lungs.

"You're a cold-hearted bastard," I said to myself.

I checked the messages on her phone. There were several texts to my father, desperate messages, pleading for him to get in touch. The last one she had sent that morning.

> Edward, please get in touch. I'll wait for you outside the bar at the usual time. Has your wife found out? Why won't you return my calls or messages? Please come and meet me. We need to talk. I miss you x

"Why did you ever get involved with him Annabel Taylor?" I mumbled. "This is the ultimate revenge for being involved with my father. It has sealed your fate."

I switched off the phone, took out the battery and threw it into the river. I put everything into my rucksack, thinking about what I had just done - contemplating the opportunistic nature of my second kill. *I need to get rid of her possessions and the clothes and the car at some point in time. This ring is mine to keep as a memento; a tokenistic gesture of my second kill and this time, I won't lose it, unlike my father's gold band.* Looking for a temporary hiding place, I buried the evidence into the undergrowth beside a bush about a mile from the house. *I'll come back and get it later.* Taking in a deep breath, I made my way up the side of the house before walking through the front door.

"Jayden, is that you? We're in here watching television," shouted my mother.

"I'll be there soon. I'm going to get changed and make something to eat."

I sat on the floor of the shower, the water gushing over my body, soothing the tension in my muscles. The mere thought of killing Annabel Taylor filled me with a feeling of euphoria. I tried to contain the excitement in my groin. Feeling self-satisfied, I dried myself then put on some clothes and made my way down the stairs towards the cellar.

Opening the door, the musty smell filled my senses with pleasure as my hand fumbled in the dark, searching on the wall for the light. Switching it on, I looked at the wooden racks dominating the small enclosure, full of his taste in vintage wine. The bottles were arranged according to age and price, from the cheaper but still expensive ones at the top to the more exclusive ones at the bottom. I selected one from my favourite winemaker in France - Chateau Margaux - from the middle of the rack. Carefully placing it in my hand, I switched off the light and closed the cellar door.

The smell of crème de cassis, blackberries and cedar filled my senses with pleasure as I extracted the cork, the elegance of the ruby liquid seducing me as it flowed into the contours of the wine glass. I tasted it. *It's beautiful.* Checking the fridge, I decided on a steak - rare with some onions, mushrooms and crusty bread. The fork sliced into it without any effort, the wine complementing the red meat to perfection. *I need to go out for a while*, I thought to myself. *I want some female company.*

First, I joined my mother and the Reverend. We watched the first half of the news. I was about to leave them both alone when the local bulletin came on and there, flashing up on the screen was my crime scene. The police tried to contain the situation as onlookers jostled in the crowd, desperate to get the best view of a bloodstained body lying on the pavement. The reporter raised his voice above the commotion to convey the information to the public:

> The police have arrived. It is yet to be confirmed, but it appears that a young woman has been killed, her throat slashed and left to bleed to death in the street. I spoke to the witness who tried to help. She is distraught and was found cowering over the body, her hands covered in the victim's blood. An ambulance has just taken the witness to hospital - suffering from shock. The scene is chaotic at the moment… it's just frantic! I will report back as soon as there is any further information. This is Kenneth Armstrong reporting from News Scotland.

"That's awful," said my mother. "Who on earth would do something like that?"

"A bloody psychopath!" cried the Reverend. "We're not safe in our own city anymore are we, Jayden?"

"We're not!"

I felt a pang of shock at his words. It took me by surprise. *Is that what I am?* I pondered over his revelation, relishing my new title. As I listened to the report, it clarified again that she had been found dead at the scene of the crime. The broadcaster appealed for any witnesses to come forward or call the incident team.

A look of terror passed across my mother's face. "You don't think something horrible like that has happened to Edward?"

The Reverend's gaze rested upon my face.

I looked at him to answer the question.

"Of course not... please don't think like that."

"Where is my husband?"

Here we go again. I'm glad he's here. I can't deal with her in this state. "We don't know. We can only wait and see if he comes home," I said.

"It's been a week. Something dreadful has happened to him. I just know it."

Charles was brutally honest. "Then all we can do is deal with it together. Try to stop thinking about it."

He switched off the television and walked over in my direction.

"I've arranged to meet a few friends from the agency for a drink. Will you be okay with my mother?" I whispered.

His hand rested on my shoulder. "Yes... off you go. Catch up with you in the morning. I'll calm her down. You have a good time."

I made my excuses and left them alone. I walked into the city, straight through the front door of a high-end strip club - Undressed To Kill. Smartly clothed bouncers were standing in the corridor, checking me out as I paid the money and entered the busy club. Sultry music played in the background, the lights low apart from the neon signs flashing on the wall, the atmosphere full of erotic tension. It was packed with men, women and single people in need of sexual gratification. The toned bodies of bartenders - male and female - paraded behind the counter dressed in a black G-string and bow tie. I ordered my drink from a topless blonde. She placed it on the glossy surface. I picked it up then ventured through to another room, sat on the stool at a round table and looked towards the raised platform.

The scene before me enthralled my already heightened senses.

The dancers dressed in a variety of different outfits; leather bodices, panties, bras, stockings, suspenders, high heels and thigh-high boots. A grungy yet provocative version of *Tainted Love* belted out through the speakers. The star attraction, Killer Queen, cavorted to the music in the middle of the stage. Her hands, with blood red nails, gripped the pole as she spun her tattooed body around it, pouting her lips at the spectators, singing to the raunchy music. Removing the skimpy outfit, she picked up a whip and slashed it through the air, parting her legs to reveal a jewelled body piercing at the top of the pubic area.

The audience erupted, shouting and whistling at the stripper's provocative behaviour.

My eyes wandered across the stage, focusing on one particular woman.

Koko Kanu was less obscure than the star attraction; her dark hair flicking from side to side, dancing provocatively to the raunchy music, teasing her body with her fingers, spreading those legs for the eager crowd. She clasped the pole then lifted her body higher, sliding down it with the shaft between her legs. The dancer continued to cavort, joining the audience, offering to perform a private lap dance.

I took a large drink of whisky as she walked over in my direction.

"Hello, handsome. Would you like me to perform for you?"

"I would.... but not here. Can we go to a private room?"

She took hold of my hand, leading me through to another area in the club and opened the door to a small room. "Sit down, lover boy." Her legs straddled across me, pressing and rubbing into my groin as her lips brushed across my mouth. "Do you like?"

I groaned in pleasure. "How much?"

"Depends on what you want?"

"I don't want a private lap dance. I want you... all of you."

"Tell me what that's worth?"

I lifted her off, stood up and took the wallet out of my back pocket. "Two hundred... here, take it."

She raised an eyebrow. "I'm all yours, handsome. I'll throw in an added treat for you at that price."

The dancer opened a drawer concealed in a table in the corner of the room, measured out two lines of cocaine and rolled up one of the notes. I bent my body down at an angle, placed the note on the table and snorted the white powder up one side of my nose, stopped, then used the other nostril. She did the same. I took in a deep breath as a sudden adrenalin rush surged through my entire body, making me feel light-headed. Her eyes focused on mine. Just for a split second, I noticed her pupils dilating and retracting back to normal as she moved closer.

I embraced her with a desperate passion, my hands wandering over those sumptuous curves, feeling the contours of her body piercings underneath the leather outfit. The thought of killing my father's mistress was never far from my mind, making the thrill even more appealing. She turned around. I unhooked the clasps running down the back of the bodice then discarded it on the floor. All that was left were the studded cuffs around her neck and wrists and black stiletto heels. I moved closer, whispering seductively, "Put your hands on the door and spread your legs, you dirty bitch."

I got undressed and slipped on a condom. I tortured myself, waiting as long as I could before entering her from behind, my body refusing to orgasm, savouring the feeling until I was unable to bear it any longer. At that moment, it all came flooding to the forefront of my mind; the killings, my bloodstained blade, his whore of a mistress, the stripper's pole dance, the cocaine and the feeling of her tight muscles around my cock. Unable to bear it any longer, I grabbed hold of her hip with one hand, gripped a shoulder with the other and exploded - waves of euphoric pleasure surging through my body. I staggered back, falling into the chair, gasping for air.

The stripper turned around. "You're so intense. Are you okay?"

Catching my breath, I ran my fingers through my hair. "Yes... I'm fine. I feel fucking great. Thank you."

Winking, she eyed my naked body up and down. "It's my pleasure."

I left the club and walked home wondering if anyone would ever put all the pieces together between his mistress, me and my father. *Are you clever enough to catch me, Inspector Canmore? Only time will tell!*

A voice through the speakers interrupts my thoughts. "The plane will be landing at Edinburgh Airport in ten minutes. Please fasten your seatbelts for the descent."

Shuffling in the chair, I clip the belt around my waist and prepare to land. *It's good to be back in Edinburgh*, I think to myself. *Now I just have to deal with my mother when I get home. She's had seven years to come to terms with this, I'm sure it can't be that much of a shock anymore. The only difference is that he's been officially declared dead. Thank fuck! We're truly free of him now. The Reverend has waited for her all this time. My mother adores him. Perhaps she'll move on.*

As the plane rocks back and forth and approaches the runway, I feel an element of excitement as I remember the newspaper article and the possibility of meeting up with Kristina Cooper once again. *So... she's a criminologist. How ironic! If we meet up, I wonder how she'll react if she ever finds out that I was one of the prime suspects in the disappearance of my own father?*

5

THE INTERROGATION

"I'm as cold a motherfucker as you've ever put your fucking eyes on.
I don't give a shit about those people."
(Ted Bundy)

Seven years ago

Six months after the disappearance of Edward Scott.

I parked the car close to the river on the Shores of Leith, admiring the barges anchored at the side of the quay, the rays of light glistening off the painted surfaces. Shielding my eyes from the glare of the sun, I searched for my sunglasses, opened the envelope and read the contents of Edward Scott's phone messages inside. *You had it all, but where are you now?* I took the ring out of the small plastic bag. I found it on the first visit to the Scott family home, tucked into the side of the skirting. Noticing the glint of metal out the corner of my eye, I took out a pen, looping it through the gold band, seeing his initials engraved on the inside. Peering closer, I noticed the distinct pattern engraved on the wedding ring matched exactly to the one on Carolyn Scott's finger. I called in a favour, testing it for DNA and fingerprint traces. All that came back were that of Edward Scott. *How did the ring end up in the hallway? Was there foul play involved? Did he drop it? Why would he take it off? Perhaps it was something to do with him spending time with his mistress?* Whatever the reason, this piece of evidence was the key to the mystery - I knew it. My experience told me that his son had something to do with his disappearance. The duplicitous nature of his behaviour - smooth, sly and insincere - set off alarm bells in my mind the first time I met him.

I delved into Jayden Scott's background, checking up on his time at university, trying to get my mind around his character. He graduated with a first class honours degree. What was it that his guidance teacher said to me: "Jayden was studious, quiet and very intelligent. He returned to Edinburgh every weekend and kept himself to himself. The boy liked his drink that much I know. I could smell it from his breath every time I spoke to him."

"So... Edward Scott's son was a dysfunctional loner who drank too much. had a drink problem. And why did he return home to Edinburgh so often? Jayden seemed quite protective towards his mother. Far too much perhaps for a man of his age," I mumbled to myself.

I also followed him on several occasions. He was a regular visitor to a strip club, seeking sexual gratification from the same woman, a pretty woman with wild hair and piercing dark eyes. She told me: "Yeah, I know him. He's handsome, loaded and intense... really intense."

You're only twenty-three. You're in the prime of your life! You should be dating girls your own age instead of hanging about strip clubs on your own. Just then, I spotted him coming out of the boat, shaking hands with a client no doubt and once alone, he lit a cigarette. I got out of the car. Jayden watched me intently as I walked towards him with the envelope in my hand.

"Inspector Canmore. This is a surprise."

I ignored his words. "Nice barge!"

"We use it as an extra meeting room. It impresses my clients. It adds to the whole creative experience. Anyway... how can I help you?"

I waved the envelope in front of him. "I've just been reading your father's phone records. He leads an interesting life."

"In what way, Inspector?"

"In every way... power, money, women."

"That sums up my father to perfection."

"One thing puzzles me though."

He sighed. "And what would that be?"

"His wedding ring..." I said, twiddling it through my fingers.

He peered closer, staring at the gold band. The colour drained from his face. "Where... the... fuck... did you get my father's ring?"

"Are you okay? You've gone a bit pale. It's just a piece of evidence that was found in the hallway of your house, the first time we met actually, when I let myself out. Why was it there, Mr. Scott?"

Taking in a deep breath, he said, "I... He... Perhaps he took it off and lost it. We both know of his extramarital affairs. I really have no idea."

"Perhaps... perhaps not."

He paused. "Why do you follow me, Inspector? I've seen you at the strip club. I didn't have anything to do with his disappearance if that's what you think."

"I never said you did, Mr. Scott. You did."

He scowled. "Now you're twisting my words. Anyway, if you do think I'm involved, you need to prove it, Inspector."

On that note, he marched off.

****

I walked through the doors to my office at Lothian and Borders police station on the outskirts of the city centre, the encounter with Jayden Scott still etched in my mind. *If you want proof then I'll find it, you smarmy little bastard.*

"Good morning, Inspector Canmore. How are you today?" said Constable Peters.

"I'm fine. Can you come and see me later? I have a new lead on the Edward Scott case. It's taken me nearly six months to make the connection, but I've found it."

"What time? I'll need to arrange cover for the desk."

"Half an hour... in my office and don't be late."

I picked up the list of phone numbers and texts from Edward Scott's mobile phone. It had taken a while to track all the numbers. There in front of me were the dates and times of his communication with Annabel Taylor. I requested the text conversations from the mobile phone company. I read them over again. He met his girlfriend on the Friday night outside a bar, not far from her flat. The witness who identified his photo was right - he was in Edinburgh. *They were lovers. Now he's missing and she's dead*, I thought to myself. *Is Jayden Scott the connection between them both?*

I pondered over the messages. She was not his only mistress. His contacts list revealed several other women, albeit in London, with whom he regularly kept in touch. "Lucky bastard," I mumbled to myself. Looking back over the historical records, the one that did surprise me the most was his affair with his business partner's wife, Rachel Fleming. *Such betrayal.*

I heard a knock on the glass window.

I waved at her to come into my office. "Sit down, Peters. I know you took the initial phone call from Mrs. Scott. I just need you to tell me about it before I decide on the team to work on this case."

"I'll try my best to help… if I can. Do you think Mrs. Scott is involved?"

"I don't think so. How did she seem at the time?"

"Distraught… a bit hysterical. I ended up speaking to a guy with a deep voice."

"The Reverend, no doubt?"

"Yes, Charles McIntyre. He gave me all the details about her missing husband."

"She told me that." I paused. "I have a link between Edward Scott and Annabel Taylor."

"Who's she?"

"The woman who was found dead in the street with her throat slit, a week after Edward Scott disappeared. They were lovers."

"Do you think there's a link between his disappearance and her murder?"

"Perhaps, but I need to speak to a few people first before I investigate this further."

"Do you have a suspect?"

"I'm not sure yet. There's something not quite right about the Scott family, especially the son. I know he's involved… I just know it."

She laughed. "And you're never wrong, Inspector."

"Most of the time! Can you get in touch with the forensic unit? Let them know that I want a search team ready for two properties, one here and the other on the west coast. Contact Sarah McLeod. She's our best forensic specialist. Let her know I want to speak to her as soon as possible."

"Do you need anything else?"

"Can you also get in touch with the Specialist Operations Division and let the POLSA know that I need to speak to him as soon as possible."

"POLSA?"

"The Police Search Advisor. It's Sergeant Jack Murray."

"I'll do that now, Skipper."

"Less of your cheek. I'm Inspector Canmore to you. Now get going!"

She chuckled. "Aye, aye, Skipper!"

I need to run this by another fellow officer, I thought to myself. *Jack Murray is an expert in his field. He's a clever one come to that for a hand:-on Sergeant. He and his dog Blade are a formidable team.* I started to write down the details of my team and what I needed everyone to do. I knew the time was right to either prove or disprove if Jayden Scott was anyway involved in his father's disappearance or murder.

Constable Peters - Co-ordinate meetings between myself, Sarah and Jack

Sarah McLeod - Forensic tests in Argyll.

Sergeant Jack Murray - Conduct the dog search in Argyll if necessary.

Me - Lead the forensic team at the Scott family home in Edinburgh.

The phone interrupted my thoughts. I answered it within three rings, knowing it was Jack, eager to arrange a time to meet.

"Hey, Skipper. I just spoke to Constable Peters. How can I help?"

"I need your advice. Is it possible to meet up sometime today? I'd rather speak to you in person, if possible."

"I'm going to be in your area this morning. Is everything okay?"

"I just need your opinion on something."

"See you about eleven o'clock."

"Thanks, Jack."

Before my meeting, I talked to Sarah McLeod, the leader of the forensic unit. She confirmed that they would be ready to go on my instruction and also arranged the team in Edinburgh, under my command. I requested a search warrant for both the properties, waiting for it to be approved. I made a strong coffee then gathered all the information I had so far on the Scott case. My experience told me that Jayden Scott had something to do with the disappearance of his father. Whether he was the link between Edward Scott and Annabel Taylor was another matter.

I saw him approaching my office and got up to open the door. "Jack, it's good to see you."

He shook my hand with a firm grip and slapped my back. "Likewise."

"Take a seat. Do you want a coffee?"

"No thanks. I'm curious. You only ever ask to speak to me in person when you have a dilemma on your hands."

"I want to run it by you first."

"Fire away. Perhaps I can help."

I took in a deep breath. "This is the situation… wife (Carolyn Scott) reports her husband (Edward Scott) missing just over six months ago. No monetary transactions have been made since he disappeared. The husband is having an affair and meets his mistress (Annabel Taylor) on the Friday night. Edward leaves his car at work. He does not come home over the weekend and hasn't been seen since."

"Have you spoken to the mistress?"

"Unfortunately, she was killed a week later. Let's leave her out of it just now."

"When did the wife report him missing?"

"On the Monday. She was expecting him home on the Friday night or early Saturday morning. She thought he might have gone to London for the weekend but he was here, in Edinburgh, with his lover."

"Do you think he stayed with her or made his way home that night?"

"I'm not sure."

"Have you checked Annabel Taylor's phone records?"

"I have requested it from the phone company. I'm just waiting for it to arrive. I need to be careful as the Taylor murder is DCI Marcus Hunter's case. You know what he's like. Up his own bloody arse! Anyway, Edward Scott didn't make any other calls or texts after seven o'clock on the Friday night. His last text was to his mistress saying he would meet her at the usual time outside the bar."

"You got a suspect?"

"Despite whether or not there's some kind of connection between them both… my experience tells me that Edward Scott's son is involved."

"Why?"

"Here are his windows of opportunity. In the early hours of Saturday morning, Jayden was with his mother until midnight and then, they both went to bed. Perhaps his father came home and something happened. Carolyn Scott might be involved, but I doubt it. She's distraught. I found his wedding ring in the hallway, a week after he disappeared, but there's no forensic evidence to link it to Jayden Scott. Anyway, her son heads off to Argyll about eleven o'clock the next day, albeit a planned birthday party for five days in the family's holiday cottage to celebrate his twenty-third birthday. His friends left on the Tuesday evening about seven o'clock and he didn't arrive home until the Wednesday night. And check this out, he sold his car for scrap two months later. It's lying in the junkyard, stripped of its parts, the metal frame crushed to a pulp. There's no way we can forensically examine it now."

"You think something happened in the early hours of Saturday morning. The ring somehow ends up in the hallway. The son bundles his father into the back of the car and gets rid of the body somewhere in Argyll once his friends leave, then disposes of his car two months later. That's what you're implying, Skipper."

"I suppose that's what I'm saying. He's hiding something. The smooth bastard is arrogant as well. I spoke to him a few days ago outside his work. He's taunting me, Jack."

"Well get the forensics team out. That's what I would suggest. If there is any evidence, you will find it."

"That's what I've got planned. I spoke to Sarah McLeod. She's agreed to conduct the tests at the cottage in Argyll. I'm leading the team at the Scott family home in Edinburgh. I've already applied for the search warrants. I'm sure I'm right. I need to find some kind of evidence. If we find anything in Argyll, I'd like you to be on standby with your handlers and dogs to search the area. It's an ideal place to get rid of a body."

"That's fine. I've always got your back, Skipper. If there's something out there, you know I'll find it."

"I understand that."

"What about the mistress? Do you think it's all connected?"

"I'm not sure. I've heard her purse, mobile phone and ring were taken. It may have been a robbery, but I doubt it." I made a gesture with a finger across my neck. "She had her throat slit with a knife. It's a bit personal for a robbery."

"It could be someone on Annabel Taylor's side. Have you thought about that? Was she married? Ex-partner? Jealous boyfriend? Stalker?"

"I need to speak to DCI Hunter about that. As I said, he's in charge of the Taylor murder. I'm going ahead with my forensic examination. I need to see if Jayden Scott is somehow involved with the disappearance of his own father first."

"I agree. I hope you're right. DCI Hunter is your superior officer. He'll be pretty pissed off if you're wasting time, money and resources. You know what he's like!"

"I'm right, Jack. I know Jayden Scott is involved. I'm going ask him to come in to see if he can help with our inquiries. Get the smarmy bastard on his own and put him under a bit of pressure. You know yourself, if anyone is going to crack, it's through cross-examination. If he agrees, can you witness the interview, just to let me know what you think? I trust your judgement."

"Sure... no problem. Just give me plenty of notice."

Jack stood up then walked towards the door. "I need to get off. I'm heading a drugs bust in the morning and need to get the unit organised. Good luck, Skipper. See you soon."

Two days later, I obtained the warrant and phoned Carolyn Scott to let her know about the search. My team arrived early on a Monday morning, dressed in coveralls, gloves and masks, armed and ready to uncover and find any pieces of crucial evidence to solving this case.

I rang the doorbell to the house.

The door opened.

He hesitated for a moment, looking at the masked faces standing behind me. "Is this absolutely necessary, Inspector? You're so out of order."

"Mr. Scott, it's just a formality. I assure you."

"Well you go and tell that to my mother."

I stared at him looking for some kind of reaction, but his face was devoid of emotion. "I'll reassure her she's nothing to worry about. You on the other hand..."

He exuded a sense of confidence. "What are you implying?"

"Nothing... please let us in to do our job."

"Sorry, it's just a bit of a shock... come in."

"We also have a team visiting the cottage," I told him. "We need to double-check both properties."

He shrugged, walked off and went to get his mother.

"Inspector Canmore, what on earth is going on?" she cried.

"It's nothing to worry about. We just need to check the house for any irregularities. Honestly, it's just a routine search. Shall we have some tea or coffee?"

"Of course," she said, making her way into the kitchen.

"Is Reverend McIntyre not here?"

"Charles has gone back to the village. He does have to attend to his parishioners and church, Inspector."

"Have you known each other a long time?"

"We grew up together. Our parents were close. He's a very good friend to my family. Anyway… what would you like to drink?"

"Coffee please. Black. Two sugars."

My phone rang. It was Sarah McLeod. "Excuse me for a minute."

"If you must…"

I went into the hall, saying in a hushed voice, "How's it going? Have you found anything?"

"It was a bit awkward when we arrived. There's an old gardener making life difficult for us. He started brandishing his spade when we arrived. Henry looks after the cottage when the Scott family are not here. His stupid dog won't stop barking at me."

I laughed.

"It's a bloody nightmare, Skipper. I suspect he's contaminated the cottage. I'll try my best to see what we can find. The photographer has taken some shots of the inside and outside of the house as well as the surrounding area. There's a lot of woodland."

"Anything else?"

"Not much. I've checked the drains and faucets in the sinks, bath and shower. Nothing suspicious there to the naked eye. We've taken some swabs just to check for any residue. I've bagged some of his clothes. We can get them tested for anything suspicious. There are lots of different fingerprints which is understandable. I found some trace evidence, dried blood to be precise and taken some scrapings to get it analysed."

My heart skipped a beat. *She's very thorough - one of the best.* "We're going to spray the house here as well to look for any traces of blood, especially in the hallway." I decided not to tell her about the ring as it was still not an official piece of evidence. Besides, it held no kind of proof on its shiny surface. Instead, I had used it to provoke some kind of reaction from Jayden Scott. "I'll let you know what we find."

"Your coffee is ready."

"I need to go," I whispered. "Keep up the good work. I'll catch up with you later. Bye for now."

She handed me the cup. "Have you found out any more information about my husband?"

I thought about it. *Do I tell her about his mistress?* "Not much more than our last conversation. When was that?"

"Out with your search warrant contact, it was about four months ago. You told me that a witness had come forward in response to your local news feed, and that my husband may have been here, in Edinburgh, on the night he disappeared."

"Unfortunately, the witness couldn't positively identify him from the photo you gave me."

"Was he here or not?"

I paused.

"Tell me!"

"We're still investigating that line of inquiry. I'll let you know when we've got some more concrete evidence."

"Is it another woman?"

"Perhaps… it's a long process checking out all the details."

Tears welled up in her eyes.

I changed the subject. "How's Jayden? Is he coping okay?"

She took a tissue out of the box and blew her nose. "As far as I know. He doesn't say very much and keeps it all to himself. He's always been like that. My son is just concentrating on the agency and helping out my husband's partner, Mathew Fleming, with the consultancy business."

"I see." *That must be Rachel Fleming's husband. One of Edward Scott's many mistresses!*

She interrupted my thoughts. "Do you suspect we have something to do with his disappearance? Why are the forensic team here?"

"It's just routine. We won't be long. Sorry about the disruption."

"Answer my question truthfully," she demanded.

"We're not sure. It's not you…"

She sighed. "I'm going to find my son. See yourself out, please."

"I need to see Jayden before I go. Can you tell him? I'll wait here."

"If you must."

"Mrs. Scott…"

"*WHAT!*"

"You need to take this."

I handed her two plastic tubes with a swab stick inside. "Can you go with my assistant? He will run it around the inside of your mouth and put it back in the container. It's just so we have a record of your DNA. It's nothing to be concerned about, just so we can eliminate you from the forensic evidence. Jayden will need to do it as well."

She stared at me, grabbing them out of my hand then marched off with my assistant.

I finished my coffee and peered out the window at the garden. It led onto the walkway along the river. I talked to one of the team. He told me they had found some trace elements of blood in the hallway. With a feeling of excitement at the news, I said to him, "Search out there as well and be thorough."

Just then, Jayden walked into the kitchen dressed in his business suit. He looked a lot like his father. "Your lab rat has my sample. For elimination purposes, no doubt?"

"Thanks."

"No problem."

"Can you come to the police station on Friday? I just need to ask you a few questions. We can do it later in the day so you can fit it around your work schedule. What time is convenient?"

"I can be with you about five o'clock. Does that suit you?"

"That's fine. Just to confirm. You will not be questioned under caution and do not need legal representation. It's more of an informal interview. Do you know where the station is?"

He nodded. "Is it the one based at St.Leonards?"

"That's the one."

He turned and left the kitchen. "I need to get to work. Goodbye."

****

I set up the audio equipment in the interview room. The heat in the small space was unbearable, almost oppressive, made worse by the stifling weather outside. I grabbed the chair and stood on it to reach the window. A slight breeze swirled through the opening, toning down the humidity of the afternoon heat. I took in a deep breath of fresh air. Wiping the sweat from my brow, I thought about how to conduct the interview. The results from the crime scene examiners would not be ready until early next week, so it had to be more of an informal interview.

I received the phone records from Annabel Taylor's phone. I was right. Edward Scott had left her flat. She had sent him a text and called him in the early hours of the morning – not long after he left - saying how much she enjoyed the evening and to call her the next day. Miss Taylor also left him a message on the night of her murder, arranging to meet him outside the bar at the usual time, but of course, he never replied.

I found it hard to contain my excitement as I leapt up the stairs to see if Sergeant Murray had arrived. *Jayden Scott is going to be a hard one to crack*, I thought to myself.

He was there, waiting. "Jack, glad you could make it."

He got up off the seat outside my office "I'm intrigued. It should be interesting. I'm looking forward to meeting the mystery man."

"I'll lead the interview. Feel free to ask any questions. What I really need you to do is note his body language. I know you can sniff out a liar just as well as your dog can detect the scent of death."

He chuckled. "That's true. I'll keep a note of his reactions to your questions."

The phone rang. "Jayden Scott is here to see you, Inspector Canmore."

"Can you take him to the interview room, Peters? I'll be down shortly."

"Is that him, Skipper?"

"Yes. I'll make us a cold drink. Let him sweat it out for a bit. The heat in that room is unbearable at the moment. It might put him under a bit of pressure." I made some iced tea and said, "He's a cold bastard, Jack."

We headed down the stairs to the interview room, watching him through the glass panel on the door. My prime suspect was talking to Constable Peters. She was placing some water on the table. He was watching her, intently.

"What are your initial thoughts, Jack?"

He peered through the window, observing my key witness. "Smooth operator. Bit of a ladies man, I suspect. He's got money and lots of it. His clothes are expensive. Look at the way he's watching Peters with that intense stare. He uses his charm to get his own way in life no doubt - especially with women."

"Just like his father, perhaps? Let's go and see what he's got to say. See how my suspect reacts under pressure."

I entered the room.

He stood up.

I shook his hand. "Glad you could make it. This is a colleague of mine. He's going to be sitting in on the interview."

Jayden stretched out his arm. "Pleased to meet you…"

"Sergeant Murray, but just call me Jack."

They shook hands.

"Do you mind if we tape the conversation?" I asked.

"I suppose not." He poured himself a glass of water and then, took in a deep breath. "Right… how can I help you, Inspector Canmore?"

"I just have a few questions. I've been in close contact with your mother. She's given me quite a lot of information already. I just want to take you back to the Friday night, the night your father didn't come home."

"Okay."

"Did you know he had a mistress in Edinburgh? He was with her that night."

"Did he? As I said to you the other day, it doesn't surprise me."

"Why?"

"It just doesn't. You have his phone records, Inspector. You must know of his affairs? He's cheated on my mother in the past and we found out about it. I'm not sure why she put up with it for so long."

"And how did *you* react to that news?"

"React? What do you mean? It was up to them to sort that out It's a private matter between a husband and wife. Don't' get me wrong, it annoyed me, but it's happened quite a few times. I just ended up staying out of it."

"His mistress was murdered a week after he disappeared."

"What? Do you think my father had something to do with it?"

"I doubt it. We believe something also happened to him the week before. He's not withdrawn any money or used his phone since seven o'clock on the Friday night. His last known whereabouts are meeting his mistress, Annabel Taylor, outside a bar. We know he went to her flat near the pub. He's not been seen since."

"How odd, don't you think?"

I looked at him straight in the eye. "Did he come home that morning, Mr. Scott?"

He looked straight back. "My mother told you, she woke up and he'd not been back."

"I mean in the early hours of Saturday morning. Did he return sometime after midnight?"

"We went to bed just before twelve. I slept right through the night until my mother woke me up the next day. It was then that she told me he'd not returned home."

"That's what your mother told us as well. What do you think might have happened to him, Mr. Scott? Annabel Taylor's mobile phone activity shows that he left her flat around one thirty in the morning. So... something happened to him between her flat and your home."

"I have no idea, Inspector."

Jack's gaze found mine. "It's been confirmed then that he did leave her flat?"

"I received the information yesterday. I've not had time to update you on everything."

"That's interesting," he said, as his eyes rested on my suspect.

Jayden flinched, but only for a brief moment.

I called his bluff. "We've found some blood samples at both of the properties. Are you sure he didn't come home?"

There was no reaction from him this time. "Not as far as I know."

"I hear you're interested in weapons-based martial art?"

"What about it?"

"What kind of weapons do you fight with?"

"A Hanbo. It's a wooden staff. Why?"

"Anything else?"

"That is all we train with. Why are you asking?"

"Just interested. When you were at the cottage, your friends left on the Tuesday evening just after six. Why didn't you make your way home?"

"I felt tired. I sent a text to my mother to see if everything was okay and she told me to come back the next day. A wicked smile passed across his face. "I was planning on leaving on Wednesday morning, but I got distracted."

Smug little bastard. "And what would that be?"

"A woman, Inspector..."

"Who?"

"One of my guests who invited themselves to my party on the first night we arrived. Alex and Grant said they told you about them. The guy I met in the layby. She was one of his friends."

"Who? Amanda? Ben's friend?" I asked.

"She came to visit me at the cottage. We spent the day in bed. I left that afternoon. Would you like her full name in case you want to track her down? Amanda Kennedy. She lives in the village just along the road from the cottage. I actually have her phone number. Do you want it?"

The heat in the room was unbearable. I felt my face turning red. "We'll get it from you before you go."

He reached into his pocket for his mobile phone, getting her number up on the screen. "Take it now."

He handed it over.

I noted down the number and gave it back.

"Is there anything else you want to ask, Inspector? I need to go soon."

I thought for a minute. "Your car."

"Which one?"

"The one that's lying in the junkyard."

"What about it? It was old. It wasn't worth selling. I sold it for scrap."

"So... you got rid of it two months after you returned from your trip to Argyll." *What else did you get rid of?* I thought to myself.

He said in a challenging tone, "Is there a problem with that, Inspector?"

"No, I'm just interested that's all."

Jack stopped writing and looked up. "How was your relationship with your father?"

Jayden looked a bit taken aback by the question. He shuffled in his chair. It was the first sign of any kind of emotion from him. "Well... he offered me some good business advice at times."

"That's not what I mean. On a more personal level, you know... as a father and son. How did you get on?"

He paused. "Okay, I suppose. He was my flesh and blood."

"What does 'suppose' mean? That would suggest that there was some kind of a problem."

"I'm closer to my mother."

"How did you feel about the way he treated her?"

"What do you mean?"

"His affairs... she must have been upset by that. Were you? Was he not quite a controlling father, Mr. Scott?"

"Not really. I agree that I didn't like him cheating. As I was growing up, I just learned to accept it."

"Accept what?"

Looking flustered, he took off his jacket and poured himself another glass of water. "Just the way he acted."

"You look nervous. Just tell the truth."

"I'm not. It's just too hot in here!"

"And how did he act? Was it the way he treated you or your mother?"

"Both. I fucking hated him at times. My father... " He quickly stopped what he was saying.

"That's a strong use of language. That word 'hate.' Did you hate him enough to harm him?"

He's cracking under the pressure, I thought to myself. *Nice work, Jack.*

"What are you implying?" replied Jayden.

Just then, I heard a commotion outside the room. Someone started banging on the door. *What's going on?* I thought to myself. A face peered through the glass window. "You open this door, Inspector," shouted a voice on the other side.

Jack immediately went into field mode. He was on his feet in a second, his hand reaching for the baton, ready to strike. I gave him a reassuring look. "It's fine. I'll handle it."

I stared at Jayden.

He gazed back and smiled.

BANG, BANG, BANG... "Let me in right now, Inspector Canmore," bellowed the voice.

I opened the door.

"I couldn't stop him," announced Constable Peters.

"Don't worry about it. Off you go."

"Reverend McIntyre," I sighed. "How can I help you?"

He barged in through the door. "I've come to get my boy. What in God's name is going on here? Carolyn told me about the forensic examiners and now this. Are you insane, Inspector? What the hell is going on?"

"Calm down," I said. "It's just routine, Mr. McIntyre."

"I'm Reverend McIntyre to you. I've told you that before."

"Sorry... but you..."

"Routine!" he cried. "You're harassing this family when you should be finding out what really happened to Edward. I'm putting in a formal complaint about you, so you better stop all this nonsense."

"It's only an informal conversation to help with our inquiries."

"Informal?" His wide eyes were full of anger as he focused on the red light. "Then why are you taping the conversation?" He stretched over to the audio equipment on the table, fumbled about and switched it off. I had no time to react to his insane outburst. He turned on his heel, made his way through the door and shouted, "Come on, Jayden. We're leaving. Right now!"

He put on his jacket. "The Reverend is a bit protective of my family, Inspector Canmore. You know that. We'll see our own way out."

Jack wiped away the sweat from his forehead, staring at me in disbelief. "What was that?"

"That... was *the* Reverend Charles McIntyre."

"Jesus Christ." He looked up at some imaginary being in the room, apologising for his choice of language. "What a formidable character. You don't think he..."

"Absolutely not. I know he's very protective of the Scott family. They have a long family history. I've already checked up on his whereabouts on the night Edward Scott disappeared. He was staying with friends before he went to the Scott family home on the Sunday. Anyway, what do you think about Jayden? Is he hiding something?"

"Definitely! He's clever. You just need to probe him where it hurts... on his relationship with his father."

"That's when he started to feel uneasy."

"There's something not quite right, Skipper. I also suspect there's more to the Scott family than just a few extramarital affairs."

"I agree. What about his body language?"

"A few flinches here and there, but not much. He's very controlled. His eye contact is impeccable, perhaps due to his martial art training. He was very composed until I got up, close and personal about his father. But... just because Jayden may have had a fractious relationship with his father doesn't mean to say he did something to him."

"If Edward Scott didn't make his way home that night, who did he encounter?"

"You need to work that one out. I still think he's hiding something."

"I think so, too. The immediate family is very secretive. However, no one that I have spoken to so far has a bad word to say about Edward Scott."

"What's your plan now?"

"I'm just going to wait for the forensic results which I should get by Tuesday. I also want to speak to DCI Hunter. He's dealing with the Annabel Taylor murder. That's all I can do at the moment."

He nodded his head in approval.

"You want to head off for a cold drink," I said. "There's a beer garden just round the corner from here."

"I thought you'd never ask. Come on… let's go."

He took off his baton, handcuffs and radio. "I'll pick them up later. They're a bit intimidating for a pub visit," he laughed.

"A big hit with the ladies, no doubt!"

"It has been known, but not today. I just want a beer and an early night."

"Remember, I need you on standby on Tuesday morning Jack, ready for the search in Argyll."

"I'll try my best. Victim recovery dogs are few and far between at the moment. I have a handler in mind that should be able to accompany me. We'll be ready, don't worry about that."

****

I arrived early on Monday morning and made my way to the other side of the building. The hot spell of weather had passed. The atmosphere was not as oppressive as it had been the week before. I knocked on the door and entered the incident room dealing with the Taylor murder. It was a hive of activity. My eyes were drawn to the board on the wall. There in the middle of all the different connections was a photograph of Annabel Taylor. Seeing her face looking back at me made it all seem so real. *She's beautiful*, I thought to myself. *I wonder what they've found out.*

"Inspector Canmore. I got your message. How can I help?"

I walked towards DCI Hunter. "Good to see you again," I said, shaking his hand. "I just want to get your advice on a missing person who has links to your murder victim."

"I suspect that would be Edward Scott?"

"Yes."

"Let's go into my office."

I followed him.

"Take a seat," he said.

"Thanks for seeing me. I know you're busy."

"How can I help?"

"Edward Scott was with Annabel Taylor the week before she was murdered. He left her flat in the early hours of the morning and hasn't been seen since."

"We know that. He's been part of our inquiry."

This is encouraging news, I thought to myself.

"I was going to contact you sooner," said DCI Hunter, "but we're now concentrating on our prime suspect, possibly for both Edward Scott and Annabel Taylor. We know that his financial activity stopped on the Friday morning. I doubt we'll ever find Edward Scott alive."

I looked over in surprise and replied, "Who's your prime suspect?"

"Annabel Taylor's ex-partner. He's been harassing her for the past two years. She obtained an injunction with the power to arrest if he broke the terms and conditions of the court order. He has crossed the line on several occasions and is known to the local police."

"That's not enough evidence to assume he killed her," I declared.

"Hold on a minute, Inspector. I'm not finished yet..."

"Sorry, for interrupting!"

He continued. "We also obtained CCTV footage on the night of her murder. The ex-partner was in the area, but we lost sight of him about eight o'clock. My team interviewed him. He claims that he made his way home, spending the rest of the night on his own at his flat. But did he? And the final piece of evidence is his obsessive nature. We searched his home and retrieved not only photographs of Annabel Taylor, but of her with Edward Scott. He also had several newspaper clippings of Mr. Scott's disappearance. Now that to me is not coincidental."

"I see." *This is not looking good for my case!* I thought to myself.

He proceeded. "Whoever killed Annabel Taylor had minimal contact with the body and there are no reliable witnesses. My team believe that her murder was made to look like a robbery, but to cut someone's throat like that is a bit personal, don't you think?"

"Perhaps," I said. *Jack was right. A bloody ex-partner!*

"What have you found out, Inspector?"

My mind was in turmoil. "Has her ex-partner got an alibi?"

"He has for the night Edward Scott went missing, but not for the night of Annabel Taylor's murder. As I said, he told us he went home on his own. Whether his alibi for the night Mr. Scott disappeared is credible or not is another matter."

I let out a huge sigh of relief. "What's his name? Just out of interest…" *I'll be checking up on you later.*

"Stewart Bailey. Totally obsessed with her. Annabel Taylor was a stunning woman."

"I saw the photograph on your wall. Well… I'm pursuing another possible line of inquiry for Edward Scott."

"Who?"

"His son."

"And what evidence do *you* have, Inspector?"

"Well… Edward Scott left Annabel Taylor's flat on the morning he disappeared. One can presume that he made his way home." My words tailed off thinking about his suspect Stewart Bailey… "Or he never made it home at all."

"Perhaps he encountered my suspect or yours? Which one do you think?" said DCI Hunter.

"No offence to your case. I think the son is involved. He left the same day his father went missing then headed to the west coast, and returned five days later. I've had the forensic team out to check the family home as well as the holiday cottage in Argyll. There have been a few trace elements found. I don't get the results back until tomorrow."

"What elements?"

"The main one is dried blood. It's been found at both properties."

"That's a start at least. We've found no forensic evidence yet to incriminate Stewart Bailey in Edward Scott's disappearance and… he does have an alibi. However, his link to Annabel Taylor is a fact because of all the circumstantial evidence."

"Is it possible to view the CCTV footage myself?"

"I'll get it to you later. Let me know if you find out anything that we haven't!"

"I will. I'm also hoping the forensic results will clear up my case. I know he's involved. I just need to prove it then try and get some kind of confession from Jayden Scott."

"Keep us informed. I'm glad you came to see me. It certainly brings another dimension to the Annabel Taylor case."

I got up to leave. "Thanks. I'll speak to you soon."

Stunned, I made my way into my office, slamming the door behind me. *I need some privacy.* I pulled the blinds shut and started pacing back and forth. *Damn. I wasn't expecting that. I need to think about this in a rational way. So… there's another suspect, but he's got an alibi for the night of Edward's disappearance. I'll be checking you out, Stewart Bailey. As for you Jayden Scott, I know you're involved. I just know it. Calm down. Get the forensic results then take it from there.*

I took in a deep breath and made a coffee.

There was a bang on the door.

"Are you in there, Skipper?" said a familiar voice.

"Just a minute."

I composed myself. Opening the door, I said, "Good to see you, Jack."

"I was just dropping by to pick up my gear." He slapped my back. "It was a great night on Friday. Bit of a sore head the next day though!"

"It was…"

He looked at the blinds then at my face. "Are you okay? What's going on?"

"I've just been to see DCI Hunter about the Annabel Taylor case. His main suspect is her ex-partner. A man called Stewart Bailey. You were right!"

"What about Edward Scott? Is it all connected to his suspect?"

I groaned. "He's not sure. There's no hard evidence yet. It's all circumstantial. Stewart Bailey was seen on CCTV footage in the area the night she was murdered. They also retrieved photographs he had of both of them together and check this out - he had clippings of newspaper articles on Edward Scott's disappearance."

"I can't see a problem at the moment. He's got his case. You've got yours. Just go with it. See what unfolds. That's all you can do."

"You're right. Are you still okay for tomorrow, if I need you?"

"It's all sorted. We're in Glasgow early in the morning. We'll make a detour past Glencoe on our way back to Edinburgh. What's the name of the house again?"

"Black Ridge Cottage. You can't miss it. It's a solitary place just off the main road about half way through the glen on the left-hand side."

"I'll go and check it out anyway and wait for your call."

I chuckled away to myself. "Watch out for the gardener."

"What are you talking about?"

"Nothing. It's just a joke!"

He shook his head. "I'll be in that area around eleven o'clock tomorrow."

"Thanks."

"I need to head off. I've a busy day as usual. Catch you later, Skipper."

"Yeah... see you soon."

I looked up Stewart Bailey on the system, typing his name into the search engine. His photograph appeared on the screen. He looked a decent enough bloke. I peered into his eyes. "It's strange what love, obsession and jealousy can do to someone," I said to him. "But did you kill Annabel Taylor and were you involved in Edward Scott's disappearance?"

I read his profile. He had broken the court order twice. At the time there were no conditions attached to it. He was given a caution. She applied to the court, with the power to arrest if he continued with the harassment. *So... she decided a married man was the better option*, I thought to myself.

There was a knock on the door.

"Come in," I shouted, agitated at the interruption.

Constable Peters had a case in her hand. "This is from DCI Hunter. Anything interesting?"

You ask too many bloody questions. I replied in an irritated voice, "It's just CCTV footage."

She got the message I was not in the mood for idle chit-chat. "I'll leave you alone. Let me know if you need anything."

On that note, she turned and left.

Placing the DVD in my computer, I waited for it to load. The note on the inside cover stated the time, date and length of the street footage. There was a total of three hours from six o'clock to nine o'clock on the night of Annabel Taylor's murder. I sat back in the chair, my eyes scanning the images before me and then I spotted him. The time indicated it was twenty past seven in the evening. Freezing the image, I zoomed in on his face. Stewart Bailey *had* been in the area on the night of her murder. *Was it planned or coincidental?* I followed his movement passed the pub where Edward Scott and Annabel Taylor normally met. He walked up the street where he greeted a man then headed into the bar. At exactly eight o'clock, he emerged at the entrance of the pub, shook hands with his companion, and crossed the street; disappearing into the depths of a side road where there were no cameras. *Did he go home or double back?* Only he knew the answer to that question. At quarter past eight, she was sitting outside the pub, nervously looking up and down the street for Edward Scott. I watched the flurry of activity in the area, my eyes scanning the crowds of people for his face. *Where are you, Jayden Scott?* At twenty to nine, she left the pub then crossed the road. Zooming in on the footage, I determined that nobody followed her from the main thoroughfare. *Damn! Her attacker must have been waiting for her somewhere along that side street*, I thought to myself. *Was it Jayden Scott or Stewart Bailey, or some random lunatic?*

I jumped out of my chair at the sound of the phone ringing. It was DCI Hunter. "Can you come and see me?" he said in a stern tone before hanging up the phone.

I closed down the screen. *Nice of you to let me reply. What the hell is going on?* As I approached his office, I heard him before I saw him. *My day couldn't get any worse.*

I knocked on the door.

He let me in. "Take a seat, Inspector."

An accusatory finger pointed in my direction. "He's been harassing the Scott family, Chief Inspector Hunter. I'm not having it anymore," he bellowed. "I want to make a formal complaint."

"Mr..." I stopped then rephrased my words before he exploded. "Reverend McIntyre, as I said to you the other day, our investigation is ongoing at the moment."

"Are you related to the Scott family?" said DCI Hunter.

"Not exactly," replied the Reverend, "but they're the closest thing I have to one. I'm not having this man intimidating them anymore."

DCI Hunter looked over in my direction. "Inspector... is there any kind of intimidation going on?"

"It's not so much that I'm accusing anyone of anything, it's more that I need to eliminate both Carolyn and Jayden Scott from our inquiry..."

He interrupted. "Don't insult my intelligence. Please stop your bullshit," shouted the Reverend. "You suspect Jayden. He's told me about your line of questioning. It stops right now. Right now! It's bloody harassment."

He ignored me, looking at DCI Hunter for a response.

"I assure you that this is part of the procedure. We need to eliminate rather than accuse the immediate family when a member of that family has disappeared. Clearly, something has happened to Edward Scott. In ninety percent of cases, it's a close family member that's involved. It's a fact."

With a deep sigh, the Reverend slumped back in his chair. "It's all been too much. Do what you have to do, but stop questioning my boy unless you have some evidence, Inspector Canmore. Do we understand each other?"

I forced myself to look him directly in the eye. "Yes... we understand each other, Reverend McIntyre."

"Just before I go, I need to ask you something. Carolyn mentioned it to me. Was *he* with another woman the night he disappeared?"

I decided to just tell him the truth. "Yes."

"Bastard," he said, marching out of the room.

"Thanks for your support, DCI Hunter."

"Just get the results back. Find out one way or another, Inspector. Please leave the Scott family alone for now."

"Agreed."

"Who's collating the lab results for you?"

"Sarah McLeod. Do you know her? She's my forensic specialist on this case."

He thought about it. "I do."

"I better go. I've a busy day ahead," I told him.

"Catch up with you later."

It's just a waiting game until I get the results back, I thought to myself.

****

I called Sarah McLeod early the next day. She was busy so I spoke to her assistant. "We've collated the results. I know she sent them through the internal mail. You should get them by eleven."

"Thanks for the information." *Perfect timing*, I thought to myself thinking about Jack. *He should arrive in Glencoe around that time.*

I had some emails to catch up on which kept me busy for the rest of the morning. Once finished, I made myself a coffee then called the reception. "Let me know when the mail arrives. I'll come down and get it. It's important, Constable Peters."

"I'll call you straight away."

I dialled his number. "Jack, it's me. Where are you?"

"We're on our way to Argyll. We'll be there within the next half an hour."

"Did you manage to secure another victim recovery dog?" I asked.

"Lady, she's a beautiful Spaniel and one of the best."

"Have you got Blade with you as well?"

"Of course. You know me and my Alsatian are inseparable."

"Just start an informal search of the area. I'll call you soon when I receive the forensic results. Speak to you soon."

I waited and waited for the call from reception. I picked up the phone then dialled the number. It was engaged. Running down the stairs, I reached the front desk just as Constable Peters was hanging up the telephone. I looked at her straight in the eye.

"What?" she asked.

Out of breath, I said, "Where's my mail? I asked you to call."

"Nothing has arrived yet. That's why I've not called you," she insisted.

Where the hell is it? I ran back up the stairs to call Sarah McLeod "She's not here, Inspector. She's out in the field," said the receptionist.

"I've got her contact details. I'll call her myself."

Becoming increasingly agitated, I dialled the number. There was no answer. "Bloody hell!" I shouted. "Maybe it will arrive this afternoon."

I phoned Jack.

"We've arrived. I'm just having a look around the outside of the cottage. Did you get the results back?"

"Not yet. I'm just waiting on them to arrive. I'm not sure where they are?"

"What do you want me to do then?"

"What do you think?"

"Now that we're here we can start a search of the surrounding area if you want. I noticed there's a path at the back of the house leading up to the forest. We'll head up that way with the dogs. I'll take the venting poles, just in case we need to check the ground."

"That all sounds good. Is anyone else there at the cottage? Did you meet the gardener?"

"We're alone."

"Keep me updated. I'll contact you as soon as I get the results."

"Speak soon."

Picking up the case file, I flicked through the evidence. My eyes rested on the number Jayden Scott had given me last week.

I dialled it.

"Hello... who's this?"

"Are you Amanda Kennedy?"

"Yes."

"Mr. Scott gave me your number."

"Who? Jayden Scott?"

"He did. My name is Inspector Nicholas Canmore. I need to verify that you were with him the day he left the cottage. It was just over six months ago now."

"Is he in trouble? Is everything okay?"

"It's all fine. I just need to check he was with you."

"He was with me, Inspector."

"On the Wednesday before he made his way home?"

"I went to the house about ten in the morning. I made my way round to the back of the cottage. I saw his car so I knew he was there. He took a while to answer the door. Actually, I was just about to close the boot of his car when he shouted down from the window."

"It was open?"

"He was getting rid of the hiking clothes smell.

My mind sifted through the information Alex and Grant had given. They'd taken Alex's car on the hiking trip. *Interesting*, I thought. *You're a bloody liar, Jayden Scott.*

"He told me to leave it then came and answered the door."

"How was Mr. Scott that day?"

"He looked awful. He said he wasn't feeling well."

"Then what happened?"

"He went back to sleep. I tidied up the cottage." She paused. "He woke up about one o'clock and we... you know..."

"He told me. That's been a great help. Thanks for the information."

"Is he in trouble?"

"No. I just need verification that you were with him."

"We were together. I've not heard much from him since. Nice guy as well. Tell Jayden I'm asking for him."

"I will. Thanks for your help."

Well, well, well. What smell was he trying to get rid of? I thought.

My phone rang.

"Hey, Skipper. We've checked the grounds around the cottage. There's nothing of interest so far. I met the gardener. He's a grumpy old bastard! He threatened to call the cops until I told him we were the police."

I laughed. "Just reassure him that it's all part of a routine search."

"I did. He's calmed down a bit. We're going to head off into the forest. It's a large stretch of land. We'll do what we can in the time that we have."

"Good. I'm off to track down the post. Catch you later."

I decided to have some lunch to pass a bit of time before the afternoon mail arrived. Sitting alone in the canteen, my head felt heavy with thought, pondering over every detail, desperate to make the connections. The evidence pointed to only one man; he had the opportunity early on Saturday morning, the strained relationship with his father, he buggered off for five days to Argyll staying there for an extra day on his own, the car with the open boot and the ideal setting in which to dispose of a body. *I'm closing in on you, Jayden Scott.*

A voice interrupted my thoughts. "Here's your mail."

"Thanks, Constable Peters."

"You okay? You seem extremely irritable today."

"I'm just waiting on the forensic results from the Scott case. It's important."

"I'll leave you to it then."

I sifted through the mail. There was nothing from the lab. I banged the table. "Where the hell is it?" I mumbled to myself.

Dashing up to my office, I made one final attempt to talk to Sarah

McLeod. The phone rang out. It went to her voice mail, so I left a message. "This is Inspector Nicholas Canmore. Where the hell are the results? I got told by your assistant that you'd sent them this morning. Get in touch soon."

This is starting to piss me off. Tapping my fingers on the desk, I contemplated my next move. *I wonder how Jack is getting on.* I heard a knock on the door. Feeling agitated, I swung it open. "What is it, Constable Peters?"

She made a circular motion with her eyes. "You have a visitor."

"Get out of my way," he said, barging past her and confronting me face to face.

This is all I need.

"You... you have crossed the line this time," he bellowed.

"Do you want me to stay?" she asked.

"Off you go."

I called him by his first name just to piss him off. "How can I help you, Charles?"

His face turned red. He ignored my jibes. "What the hell is going on?"

"What are you referring to?"

"You know exactly what I'm talking about. I'm referring to the cottage, the police and the dogs. Have you lost your mind?"

I glimpsed out of the window, becoming conscious of the prying eyes focused on my office. "That's just a routine search, Reverend McIntyre."

"Stop saying that word 'routine'. It's more than that. Do you have any evidence at all to support this type of action?"

That's a good point, Charles. Not exactly, I thought to myself.

"Answer me," he demanded.

I decided to tell him the truth. "I do suspect that Jayden may be involved. I just need to go with my instinct and either eliminate or charge him with the disappearance of his own father."

His voice got even louder. "This is ludicrous. I will ask you again. What evidence do you have?"

My door opened.

"DCI Hunter... " he bellowed. "Thank God you're here. This man has crossed the line this time. There's a search team at the cottage in Argyll. There are dogs there as well..."

"Reverend McIntyre, calm down," said DCI Hunter. "I think

there's been some kind of misunderstanding. Please... let me deal with it now. I'll be in touch with you shortly. My officer will see you out. I'll speak to you once I have cleared up this matter with Inspector Canmore."

Constable Peters appeared at the door.

The Reverend pointed in my direction. "You better sort him out!"

"I have it all under control Reverend McIntyre," said DCI Hunter. "I'll speak to you soon."

"Good!" he bellowed, marching out of the door with my junior officer.

Just then, I noticed the envelope in his hand.

"What's going on? I told you to leave the Scott family alone for now."

"Jack was in the area. I wanted him on standby. I've been waiting on the results, but I've not received them yet," I said, staring at his hand.

He sat down. "I have them. I spoke to Sarah McLeod this morning. I asked her to send them directly to my office."

Is that why she's been avoiding me? "Why? It's *my* case."

"Don't question me. I'm your superior officer," he warned.

"Well... what did you find out about *my* results?"

"There's no incriminating evidence. None at all..." he declared.

"What? Are you sure?" I said in disbelief.

"There was nothing found in the faucets, sinks or drains at both properties. His clothes are clean and there is no supporting evidence at all."

"What about the blood samples?" I asked.

"Well... the blood found at the family home belongs to Jayden Scott. I spoke to him today. He collapsed in the hallway after a night out. It was a nose bleed."

"What about the blood sample at the cottage?"

"In the wheelbarrow? Did you seriously think he put his father in there and disposed of his body somewhere in Argyll," he said. "It's animal blood. A damn fox to be precise."

"There's nothing at all? Absolutely nothing?"

"Correct. You're gut instinct is wrong!"

My gut instinct is never wrong, DCI Hunter.

"You need to call off the search," he demanded.

"I know he's involved. I'm not calling it off. Not just yet," I replied.

"DO NOT challenge a superior officer," he warned. "Call Sergeant Murray and stop the damn search. This is an embarrassment to our department. Do it now," he shouted.

I stared at him in disbelief.

He grabbed the phone. "Give me his number." DCI Hunter put it on speaker mode.

I continued to stare at him. *Interfering bastard*, I thought to myself.

"Hey, Skipper. It's going well. We've covered quite a lot of ground. Nothing of any interest yet, but it's still early."

"Sergeant Jack Murray, you're speaking to DCI Hunter."

"Is this not Inspector Canmore's number?"

"Yes, but you're speaking to me. Please call off the search. Right now."

"Why?"

"Don't question me. Call it off. Make your way back to Edinburgh. Come and see me when you return."

"Yes Sir. Is Inspector Canmore there? Can I speak to him?"

"He's not here. Make your way home, Sergeant Murray."

He hung up the phone. Glaring at me, he said, "And you... you need to apologise to the Scott family *and* account for the waste of resources."

Not a chance! I thought to myself.

On that note, he turned and left my office.

6

NATURE OR NURTURE

Look down on me, you will see a fool. Look up at me, you will see your Lord. Look straight at me, you will see yourself."
(Charles Manson)

One is innocent until proven guilty.

I make my way out of the airport to find a taxi. I give the driver instructions, settling down for the half hour trip. I think about how near he came to catching me. I shudder, dismissing the thought from my mind. *Inspector Canmore, you were so close*, I think to myself, *so very close*. I heard that her ex-partner - Stewart Bailey - was charged with Annabel Taylor's murder, but due to lack of evidence and some technical glitch with the timing of the case, it never made it to court. Shortly afterwards, we received a letter of apology from DCI Hunter. My nemesis continued to follow me, albeit periodically, appearing almost obsessed by his own failure to prove my guilt. I ignored him, continuing with my killing spree over the next five years, all in the name of revenge. If only he knew, about my other victims. There was a greedy embezzler in America who stole my investment, a Brazilian businessman who had no respect for his family, and the worst kind of human violation from a filthy bastard called Raymond Cartwright, along with his dealer sidekick, Jake 'the dealer' Driscoe. At this moment in time, I have come full circle to where it all started, back to my father, who still remains missing. Seven years later, he has been declared 'dead' by the High Court.

And now, I have to deal with my mother… again.

The taxi pulls up outside the house. I pay the driver and grab hold of my bag. Handing him the money, I say, "Keep the change."

He nods his head. "Thanks, mate."

I stand alone in the street, staring at the front of the house, a knot developing in the pit of my stomach, dreading the conversation. I light a cigarette, inhaling the smoke deeply into my lungs. I start to relax, finish it, draw in a sharp breath then walk through the front door.

"Jayden, is that you? I'm in the kitchen making a cup of tea." She hugs me as I walk through the door. "I'm glad your home. I've missed you."

Startled by her calm attitude, I ask, "Are you okay? How are you feeling?"

"I'm fine. I've had time to think about it. Now that he's been declared dead, did you know that my marriage is annulled? I'm reverting to my maiden name of Carolyn Stewart."

I stare at her in disbelief. "Are you okay with that?"

"To be honest, I just feel a sense of relief. I've been trapped in between the unknown for seven years. I need to move on."

A smile passes across my face. "Good for you. It's about time."

She has a confidence in her voice that I've not heard for a while. "I'm moving back home to the village. That's where I belong. We should never have moved here in the first place... with *that* man."

"Are you? When?"

"As soon as possible. I spoke to Mathew Fleming... you know he's the executor of your father's estate. Your father has left everything to us; the house, our flat in London, the consultancy business and his savings, shares and investments. I'm moving after the memorial. I've arranged it for the beginning of next week."

I gaze at her for a moment. "What memorial? Where about?"

"I've arranged a lunch in the George Hotel with his close business associates and friends. Several of his colleagues are going to prepare a speech in honour of his life."

"You've been busy while I've been away."

"Mathew is handling most of the guest list. Charles helped to sort out the venue with the help of the event organiser at the hotel."

"That's good of them. What about you and the Reverend?" I ask. "Do you both have a future together?"

She was silent for a moment, her eyes avoiding my fixed gaze. "Well... "

The expression on my face turns to disappointment. "I just thought since you were moving back to the village... "

She smiles. "Of course we are. I'm so happy. He gave me this. Look!" My mother fumbles about with a chain around her neck and produces a gold ring with a solitary diamond on it. "It's an eternity ring. He really *does* love me. I'm not going to wear it until everything settles down."

He's been waiting for this moment all his life. I made this possible, I think to myself. "At last! That's fantastic news."

"Not a word to anyone," she warns. "After the memorial, I just want to leave here to start my new life with Charles. I can't wait to move back home to the village. It's been nearly twenty years that I've suffered living in this… *this* house."

My mouth opens, but I am unable to find the words to express how elated I feel. "Finally," I say, "I can't believe it."

"What about you? Do you want to live here, come with me or are you content with your place in Leith?"

"I'm fine in my own flat. However, I do want the apartment in London. I use it all the time anyway. I think we should just sell this house along with all the bad memories."

"I'll arrange for it to be sold as soon as possible." She steps forward and places a delicate hand over mine. "It's a new start for us all. Charles has made me realise that. It's time to go home."

****

It is late. My mother has gone to bed. I feel tired and decide to stay at the house rather than return home to my own flat. Besides, I want to be there for her in the morning to make sure she does not change her mind. I pour myself a glass of red wine, light a cigarette and make my way towards the sitting room to top up the fire. I stare at myself in the mirror. *I look like him*, I think to myself, *I am him, but worse*. I wonder how my mother would feel if she ever found out it was me who killed him. The way I see it, I did her a favour, freeing her from a life of mental and physical torture, allowing some happiness with a man she deserves. I think about the eternity ring and smile to myself.

You deserve to be together, Charles.

Scrutinising a photograph of my father hanging on the wall, I say, "You're a fool, Edward. Why did you treat us the way you did? What did she ever do to you apart from put up with your vile behaviour?"

I can only guess what his answer would be to my own question. All I know is that he was fostered as a child at six years old. His middle-aged parents - whom I never met - adopted him when he was ten. Edward then became part of the Scott family. They left him our house in Edinburgh when they both passed away not more than a year apart. I never heard him talk about the early years of his life. He made no attempt to find his birth parents. What I am certain about is that my father made our lives unbearable more often than not to make him feel better about his own existence.

Controlling bastard, I think to myself.

I laugh out loud. "We're free of you forever. And now she's found someone else. He's a man of God, for fuck sake." I raise my arms up in the air and say, "Look at me! Look what you've helped to produce, Edward."

I think about Charles, comparing myself to him.

"He believes in Christ. I am the Antichrist. He is good. I am evil. He resides in heaven. I belong in hell. Damn you! Can I blame my actions entirely on you? No! I have a natural propensity to kill, I know that. I'm the one who has chosen this life. It didn't stop with you and your mistress. I had no choice, Edward. They were vile people like you. Everyone I have killed so far has deserved to die. That's how I justify it in my mind."

I pour myself another glass of wine, wondering why I am speaking to a photograph of my father. I put it down to the pressure of having to deal with this again. "It will all settle down after the memorial," I reassure myself.

I light another cigarette, take his picture down off the wall then sit on the chair next to the fire. I look into his eyes: they are my eyes staring back at me. I shudder. Opening up the frame, I take one last look at him, light the edge of the photograph and with a sense of relief watch it burn before throwing it in the fire. I see his charred face looking back at me, disappearing into the flames before turning to ash.

"That's enough now, Edward. I'm not going to think about you or what I've become anymore. I'm fucking exhausted… mentally drained to be honest. I don't care if I was born this way or if you've shaped what I am. All I know is that I'm so tired - tired of living a lie. I reside in such a dark place in my mind. I've decided it's time for me to come out of the dark."

I place the empty frame in a drawer, finish the glass of wine, unbutton my shirt on the way up the stairs, take off my clothes and collapse into bed.

I awake the next day to the sound of the telephone ringing in the hallway. I hear my mother's voice arranging an appointment at the house for this afternoon at two o'clock. I decide at that moment to stay for the next few days, to help sort everything out, ready for the memorial next week. I have someone in charge of the agency that I can trust, safe in the knowledge that it will run perfectly well without me. *I'll give Jessica a call later*, I think to myself. Besides, I need to concentrate all my effort on the London agency to get it up and running over the next few weeks. Then I can settle back into the one in Edinburgh and hopefully, return to some kind of normality. *Normality?* I remember the conversation with my father last night and chuckle away to myself. "You're bloody mad, Jayden Scott." Feeling better about everything, I put on a pair of jogging trousers, throw on an old t-shirt then head downstairs to get a coffee.

"Who was that on the phone?"

"It was the estate agent. Someone is coming to value the house this afternoon. They're going to take some pictures. I better make an effort to tidy up a bit. What are your plans for the day?"

"I'm not sure. I need to make a few phone calls. Check up on the agency in Edinburgh. I never told you. Richard McKenzie is going to run the one in London."

"That's fantastic news. He's *so* good at what he does."

"I know."

She fiddles with the ring around her neck. "Jayden…"

"What?"

"We need to decide what to do about your father's consultancy business. Whether we should keep it or sell it?"

"I'm not sure. I've not really thought about it."

"Do you want to run it?"

"I like dealing with his clients. I'm actually quite good at giving leadership advice. I've learned a lot in the last six years. I'm not sure I want to commit myself to it on a regular basis."

"I understand."

"What about Robert Fleming? He fills in for me when I'm not there. I'm sure we can do some kind of a deal. What do you think?"

"It's a possibility. I'll think about it. It may just be easier to sell his part of the business, preferably to the Fleming family. He is your father's business partner after all. We don't need it, do we?"

"Not really. Let's have a think about it."

I pour myself a coffee. I breathe in the smell and relish the taste. It feels good that she is back in control. It makes my life a lot easier. "Do you want one?"

She shakes her head. "No thanks. I need to get the house sorted for this afternoon."

"I'll be in the study if you need me. I have to catch up with my work."

I spend the rest of the morning making phone calls to sort out the delivery of the furniture and equipment to the London agency. I talk to Richard about the layout, letting him decide upon the interior designer. I also call Jessica to check that everything is running smoothly in the Edinburgh agency. She tells me that we have just won a lucrative pitch for a perfume brand. We having nothing like it in our client portfolio. I look forward to working on the ideas to produce the media campaign. *Very glamorous*, I think to myself. I already have a team in mind. *We can work on this from the London agency as well.*

I go upstairs to get the newspaper out of my bag. I scan the article to find out more about Kristina Cooper. She teaches on a criminology degree at Lincoln University. I type the information into the search engine then follow the link to the School of Social and Political Sciences. Searching through the staff list, my fingers fumble over the keys, shaking in anticipation. My heart skips a beat. Her name, position, telephone number and email address appear on the screen.

I pick up the phone, my wide eyes gazing at the details on the monitor, contemplating on whether I should call her or not? Apprehensive about the situation, I feel a nervous flutter of excitement develop in my stomach. I dial the number and then, put the phone back down. Instead, I scan the article once again. She is due to give her keynote speech next Friday. *I need to find out more about her before then.* I check the main social media websites, but there is nothing of any relevance. I contemplate my next move. I type the information into the search engine, waiting for the details to come up on the screen. My eyes are drawn to a particular company. I click on it, reading the advice on the website.

Insightful Solutions provide a confidential service to our business and domestic clients. We give advice on corporate as well as commercial affairs such as matrimonial/relationship investigations. Our company has over fifty years' experience. Our specialists are trained to a high standard in surveillance techniques, data collection and high-tech spyware equipment. We comply within the legal boundaries of the law and provide service solutions to meet our clients' needs. Please call our confidential advice line for a free, no obligation quote.

I have no hesitation and dial the number. Taking in a deep breath, I wait for someone to answer the phone. It rings for what seems like an eternity. I become restless about the delay, pacing back and forth in my office. "Come on... someone answer it."

"Good afternoon. Insightful Solutions. How can I help you?" says the voice on the other end of the phone.

"I'm calling to get some advice about finding a friend of mine."

"Male or female?"

"A female."

"Is this a relationship or matrimonial situation?"

"I want to find someone that I've not seen for the last twenty years. Just background information before I get in touch."

"Hold the line please. I'm just going to connect you to one of our specialist investigators. Can you give me your name, please?"

"Jayden... Edward Scott."

"One moment, Mr. Scott. I'm just going to put you on hold."

I tuck the telephone under my chin, read a bit more about the company and hear his voice say, "I'm just transferring you through to Sam."

"Thanks for your help."

"Hello... Mr. Scott. My name is Samantha Banks. How can I help you?"

A woman? "Sam... I mean Samantha. I require some information on a friend of mine."

"What kind of information?"

"I'll be honest with you. I've not seen her for a long time. I want to contact her. I need to know where she lives, does she live alone, whether she's married or in a relationship and if she has children? Are you able to help?"

"Yes, Mr. Scott. This is classed as covert surveillance. I take it you have some general details about your friend?"

"I do."

"What is her name?"

"Kristina Cooper. Thirty years old. She works as a criminology lecturer at the university."

"Where? Here… in Lincoln?"

"Yes."

"That's convenient. And where are you? You have a distinctive accent."

"It's Scottish. I live in Edinburgh."

"Nice…"

I ignore the comment. "She's actually due to come here next week with her work. I want to meet up. If she's settled with someone else, I'd rather leave it alone."

"You need a quick turnaround?"

"I do."

"I'll see what I can find out."

"You will be discrete? I don't want Kristina to know I'm looking for her."

"Of course we are. It's one of our core values. Considering how long it takes to find out the information is dependent on the cost. We review this on a day-to-day basis."

"I don't care how much. Just let me know. I'll pay the money when and if you need it."

"I've enough information to go on for now. I'll keep in touch. Can you give me your mobile phone number? We can keep in contact that way. I need to transfer you back to our receptionist. He can take all your details. We require a payment upfront just as a deposit. Is that okay?"

"Yes, that's fine."

"I'm transferring you now. I'll be in touch soon."

"Thanks."

I give the assistant my details, thank him for his help and hang up the phone. I gather up my work, putting it back in my briefcase. *I can only wait to hear from the investigator*, I think to myself. *Until then, I need to help my mother with the memorial. However, she seems to be in control of the situation.*

I hear the doorbell. Leaving the study, I go and answer it.

"Can I speak to Mrs. Scott? I'm the estate agent. She's expecting me."

"Come in."

I leave him standing in the hall, bound up the stairs and go to look for my mother. I find her cleaning out the bedroom. I switch the hoover off at the socket in the hallway. She clicks the button on and off, banging the side of the machine. "What the hell is wrong with this?"

I peer round the door, finding it hard to contain my laughter.

"What is it, Jayden?"

"I turned it off! The estate agent has arrived. He's waiting for you downstairs."

She looks flustered. "I've not finished yet! Tell him I'll be down in a minute."

I turn it back on, head down the stairs and offer him a coffee.

He follows me into the kitchen.

"I'm Jayden Scott."

"Alistair Campbell. Pleased to meet you," he says, shaking my hand. "What a fantastic house you have. This won't be on the market for long. It's in a sought after location. I have several clients interested before it even comes on the market. Once I have a look around and take some photographs, I'll let you know the value."

"How much do you think… just a rough estimate?"

He ponders over my question. "My guess would be… about eight hundred thousand."

"As much as that!"

"Yes… or even more."

She enters the kitchen. Her voice sounds strained. "Sorry, to keep you waiting. I'll show you around. Finish your coffee first."

"Thank you, Mrs. Scott. I'll be dealing with your schedule as well as organising the viewers. I've just been saying, we have several clients with a keen interest already."

My mother looks upset. "It's all happening so fast."

I put my hand on her shoulder. "It's fine. It's going to be emotional. You know it's the right thing to do. Be strong. Now off you go. Show him around."

They leave me alone in the kitchen. I make myself a light lunch, my thoughts focusing on the moment we meet rather than the sale of the house. Once he leaves, I spend the rest of the day helping my mother clear up the house with Kristina Cooper never far from my thoughts.

****

The day of the memorial arrives. I feel nothing. Standing on the edge of the pavement, I take her hand, helping my mother out of the taxi. I am dressed in my best suit. With impeccable taste, she is dressed in black and looks exquisite. The dress hangs gracefully on her tall frame, layers of radiant silk fabric gathering in pools around her feet. She wears an intricately woven shawl draped around her elegant shoulders, with hands covered by long, dark gloves and resting on her arm is a textured, leather tote bag. Her hat sits at an angle, shielding her eyes, but they are just visible through the fabric mesh. Despite the sophisticated appearance, she appears nervous, overstrained and close to breaking point.

For a brief moment, we stand together in front of the hotel, staring at the grand entrance. She grips hold of my hand, inhaling sharply as her eyes focus on mine and then, she lets out a deep breath and says, "Let's get this over and done with."

My mother asks at reception for the event organiser. We wait in the lounge for him to arrive. I order a whisky. She insists on having a small shot as well. Staring, I watch her gulp it down in one go.

"What? Trust me, I need it! I just want this day to be over."

"I feel the same. What time is everyone arriving?"

"Twelve o'clock. We'll have some drinks, lunch and then the speeches. That is the itinerary for the day."

"Mrs. Scott," shrills a voice from the entrance of the bar.

"That's Oliver," she whispers.

He waves at my mother, striding towards us with a sense of purpose. "Good to see you again. Follow me," he says, taking hold of her arm. "I must admit, it looks amazing."

He ignores my presence.

I walk behind them, passing through the King's Hall. The magnificent domed room exudes an air of opulence with grand pillars surrounding the perimeter of the vast space. The arch-shaped windows - dressed in luxurious velvet drapes cascading all the way to the ground - provide a panoramic view across the city. I stare in awe at the crystal chandelier, the centrepiece of the hall, hanging from the glass dome on the ceiling. *This is pure indulgence.* Reluctant to leave, I see them out of the corner of my eye, disappearing through a door. I quicken my step to catch up and enter the adjoining room.

It takes me by surprise.

There are waiters putting the finishing touches to the elaborately dressed table, arranging flowers, filling up champagne flutes on silver trays and setting up the audio equipment on a table at the head of the suite. There are enough seats for at least forty people, each one with a name card next to the place setting.

Oliver stretches out his arms, looks up at the ceiling and swirls round to face us. "This is the George Suite," he declares. "Smaller but just as grand as the King's Hall."

He's funny, I think to myself.

"Do you like it, Carolyn?" he says, staring at her for recognition. "It has my own personal touch."

"It's lovely," my mother tells him.

He eyes me up and down. "Sorry, I'm so rude. Is this your son?"

She nods. "This is Jayden."

"What do you think?" he asks.

Who fucking cares! "It's just what my father would want. It's fantastic. Well done."

His face lights up. "Excellent! Let's get you a drink." He stretches his arm in the air, clicking his fingers at a waiter. "Can I have two glasses of champagne for our guests?" He leaves us alone, shouting at the top of his voice to everyone in the room. "We only have ten minutes… finishing touches, *please*. Quick, quick!"

"What a character," I declare.

My mother rolls her eyes. "I know! Anyway, here's to your father," she says, as the glasses clink together.

"Here's to Edward!"

As the guests start to arrive, I do my duty, shaking hands with people I have never met before in my life. After the drinks are served, the event organiser announces for everyone to take a seat. My mother is sitting on my left and Mathew Fleming on my right. The three course lunch is delicious. When the coffee and mints are served, Oliver's announcement dispels the chattering of voices.

He claps his hands. "This is just to let you know the order of speech. First, Edward's business partner wants to commemorate his life, then his wife Carolyn adds a more personal touch with her tribute to her husband and finally, several of his business clients want to say a few words about his character, life and work. Mathew Fleming, please step forward to address the audience."

There is a round of applause.

Ladies and gentlemen, I'm sure you'll agree that it is necessary to remember the life of Edward Scott. He was not only a friend, but my business partner as well. At the time when we invested in the consultancy firm, I had no doubt that he would make it a great success. His business acumen is impressive. Edward was not only a colleague, but also a successful venture capitalist. All that he did in his life was for his family. We also had the pleasure of meeting Carolyn and Jayden who are now our closest friends. I'm sorry my son Robert and my daughter Emily are unable to make it today. They both send their condolences. I think all that is left to say is that he was a remarkable man; intelligent, honest and caring. We all miss you, Edward. Finally, just as a token of our admiration, I have a plaque to commemorate his life. With Carolyn's consent, we decided upon the following inscription. It will take pride of place in our consultancy office. It reads: In memory of Edward Scott, a shrewd business partner, loving husband and loyal family man.

What bullshit. This is unbearable, I think to myself.

Oliver claps his hands again. "Carolyn, do you want to say a few words?"

All attention turns towards my mother. She looks around the room at the prying eyes - the audience waiting for her to say something - and starts to fiddle with the chain around her neck. From out of the blue, I hear the sound of erratic breathing as she clutches her throat, struggling to gasp for air. I fear that she is experiencing some kind of panic attack.

I lean closer. "Are you okay?"

She whispers in my ear, "I can't do this."

I take control of the situation, stand up and address the audience. I give her a reassuring smile. She takes hold of my hand. I ignore Oliver who is holding out the microphone. Instead, I decide to stay by my mother's side.

"It has been a testing time for both of us. All we would like to say is thank you for your support. It means a lot to our family. It's reassuring that my father has so many close friends and colleagues.

It's been a difficult time. There's not a day goes by that we don't miss him. I'm sure you'll agree that he'll always be in our hearts and in our minds. Thank you for attending the memorial today to commemorate his life. Oliver, can you introduce the next speaker please."

Several of his colleagues talk to the room. I switch off. The voices become a faint murmur in the distance. I check my phone, hiding it under the table, so not to appear rude or disinterested. There are several texts; two from Jacques, one from Alex and the other from Richard.

> I hope it all goes well today. Tell your mother I'm asking for her. I'll be thinking of you. Be strong. Sorry about my abrupt departure last week. I miss you so much. Catch up with you soon. Jacques x
>
> P.S. I really do love you. I always have. ☺
>
> Hey Scottie. Good luck. Hope it all goes well today. Alex.
>
> My condolences to your family. See you next week in London. Don't worry about anything. I have everything under control for the opening of the new agency. Richard.

Time passes by as I read the messages. The clapping of the audience snaps me out of my reverie and at last, it comes to an end. More coffee is served. The guests settle back into conversation. *What a relief that's over.* I check with my mother to arrange for her to share a taxi home with the Fleming family. She needs to speak to Mathew anyway and make up her mind about what to do about the consultancy business. *Just get rid of it.*

I turn towards her and say, "I have to make my way home as I have a few business matters to sort out. Will you be okay?"

"I'm fine. I'm just glad it's all over."

"I'll call you later. When does Charles arrive?"

"Tomorrow morning. We'll see you for dinner at seven."

I kiss her on the side of the cheek. "See you then."

I leave my mother with Mathew and Rachel Fleming. I head towards the bar. *I'll have one more drink before I leave.* I order a double whisky. Siting on the bar stool, I gaze around the room.

Our eyes meet.

What the fuck! I nearly choke on my drink.

My nemesis approaches the bar.

With a grin on his face, he says, "Mr. Scott, good to see you again."

I compose myself, nodding in his direction. "Inspector Canmore, this is a surprise. What brings you here?"

"Just passing by when I heard about the memorial taking place in the George Suite. I heard both of your speeches. It was rather… touching."

"Were you eavesdropping? Just passing through were you?"

"I thought I would pay my respects while I'm here."

"That's very considerate of you."

"He doesn't have a clue, does he?"

"Who?"

"Mathew Fleming."

"What do you mean?"

"His wife… Rachel Fleming. Now that did surprise me, I must admit. Were there no boundaries to your father's extramarital affairs?"

I look at him in disbelief. *What a deceitful bitch. She's in there with her husband, speaking to my mother.* "Are you sure?"

He nods.

"As you point out, there were no boundaries with him."

"And… what about your boundaries? Were you involved in his disappearance? If you were, it's just a matter of time before I find some solid evidence. You do realise that," he says, fiddling with my father's gold ring.

I look at the gold band, my mind sifting back to the events when I returned home from our holiday cottage; the bloodstained handkerchief, the nose bleed and my delirious state of mind. *He has no evidence from the ring or the silly bastard would have played his trump card by now*, I tell myself. I take another drink, looking at him out the corner of my eye. "What evidence? There is *no* evidence to find, Inspector. I'm not involved in any way whatsoever. I'm being rude. Can I get you a drink?"

"I'm fine."

He leans closer. "I know he's somewhere in Argyll. I'll find him."

"You're rather delusional!" I finish my drink. "Nice to see you again, but I need to go. If I were you, I would avoid my mother. I have no doubt that she'll put in another complaint. I wouldn't want you getting into trouble with what's his name... Detective Chief Inspector Hunter."

He smiles. "We have someone to replace him. Actually, we have a whole new structure to the force. We're now part of Police Scotland. We're reopening unresolved files. DCI Grace MacFarlane wants results on our backlog of unsolved cases."

I hold my nerve. "That's interesting. Perhaps now you'll find out what really happened to my father."

"I will find out. Good to see you again," he says, still fiddling with the ring. "Take care of yourself, Mr. Scott."

"Likewise, Inspector Canmore."

I feel his eyes boring into my back as I leave the bar. *Fuck you, Inspector Canmore*, I think to myself. *You're playing a dangerous game with the wrong person, you arsehole. You're never going to let this go are you? I'll deal with you when the time is right, and... I want my father's ring back. It's mine.*

I go outside, hail a taxi and head home. It is only a fifteen minute drive from the hotel. I pay the driver and get out of the car, feeling relieved the commemoration is over. In the privacy of my apartment, I dismiss the thoughts of the memorial and the encounter with my adversary. I get the equipment organised to contact *Insightful Solutions* to speak to Samantha Banks. With a feeling of excitement, I click on the icon then connect the call. A figure comes into view on my screen. I am taken aback by this woman's polished appearance. Her copper hair is cut in an elegant style with a subtle wave flowing through it. She is dressed in a masculine way, which is not out of place considering her profession. The contrast of Sam's fiery hair against those gorgeous hazel eyes is a heady combination. I try to ignore the enticing image staring back at me.

She smiles. "It's nice to see you at last!"

I say in a professional manner, "Did you find out much about my...?"

She interrupts with a sense of excitement. "I have indeed, much more than I thought I would despite the time constraints."

My heart is thumping in my chest. I light a cigarette and say, "What did you find out?"

"I've been following your friend for the last five days. I've also checked all the leading databases and found her marriage certificate."

My heart sinks.

Sam must notice the disappointment on my face. "Don't worry.

She's not married now. Kristina filed for a divorce two years later. Her husband didn't contest it because he was cheating."

What a bastard! "Anyway, how long ago was the separation?"

"It was just over a year ago."

"Did you find out anything else? Does she have children?"

"As far as I know, your friend lives alone in a two bedroom apartment overlooking the marina near the university. She works late and always seems to be on her own. Well... apart from one night last week when she went out for a drink with a colleague to celebrate her birthday in a cocktail bar in the centre of Lincoln."

"How do you know all that?"

"We girls talk to each other when we're out!"

"You spoke to each other?"

"We did. I followed Kristina into the bar, called a friend of mine to meet up with me, and you know what women are like, we started speaking to each other, as you do in a busy bar. It was a good night out. We attracted quite a lot of male attention. She's a beautiful woman, Mr. Scott."

I feel a pang of jealousy. "That's a bit too much information, Samantha."

"Sorry."

"What else did you find out?"

Sam has a smug grin on her face. "I know where Kristina's staying when she arrives in Edinburgh on Thursday. The keynote speech is on Friday morning with a formal dinner in the evening then some sightseeing over the weekend."

"Where's she staying?"

"The Balmoral Hotel. It's on Princes Street..."

I interrupt. "I know where it is. I do live here."

"My apologies." She pauses. "Miss Cooper is a lucky lady..."

I laugh. "Thanks for all your help. It means a lot to me. You've done a fantastic job. I really do appreciate it."

"No problem. I've enjoyed this one. Good luck! I've sent her file to you by post. You should get it in the morning."

"Thanks."

She disconnects the call.

Shit! I only have two days to get my head around all of this, I think to myself. I light another cigarette, checking my diary on what I need to do before her arrival. I have a meeting at the agency in the morning with Jessica to go over the brief for the perfume brand followed by a conference call with Richard to finalise the plans for the London agency. I also have to meet my mother in the evening. Charles is arriving to help pack up the house as they are leaving the next day to return to the village. That leaves me with Thursday night and Friday morning to concentrate my efforts on Kristina. I check the time. It is just before nine. It has been an exhausting day so I decide on an early night and head off to bed.

I keep myself busy at work the following morning. The agency is a hive of activity. I help Jessica to choose the team for the perfume brand, generating some good ideas for the client. The essence of the media campaign is one of femininity, eroticism, desire, passion and seduction which are to be captured in the brand name, packaging, bottle design and smell of the perfume. We have a huge budget for this. It brings some glamour into our portfolio as well as a lucrative profit margin for the agency. I also speak to Richard, completing all the last minute plans for the new agency.

As the day continues, I look forward to having dinner with my mother and Charles. I decide to buy them a gift. As I leave the office, there is a slight chill in the November air. I wrap my overcoat tighter around my body, put on my leather gloves and cross the cobbled street towards the waterfront. It is lined with boutiques, bistros, upmarket bars, traditional pubs, quaint shops and a diverse range of first-class restaurants.

I stop outside an art gallery to admire the different styles of paintings in the window. As I reach to push open the door, the tinkling noise of the bell alerts the owner that someone has walked into the deserted shop. A bearded figure of a middle-aged man appears from the back of the gallery. He is very well-spoken. "Good evening, young man. How can I help you? Are you looking for anything in particular?"

"I want to buy a gift for my mother. Can I just have a look about?"

"Of course. Call me, if you need any help."

"Thanks."

The gallery is a treasure trove of trinkets. My eyes dart around the shop as I absorb the eclectic mix of art; jewellery, sculptures and paintings. Scratching my head, I ponder over what to buy. I scrutinise the different types of images hanging on the wall. My eyes are drawn to an acrylic canvas with white-washed cottages. I brush a hand over the contours of the buildings, my fingers following the path leading to the harbour where the reflection of the sun casts illuminating shadows on the soft currents of the water. I recognise his name. He is a local artist, retired and living in a town not far from our village.

"Do you like it, young man?"

"It's perfect. I grew up there," I declare. "My mother will love it. She's moving back home after living in Edinburgh for the last twenty years."

"It will have some kind of personal value."

"It does. I'll take it."

"It's an expensive piece of art."

That's fine… money is not an issue. Can you wrap it up?"

"No problem. I'm glad it's going somewhere where one appreciates the artwork."

"She'll love it, that much I know. Thank you."

I tuck the painting under my arm and leave the gallery, intent on buying some champagne. Tonight is the night to celebrate the start of her new life with Charles. I buy a bottle of Veuve Clicquot and make my way back to the agency, noticing the extravagant display of freshly-cut flowers in a shop window.

"What will Kristina like?" I mumble to myself.

I open the door. The atmosphere is thick with the sweet scent of blossom. I breathe in the fragrance, admiring the formation of colours grouped together in water-filled containers on shelves throughout the shop. I decide upon a more discrete bouquet of wild flowers rather than the lavish arrangements.

"I love them," says the assistant. "These are wild orchids. These ones are actually native to Scotland at this time of year. They look gorgeous next to the thistles, wild fern and rich green foliage, don't you think?" She does not wait for my reply. "I like the tartan ribbons holding it all together. Do you want me to wrap them up for you?"

"I don't need them today. Can you send them to the Balmoral Hotel tomorrow?"

"Who are they for?"

"Kristina Cooper. She'll be arriving later in the day. I want them delivered before she gets there."

"We can send them just after lunch. What message would you like on the card?"

The shop assistant waits for my response, the pen poised in her hand.

"I'll choose a card and write it myself."

She smiles. "If that's what you prefer."

I leave the florist, head back to the office, close everything down, say goodnight to the receptionist and walk to my car parked at the back of the building. Taking the key out of my pocket, I press it down and the lights on the Noble flicker on and off - awaiting its owner. *It's a bit of an extravagance. I've got to look the part for my job*, I think to myself. *I bet she'll hate the car, but I'm more than sure that she'll love the flowers.* I place the gifts for my mother on the passenger seat. I light a cigarette, my fingers reaching for the button to wind down the window. I blow a cloud of smoke out of the opening, watching the wisps of vapour float up into the night air. I check the time to make sure that I am not going to be late. It is just after six o'clock, so I should arrive early. I finish the cigarette and drive to my mother's house. The traffic is horrendous. Arriving just before seven, I walk through the front door. Breathing in the powerful aroma, the distinctive smell of spices fills my senses with pleasure. I put the picture down in the hallway. The familiar tones of classical music drift into the hallway from the sitting room. I tilt my head around the door. The place is stacked with boxes. He is standing in front of the fire, deep in thought, gazing around the empty space.

"Hello..."

I startle him from his reverie. "Jayden, my boy," he says, marching towards me.

"Charles, it's good to see you again."

I give him the champagne. "This is for you and my mother."

He slaps my back. "Let's open it up. Carolyn is in the kitchen preparing dinner. She tells me it's your favourite Indian food."

"How is my mother anyway...?"

"Just relieved that it's all over. She talked to the Fleming's last night after the memorial and decided to sell your father's business. You both need to put this all behind you. It's for the best."

I think about Inspector Canmore's revelation about Rachel Fleming. *Bloody two-faced bitch!* "Let me think about it," I tell him. "I'm not sure about selling the business to that family."

"Why?"

I lie. "We might get a better offer elsewhere." I quickly change the subject, look around the room and say, "You've been busy!"

"We've spent the day packing. I just want to get Carolyn out of this house. Tomorrow my boy and she'll be heading home with me."

"It's great news. I'm really happy for you. I mean that."

His eyes start to glaze over. "I know you do, Jayden. You're like a son to me. What more could I ask for. I have a family at last. God has answered all my prayers."

With my mother, yes, but if only you knew, I think to myself.

We open up the champagne, overindulge in the delicious meal my mother has prepared and settle down for the evening with some white wine.

I raise my glass. "Here's to your future. To both of you," I declare. "Before I forget, I have a present for you."

I go out to the hallway and pick up the painting.

My mother opens it. Catching her breath, she says, "It's beautiful. Look Charles, it's our village."

He puts on his glasses, peering at the signature. "It's lovely. I see it's painted by a local artist. We can find a place for it in the parish house."

Charles wraps his arms around her neck. My mother sinks into his shoulder. I feel a pang of jealousy, wishing those protective arms were part of my life when I was growing up. How much different my life might have been. Why did she never protect me from my father? And how could she allow him to treat me the way he did, to hurt her and do nothing about it? A deep feeling of sadness engulfs my entire existence as I gaze into my mother's eyes for longer than necessary.

Time stops.

The Reverend looks over with concern. His voice sounds like an echo, sluggish and barely audible. "What's wrong, Jayden?"

I can feel the blood draining from my face and try to control the tears. My breathing becomes erratic, the attack, sudden yet severe. I place a hand on my chest, gasping for air, struggling to find some kind of coherence. He rushes forward, wrapping his protective arms around my body, reassuring me that everything is going to be okay. I cry into his shoulder, releasing the last remnants of pain lodged deep within my soul.

"You're fine. Let it out," he says, "let it out, boy."

I cling to him for what seems like an eternity. *Get a bloody grip of yourself!* I inhale deeply, trying to compose myself as my breathing struggles to return to some kind of normality. "Sorry... I'm not sure what came over me. It's the memories of my father... "

The Reverend says in a calm voice, "There's no need to explain "

My mother tilts her head, looking at me with pity. "No need at all."

"Enough!" he bellows. "This is a night to celebrate the future not for sentiment about the past. Do you fancy a whisky before we retire?"

I sit down on the sofa, regaining some kind of control. "That would be nice. Thanks, Charles."

"I'll leave you both to it," says my mother, "I'm heading off to bed. Are you staying tonight, Jayden?"

"Yes, I'll help you finish the packing tomorrow."

"Are you sure you're okay?"

"I'm fine. Off you go to bed. Now go!"

Charles pours us both a whisky, takes a cigar out of the box, lights it and puffs out a huge plume of smoke into the air. "That's better," he says. "Do you want one?"

"No thanks. Sorry, about before..."

"It's not a problem. I think once you are both away from this house, everything will get better. There are viewings scheduled for next week, so it's not going to be on the market for long. We'll lock it up tomorrow. I want you to never look back. Agreed?"

"Agreed."

"God help us all if Edward ever comes back."

"He won't, Charles. He'll never do that."

He stares in my direction. "How can you be so sure?"

"If my father was coming back, he would have returned a long time ago."

"I hope you're right."

I finish up my whisky, leaving him sitting in front of the fire to finish his cigar. "It's been a long day. I'm heading off to bed. See you in the morning, Charles."

"Goodnight, Jayden. Sleep well."

****

The following day, I help to pack up the boxes, ready for the removal men at four o'clock. I help my mother with the remaining items in the kitchen. I notice the ring on her finger. "So you're wearing it now, are you?"

She smiles. "I can't remember the last time I felt so happy. I know how miserable my life was with Edward. I hope it's not affected you too much. You seem such a well-grounded individual despite your upbringing."

Well-grounded? Your son is a serial killer! "I'm fine."

"Jayden..."

"What?"

"I regret not being a stronger mother, for letting him..."

Realising that this is the first time she has ever apologised, I say, "Stop! Let's not go there. Today is about your new life. I can take care of myself. I always have."

"I know that. Have you got all your belongings out of the office?"

"It's all packed in the car, ready to take back to my flat."

"Good."

The doorbell rings. The removal men arrive. Charles is busy helping to load the van. Apart from a few pieces of furniture, the rest is to be auctioned or sold with the house. It is not long before the driver slams the door shut and announces, "We're ready to go."

She grabs the shawl, picks up her bag then hands the keys to the Reverend to secure the house. Charles turns the key in the lock, looking relieved that it is finally over. He nods in my direction, knowing we need a moment together and says, "I'll wait for you in the car."

She wraps her arms around my neck. "Take care of yourself. See you soon."

"I'll see you next week before my trip to London for the opening of the new agency."

"Perfect." She turns, making her way towards the car and looks back. "I'm so proud of you, Jayden."

Charles peeps at the removal man, indicating they are ready to leave for the village.

I stand alone in front of the house, watching the car drive away. *What a week. Thank fuck, it's all over!* I drive towards my flat on the other side of the city not far from the agency. I reverse the vehicle into my space in the private car park then ask the concierge to help with the boxes. Loading up the lift, I press the button to the sixth floor. It is a modest, but spacious apartment with views over the Firth of Forth. I pick up the post, noticing a brown envelope from *Insightful Solutions*. Once everything is in the flat, I make my way towards the balcony and light a cigarette. I press the button on the wall. The red glow of the heaters above my head burst into life. Before opening the letter from the private investigator, I phone the Balmoral Hotel.

"I'm calling to check that you received some flowers for one of your guests today."

"What is the name, please?" says the receptionist.

"Kristina Cooper. I'm not sure whether she's arrived yet."

"Miss Cooper got here an hour ago. She received the flowers and phoned me to find out if I knew who had sent them."

"Thanks very much for the information."

"My pleasure. Thank you for your enquiry. I'm glad I could be of assistance to you Mr...?"

I ignore his request for a name and hang up the phone. I finish my cigarette then reach for the envelope lying on the table. *Open it!* With trembling hands, I peel open the seal. Discarding the contents on the table, my fingers trace the contours of the image staring back at me; Kristina's olive skin-tone is subtle yet smooth and complements an oval-shaped face with dark hair that appears as vivacious and wild like her character. That carefree smile is exquisite and those beautiful green eyes seduce me in an instant. She *is* gorgeous. I try to think of the moment we meet, but refuse to schedule the incident for fear of failure. It is not something that can be meticulously planned. "I'll just go with the flow tomorrow," I reassure myself.

I am aware that I have not eaten all day and decide on some Japanese cuisine, placing an order for some miso soup, squid, chicken teriyaki and a bowl of noodles. I have a shower, devour the food, smoke a few cigarettes, listen to some music then drag my weary body through to the bedroom.

I feel unsettled.

My mind refuses to shut down as I toss and turn in bed; Kristina's tantalising image never far from my thoughts. As a distraction, I roll out of bed, opening the doors to the closet. *What shall I wear tomorrow?* My fingers brush over the soft fabric. I decide on a suit made of merino wool then add the finishing touches with a pale shirt and my favourite tie. *Perfect*, I think to myself, *now go to bed!* I try to clear my head with a series of breathing techniques. I begin to relax and eventually drift off to sleep.

7

LOST AND FOUND

"I like not only to be loved, but also to be told I am loved."
(George Eliot)

Welcome to my world of criminology.

I stretch an arm out of bed, thumping the alarm button, trying to make it stop. The noise is starting to really annoy me. I open my eyes and glance at the clock. It is seven thirty in the morning. I sit up, familiarising myself with the surroundings of the bedroom in one of the most gregarious cities in the world. I have a social event organised for later in the evening, but right now, I must get ready for my keynote speech at one of the most prestigious universities in Edinburgh.

Dragging myself out of bed, I look at the reflection in the mirror. *Oh dear! What a mess!* After a restless sleep, my curly hair is matted, especially at the back. I try to force the brush through it, pulling on the tugs. My eyes wander over to the beautiful arrangement of wild flowers sitting on the dressing table. *Who sent them?* I pick up the card then read the message… again.

Good luck with your speech tomorrow. I'll be thinking of you x

I really have no idea who they are from. The receptionist called. He told me that a man had phoned asking if I had received them. *Could it be someone at my work, my father or a secret admirer?* I dismiss the thought. I step into the shower, focusing on the speech as the water cascades over my body.

"Good morning. My name is Dr. Kristina Cooper. It's a privilege to be asked to deliver this seminar." *That's too formal.*

"Good morning, thank you for your attendance…" *No!*

"Thank your attending the conference today. My name is Dr. Kristina Cooper. Based on my experience as a criminologist, I want to focus on the personality traits of psychopathic killers. My argument is that many of these traits can be found in some, I say some and not all, sociopathic leaders in the corporate world." *I like that.*

Getting out of the shower, I go and write it down. I have most of my talk prepared, but not the opening lines. Feeling excited about the day, I diffuse my hair; creating soft yet delicate curls then spritz in the holding spray to keep them in place. *That's better*, I think to myself. I decide to have something to eat first. I put on some casual clothes and make my way down to the breakfast room. Passing the reception, I book a beauty treatment as well as a body massage for later in the day. *I'll need it*, I think to myself.

I choose the light continental breakfast accompanied by a strong coffee. Although it smells delicious, I nibble on the freshly baked bread, my nerves stifling my appetite. I push the plate away, order another coffee and take it up to my room. I have an hour left to get ready before the taxi arrives to take me to the university campus.

I stare at the suits hanging on the rail in the cupboard, my mind struggling to decide on which one to wear. *Grey or black?* Both are of a similar style with a fitted mid-length skirt and tailored jacket. *Black!* I ponder over the choice of blouse, deciding on a pale shade of green. I put on some makeup, subtle yet suitable for the occasion and get dressed. I take my court shoes out of the case to finish off the outfit. Staring into the full length mirror, I am pleased with the image staring back at me. I think to myself, *Right Kristina Cooper... you're ready.* I leave my room, press the button for the lift to arrive then notice that I have left my briefcase. Rushing back along the corridor, I put the card in the slot, open the door, gather up my notes and grab my case.

I check at the reception. The taxi has still to arrive.

As a distraction, I text my father.

> I'm ready to leave the hotel for the conference. Wish me luck! By the way, did you send me some flowers yesterday?

I hear a voice shouting, "Taxi for Kristina Cooper."

"Yes, over here!"

I climb into the black cab, give the driver the address for the Law Department and sit back to admire the view of this historical yet vibrant city. From what I have read, I can tell that we are heading across South Bridge towards the Old Town, home to the city's most iconic landmark - Edinburgh Castle. *I must go there before leaving the city.* Just then, I notice the cars have come to a standstill.

"Is it far from here? I need to get there by nine-thirty."

"Don't worry. We'll be there in ten minutes. It's just the traffic at this time in the morning. It's a bit crazy."

"Thanks."

The text alert on my phone goes off with a single beep.

> Good luck today from both of us. Have a lovely break. See you when you get back. We must all make the effort to meet up. What flowers? I never sent them x

"We're here," says the driver.

Deep in thought, I hand him some money and say, "Thanks very much."

"No problem, love. You make your way through that stone archway. That will take you to the entrance of the building."

"Thanks for your help. Before you go, can I book you to pick me up at two-thirty? I'll just meet you here."

"That's fine. See you then."

I push open the wrought iron gate, the daylight fading away as I enter the dark passage. I quicken my step, eager to reach the other end. The sight before me takes my breath away as it opens up into a quadrangle. Historical buildings overlook the grass lawn where a stone path encircles the rectangular space, providing a walkway to the numerous entrances perched upon the elevated terraces. My eyes wander up to the stone columns sweeping around the curved structure on the second floor of the old buildings. *Which way? Where is the Law department?* I spot two people sitting on one of the benches, approach them and ask for directions.

She points a finger towards my destination. "That's it over there. Are you going to the lecture series? There are some really interesting people on the guest list. I'm so excited."

"I'm one of the speakers! See you in there."

I do not wait for a reply. Instead, I turn to leave, conscious that I am running late, eager to meet the organisers and get to know the surroundings before my speech. I follow the path leading around the edge of the quadrangle; the bulbous shaped carvings in the wall surrounding the terrace spans the enclosure and comes to a halt at the bottom of a stone staircase. I make my way up the steps towards the solid wooden door, push it open and enter the building. I notice the sign for the reception on the wall and follow the main corridor. Finally, I speak to a woman behind the desk.

"My name is Kristina Cooper. I'm here to meet Professor John Carmichael. He's expecting me."

"Hold on one moment, please." She runs her finger down the list of names on the piece of paper in front of her, picks up the phone, presses a button and says, "One of the guest speakers has arrived Professor Carmichael. It's Kristina Cooper." She nods her head. "I'll let her know."

"Is everything okay?"

"He's just coming to meet you. Here is your pass for the day."

I sit on the chair, clipping it to the lapel on my jacket and wait.

"Dr. Cooper," he declares. His glasses are perched on the end of his nose. A black gown drapes over his slender frame, flapping behind him as he strides towards me. He is very well-spoken. "It is a *pleasure* to meet you at last." Stretching out his arm, he shakes my hand with a firm grip, ushering me to follow him.

"It's nice to meet you too, Professor Carmichael."

He smiles. "I will introduce you to the rest of the guests. You can help yourself to tea or coffee before we start. Everything is set up in the lecture theatre ready for the conference." He hands me the itinerary for the day. "You will be the first speaker. We have over a hundred guests. Not just from the Law Department, but also from our Business School as well as practitioners and leadership consultants. Your subject area has created quite an air of excitement *and* controversy."

"Well... that will make it more interesting then."

He laughs. "It certainly will. I have arranged a light lunch in the Library Hall. We will also be having dinner there later on tonight."

"I'm looking forward to this evening very much."

We reach the reception area where he introduces me to the other guests. I excuse myself, then go and get a coffee before the audience arrives. Wandering over to the door leading to the lecture theatre, I open it and go inside. My first slide is on the huge screen, overlooking the tapering seats that stretch all the way to the back of the room. Hearing the alert on my phone, I see a text message from my mother.

> Good luck today. We're thinking of you. Call me when it's all over to let me know how you get on. You're father

mentioned the flowers. I wonder who sent them. Is there something you're not telling me? Speak to you soon xx

Someone taps me on the shoulder.

I turn to look at my pursuer.

He looks over his glasses. "There you are. I will be starting in five minutes." He points at the seats behind a table at the front of the theatre. "You will be sitting there along with the other speakers. Are you okay?"

"Yes, I just like to familiarise myself with the surroundings first."

"I understand. I will be back in a minute. I am going to tell everyone to come in now."

Pouring myself a glass of water, I settle into my seat. Taking the notes out of my case, I read over the speech as the crowd of people jostle through the doors into the lecture theatre, the excited chatter of the audience becoming louder as people shuffle along the wooden seats. The atmosphere is thick with excitement.

He walks into the room and in an instant, there is a deadly silence.

Good morning. My name is Professor John Carmichael. Welcome to the Law Department. Today, we have a special lecture series devoted to Criminology, Serial Killers and the Law. We have three guest speakers – Professor Jackson Miller who outlines an American perspective to the law and capital punishment. Then there is a more practical approach to our series. We have Superintendent Marcus Hunter from Police Scotland. But first please give a warm welcome to Dr. Kristina Cooper who brings a modern management twist to her research.

The clapping of the audience erupts around the lecture theatre. I take in a sharp breath and then, settle myself behind the lectern at the front of the auditorium.

Thank you for attending the lecture. I work closely with the Metropolitan Police as a criminal profiler and based on my experience as a Criminologist, I want to discuss the personality traits of serial killers. My argument is that many of these traits can be found in some, I say some and not all, sociopathic leaders in the corporate world.

A wave of laughter echoes around the room.

I continue with my speech.

I'm sure that you are aware of the Holmes classification. People can be categorised into act-focused killers and processed-focused killers. The act-focused murderer focuses on the act itself, kills quickly and includes both visionary and missionary style behaviours. A visionary killer hears voices that instruct him/her to commit the crime. As such, he/she shows signs of psychotic behaviour. On the other hand, the missionary killer wants to kill a certain type or group of people. The murder is premeditated and is based on his/her moral or ethical stance. In contrast, the process-focused killer is grouped into three types: lust, the thrill of the kill or he/she gains some kind of profit from the act. All of these are classed as hedonistic killers. Finally, the power killer likes to play God, deriving pleasure from the control that he/she has over the life and death of the victim. Many of these classifications can be used to understand different types of serial killers; both from the past and our present. With regards to human behaviour, it is important to know that serial killers can and do transcend across several of these different classifications. So… out with the classification, serial killers can also share similar behaviour and personality traits. If I may, I will ask you. What do you think these traits are?

Looking into the audience, I wait for a response, keen to get some kind of participation.

"Intimidation and manipulation," shouts a voice from the front of the audience.

"Control," says another.

"Narcissism," cries a female voice.

"Lack of empathy," says Professor Miller.

"Egocentric and self-centred," exclaims someone else.

I nod in agreement. "Anything else?"

A hand stretches up into the air at the back of the theatre.

I strain my eyes to see his face.

"Charming yet devious," he shouts.

"For example… who?" I ask.

His eyes focus on mine in an unnerving way.

"I've been reading about Ted Bundy. He was charming, charismatic and handsome. Was his behaviour not and I quote: "An insane cesspit of devious acts?" Did he not manage to use his charm to kidnap more than thirty young girls? Bundy then raped and killed his victims only to perform necrophilia on the decomposing bodies."

"You're right. He was charming, but extremely devious. According to the Holmes classification, he can be categorised as a process-focused killer, more specifically, someone who kills for lust, pleasure and sexual gratification."

I tear my eyes away from his gripping stare.

"Let me summarise. Your key words to describe the personality traits of serial killers are; charming, devious, charismatic, egotistical, narcissistic, self-centred, intimidating and manipulative with a lack of empathy for his/her victims. If we take those traits and transfer these to leadership roles, then we have an interesting argument for sociopathic behaviour in the corporate world."

"Are you doing any field research to support this at the moment?" asks Professor Carmichael.

"It's in working progress. It's a longitudinal study over five years. We have some interesting findings so far from observing leaders in action through covert surveillance as well as storytelling in the form of narratives from employees."

He looks over his glasses. "It is very interesting. The academic and practitioner world looks forward to your findings. Does anyone have any questions?"

"I do," declares the young lady from the quadrangle.

"Please speak up so everyone can hear you," he says.

"What industries are you looking at, Dr. Cooper?"

"At the moment, our focus is on the banking sector, consultancy firms and the fashion industry."

"What have you found out so far?" she says with excitement.

I think about her question and reply, "I have observed first-hand the behaviour of some individuals through our covert surveillance such as the desire to treat competitors in an unethical way as well as intimidating behaviour towards employees with a distinct lack of empathy for those individuals. People in powerful positions have egotistical traits as well as charm, wit and intellectual manipulation to get the results they want, both men and women, but predominately men in leadership roles."

"That's very interesting. Thanks."

"Are there any more questions?" declares Professor Carmichael.

"I have one," says Superintendent Hunter. "Your use of covert surveillance. Is that not unethical in its own right to obtain information?"

"It's necessary to secretly observe these people because if they knew the truth then nobody would cooperate with the research. You must use that form of surveillance to obtain information?"

"I do, but we are Police Scotland. You're talking about the immoral behaviour of leaders in the corporate world yet you indulge in unethical surveillance techniques to find out the information you need to be able to publish your research."

I think about his question for a moment.

Just then, a voice shouts from the back of the audience and says, "If covert surveillance is good enough for the police then it's good enough for researchers to uncover immoral practices in the workplace. As a leadership consultant, I have observed this type of conduct. If this is what is needed, then so be it. Are you not taking the moral high ground, Superintendent Hunter?"

"That's a fair point," he declares.

There is an awkward silence.

Professor Carmichael fumbles with his glasses. "Are there any other questions? No... then we will proceed to the next speaker. Thank you very much Dr. Cooper.

I sit back down on my seat, putting the notes in my case. *Well that was challenging*, I think to myself.

He continues.

Our next speaker talks about capital punishment in some of the dominant states in America including Texas, Oklahoma and Virginia. Do you agree with capital punishment? Is there a place for this in our society, and what method of execution is acceptable? Lethal injection, hanging, gas chamber, electrocution or the firing squad? Interestingly, only Utah and Idaho authorise the firing squad. Is this more humane than the other forms of execution? These are some of the controversial issues covered by Professor Jackson Miller. Please welcome him to our university.

The sound of applause echoes around the theatre.

I listen with interest for a while, but the rest of the lecture goes by in a haze, my mind refusing to listen, exhausted by the preparation of my own speech. I need to thank the mystery man for his support. However, I could have answered the question myself. The speeches eventually come to an end. Professor Carmichael announces that a buffet lunch is to be served in the Library Hall. He approaches the table at the front of the theatre, shaking each of our hands in turn.

"That went extremely well. Thank you... thank you so much for an interesting debate. I will take you for lunch."

I look around the empty theatre then follow them out.

"Sorry, if my question was a bit challenging," says Superintendent Hunter.

"There's no need to apologise," I retort. "There is a moral dilemma with covert surveillance. However, I think in this case, the subject area warrants such a method."

"You're right, Dr. Cooper. It's very interesting."

"Thanks."

"I did want to ask you a favour since you mentioned you work as a criminal profiler for the Metropolitan Police. Our new structure at Police Scotland has allowed me to open up unsolved cases. I have one in particular that may interest you. I am keen to get your opinion on a murder that happened seven years ago. Beautiful woman... her name is Annabel Taylor. If I send you her file, can you look over the details? I would value your opinion on this case."

"Of course. I'll have a look at it. It's my area of specialism. Here is my card. Contact me as soon as possible with the details. I will put together a dossier of the killer. It might take some time to get my head around all the information, but a profile you will have."

He shakes my hand. "Thank you very much. It's much appreciated."

"It's my pleasure, Superintendent Hunter."

"I actually need to go now," he declares. "We can catch up with each other at the dinner."

He makes his apologies and leaves.

By the time we reach the Library Hall, I am ravenous, pile the food onto the plate, but somehow have no desire to eat it. Instead, I have another coffee and participate in small-talk with several law lecturers from the university. Feeling restless, I offer an apology and leave. Jostling through the crowd of people, my eyes dart around the room searching for my advisor. *He's not here*, I think to myself. I take my drink, follow the corridor back to the reception area and find the exit sign. Pushing open the door, I sit down on a bench in the quadrangle.

Despite the chill in the November air, the sun is suspended in the clear blue sky, beating down into the enclosure. Shutting my eyes, I point my face towards it, feeling the warm rays of light on my face. I start to relax. Checking the time, I note that it is twenty past two. I gulp down my coffee, tuck the cup under the bench, head towards the archway and wait for the taxi.

****

As I enter the hotel, the receptionist shouts over, "I have a message for you, Miss Cooper."

I approach the desk. "What is it?"

He smiles, producing an envelope out of the rack on the wall. "This is for you."

I take it and go up to the comfort of my own room. I look at the bunch of wild flowers then notice that the handwriting on this envelope, **Dr. Kristina Cooper**, is the same as the one on the gift card. My hands start to tremble as I unfold the note, slowly revealing the words concealed inside.

Well done. What a fantastic speech. Meet me in the Whisky Bar in the hotel when you get back. I'll be waiting for you x

Curiosity gets the better of me. I decide to find out. I brush my hands over the suit, ruffle my hair then take in a deep breath. Before leaving the room, I grab the key card, slipping it into my purse. I make my way down the stairs, pass the reception and ask the young man directions to the bar.

"It's just down the end of the corridor… on your right hand side."

I find it easily enough and walk through the entrance, the loud noise of my court shoes clicking on the tiles as my eyes frantically search around the room for my suitor. I stop. It is busy at this time of day - tourists no doubt trying out Scotland's national treasure. Scanning the room, I fail to find a solitary figure and then, I see him sitting by the window. *It's the leadership consultant from the lecture theatre!* I stand like an idiot in the middle of the busy bar, not knowing whether to stay or go. I decide to stay, needing to tackle this head on.

The mystery man walks over in my direction. As he comes into focus there is a familiarity about him that I am unable to place. "I'm glad you could make it," he says. "Come and join me."

I hesitate.

"Can I get you a drink?"

I feel uncomfortable, but look him straight in the eye. "I don't drink whisky. Can you get me a glass of sparkling wine?"

I sit down and watch him talking to the bartender. He leaves, returning a few minutes later with a bottle of champagne in a wine cooler, immersed in frozen ice. My admirer picks up the glasses in one hand and with the other, lifts up the ice bucket, placing it on our table. With an expert touch, he pours the champagne into the flutes.

"To you," he says.

"To me," I reply, as the glasses clink together.

I take a small sip. "Thanks for stepping in today. I appreciate it. However, I'm more than capable of dealing with awkward questions."

"I know you are."

I have another drink of champagne and then, it all comes flooding out. "How do you know? Who are you? Why did you send me flowers before I even arrived? How did you know I was staying here?"

He laughs. "Covert surveillance!"

I try to hide the smirk on my face. "Very funny... who the hell are you to attend my lecture, leave me a message and buy expensive drinks?"

I get up to leave.

He grabs hold of my hand. "Sit down, Kristina."

Reaching over the table, his fingers tuck a stray lock of hair behind my ear. I am just about to slap him across the face when he looks at me with his piercing brown eyes. At that moment, the truth hits me like a hammer blow to the heart.

"Is that you, Jayden?"

I begin to experience a reeling sensation in my head. The room starts to spin around, making me feel dizzy. I grip onto the side of the table, the knuckles on my fingers turning white from the strain of trying to support the weight of my body.

In a flash, he gets out of his seat and sits next to me, puts an arm around my waist, helping to prop up my body before I threaten to pass out. "Take a deep breath," he says, "breath in, breath out, breath in, breath out... keep doing it until you feel better." Jayden shouts at the bartender to bring over a glass of water. "Hurry up!"

I take a drink and start to calm down. I try to compose myself, but I am aware of his body next to mine, arousing my already heightened senses.

"Sorry, Kristina... it must be a bit of a shock."

I wrap my arms around his neck. "It's so good to see you again. You're lucky I didn't slap you across the face."

He smirks. "I know!"

I am lost for words, not sure what else to say.

He breaks the silence. "Now we've got that out of the way, do you want another glass of champagne to celebrate your keynote speech?"

"Thank you. That would be nice."

I touch his face with my fingers. "Is it really you?"

"Of course it is!"

"I still can't believe it."

"Well believe it, Kristina... it's me!" He takes my hand. "Let's find somewhere more comfortable to sit. We can catch up properly. Can you bring the drinks through to the lounge," he tells the bartender. "And can you bring a mixed selection of sandwiches."

We settle onto the fabric sofa, sinking into the soft cushions, drinking our champagne. He tells me about his life, advertising business, his father, mother and Reverend McIntyre. I tell him about my parents, Lincoln University, my job as a criminology lecturer, the covert research and my divorce.

"It was an emotional time in my life, such an act of betrayal. It was a messy separation... a waste of three years of my life. Why did I not see the signs? I feel such a fool."

"Don't say that. You're a strong woman." He strokes my face with his fingers. "Don't ever say that about yourself again. You're not a fool."

"I know that." I check the time. "Damn! I have my beauty treatment and massage. I need to go. I'm going to the dinner at the Law Department tonight. Did you get an invitation?"

"What do you think? I work in one of the best leadership consultancy firms in Edinburgh, albeit my mother is in the process of selling it. Of course I got an invite!"

"Are you going home first?"

"No."

"You can stay in my room until I get back. Room 3/20." I give him the card. "I need to go for my beauty therapy."

"Are you sure?"

I smile. "Yes, see you soon."

I wander about the lower ground floor, looking for the spa room and eventually find it. "Miss Cooper, I've been waiting on you. My name is Heather. I'll be doing your treatments today. What would you like me to do, my dear?"

"I definitely want a manicure. I also want a massage. Is that okay?"

"Of course, I'll do your nails first. Let me see them. They're beautiful. What colour would you like?"

"I'm not sure. I'm wearing a black dress tonight. I might indulge in some ruby red lipstick to brighten up the outfit. You can do my nails the same colour."

"Perfect." She looks at my eyebrows. "I can tidy them up for you. You have such a pretty face. Let's get started. Do you want something to drink?"

"Can I have a glass of water?"

"Of course, my dear." Heather points towards a door. "Can you just go in there? I'll be back in a minute."

The scent of burning candles permeates through the air in the small room. It smells like the ocean; reminding me of my life in the village, the beach and hunting for crabs with Jayden Scott. The sound of pan pipes play in the background. I close my eyes, losing myself in the haunting tones of the music as it transports me to another time and place - to our secluded bay in the village. I can hear the gentle flow of the waves, smell the fresh sea air and feel the whispering noise of a breeze as it caresses my face.

She walks through the door interrupting my daydream.

"Here's your water. Let's get started on your nails then we can get you settled for a massage. Are you going somewhere nice tonight?"

"I'm attending a dinner at the Law School."

"At the Old College?"

"Yes."

"That's lovely there. Are you going alone?"

"Someone *very* special is taking me."

"In that case you need to look your best."

Heather files, buffs and paints my nails a deep shade of red then shapes my eyebrows before giving me a massage. The tender stroke of her hands helps me drift off to sleep. Half an hour later, she whispers, "That's us all finished."

I open my eyes and quickly put my clothes back on eager to spend time with Jayden. "Thank you so much. That was lovely."

She winks. "No problem dear. Have a good night!"

"I will... thanks."

I stop at the reception, ask for another key card then make my way up the stairs. As I enter the room, I notice his jacket lying on the chair. He is fast asleep on top of the bed. I decide to leave him alone and go for a shower, relishing the water running over my body. I get out and look at myself in the mirror. Peering at my eyebrows, the arched appearance brightens up my eyes, complementing the shape of my face. *She's done a really good job!* I pull the towel off the rail, dry myself then unhook the complementary robe hanging on the back of the door. For fear of waking him up, I tip-toe into the bedroom, conscious not to disturb his peaceful sleep.

I take the cocktail dress off the rail and place it on the bed along with the lacy underwear. Choosing my makeup, I decide on a bolder more daring look, finishing it off with ruby red lipstick. I spray some perfume on my neck and wrists. I see him stir as I look at his reflection in the mirror then wrap the robe closer to my body.

"Hey, sleepy head. It's time to wake up!"

He stares in my direction. "Come over here."

I ignore his demand. "Did you have a good sleep?"

"I did." He takes in a deep breath. "You look gorgeous. Kiss me with those luscious red lips... *please.*"

"Not a chance! I've just put on my makeup."

I lift the outfit off the bed, deciding to get changed in the bathroom to avoid his prying eyes. I have trouble sticking the deep-plunge bra to the side of my breasts, but somehow manage to keep it in place. I slip on the backless dress. It hangs elegantly on my slender body. I untie my hair, smoothing out the curls into a classic style. Slipping on the court shoes, I stand in front of the mirror admiring the image staring back. *You scrub up well.* I open the bathroom door, peering into the room. *He's gone. Where is he?* At that moment, I hear the card sliding in the lock. I see him push open the door with one hand and in the other he is holding a small tray with two glasses of wine.

He stares over in my direction, placing it on the dressing table. "I just… went… to get… these. You look gorgeous. You're very beautiful."

"Thank you."

"Come over here and get your drink."

I move closer to him.

He hands me the glass. "Here's to a good night."

I raise my arm up in the air. "Remember, we only have a few minutes before the taxi arrives. So drink up."

"That's long enough." He moves closer, breathing in my scent, losing himself in the moment. "You smell gorgeous," he says, kissing the side of my neck.

He's tempting me, but we need to go. "Jayden…"

"What?" he mumbles.

"Finish your drink. We have to leave soon."

"I know."

Just then, the phone rings from reception. "Your taxi is here, Miss Cooper."

I put on my winter overcoat and pick up the clutch bag. He takes my hand - pulling me out of the room - as we run towards the lift. My fingers reach for the button. When it arrives, he drags me through the doors, staring out the corner of his eye and then, makes a claw-like gesture with his hands as his body jolts forward, pretending to pounce.

"Behave yourself!"

"I'll try my best. I'm not promising anything!"

Rushing through the entrance of the hotel, we are met by a cold burst of wind, the force of the bite sending shivers through my body. "It's *so* cold, Jayden."

He laughs, helping me into the cab. "Welcome to Scotland!"

The taxi driver makes the short trip to the Law Department, dropping us off outside the quadrangle. I pay the fare. "Have a good night, love," he says, as the taxi pulls away from the kerb.

"You too!"

We arrive at the Library Hall. I notice for the first time the magnificent nature of the surroundings. The pillars of stone carve out the rectangular shape of the hall, stretching all the way up to the barrel-vaulted ceiling, the single arched surface spanning the length and breadth of the vast space.

Looking in awe around the hall, I say, "It's breathtaking."

He nods in agreement.

Just then, a voice interrupts the moment. "Dr. Cooper," he says, striding towards us. "Come and join me at the head of the table with our other guest speakers."

I let go of his hand as Professor Carmichael pulls me away from my dinner date. My eyes lock onto his as he stands alone at the entrance of the hall. He shrugs his shoulders and proceeds to find a table at the other end of the room.

My host peers over his glasses and says, "It is good to see you again, Dr. Cooper."

"And you…"

I end up sandwiched between Professor Carmichael and Superintendent Hunter, indulging in conversation about the criminal justice system, but it bores me. My interests lie in the criminal mind rather than the formal structure of the legal system. However, I make the effort to look interested in the conversation and the meal is delicious. A seafood starter is served, followed by a beef medallion with roasted vegetables, finished off with a trio of small desserts.

I peer over at Jayden, noticing that he is engrossed in conversation with another woman. To my surprise, I feel a pang of jealousy. *She's leaning a bit too close to him*, I think to myself. He catches my attention and smiles. With a subtle flick of the head, my eyes move to the side, beckoning him to meet outside the room. I excuse myself, make my way out of the hall towards the bathroom and wait.

He does not come.

I go to the toilet then head back to my seat. He is still speaking to the lady sitting next to him. As the evening progresses, the conversation flows at our table and the waiter fills up the glasses - on more than one occasion. Periodically, I stare over in his direction. He is still engrossed in deep conversation. At last, the tables begin to empty as the guests start to leave.

"Professor Carmichael, it's been a privilege to meet you. Thanks for the invitation," I say.

"It is my pleasure. You are an inspiring criminologist."

"Thank you." I turn towards Superintendent Hunter. "Goodnight Marcus, it was good to see you again. Remember to get in touch with me about your murder case."

He shakes my hand. "I will, Dr. Cooper. Take care of yourself."

I notice the woman leaving his side as she makes her way towards the bathroom. Seeing my opportunity, I approach Jayden's table and sit down next to him. "I thought your companion was never going to leave you alone!"

"She's a consultant in Edinburgh. We have quite a lot in common. Sorry, but she just wouldn't stop talking about her business." He takes my hand. "Let's get out of here. She's boring me anyway."

Just as we are about to leave, the woman returns to the table, looks me up and down then turns her body towards my date. "Are you leaving already? Here's my business card. Give me a call... anytime."

He wraps a protective arm around my waist. "Thanks, my consultancy fee is expensive. If you can afford it, I'll be glad to give you advice. I need to leave now. It's getting late."

We walk out of the hall into the quadrangle. The blast of fresh air makes my head spin. I feel his arm grip hold of my waist, helping me down the steps.

He laughs. "Watch what you're doing! Has someone had too much to drink?"

"Guilty your Honour!" I wrap my arms around his neck. "I'm ready to let you kiss my red luscious lips now," I say, in a playful manner.

"Not tonight. Let's get you home."

He hails a taxi. Once we are in the hotel bedroom, he gives me a kiss goodnight. "See you in the morning. Sleep well."

****

I wake up just after ten o'clock. I smile to myself, noticing the glass of water on the bedside table. I take a drink to relieve the heavy feeling inside my head and then, peer under the covers at my naked body. It comes flooding back as I remember falling into a heap on the bed, laughing at him in a hysterical manner as he tried to help me undress. *I wonder if he'll get in touch today.* Stretching out in bed - feeling relaxed for the first time in a long time - my hands wander over the curves of my body, yearning for his touch. I start to become aroused as my fingers drift towards the top of my legs.

Ring ring, ring ring, ring ring...

"Damn!" I mumble to myself. Picking up the phone, the

receptionist states there is a call. I hear a clicking sound as she transfers the line.

"Are you okay? What are you doing?"

Feeling embarrassed that she nearly caught me, I say, "I've just woken up! How are you?"

"I'm fine. How did it go yesterday? You never text back."

"I've been really busy. I gave a good performance. It went really well."

"We're so proud of you. Your father sends his love."

"Thanks."

"Did you find out who sent the flowers?"

"You're never going to believe this…"

"What?"

It all came bursting out. "Jayden sent them to me *and* he was at the lecture *and* he sent me a card *and* he was waiting for me at the hotel *and* we went dinner last night at the Law School *and*…"

She interrupts. "Slow down. Jayden who?"

"Jayden Scott. You must remember the Scott family from the village?"

"Edward and Carolyn's son?"

"Yes! He's not changed at all. He brought me home last night."

"Wait a minute…"

"Don't worry mother. He left. I'm waiting for him to get in touch today. You need to go just in case he's trying to call. I'll catch up with you when I return home on Monday."

"Have a good weekend, darling. Speak to you soon. Take care of yourself."

"I always do, so don't worry. I can't wait to see him again. It's like we've never been apart. See you soon."

I hang up the phone. All my thoughts of sexual gratification have disappeared. Rolling out of bed, I grab an oversized cashmere jumper out of the case then pull on a pair of sweat pants. Looking at myself in the mirror, remnants of makeup still cling to my face. I take a cleansing wipe to remove the smudges, struggling to get rid of the ruby red colour on my lips. Putting on a pair of comfortable shoes, I decide to go for breakfast. I am conscious of how bad I look and rush through the doors of the room, snatching an orange juice from the cooler on the way to my table.

I decide on some muesli first, then eat some toast smothered in raspberry jam and finally, order eggs benedict. I twist over a generous helping of pepper. My knife slices through the muffin with ease. I relish the creamy taste of the hollandaise sauce as it melts in my mouth. *This is lovely*, I think to myself. Once finished, I decide on a peppermint tea rather than a hyperactive-infused coffee. Breathing in the refreshing aroma, the relaxing taste of the mint leaves lifts my spirits, ready to face the day ahead.

In the comfort of my own room, I read the brochure provided by the hotel, my eyes focusing on the street map, keen to understand the layout of the city in relation to the position of the hotel. I look out of the window - not a single cloud clutters the clear blue sky. *It is beautiful, but still very cold*. I decide to go for a walk, browse the shops on the Royal Mile, finishing the day off with a visit to Edinburgh Castle.

I put on my coat, hat, gloves and scarf, armed for the wintery weather outside. I check at the reception. There are no messages. With a feeling of disappointment, my heart sinks, upset that he has not taken the time to get in touch. *Maybe he's working today*. The voice inside my head tells me off. *It's your own fault. If you hadn't been so tipsy you could have arranged something last night!* "You're right," I mumble to myself, "it is my own fault."

I leave the hotel, deciding to walk the short distance to the Royal Mile. *I'll go to the castle first, and then do some shopping on my way back*. My journey leads me up the steep hill to the esplanade at the front of the castle, where I pay the entrance fee and buy a guide book. Perched on top of an extinct volcano, its unique defensive position allowed it to be used not only as a protector of its land and people, but also as a prison of war and royal residence. There is a Latin inscription at the entrance of the castle:

Nemo me Impune Lacessit (No one attacks me with impunity)

I shudder. *Those brutal words are enough to put off any attacker for fear of the consequences*. I walk across the stone bridge, heading towards the narrow opening leading to the Portcullis Gate. I look up at the iron grate suspended over the archway; deadly spikes hang from the end of the gate, pointing towards the ground, ready to be lowered if attacked. I proceed to the Lang Stairs, climb up the winding steps and explore the battlement area at the top. It is armed with guns and cannons. A crowd of tourists gather around to hear the one o'clock gun. The deafening noise booms out across the city. Eager to get out of the cold, I find myself in The Great Hall then head towards the underground vaults of the prison, the war memorial and find the Crown Jewels in the Royal Palace and take a photograph of the crown, sceptre and sword of state enclosed in the glass case. I make my way back outside to take one last look at the city from the top of the crag.

In the fading winter light, high above the city on the Castle Rock, I absorb the image of the skyline, admiring the neo-classical buildings of the New Town; the landscape littered with green open spaces, juxtaposed against the urban architecture, complementing each other to perfection to accommodate city life. Reluctant to leave, the strength of the biting wind is fierce, nipping and stinging the surface of my skin, forcing me to move on.

I wrap the scarf tighter around my neck, walk across the cobbled path, through the wrought iron gates and meander down the main thoroughfare, gazing into shop windows at the souvenirs. The whisky tumblers catch my eye. I enter the shop, peruse the different types of locally made glass before deciding on a set of two. Thinking of Jayden, my fingers brush over the soft velvet interior of the box.

I lift it up and give it to the shop assistant. "I'll take these."

"Shall I gift wrap it for you?"

"That would be lovely."

On leaving the shop, I notice a small arrow on the wall at the entrance to an alleyway pointing towards Princes Street. I leave the Old Town behind and walk through the lane. It leads to a steep gradient, the old stairs twisting down, down, down towards the New Town. By the time I reach the bottom, I emerge from the underground passage at the start of South Bridge. The noise of the traffic is almost unbearable compared to hushed tones in the alleyway. *Not far now*, I think to myself.

The warm air inside the hotel is comforting. My body feels numb. Shivering, I approach the reception to check if there are any messages.

"Not today," he declares.

I head up the stairs and push the door open to my bedroom. I see him sitting on the chair. *He must have kept the key card to my bedroom.* At that moment, a huge smile passes across my face. "Jayden!" I thought... I thought... "

"Thought what?"

"I thought you didn't want to see me again. Sorry, about last night."

"Don't be silly! You were actually very funny."

He walks towards me, wrapping his arms around my body. "Bloody hell, you're freezing. I'll get you a warm drink," he says, switching on the kettle. "Where did you go?"

"I visited the castle. Beautiful but cold! I did wait until about twelve o'clock for you."

"I had to go to work today. Bit of a problem with an awkward client. I also need to meet him tonight. His account is worth a lot of money so I can't refuse his offer."

"I understand."

"I did want to see you today… and be with you tonight."

"I'm tired anyway. I need to recover from last night. I'll just have an early night."

I peel off my layers of winter clothes.

He watches me, intently.

"Do you want tea or coffee?"

I pull the blanket down from the top of the cupboard, wrapping it round my body. "A hot chocolate, please."

Several minutes later, he says, "Here you go, Miss Cooper."

I sit in the chair next to him, tuck my legs into the side of my body and breathe in the smell of the intoxicating aroma. Taking the first sip, the sensation of the steaming liquid fills my mouth with pleasure as I savour the deep, rich tones of the melted chocolate. Wrapping my hands around the cup, I start to feel warmer then take another mouthful.

"Better?"

"Yes… thanks."

"Will you be okay on your own tonight?"

"Of course I will."

"I want to take you out in Edinburgh tomorrow. Would you like to accompany me?"

"That would be lovely. Where are we going?"

"You'll just need to wait and see. Be ready by seven. I'll pick you up. I need to go."

"That's fine." I hand him the present. "This is for you. Open it later when you have time."

"What a lovely thought. Give me your mobile number. I'll text you tonight."

I tell him the number and he punches it into the phone.

"Get some rest, have something to eat and settle down for the night." He kisses my forehead. "See you soon."

"Okay... tomorrow at seven."

His hand brushes across my shoulder as he leaves the hotel room.

****

I read over his texts... again and again and again. I place the mobile on the dresser, trying to concentrate on getting ready rather than the messages in my phone. But his last text is imprinted on my mind.

> I'm taking you out for dinner to one of my favourite seafood restaurants on the Shores of Leith. Then Miss Cooper, you're coming home with me. Be ready by seven
> x

Trying to dismiss the thoughts, I prepare to get ready. I only have one outfit left that is suitable for a night out. It is my grey suit albeit tailored yet feminine in its own right. It is a bit formal, but I have nothing else to wear. *I never prepared or packed my wardrobe for this*, I think to myself. I remove the ruby red varnish and repaint them. I try to soften the formality of my suit with subtle makeup, glossy lips and a pale pink blouse to match my nails. Smoothing my hands over the mid-length pencil skirt, I tuck in the blouse before putting on my jacket. *I'm ready*, I think to myself. *Perfume!* I spray it on, pick up the clutch bag then make my way down towards the lounge.

I text Jayden.

> Meet me in the bar when you get here. I'm just having a quick drink. See you soon x

I check the time. I have ten minutes until he arrives so order a small glass of prosecco, settle onto the bar stool and wait for him. To pass the time, I contact my mother.

> How exciting. I'm going out to dinner with Jayden tonight. Tell you all about it when I get home. Hey, I visited Edinburgh Castle yesterday. I have some great photos to show you. See you soon x

Just then, I feel a pair of arms sliding around my waist. His warm breath brushes against the back of my neck, inhaling my scent. "Good evening Dr. Cooper," he whispers, "you smell gorgeous."

I swivel round on the chair to face him head on.

His eyes stare at my glossy lips. My date has a playful look on his face as he kisses my hand. "I could have been anyone!"

"It could only have been you. Do you want a drink before we leave?"

He holds his hands up in the air. "I'm driving."

"Okay."

"You look lovely."

Ignoring his attempt to flatter me, I change the subject and say, "So… we're having seafood tonight?"

"Yes, drink up. I've booked us in for seven-thirty."

He takes hold of my hand. Leaving the warmth of the hotel, we run towards his car, trying to avoid the cold weather.

I whistle. "Very nice!"

"It's a Noble M600. Do you like it?"

"Not really," I declare, "but it's definitely you!"

Jayden drives through the busy streets. I get a tour of the East End before he veers off down a side street emerging at the waterfront. Getting out of the car, I watch him unlocking the chain which protects the parking place at the edge of the quayside. He gets back into the car and reverses into the space. "We're here. Do you like the barge?"

"Is it yours?"

"It belongs to the agency. We hold social events and meetings there. Our clients love the boat. It's something different than a boring office environment. There's the agency up there and the restaurant is just along the road. Let's go or we'll be late." He lifts the chain then clips it back onto the metal pillar. "I'll get the car in the morning."

I find it hard to walk on the cobbled street in my court shoes so we cross the road onto the pavement. He takes my hand, leading me towards the bistro. "It's the best seafood restaurant in Edinburgh. You do like fish don't you? Sorry, I never asked!"

"I love it. How can we come from where we were brought up and not like it?"

He laughs. "That's true."

"Let's go in. It's freezing," he says, stomping his feet on the ground.

The ambience in the bistro is sultry, the low chattering of voices blending in with the flow of the soft music. Candles flicker around the room creating a warm glow in the spacious yet intimate atmosphere.

"Hello, Mr. Scott. How are you this evening?"

"I'm fine, thanks. Kristina, this is Tom Ritchie. He owns this wonderful restaurant."

I smile. "Pleased to meet you."

"Can we get a bottle of sparkling wine?" asks Jayden. "A nice bottle and a pitcher of water."

"Of course. Take a seat over by the window. I'll get someone to bring it over."

The waiter pours the shimmering liquid into the glasses, and leaves.

"To fate," he says.

"To fate," I reply.

I pick up the menu and nearly choke on my drink. *It's so expensive.* "Sorry, it just went down the wrong way!"

The waiter comes to take our order.

"Jayden, you can choose."

"Are you sure?"

"Yes!"

I pour myself another glass of wine while the food is ordered.

"Watch what you're doing tonight, Kristina. I don't want a repeat of the other evening."

"Very funny! I just got caught up in the moment at the dinner."

He raises an eyebrow. "I noticed."

I ignore him and pour myself a glass of water but leave it, staring at him in defiance as I take another sip of wine.

He eyes me with suspicion.

He's so controlling. "Well... I'm on holiday! I am allowed to relax every now and again. Just because I have a serious job, doesn't mean to say I have to be a serious academic... all the time!"

"I see."

The waiter interrupts the moment, placing the silver platter on the table, laden with different types of seafood to share; lobster, crab, oysters, squid and shelled prawns. There is also a bowl of crusty bread and butter along with some salad.

"This is beautiful. Thank you, Jayden."

"Only the best for you."

The evening passes us by as we eat the delicious meal and find ourselves reminiscing about our childhood; remembering the days we went hunting for crabs, yearning to be back in the village. As the end of the night approaches, I insist that we both contribute to the meal, but he pays for the bill on his credit card.

"Are you ready to go?"

"All set. Jayden… the other night, did you help to take off my clothes before I went to bed? "

"Yes. I wanted to stay. You wouldn't let me."

"Good."

He leans closer, caressing my face, the gentle stroke of his fingers sending shivers down my spine. "And tonight… will you stay at my flat?"

I pause. *It's too soon. We've only just met, but the chemistry is undeniable. It feels like we've never been apart. I feel safe in his company. It all just seems so right.*

He waits.

Eventually… I nod my head in agreement.

"Let's just walk. It's only ten minutes away."

We link arms and head out into the cold night. There is a hushed silence as he leads me towards a lavish apartment block. "This is my home, Kristina."

"It's definitely you!"

He chuckles.

"Good evening, Mr. Scott," says the concierge.

I nod in his direction. "How are you tonight, Michael?"

"I'm fine. Pretty quiet though… have you been anywhere nice?"

Jayden looks across at me then back at him. "We just went out for a meal. I had a lovely time."

As we wait for the lift to arrive, he looks troubled. "Are you sure you want to stay tonight? We can wait. Do you think it's all happening too fast?"

"I'm positive. I've never been so sure about anything in my life."

He unlocks the door.

I enter his flat.

He turns towards me.

I know the moment has come. I know that I have wanted this man all of my life. Fate has brought us back together. We stare at each other in awkward silence. The intensity of his brown eyes takes me by surprise, staring, absorbing the contours of my body. His hands gently stroke my face, wander down my body and come to rest in the hollow of my back. I feel his desire as he presses his body into mine. He takes my hand, leading me towards his bedroom then closes the door.

"You're very beautiful. I want you so much."

His head tilts to the side as he buries it into my neck. Taking in a deep breath, he says, "I've waited so long for you - to feel you, to smell you, to taste you, to touch you."

His lips find mine.

Our first kiss is tender.

Jayden holds my head in his gentle grip, parts my lips, kissing me as his hands move to find the zip at the back of my skirt. The anticipation of the moment is exhilarating. He continues to kiss my neck, removing the jacket and then, it falls to the ground. I wriggle out of the skirt and it too, ends up on the floor. His hands undo the buttons on the blouse; one-by-one. He pushes it from my shoulders, down past my arms and it also falls to the ground.

I stand in front of him in my lacy underwear and sit on the edge of the bed. Jayden kneels down, lifts each leg up in front of him, takes off my court shoes and puts them under the bed. Looking at me with his piercing brown eyes, he places his hands on my thighs, parts my legs then moves closer, his mouth finding my lips, kissing with more passion this time.

My body aches for him.

With a gentle push, he lowers me down on the bed. Lying on my back, I look up at the ceiling. His hands wander up to the straps on my black camisole, peeling it down my body and over my legs. He stands up, removes his clothes, devouring the image before him.

I take in a deep breath.

Resting his hands on the pillow, he looms over, kissing me on the lips. My legs instinctively part to invite him to penetrate my body. He refuses. Instead, his mouth finds my pleasure, his hands wandering across the curves of my body. It does not take long before I feel myself building up towards an orgasm; the intensity of the climax rushing through my entire body, wave after wave after wave of pleasure. My arms stretch out across the bed, rising above my head as the feeling overpowers me. I open my eyes. He stares, watching my reaction with a sense of satisfaction on his face.

I let out a deep breath. "Make love to me now… please."

His toned body limbers over mine as his mouth finds my lips, kissing me with passion - demanding and almost feral. I find myself responding in the same way, the sexually charged tension between us fuelled by the events of the past few days. I kiss him back, my hands gripping his hair, pulling him towards me, losing myself in the moment, wrapping my legs around the lower half of his torso, forcing him to penetrate my body. He builds up towards the point of no return as I lose myself in the rhythm of his thrusting body, his release overpowering his sweat-infused body.

Breathing heavily, he lies down beside me, wrapping his arms around my shoulders, realising that there is no need for anymore words as we cling onto each other and drift off to sleep.

8

SECRETS AND LIES

"I wish it would go away, I wish there were some way to completely get rid of the compulsive thoughts."
(Jeffrey Dahmer)

It wakes me up.

I hear the sound of rain hitting the window. I roll over. She is lying to the side with her arms wrapped around the pillow. My hand runs down her back, enjoying the feel of that soft skin on the tips of my fingers. I think about Kristina's keynote speech. *According to the Holmes classification, I am an act-focused murderer; a missionary killer who eradicates a life in a split second, focusing on a certain type of person - people like my father - in a premeditated act of violence.*

I reach over into the bedside drawer, retrieving a small silver box and open it, caressing the different types of rings concealed inside, stolen from my victims' fingers, a keepsake to relive the glorious nature of the kill, over and over again in my mind. Everyone I have murdered so far was like my father, but worse and all deserved to die at the hand of my blade – all in the name of revenge. *It's all very clever. The Holmes classification sums me up to perfection.* Do I transcend across the different types of categories? I surmise, that although I am not a process-focused killer, I do enjoy the thrill before (planning and stalking) and after the act itself (fine dining, sexual gratification and the sense of euphoric pleasure as I release myself inside a woman's body - any female body).

My childhood sweetheart is different, I think to myself.

She stirs.

I place the box back into the drawer. Dismissing the thoughts from my mind, I continue to stroke Kristina's delicate skin, remembering the feel of her beautiful body from the night before. She is gorgeous, so eloquent and belongs to me now. I shift closer, moving her hair out of the way, kissing her exposed shoulders and neck.

The rain stops.

A tender ray of sunlight radiates through the window as she turns towards me. I wrap a thigh around my hip, parting her legs, ready to penetrate that luscious body. I close my eyes, feeling her warm breath caressing my face. My hand moves towards the back of her head, gently pushing it into mine as I kiss those soft lips. She moves closer, rubbing herself on my erection. I enter, wrapping my arms around her neck, pulling her down - down onto me - as I go deeper into her body. Our intimate lovemaking is exquisite. We stay in the same position for what seems like an eternity. I feel myself building up towards an orgasm as her tight muscles wrap around me. I am unable to bear it any longer. I groan with pleasure, ejaculating inside her beautiful body, kissing her luscious lips, all at the same time.

****

I take the glasses out of the glove compartment, shielding my eyes from the glare of the winter sun, turn up the radio and sing along to the lyrics.

She shouts over the music. "You can't sing."

I laugh. "That's true!"

Where are we going, anyway? Tell me!"

"It's a secret, Dr. Cooper."

"Well... I'll find out when we get there!" she exclaims. "Thanks for changing my flight details. I don't have to be back at work until next week anyway. Then I can wrap everything up before Christmas. It'll be nice spending another few days with you. We've lots to catch up on!"

Feeling happy, I wink in her direction. "We do indeed."

I drive across the Forth Road Bridge, remembering the journey with my mother - just over twenty years ago now - and wonder why I was so scared. The beautiful structure is an iconic Scottish landmark, one of the world's most impressive suspension bridges. It is part of my heritage - part of who I have become. Reaching the other side, I veer off towards the countryside, taking Kristina past the coastal villages towards our destination. As the landscape becomes more familiar, she stares out the window at the vast ocean and catches a breath.

"Jayden... are we going home?"

"Yes."

She throws her arms around my neck, kissing me on the cheek. Trying to concentrate on my driving at the same time as her outburst, the car swerves into the middle of the road, narrowly missing another one coming towards us in the opposite direction.

I jerk at the steering wheel. "*WHOOOAH!* That was close!"

"Sorry… I'm just *so* happy."

"Have you been back since you left?"

"It just never seemed to be the right time. I have spent a lot of effort focusing on my career. I have worked hard to get where I am now. Sometimes, I feel that is all I live for at the moment. I also had to deal with the divorce. It has knocked my confidence slightly, but it's nothing I can't handle. Sometimes I get tired of being in control all the time. Meeting you has been a bit of light relief to my structured life. I think I need to have a bit of fun for a change!"

"I want you to wind down completely on our break. Everything will be waiting for you when you go back. Relax for a few days. It's not a crime to have fun, Kristina." I laugh at my choice of language. "I'm like that as well. I suppose in our profession, work just takes over your life. I think it's the right time to go back home."

"Of course it is, because I'm with you."

"Flattery gets you everywhere."

She laughs. "You can show me later!"

I roll my eyes in delight. "I will indeed."

"We're nearly there, Jayden."

As I drive through the centre of the village, she turns and says, "It's not changed one little bit. Look! The flower shop is still here and there… over there, it's the memorial. There's the school and along the lane, it's our church."

I squeeze her hand. "Welcome home."

I approach the driveway leading up towards the house. I gaze up at the old mansion with a warm feeling in my heart. Although it is unfamiliar, it somehow feels right to come here - to his home - and visit my mother.

I wonder if they're settling in okay, I think to myself.

The door opens.

She is waiting at the front of the house. He is standing by her side.

As I walk up the path, my mother runs forward, throwing her

arms around my neck. "I'm so glad you came. Come in, sweetheart. It's cold out here."

"It's only been a few days! I've brought a visitor. I hope you don't mind. I didn't tell you because I wanted it to be a surprise."

"Who?"

I wave to Kristina to get out of the car. She briskly holds out an arm, waiting to shake my mother's hand. "Hello, Mrs. Scott."

My mother looks at me with a questioning glance then stares at my companion. "I've changed my surname back to my maiden name. It's Carolyn Stewart."

"I never knew that. It's nice to see you again." "

Do we know each other?"

I interrupt. "This is Kristina... Kristina Cooper," I declare.

A look of recognition passes across my mother's face. She finally takes hold of her hand. "Kristina! Look at you. You're so pretty."

Charles and my mother both fuss over her on the driveway as I take the bags out of the boot of the car.

"Come in both of you," says the Reverend. "Let's get you settled."

He stops at the bottom of the stairs, then turns, staring at us both. In a blundering way, he says, "Do you... shall I give you a single room each or..."

I interrupt, dispelling the awkwardness of the situation. "A double room is fine, Charles."

He leads us into a bedroom on the second floor at the back of the house. The four poster bed dominates the room with heavily carved patterns etched into the mahogany wood. It is surrounded by matching furniture, a woollen rug, open fireplace and luxurious accessories.

"Come down when you're ready. I'll show you around."

He closes the door.

I look at Kristina out of the corner of my eye then pounce, pushing her into the sumptuous folds of the covers on the bed. My hands wander over her curves, sliding up the cashmere jumper, feeling her soft flesh.

With a serious look on her face, she says, "Slow down. You're so intense. They might hear us anyway."

"Remember you're under orders to have some fun!"

"Not today. We've only just arrived. It doesn't feel like the right moment. Besides, we need to unpack first."

I agree, helping to hang up our clothes in the wardrobe. When we are finished, she must notice the look of lust in my eyes, and drags me out of the room. She laughs. "Behave!"

My mother and Charles are in the living room sitting in front of the blazing fire. Although I know she is happy, it does feel odd, seeing her with another man in a strange house. *I'll get used to it*, I think to myself.

She jumps up. "Kristina, I still can't believe you're here after all this time. Let's go and make some tea. You can tell me all about how you both met up."

He looks in my direction. "You look well. It's nice to see you happy."

"Thanks. How are you?"

"I'm fine... more than fine."

"Is my mother settling in okay?"

"She's like a different person and belongs here with me now."

"I'm so pleased for you both."

He squeezes my arm. "I know you are, Jayden."

They both enter the room with a tray of tea and biscuits.

"Charles! Kristina's a criminology lecturer in Lincoln and has just given a keynote speech in Edinburgh. That's where they met. Look at her... so clever as well as beautiful." She pats the cushion on the fabric sofa. "Come and sit next to me."

My mother spends the rest of the afternoon catching up with Kristina. We leave them alone and head off to the drawing room where he pours us both a whisky.

"To our future," says the Reverend.

"To us," I confirm.

"I think it's time for a quick cigar, Jayden. Pass me the box. It's just on the sideboard behind you."

I hand it to him. "I think I might join you. I've not had a cigarette in days! I'll be back in a minute. I've got some upstairs in my bag."

When I return, he is filling up the glasses with another shot of whisky, puffing away on his cigar. I light the cigarette, inhaling the smoke deeply into my lungs. It feels good - bad for me but good.

"You and the lovely, Miss Cooper. Is it not all happening a bit fast?"

"No, we were always meant to be together. I can't believe it. It's like we've never been apart. She's everything I want and much, much more."

"That's how I feel about your mother. I always have. We were once like you and Kristina in your early childhood years... until your father came along. Anyway, I'm *so* pleased you're together."

"Thanks."

"What are your plans for tonight? Are you having dinner with us?"

"I think I'll take her out. She has a pretty stressful job and needs to unwind. We can head off up the coast to my old university town. I know she'll love it there. I can take her to some of my old haunts."

"Oh yes... that's where you did your degree. You're right. It is beautiful."

"You don't mind, do you?"

"Of course not!"

"We can all spend the evening together tomorrow night. I need to get back to Edinburgh on Wednesday afternoon. She's flying back to Lincoln."

"Okay."

"Thanks for the drink! I better go and rescue her from my mother."

"Good idea. I'll be there shortly."

I realise then how much I have come to respect him. *He's been there for both of us over the last seven years.* I turn towards him as I reach the drawing room door and say, "You're such a good man, Charles."

He nods his head in agreement.

My mother is still gushing over Kristina as I enter the sitting room, her beaming smile as bright as a half crescent moon. *It's good to see my mother so happy. She deserves it.*

I interrupt. "We need to get ready for a night out. I'm going to take you up the coast. You're not too tired, are you?"

"I'm fine."

I grab Kristina's hand, tearing her away from my mother.

"I'll catch up with you later, Carolyn," she says, as I drag her through the door. "That was a bit rude, Jayden."

"I don't care. I want you all to myself."

Running away from me, she dashes up the stairs. I chase after her, eager to get ready and go out. She has a bath while I take a shower. Her body is irresistible, but I resist the temptation. I decide on some casual clothes. She does the same, looking gorgeous, even in a pair of jeans and cashmere jumper. Before we leave, Kristina puts on a winter coat, boots, hat, gloves and scarf, ready to embrace the cold weather outside.

Charles drops us off outside the hotel. "Have a good time! See you later or we can catch up with you both in the morning."

"Thanks for the lift," I say, as he drives off.

She looks adorable. I grab hold of the scarf around her neck, pull her towards me and kiss her lips. "Mmmm hmmm… de-lisc-ious!"

Laughing, she slips an arm through mine as we make our way to the bistro in the basement of the hotel. "I have a reservation for two people… for Scott," I tell the waiter.

We decide on some white wine accompanied by a bowl of Cullen Skink and some wholemeal bread - finishing off the delicious meal of smoked haddock chowder with some coffee and mints.

"Thanks Jayden, that was lovely. Believe it or not, I've never tried it before despite it being a national treasure! It was *so* tasty… such a hearty bowl of creamy heaven."

"I needed that," I say, patting my full stomach.

"Me too!"

"I'll take you up to the lounge. We can have a drink in there if you want? It has a stunning view over the North Sea."

I order us another small glass of wine. I take the drinks over to a table near the window. It overlooks the golf course next to the beach. Beyond that, I can just make out the outline of the curving slopes of wind-blown sand dunes stretching up the side of the coastline for at least two miles.

"Jayden, it's beautiful."

"I spent four years of my life here studying for my commerce degree. The university has an excellent reputation for science, politics and history, but the management school is also fantastic."

"You're a very clever businessman. You've done well for yourself."

"And so have you." I take hold of her hands across the table. "I know that it's cold outside. Walk with me for a while. I want to show you some of this beautiful town."

She nods in agreement.

We leave the hotel by the back entrance. It leads onto the

cobbled street at the edge of the golf course. She links her arm through mine and walk across the fairway then sit on the wall, listening to the lapping sound of each incoming wave as it breaks near the shoreline, gently caressing the rocks below us before rushing back out to sea. My quiet voice interrupts the peaceful moment. "I'll take you on a short walk up there, just behind those cliffs and show you where I used to stay."

I grasp hold of her hand as we climb up the steps to the top of the steep hill, peering through the wrought iron railings down towards the rock pools, hearing the noise of seals splashing around in the water, free from the prying eyes of daytime visitors. We pass a small church, down a tree-lined street and walk through a dimly lit lane. She holds on tighter to my hand. I push open a gate which leads into a courtyard. The student residence is surrounded by old trees, the creaking branches hovering overhead, swaying in the gentle breeze. I smell the familiar musty odour of wood clinging to the damp, winter air. Creeping along the side of the building, I place my hands on the ledge, stand on the tips of my toes and gaze through the window. In a hushed tone of voice, I say, "Over here. This was my bedroom."

Just then, a figure of a young lady appears at the window, staring down at me. There is a loud knock on the glass and we run as fast as we can through a stone archway onto the main street – laughing uncontrollably.

"Stalker!" she says.

"Ha bloody ha!" I reply.

"That was *really* funny."

As our laughter subsides, she slips her arm through mine. We approach the bustling town centre, pass a row of boutiques then hear the beat of the loud music streaming out of a busy café.

"Let's go in for a drink!"

"I'm not dressed properly for a night out like this."

"You look gorgeous. Trust me!"

I drag her through the door, making our way up the winding staircase to the busy bar. Jostling through the crowd, I order the drinks and we dance - dance the night away.

****

I wake up the next day and remember collapsing into bed when we returned home. I also remember our sleepy sex during the night. *I can't get enough*, I think to myself. *Well... we are at the start of the honeymoon period.* Wrapping my arms around that beautiful body, I spoon into her back. My breathing becomes slower, my mind drifting from one thought to another as I nod off back to sleep.

Sometime later, I hear a loud knock on the door.

"Jayden, it's just after one o'clock. Is it not time to get up? You don't want to waste the day in bed. It's a lovely day outside," declares my mother.

Yes I do! "We'll be down soon."

I nuzzle into Kristina's neck. "It's time to wake up sleepy head."

She stretches, raising both arms into the air and turns towards me. "What time is it?"

"Time we were getting up according to my mother!"

She opens her eyes. "I don't want to. It's *so* comfortable in here."

We cuddle into each other for a while. Despite her earlier protest, Kristina is the first one out of bed. I watch as she slips on a pair of jogging trousers and pulls the jumper down over her body, the faint outline of her nipples protruding through the fabric.

"Come over here."

"No way! I know that look." She picks up a discarded cushion on the floor from the bed, hurling it towards me and cries, "UP!"

"I am UP!"

"Behave.... you've hardly seen them since you got here!"

We make our way down the stairs. They are both in the kitchen. My mother is sitting at the table eating a sandwich while the Reverend fills up the kettle.

"There you are. Did you have a good night?" she asks.

"We went dancing until the early hours of the morning," I reply.

"Sounds like a lot of fun!"

"It was a great night."

"Kristina, do you want some tea and toast?" asks Charles.

"That would be lovely... thanks."

"Sit yourself down. I'll get it for you."

"Jayden, coffee or tea?" he says.

"Coffee thanks."

Several minutes later, he places it on the table. "Sorry, I need to leave. I have a meeting at the church with the community choir. See you at dinner."

I nod in his direction. "Thanks."

"What are your plans for today?"

"I want to take Kristina for a walk around the village. We'll be back for something to eat. We might go to the pub for a hot drink on the way home."

"I'll leave you to it. I've joined the horticultural society. We're already planning the spring blooms for the village with Mrs. Cameron. Do you want anything else before I leave?"

"This is lovely," says Kristina.

"I'll see you both later."

We finish our breakfast and head off out into the cold November afternoon, stopping at the pottery shop. After much deliberation, Kristina buys her parents a glazed earthenware teapot - with blue and white patterns - and a set of four sturdy mugs.

"I'll pick them up on the way back," she tells the shop assistant. "We're away for a walk."

Strolling along the terrace high above the harbour, she looks out over the ocean, takes in a deep breath, smelling the fresh sea air and says, "It's so good to be home. Look! Over there is our beach." She points over to the top of the cliff. "And there... I can see your house from here."

I gaze up at my old home. "I loved living there, most of the time."

"I know you did. Let's go down to the harbour."

We walk down the narrow stairs leading to the start of a steep decline, pass the gallery tearoom and emerge at sea level. The smell of cooked fish lingers in the air from the stall next to the old museum - feeding locals as well as visitors to the village. I ask the vendor for some fresh crab and lobster. We eat it sitting on the wrought iron bench overlooking the ocean. Licking her fingers, she looks into the pot and then, helps herself to some more.

Kristina plants an oily kiss on my lips. "This tastes amazing."

"Glad you like it. It's so peaceful here, don't you think?"

"It is beautiful. Where shall we go? Do you want to take a walk along the coast?"

"That would be nice. Are you warm enough?"

"I'm not too bad at the moment."

I take hold of her hand. We meander up the stone staircase

leading towards the clifftop, passing the spot where I left her sitting alone as I walked away with such a deep sense of sadness in my heart.

"Do you remember?" I ask.

"Of course I do."

I hold on tighter, never wanting to let her go. We follow the track for at least two miles, towards the grassy mound just before the coastal path, sit on a bench at the highest point and look out across the water. Huddled together, we sit there for a while - not saying a word - fixated by the rise and fall of the waves. I listen to the crashing noise of the swirling sea on the rocks until her voice breaks the silence.

"It's strange how our lives have come full circle."

I stroke her cheek with my fingers. "It's fate. We're meant to be together."

Just then, Kristina's head turns away from my touch. She shudders as it convulses through her entire body. "Someone just walked over my grave."

What is it they say about that remark? It is a sense of foreboding... a sign of impending doom. Such superstitious nonsense! I dismiss the thought from my mind. "You're just cold. Let's go to the hotel for a warm drink before heading home."

As we approach the centre of the village, she runs into the pottery shop to pick up the present. Taking a short cut, I lead her through a lane that takes us onto the main street. We enter the hotel through a side door leading to the bar. The heat in the pub instantly warms up my numb face, my fingers tingling from the unexpected change in temperature.

"Take that table next to the fire," I say. "I'll get the drinks."

I order a hot chocolate and get myself a cappuccino. She takes off her layers of winter clothes and settles in front of the fire, rubbing her hands together in front of the warm flames. I take over the cups of steaming hot drinks. She smiles, the glow of the fire brightening up her face, those green eyes sparkling in the light.

I look at her with affection. "Here you go. This will heat you up."

"Thanks."

"Is it good to be back, Kristina?"

"I love it here."

"I'm glad you're enjoying yourself."

"I don't want to leave, but I need to get back to work!"

"Are you free next weekend? I want you to come to London for the opening of my new agency."

"That would be lovely. Is it on Saturday?"

"It's the Friday night. Is that a problem?"

"Not really. All my teaching is finished. I can request the day off. I'll travel back on Sunday. How exciting. I can't wait to see it."

"My partner, Richard McKenzie, is working hard to get it all finished on time."

She takes a sip of hot chocolate and says, "It's a date."

"I'll sort out all the details. I'll book your flight."

"I can do that myself."

"I know but I want to," I say, taking hold of her hand. "You mean everything to me. You do realise that?"

She nods.

Snuggling into each other next to the fire, we finish our drinks. Kristina takes in a short breathe of air then a deep, thick breath escapes from her lungs, letting out a huge yawn.

"You're sleepy. Let's finish our drink. It's nearly time for dinner anyway. I think we need an early night tonight. It's been an eventful four days."

"I think it's just catching up on me," she says, trying to stifle another yawn.

Kristina decides to go for a lie down when we get home. I help my mother prepare the meal. She is making a roast dinner. I offer to peel the vegetables then set the table in the dining room. As I am opening the wine, I hear the front door slamming shut. His familiar voice roars at full volume through the house.

"Something smells good," he bellows.

I chuckle away to myself.

"We're in the kitchen," she shouts.

His arm touches my mother's shoulder as he places a tender kiss on the side of her cheek. "You two have been busy. Where's Kristina?"

"Sleeping... it's probably all that sea air! I'll go and wake her up."

"Fifteen minutes. Then we'll serve up the food," warns my mother.

I enter the room. Kristina is curled up on the bed. I kneel down on the floor and run my fingers over the surface of her soft skin, pushing aside a few locks of hair and then, brush my lips over her mouth. She flicks open her eyes, staring at me for a moment, then kisses me back. "Is it time to wake up already? Is the dinner ready?"

"I'm afraid so."

"Right now... like now... this very minute now?"

I laugh. "You have ten minutes!"

Kristina groans and rolls onto her back, stretching out that beautiful body. I lie down on the bed. She wraps an arm around my chest, cuddling into me, resting her head on my shoulder. I look around the room. *This is perfect, just perfect,* I think to myself.

"I can light the fire later on if you want. We can just relax for the rest of the evening. How does that sound?"

"That would be lovely."

"We better go," I say, pulling her off the bed.

"Do I look okay?"

"You look gorgeous, so don't worry."

We make our way to the dining room. Charles is already there, running his finger down the music rack. "There you are! Help me choose something, Kristina. Jayden, can you give your mother a hand?"

"Okay... no problem."

I go into the kitchen just as she is placing the vegetables into serving bowls. "Can you pass me the jug for the gravy? It's in that cupboard over there."

"Sure, here you go."

"Can you also carve the joint?" she says. "Bring it through to the dining room when you're finished."

Standing alone in the kitchen, with the knife in my hand, I feel at peace with the world. *This is what family life should be like,* I think to myself. When it is sliced, I take the tray through to the dining room, put the plate of meat in the centre of the table and settle into my chair next to Kristina.

He says a prayer before we eat.

"Do not neglect to do good and to share what you have, for such sacrifices are pleasing to God (Hebrews 13: 16). Bless us, O Lord, for what we are about to receive. For this lovely food and to Carolyn and Jayden who prepared it. I am truly blessed to share it with my new family. I thank you, Lord. Amen."

"Amen," we all say in unison.

"Thank you, Charles," says my mother, squeezing his hand, "that was lovely."

"My pleasure," he replies.

As the sentiment of the moment passes, he hollers, "Let's tuck in!"

Kristina chuckles at his joviality. "They are so right for each other," she murmurs.

"No whispering at this table. Here, you can pass the vegetables around. Jayden, can you serve the meat. I'll pour the wine. Carolyn, you can relax."

The plates of food look delicious - piled high with beef, gravy, roast vegetables and my mother's delicious home-made puddings. It does not take us long before we devour it all.

"That was lovely... thanks. It just melted in my mouth," I declare.

"It was delicious, Carolyn," says the Reverend.

"Thank you, Mrs. Scott. Sorry... what shall I call you?"

She smiles at Kristina. "Just call me by my first name."

"Thanks, Carolyn."

I look over at my mother. "How's the sale of the house going?"

"We've had an offer already. The family wants to move in just after New Year."

"That's fantastic news. What about the business?" I ask.

"It's all in the process of being sold. Mathew and Rachel want me to come to Edinburgh next month to finalise the contract. They're going to buy it from us."

Taking in a deep breath, I feel the anger welling up inside. My fists clench together, ready to bang them down on the table. I look at their faces, staring at my reaction, and decide against it. Instead, I tap my fingers on the wooden surface and tell her this: "You're *not* going and they're *not* buying the business from us."

"Don't speak to you mother like that," warns the Reverend.

"Charles, this has nothing to do with you."

"Like hell it does! Explain yourself, boy!"

Kristina stares into my eyes. "What is it? Why are you so angry?"

Picking up the glass of wine, I take a large mouthful. "I can't say, but they're not, and I repeat NOT, buying that business."

"Tell me why?" cries my mother.

"It's her..."

"Who?" says the Reverend.

"Rachel Fleming.... is a lying, two-faced bitch, acting as if she was your friend all these years. When in fact, she..."

"What?" shouts my mother.

A look of realisation passes across the Reverend's face as his wide eyes stare in my direction, shaking his head, his eyes pleading with me not to tell her, but it is too late.

"She was *fucking* your husband. That's the reality."

My mother takes in a short intake of breath, placing a hand across her mouth.

Kristina squeezes my arm and says, "Calm down."

"I didn't mean to say it like that. Sorry..."

The Reverend takes control of the situation. "Kristina is right. Let's just all calm down."

He takes a firm hold of my mother's hand. "We shall deal with this together."

My mother turns her head towards him and sighs, "Thank you."

"None of Edward's behaviour surprises me anymore. I don't know the Fleming family personally, but Jayden is right. You're not going. We can find another buyer for the business." He looks over in my direction. "Will you sort that out?"

"Of course I will."

"Secrets and lies," declares the Reverend. "This is such an act of betrayal from both of them - that of infidelity with your neighbour's spouse. Carolyn, you stay away from Rachel Fleming, do you hear."

"I will. I still can't believe it. Are you sure, Jayden? How do you know?"

"I spoke to Inspector Canmore at the memorial. It's all documented in Edward's phone messages, well before the time of his disappearance."

"That man's a bloody lunatic. What was he doing there?" he bellows.

"He was having a drink in the bar. Tormenting me as usual."

He rolls his eyes. "Jayden, you can deal with the sale of the business. We'll sort out the house in Edinburgh. For now, the subject is off limits. I am not spending any more of my time talking about that man. No more! We won't let Edward ruin everything for us. Agreed?"

"Agreed," we say together.

"You two go and relax. We'll tidy up in here then just head off to bed. I need to leave early tomorrow to take Kristina to the airport."

"Thanks."

They both head off to the sitting room. I leave him to deal with the fallout.

"Are you okay?" asks Kristina.

"I'm fine. Sorry, you had to witness that. I had to tell her."

"I know you did, but you could have said it in a better way! Fucking your husband!!?? Jayden…"

I chuckle away to myself. "It just came out!"

When we finish the dishes, I wrap my arms around her body, whispering seductively in her ear. "Let's have an early night, just the two of us. I'll light the fire in the bedroom. We can take a bath together, light some church candles and share a bottle of wine. What do you think?"

"You're so romantic. It's a deal!"

I take her hand, leading Kristina upstairs.

****

The day of the opening arrives. I put on my overcoat. I have an hour left until she gets here. Checking the apartment, it feels warm and inviting, ready for her arrival. Just then, I hear the buzzer from the intercom. *Who the fuck is that?*

"Hello…"

"Hey baby, it's me."

Oh no! "What is it, Jacques?"

"I heard you were in London for the opening of the agency. Alex mentioned it. Let me in. It's really cold out here."

I hesitate then press the buzzer. *This is bad timing!*

I open the door as she gets out of the lift.

Jacques runs in my direction, throwing her arms around my neck. "It's good to see you again." Her lips move towards my mouth.

I turn my head away.

"What's wrong?"

"Nothing! I'm just about to go to the airport. I'm running late."

"Who are you picking up?"

"Just a friend."

I'll come to keep you company.

"Sorry... that's not possible."

"Why?"

"It's just not. Sorry... I need to go."

She scowls at me. "Stop saying sorry! Is it another woman?"

I am unable to look her in the eye.

"Who is she?"

"I've not got time to explain. I need to go. I'll call you later. Okay!"

"No, it's not okay. Who the hell do you think you are? Tell me and tell me now."

"I met her in Edinburgh a few weeks ago..."

She interrupts. "And you're already inviting her to social events to do with your business?"

"It's not like that. She's a childhood friend. We grew up together before I moved to Edinburgh. Way before I met you."

"So that makes it fine then! What about me?"

"What about you, Jacques?"

She slaps me across the face. "You're a bastard."

I rub the side of my burning cheek. "Hold on a minute. We've never been exclusive. We meet up two or three times a year. That's not the basis for a relationship."

"And... she *is* relationship material? What makes her *so* special?"

"It just is, Jacques... sorry."

She opens her mouth to say something, but decides against it. The only noise I can hear is the rise and fall of her heavy breathing. Without another word, she turns on her heel, presses the button, waits for the lift and is gone.

I deliberately didn't tell her about the opening for this reason. Thanks, Alex! I wonder if he'll make it tonight as I've not heard from him. Grant and Phil are busy. I never told Jacques – she knows now! I rush out of the flat, run towards the car, pointing out the key to unlock the Noble. I light a cigarette, trying to calm down as I drive through the busy streets of London towards Heathrow airport. The traffic eases once I am out of the city. I check the time. *Shit, I'm going to be late.* To make matters worse, the vehicle in front of my car grinds to a halt at the barrier as I approach the airport and then, I hear the loud noise of horns behind me... *HONK, HONK, HONK!*

A woman approaches my vehicle.

I wind down the window.

"Excuse me, love. I don't have any change. Can you give me some money to put in the meter?"

Jesus Christ! You couldn't make it up! Rummaging about in my pocket, I produce a handful of coins. "No problem."

She takes the change, smiles and says, "Thanks, love. Much appreciated."

Just bloody hurry up!

Once inside the airport, I end up going round and round in circles looking for a parking space. I feel my face turning red and cry out in frustration, "FOR FUCK SAKE!" Just then, I spot one at the far end of the car park. It is a tight space. I manage to manoeuver the Noble between the two cars but have to squeeze my body out of the door. Running towards the front of the airport, Kristina is standing at the entrance, her head shifting from side to side, looking for me.

"Over here," I shout.

She waves then crosses the road, wrapping her arms around my neck.

I let out a huge stress-induced sigh of relief. "It's good to see you again. I've missed you." I kiss her warm lips. "Sorry, I'm late. It's the rush hour traffic."

"I only arrived ten minutes ago! Are you okay? Your cheek looks a bit red."

"I'm fine. Just a bit flustered that's all. Let's get you home," I say, grabbing her case.

The journey back from the airport is more relaxing. As I drive into my parking space, she looks up at the apartment block and says, "It's definitely you!"

I laugh. "I recall you've made that comment before!"

She chuckles. "I know!"

We take the lift to the apartment. "I hope you like it."

I take her coat, dump the bags in my bedroom and give her a guided tour of the flat.

"Jayden, it's beautiful. I love it."

"It's important to me." "Let's open a bottle of wine. You can choose." I open the fridge. "Dry, sweet, sparkly, rose?"

She is standing in front, peering at the bottles, deciding on what to select. I wrap my arms round her waist, resting my chin on the back of her shoulder. I inhale short breaths of scent through my nose, sniffing like an animal seeking out a mate. Kristina's perfume smells gorgeous. I lose myself in the sensual tones of citrus, vanilla, musk and ginger which combine together to provide layer after layer of different oriental spices - setting my senses on fire.

"Sparkling!"

I let go of her as she reaches for the bottle in the fridge, turns round and places it in my hand. I can feel my eyes glazing over. The intensity of my stare seems to startle her for a moment - just a fleeting moment. With a serious look on her face, she announces, "I know that look!"

I put the bottle on the worktop and move closer. She steps back as I move forward. "It's your smell. It drives me insane. I need one kiss. Just one..."

I trap my prey in a corner.

We embark on a long, slow, sensual kiss and then, I stop. Kristina's body presses into mine, moving closer for another one.

"No, no, no... just one, Dr. Cooper."

"That's so unfair! You're such a tease."

I wink. "That's your ration until later on."

"How much later on?"

"Let me see. I might let you have one when you return home from our night out. You need to get ready or we'll never make it there on time. You're too much of a distraction so we need to behave. I can't be late for my own party!"

She blows a playful kiss in my direction. "It's a deal! Can I have a shower?"

"Off you go. I'll pour us a glass of wine."

By the time she comes back into the bedroom, I have already chosen my suit, shirt and tie. A towel is wrapped around her head. I notice the fabric of the silky bathrobe, caressing the contours of her body. *I want you so much*, I think to myself.

"Here's your wine. I'm off to take a shower. Just help yourself to anything you need."

I lower the temperature dial, trying to calm down. My body refuses to comply. To be honest, I am finding it hard to control myself. It has been well over a week since I touched her beautiful body. *Fuck it! I don't care if we're late.* I quickly have a wash and grab a towel, drying myself as I make my way back towards the bedroom.

I push open the door.

She is standing in front of the mirror brushing her hair.

Throwing the towel on the floor, I grab Kristina by the hand and pull her onto the bed, giving my lover no time to refuse. I kiss her soft lips. She responds - passionately kissing me back. My hands find the tie on the robe and pull it open. My knees push her legs apart. Taking hold of my erection, she guides it inside her body. In the classic missionary position, I lose myself in the rhythm of our lovemaking. She digs her nails into my back, pulling me closer, pushing harder onto my shaft, turning my head towards her face, kissing my lips - over and over again - as I climax inside her beautiful body. It is overwhelming. I roll over and lie on my back, looking up towards the ceiling, trying to catch my breath.

"That was *very* unexpected considering your one kiss policy!"

I chuckle. "I just couldn't help myself! I was thinking about you in the shower and this is the result!"

Running her finger down the middle of my chest towards the line of hair at the base of my stomach, she says, "And a good result come to that."

I shudder with pleasure. "Stop it or we'll never get out of here! Let's have another shower together then get ready. I really don't want to be late. We need to arrive at least half an hour before everyone else so I can check that everything is ready for my guests."

Kristina takes hold of my hand, dragging me off the bed. "Let's go then!"

I am ready first. Sitting on the chair, drinking my wine, I watch as she puts on her makeup, unzips the clothes bag and pulls out a red chiffon dress; a timeless classic which is simple yet exuberant.

"Stop staring. You're putting me off!" she declares. "Do you like it? I bought it especially for tonight."

"It's definitely you," I say. "It's beautiful!"

I watch as she puts on some lacy underwear, steps into the dress, pulls it up and wriggles her arms through the holes. Straightening the neckline, she reaches for the loose curls hanging down her back, wraps them around her fingers then moves her hair off to one side. Looking at my reflection in the mirror, she says, "Can you zip me up?"

As my fingers pull on the clasp, Kristina fastens the belt. I stare at her reflection in the mirror. The silky fabric hangs delicately around those lovely breasts and nips in at the waist; the full flow of the skirt gliding in the air as she twirls around. *Stunning*, I think to myself.

"I'm nearly ready. All I need now is red gloss for my lips, shoes, clutch bag, perfume, winter coat and there's something else... what could that be? "That must be... YOU!"

I laugh. "You're not funny. Well... maybe just a little."

I decide to change my tie and call a cab. "Ready?"

"Yes, I'm looking forward to this."

We arrive outside the agency bang on time despite our sexual encounter. Richard McKenzie is instructing the caterers to set up the food on the fourth floor. I am keen to have a look around - to see the décor rather than from the digital images he sent.

He shakes my hand. "Jayden, it's good to see you again. Wait until you see the layout... it's fantastic."

"I can't wait. Richard, this is Kristina Cooper."

He kisses her hand. "Pleased to meet you."

"You too."

"I'll show you both around before everyone arrives."

He has done an amazing job. It is stylish yet full of character. The reception area dominates the third floor. It is surrounded by work stations with break-out areas for Account Management and Planners. Images of our existing campaigns hang on the wall, contrasting perfectly with the bright yet bold colours of the décor. The use of light, glass and clean lines gives the agency a contemporary feel. Upstairs on the fourth floor, the open space is vast, the clutter kept to a minimum. Glass-infused offices surround the perimeter equipped with state-of-the-art technology. There are groups of four sofas littered around the room with a table at the centre for meetings. A small office in the corner houses a library - a quiet place for creative thinking time. The caterers are setting up the buffet as waiters pour champagne into flutes, ready for the busy night ahead.

A wave of emotion wells up inside, catching my normally composed demeanour off guard. I have worked hard for this all my life. Now it is real. For once, I am lost for words. "Richard... I... I'm not sure what to say!"

He laughs. "It looks amazing or something along those lines."

"It really does. Do you like it, Kristina?"

She smiles. "I love it."

"We will have at least sixty people here - staff, friends, family as well as existing and potential new clients," says Richard. "It's going to be a huge success. I just know it."

I stretch out my arm, squeezing his shoulder. "Thank you so much. You've done a fantastic job."

"I have just been working from your insight, that's all."

"I know but you've added some of your own personal touches that just bring the whole place to life."

I turn towards Kristina, placing a soft kiss on the corner of her mouth. I shout over to the waiter to bring us some drinks.

"Have you known Jayden long, Miss Cooper?"

"All my life," she tells him. "We grew up together, lost touch then found each other again."

"How exciting! Do you live in London?"

"Lincoln. I teach criminology at the university there."

"So... you're intelligent as well as beautiful."

"That's a comment I hear a lot. It's becoming quite a cliché..."

He falters, not sure how to reply.

I interrupt the conversation. "Back off McKenzie."

The champagne arrives. "Here's to the success of the new agency," I say, as the glasses clink together.

The room soon fills up, the excited chatter of voices drowning out the music in the background. I leave Kristina with Richard and talk to some prestigious clients interested in our creative work. Just then, I notice Alex coming through the door. *He's made it!* But draped over his arm, dressed in an outrageously tight black dress with a thigh-high split along with overindulgent makeup is Jacquelyn. *Oh no! This is all I need.*

Alex catches my eye. "Scottie!"

I squeeze my way through the crowd of people, stretch out my arm, shake his hand, embrace him then slap him on the back. "Good to see you Alex. I wasn't sure if you were going to make it. I've not heard from you!"

"I sent you a message about two hours ago. Did you not get it?"

"I've not checked my phone. Anyway, I'm glad you're here. What do you think?"

"I think it's bloody amazing!" replies Alex.

"Well done," declares Jacques.

I nod my head, acknowledging the comment. "Are you okay?"

Her eyes dart around the room. "I'm absolutely fine."

I peck her on the side of the cheek, whispering, so no one can hear, "What the hell are you dressed like that for?"

In a hushed voice, she says, "I can dress anyway I like. What do you care?"

I ignore the comment. "Let's get you both sorted out with a drink. We've got a buffet table as well. Help yourself. I'll be back in a minute."

I go and find Kristina. She is talking to some of the new employees from the creative department, engrossed in conversation when I interrupt them.

"Excuse us for a minute," I say to the staff.

Placing my hand on her arm, I turn her towards me. "I've been caught up with other people. Are you okay?"

"Yes. I've just been discussing the new perfume brand with your employees. They're full of wonderful ideas. It's all so exciting! They think I have the face that fits the essence of the brand – whatever that means? But how exciting would that be?"

I smile. "It means that you have the perfect characteristics that represent the brand - the scent *is* you Kristina. The way you look, dress and act. You're my own personal brand of perfume and... you're all mine."

She laughs.

I kiss her on the side of the cheek. "I'll leave you to it. I need to catch up with a few friends."

"Don't worry. I'm having a great time."

I make my way towards the buffet, eat some food and get another flute of champagne. Jacques is hovering around the make-shift bar, gulping down the contents of the glass.

"Slow down," I say.

She ignores my words, taking another mouthful. "Is that your girlfriend? The one dressed in red? I just know it is!"

"Why are you asking then? Please don't drink too much."

"I might, might not. And... how sweet, you have on a matching red tie to go with your female accessory."

"Stop it. Right now!"

She glares at me in defiance.

"Fantastic spread," Alex says, holding up his plate of food.

Jacques hands him another glass of champagne and takes another one for herself.

I roll my eyes. "We all need to get together soon and celebrate properly don't we Jacques... me, you, Grant, Phil and Scottie."

"Possibly... it depends on whether I have the time," she retorts.

"Where are you staying, Alex?"

"With the lovely, Miss Hayes," he declares.

She drapes her arm over his shoulder, kissing the side of his cheek, staring in my direction, trying to make me jealous, but it does not have the desired effect. At this moment in time, her behaviour is less-than-ladylike.

I feel someone touching my shoulder. "Jayden come and meet some of our potential new clients. It's important to make a good impression," says Richard.

"I'll catch up with you both later. Okay..."

"Sure, Jayden," she declares.

I forget about Jacques. Instead, we have an interesting conversation with several clients about the possibility of pitching for new business; one for a beer brand and one for a fashion label. I have no doubt in my mind that the agency is going to be a success. I search the room for Kristina, but have no idea where she has gone.

Excusing myself, I say, "It was nice meting you. I'll leave you in the capable hands of my partner." I make my way over to the creative clique gathered on the sofas. "Have you seen Kristina?"

"She went to the bathroom," piped up a young woman.

"Thanks!"

Heading towards the restroom, I pass Alex who seems a bit unstable on his feet. I sit him down on a chair and get him some water.

He sniggers. "We had a little too much to drink before we left!"

"Don't worry about it. Where's Jacques?"

"She's gone to the bathroom I think."

Fucking hell! I am just about to burst through the door when two women - from Account Management - come out of the bathroom.

"Good evening, Mr. Scott," they say in unison, sniggering at each other as they pass.

"I hope you're enjoying the party," I reply.

"We are!"

They disappear down the corridor leading back to the reception. When they are gone, I press my ear to the door and listen.

"You're so pretty, Kristina. How long have you known Jayden?"

"It's a long story. We met up with each other a few weeks ago. It was a complete shock to see him again. We stayed with his mother last week. She's hardly changed at all. I absolutely adore Carolyn."

"His mother? You've met her already?" Jacques gives her no time to reply then changes the subject. "Did you hear about his father?"

"He mentioned it."

"Did you know he was one of the main suspects? They searched his family home in Edinburgh as well as the cottage in Argyll. There were even police dogs involved in the hunt for his father's body."

"No... I didn't know."

"He told *me*. I didn't believe Jayden was connected in any way whatsoever to his father's inexplicable disappearance. We've been friends a long time. We were at school together and..."

"I really must go. It was nice to meet you...?"

"Jacques. Jacquelyn Hayes."

I hear footsteps coming towards the door, dash along the corridor back to the party and blend in with the crowd, trying not to look suspicious.

Richard comes and finds me. "It's speech time, Mr. Scott. Time to welcome everyone to the agency."

There are no formal arrangements made so I stand on top of a table.

"Can I have your attention, please," I shout over the humdrum of chattering voices.

It eventually goes quiet. I hear a few wolf whistles in the audience. Stifling a grin on my face, I address the audience. "I just want to say to my employees that I hope you'll enjoy your time at the agency. Work hard, get results and you can all keep your jobs."

A sudden outburst of laughter echoes around the room.

"To all our potential new clients, we hope you choose us because we have something special, a creative twist to match and beat any of our competitors. Finally, I would like to say a very big thank you to our Managing Partner - Richard McKenzie - who will lead you with an iron fist in order to make the agency a success. Here's to our business."

"To our business," they shout.

"Thank you."

"Richard, can you call me a taxi. I'm going to find Kristina."

I get back down off the table. My eyes scan the room for a red dress. I catch sight of her, sitting alone in the corner next to the buffet table.

I kneel down, reaching out to stroke her face.

She turns away. "Don't touch me."

I take hold of her hand. "We're leaving."

There is an awkward silence as we sit next to each other in the taxi. Not a single word is spoken on the way home until I close the front door. She explodes, shouting at the top of her voice in the hallway, "Why did you not tell me about your father? Why did you lie?"

"What are you talking about?"

"You... you were a suspect! Why did you keep it a secret?"

"It's not a secret. It's just not important."

"How can you say that?"

"Listen! We received a letter of apology about that from Lothian and Borders police from DCI Hunter."

"Marcus Hunter... he's now a Superintendent and was one of the speakers at my keynote speech. He's asked me to do some work for him. Anyway, why did you not tell me? That's more lies!"

"I didn't tell you because it's all in the past! I'm tired of it, Kristina. It was all in the mind of that lunatic, Inspector Canmore, obsessed by finding evidence that didn't exist. And, it didn't exist because I had nothing to do with his disappearance."

"She told me..."

"Who told you?"

"I spoke to that awful woman, Jacquelyn Hayes. Have you... is she..."

"I have seen her in the past."

"Well... go back. She clearly wants you."

"I don't want Jacques. I want you. This is about you and me now. Stop being so dramatic! Everyone has a past, Kristina. I have to deal with the fact you were married. That you once loved someone else, and trust me, I find that *very* hard."

She looks me straight in the eye. "I suppose so."

"Now stop it. Please let's not argue. Not tonight. Agreed?"

She sighs. "Agreed, but don't ever lie to me again."

I peck her on the cheek. A faint smile flickers across that pretty face.

I cup my hands around her face, gently kissing her lips. She is hesitant at first, and then responds, taking a small step forward. This time, our sweet kisses are laced with a tinge of hunger as she presses her lips against mine. I pull Kristina towards me, pushing her against the wall, teasing her mouth with my tongue. I catch my breath and then, continue with such a deep sense of desperation. Her positively charged response to the urgency of my kisses is like an electromagnetic force surging through my veins. I take hold of Kristina's hand, leading her from the hallway towards the bedroom.

****

I watch the plane taking off then disappear through the clouds in the sky. *I'm going to miss her*, I think to myself, *but it's not that long before we'll see each other again.* She is spending Christmas with her parents before coming to stay with me over New Year.

Right now, I need to head back to the London agency, to make sure that everything is running smoothly. First, I light a cigarette and climb into the Noble. My mind wanders back to her keynote speech. I keep thinking about that bloody Holmes' classification, knowing that it is time to draw a line under my shady past. She is too important. It is time for a new start. I am unable to feel any kind of remorse for what I have done as I believe there is nothing to forgive. However, the rational part of my mind knows that I somehow need redemption - someone to forgive me - in order to move on. Out with my own father and Annabel Taylor, I remember the bastards who perished at the hand of my blade.

Victim 3: Martin Harris ripped me off for money. He was a businessman in New York, an entrepreneur looking for a silent partner in his high-tech company offering software solutions to his business clients. He needed a *substantial* financial investment to extend the business in China. Although his domestic market appeared to be legitimate, after much negotiation and persuasion, he told me his plans for the Chinese market - that of reverse engineering to rip off some of the biggest software brands on the market with sky high margins. On that basis, I became an anonymous donor and silent partner in the company. At first, the returns were extremely lucrative but then, the money stopped. I demanded back my investment. He ignored me. In preparation for his demise, I cut all contact two years before I killed him. Every time I was in America, which was at least three times a year, I followed him, waiting for my opportunity to kill the thieving bastard. I got him one night, outside a bar, pissing my money up against a brick wall.

Victim 4: My next victim I met in Brasilia. Again, it was a possible business investment with three other venture capitalists. We met twice to decide whether to place a stake in his distribution company. Luiz Rodriguez invited us to his extravagant home on the outskirts of the capital city. I observed the way he treated his wife and children; recognising those flinches, the name calling, humiliation and degradation. On the way out of the bathroom, I heard crying from the bedroom, opened the door, noting the bruises on her arms and legs as she got changed. I shut the door. I never went back, declining his offer to invest in the company. I stayed there for an extra few days. I followed him, witnessing his vile behaviour as he picked up prostitutes while his wife was at home taking care of the children. And when he did return to the house, I heard screams as he beat her up. One year later, I killed him, slitting his throat as he emerged from the backstreets of Brasilia, after a night of debauchery with a dirty whore.

Victim 5: Raymond Cartwright was a vile, sleazy bastard and he nearly killed me.

9

THE TRAFFICKER

The interest in the child is sinister."
(Marilyn Hawes)

Two years ago

The sweltering summer heat is unbearable.

I bang my hand down on the horn of the car - again and again - as I approach the roundabout. "Come on you fuckin' dickhead. Go!" Revving my car behind the driver, he sticks his middle finger up in the air, deliberately taking his time to move on. I overtake the bastard on the flat stretch of road. I shout over to him, "Asshole!"

I press the button to wind down the windows. I'm sweating like a fuckin' rapist. Pools of water cover my body, clinging to the fabric as yellow stains appear around the armpits of my shirt. I wipe the beads of sweat off my face with my sleeve, unloosen my tie and turn down the dial on the dashboard - the continuous stream of cold air providing some relief from the stifling weather. Then, I slam my foot down on the accelerator, speeding down the dual carriageway towards London.

One of Australia's richest people, an iron ore magnate, is visiting the casino tonight with several of his business associates. I want to be there to meet, greet, wine and dine them - to butter them up to part with their fuckin' cash. Just because I'm an East End lad, it doesn't mean to say that I can't turn on the charm when I need to, especially when there's money involved.

It's going to be a lucrative night, I think to myself, *I just know it*.

I drive like a lunatic through the busy London traffic towards the West End into the heart of Soho. I reach my destination covered in sweat. To make matters worse, the stink of pollution in the smoggy air along with the rancid odour from my body smells like a fuckin' sewer. As I get out of the car and breathe in the city air, the taste in my mouth is vile. I wipe my nose with the back of my hand, hawk and then spit out a thick gob of phlegm onto the side of the pavement. Rushing up the steps towards the entrance, I walk through the doors of The Diamond Life casino.

"Good evening, Mr. Cartwright," says the receptionist. "How are you tonight?"

"Hey there, Crystal. I feel bloody shit!"

"What's up?"

"It's the fuckin' heat! I'll be upstairs in the flat. I need to take a shower. Can you check the VIP room is all set up for me? I've bagged myself some wealthy Diamond Deal customers tonight, so make sure everyone knows they've got exclusive rights to the cash desk. And can you check with the kitchen? I want a full spread of our finest food served when they arrive. You're a gem!"

"Certainly, Mr. Cartwright."

The water is refreshing as it washes away the grime of the day. Finding a lightweight shirt and a pair of trousers, I get dressed, ready to face the busy night ahead. I've worked hard to build up my empire, but rely on losers - addicted gamblers - to increase my profit margins. *Silly bastards*, I think to myself, *it's a fuckin' mugs game unless you've got money to burn.* And tonight, the stakes are high.

The telephone rings. "They've arrived. One of our hosts is taking them to the VIP room now."

"Thanks, Crystal. I'll be there in a minute."

I make my way down the stairs to the casino. I've managed to create the ultimate gambling experience in one of the most sought after locations in London. I fuckin' have it all; poker, brag, roulette, black jack and huge cash prizes to be won on the slot machines. Slow jazz music plays in the background. The lights are low at this hour, but as the night progresses it livens up, the music thumping like the beating hearts of gamblers, quickening the pace as more and more money is lost and won. The atmosphere is electric - buzzing with nervous excitement.

The restaurant is packed full with punters stuffing their faces before the ultimate showdown. I've got the best trained croupiers in London who know how to pump money out of those goddamn losers. I walk through the Diamond Lounge - which is filling up with groups of cocktail drinkers - and make my way to the VIP room on the balcony to meet Sebastian King. *He's fuckin' loaded. Good looking bastard as well. He's got it all!*

His Australian twang is very distinct. "Raymond, good to see you again," he says, shaking my hand.

I revert to my business voice. "It's a pleasure... as always."

"These are my associates. This is Oliver, James, Harrison, Jake, Charlotte, Grace and Natalie."

I nod my head in each direction as he introduces his entourage. "I see you've met your personal host for the night. He'll be taking care of you."

"Great! It's fantastic champagne by the way. Thanks, Raymond."

"It's the least I can do. I've ordered you a mix of our finest cuisine from the restaurant. It'll be here, shortly."

"Perfect. Thank you."

"I'll leave you to it. I hope you all enjoy your evening." *It's perfect for one reason and one reason only - for fuckin' money!*

I make my way down the stairs, catching up with one of the security guards in the main hall. "You got anything to report, Charlie?"

"No. Everything is fine at the moment, but it's still early."

"Good. I'm off to get a cold beer. Contact me if you need me."

I grab a bottle out of the fridge in the Sports Bar. Taking it with me, I slouch down onto the swivel chair in the security room - cameras capturing every angle of my casino - to watch the punters. My eyes focus on the blackjack table. I see his stash of chips mounting up in front of him.

I put in the earpiece.

"Charlie, go and check out the blackjack table, the one in the main thoroughfare. There's a smooth looking bastard with a stash of chips, winning quite a bit of my money. Report back to me as soon as you can."

I zoom in on the VIP room. Large stakes are being placed on the roulette wheel as the iron ore magnates drink my champagne and wait for the food. *Spend, spend, spend, you bastards!* All I can see at this moment in time is pound signs in my eyes!

He interrupts my thoughts. "Hey boss, it's me... Charlie."

"What's happening at the table?"

"The punter's on a winning streak. He must have at least twenty black, five burgundy and a few light blue chips. I spoke to one of the other security guards who told me he's been hanging about all afternoon. He's just leaving the game now. Do you want me to follow him?"

"Leave him to me. Do you think he's card counting?"

"Possibly. I'm not sure."

As I make my way through the throng of punters, I see him standing at the Diamond Bar having a whisky, running my chips up and down in his hands.

I sit on the bar stool next to him. "Get me a cold beer," I ask the bartender.

"Certainly, Mr. Cartwright."

Eyeing up the stash in his hand, I say to him, "You're doing well tonight."

He grins. "Not bad for a day's work!"

Scottish eh? I stretch out my hand. "Raymond Cartwright. I own the casino."

"Jayden Scott. Pleased to meet you. This is an amazing place."

"Thanks. What brings you to London?"

"Investment opportunities."

I take a large swig of beer. "You like to take risks?"

"Sometimes. I only invest if there's a guaranteed rate of return."

"Do you now? You're also quite a dab hand at blackjack."

He laughs. "I just got lucky today. I'm off to play some roulette. Maybe a few purple chips on black perhaps? Odd or even? What do you think?"

"That's entirely your decision."

"Odd it is then. Nice to meet you… Raymond."

"If you're still here later on, come and join my party. It's in the VIP room just up there. Here's a pass for you." *I'll get my money back you smooth bastard. The tables up there are fuckin' rigged anyway!*

He takes it. "I might just do that."

I watch him from the bar as he places a thousand pound bet on one spin of the wheel. His cry of delight tells me the outcome. He hangs about the casino for the rest of the evening - drinking, gambling and winning my money on the blackjack table.

Once my business guests leave, I spread the word to all my regulars about a private party in the Diamond Suite. It's not long before everyone arrives. The room fills up with the usual suspects; friends, family, guests, escorts and dirty whores waiting to make a quick buck. The booze-laden party is laced with lines of cocaine. I snort some and join my young bitch who is just old enough to indulge in some of my extreme sex acts. He follows me around like a fuckin' lap dog, eager to please for filthy drugs and dirty money.

Just then, I spot my dealer out the corner of my eye - Jake Driscoe.

"I'll be back in a minute," I say to my escort. "Go... piss off and hang about somewhere else for a while, but don't leave. I want you here later on. I need some of your fuckin' hard cock."

My bitch nods his head in agreement.

I wave my arm in the air at my dealer. "Driscoe! Over here!"

He slaps my back. "Raymond! Good to see you again."

Leaning closer, I say in a hushed tone of voice, "It's finally been produced on disc. It's as hardcore as it gets for a DVD of that calibre. I got the first batch delivered this afternoon. Let me know how many copies you need? I'll get them to you as soon as I can. You'll get your usual cut."

"Sounds good. I'll let you know the numbers tomorrow. I've got lots of punters waiting for this one! And, they're willing to pay a lot of readies for that kind of hardcore kiddie porn."

"For fuck sake, keep your voice down!"

"What's hardcore?" says a voice.

I turn around. His lips are wrapped around the glass, swigging on a whisky.

He smirks. "Kiddie porn, did you say?"

Fuckin' hell! What do I say to him? He's heard us now. "This is a private conversation."

His eyes glaze over. "Sorry, is it bad timing? I couldn't help but overhear,"

I ignore his comment. "Driscoe, this is Jayden Scott. This young man won a lot of my money today. He's a cool hand at blackjack. He's been running circles around one of my best croupiers."

"You must be good then..."

He slurs. "I am... *the*... best!"

"Bloody card counter," I mumble.

"Raymond, I need to go. I'll catch up with you tomorrow. I look forward to viewing the merchandise."

"See you soon, Driscoe."

I quickly change the subject. He'll never remember anyway. He's out of his goddamn face on drink and drugs. "So... Mr. Moneybags. Are you enjoying the party?"

"It's fantastic. You're coke is good stuff. It's blown my head off."

"Nothing but the best here!"

"I can see that," he says, eyeing up Candy, the prettiest whore in the room. "Where's the bathroom? I need to go for a piss. I'm about to burst."

I snigger. His well-spoken accent has taken a nosedive into the gutter. "Take your pick. That one over there is usually pretty quiet. It's just through the doors and down the lobby."

He's unstable on his feet, clutching onto my arm. "I feel a bit out of it. It's not like me. That coke is strong shit!"

I see him staggering towards the other end of the room. He pushes open the door leading towards the toilet. I nod in Candy's direction to go and make some money. I follow my escort down the long corridor and linger in the shadows. She intercepts him coming out of the shit can, stretching both her arms against the wall, blocking the passageway.

He tries to pass. "You're in my way!"

She pouts her lips and says, "Hey, lover boy... you fancy some fun?"

His eyes roll to the back of his head. "Not tonight. I don't know what's going on anymore."

Checking out the boundaries, Candy moves forward, rubbing her hands over his groin. "Well your cock knows exactly what's going on." Pushing him against the wall, she teases his mouth with her pierced tongue. My whore bends down, unzips his trousers, releases him and then, her tongue runs up and down the length of his shaft, licking the rim of his cock.

You're a big boy, I think to myself.

He groans with pleasure.

My slut wraps her lips around the head of his penis before giving him deep throat pleasure. It's not long before he explodes into her mouth. Zipping him back up, she searches for his wallet in his trouser pockets, pulls out a wad of notes - flips it shut then puts it back - and leaves him leaning against the wall. She winks, walking towards me, slipping one arm through mine - flashing the money in the air.

****

My eyes flicked open. *For fuck sake! Where am I?* The agonising pain in my head was almost unbearable, not a razor-sharp stabbing pain, but more of a dull ache like a repetitive hammer blow to the head - pounding over and over and over against my skull. My hand instinctively reached towards my forehead, pressing on it to relieve the pressure behind my eyes. As I tried to sit up, the room started spinning around. It took several minutes for the reeling sensation to stop. Ever so slowly, I started to recognise the familiar surroundings of my apartment.

Lifting my head off the pillow, I saw one shoe lying on the floor, the other still on my foot. I tried to take off my unbuttoned shirt, but the tie was still wrapped around the collar. I loosened it, throwing it on the bed then took off the rest of my clothes, chucking them on the floor. I sank back onto the bed, staring up at the ceiling, remembering bits and pieces of the previous night.

"What a bloody state," I mumbled to myself.

I dragged myself out of bed. Picking up a pair of jogging trousers on the chair, I pulled them over my legs and shuffled through to the kitchen with a hand leaning on the wall for support. *I need something for my head before I can think straight*, I thought to myself. I opened the kitchen drawer, found some painkillers and popped them into a glass of water. I watched the soluble tablets sink to the bottom of the clear liquid then burst into life. Once the bubbles had settled down, I forced the contents down my throat. I hobbled back to the comfort of my bed, falling into a deep sleep until the shrill of the telephone woke me up several hours later.

"Go away and leave me alone!"

It rang out. "You're through to Jayden Scott. Please leave a message. I'll get back to you as soon as I can."

I heard the echo of her familiar voice. "Hey baby, it's me! Where are you? I'm waiting for you at the restaurant. I've text and called your mobile. There's no answer. Call back. Soon!"

I checked the time. *Shit! I've slept most of the day!* Reaching for my trousers on the floor, I took the mobile phone out of my pocket and read her texts.

You're half an hour late! Where are you?

Jayden where the hell are you?

I replied.

> Jacques, I'm really sorry. I've been held up in a business meeting. I'll call you tomorrow x

My limbs felt heavy, refusing to respond to the feeble attempt to get out of bed. To make matters worse, my skin was covered in a film of sweat due to the oppressive heat in the flat. I felt more coherent though, my mind reliving the events of the previous night; the blackjack win, Raymond Cartwright, the child pornography conversation, the party, her dirty mouth around my shaft and the money... my money! I opened up my wallet. There was at least two grand missing. *Fucking dirty bitch!*

The bleep on my phone went off, again.

> Thanks very much. I'm sitting here on my own like a right idiot. Let me know when you get back. I'll come round for the night. Jxx ☺

I texted back.

> Not tonight Miss Hayes. Another time? I'm too tired x

She responded.

> You really are a bastard. Why arrange to meet me then stand me up? You drive me mad. Whatever!

I threw the phone across the bed. Forcing myself to get up, I went for a shower then made my way towards the kitchen to make a coffee, drinking it out on the veranda, soaking up the last rays of the evening sunshine. The caffeine hit started to clear my mind.

I lit a cigarette and began to plan my next move.

I went back into the apartment to get my laptop. Placing it down on the table outside, I typed in his name, retrieving pages upon pages of images and reviews. My eyes focused on one picture. His hair was swept over the crown of his head. That smirking face emphasised his devious grin. I stared at his sleazy face staring back at me, knowing that his fathomless eyes hid a bottomless pit of secrets. I clicked on a review.

> Casino tycoon, Raymond Cartwright, is an inspring member of the local community. Not only does he support international gaming competitions, he is also a strong supporter of local charities. He recognises that most of his customers use the casino for the

ultimate gambling experience. However, he does acknowledge the more serious side of this industry and is an advocator of responsible gambling. A direct quote from the founder of GamblersDirect reinforces this commitment: "Raymond Cartwright has a strong sense of duty to our mission. Not only does he provide financial support, he is an Ambassador for the charity in order to provide help to some of the most vulnerable people within our society."

This is just bullshit! I shouted at the computer. "It's nothing but a public relations exercise." I closed it down, then go to get changed. I felt back in control. *You've picked on the wrong person! If you live on the edge Raymond Cartwright, you're eventually going to fall off it.* There and then, I decided to set him up and get to know him better. I chose to infiltrate his business, to do a deal with him related to his sordid DVD distribution and then, eventually kill him. *No one treats me with impunity and gets away with it*, I thought to myself.

I lit another cigarette, left the flat and drove to the Diamond Life casino.

"Hello. Are you back for more?" said the receptionist.

"I am indeed!"

I made my way towards the blackjack table. I intended to get him where it hurt the most - in his back pocket. Taking out my wallet, I traded in over ten thousand pounds of his filthy money in chips. I settled down at a table with a minimum bet of a hundred pounds. Several hours later, I was running circles around his croupier, placing small bets when I knew I would lose and large bets when I knew I would win. *I hope you're watching me on your security cameras, you asshole.* I also placed a huge sum of money on the roulette wheel. Luck was on my side as I won over and over and over again. Like a moth to a flame, he appeared as I sat in the restaurant looking at the menu.

"How are you tonight, Mr. Scott? I see you're luck is still with you."

"I'm fine. I am indeed on a winning streak!"

"So I see," he said, eyeing up the stack of chips on the table.

"Come and join me, Raymond. I want to speak to you about last night. I think I might be able to assist you in a lucrative business deal."

He sat down. "And what would that be?"

"I know a distributor who's interested in your merchandise. You know what I'm talking about. The kiddie porn DVD's. At the right price of course."

He hesitated. "I already have a dealer."

"I know that. Depending on whether the content is suitable for my client base, I need a thousand copies in the next few months."

His eyes flashed with greed. "A thousand! It'll cost you. It's not cheap."

"Money isn't a problem. Trust me."

"You're full of surprises. I think I might be able to do a deal with you."

"Might? Look… I'm a businessman, Raymond. Legitimate or not, I'm out to make as much money as I can get my hands on. I'm a middleman just like you. I need a sample first, just to check it out. We need to keep this low key. This is just between the two of us. Nobody else. I have my reputation to think about."

"I keep all my business dealings of this nature private. Stay there. I'll be back in a minute. Don't go away."

I ordered a glass of water and some food, deciding on steamed dumplings, rice and crispy duck. By the time I finished the meal, he had still not returned. *Perhaps he's checking me out?* I wandered through to the casino, making my way back to the blackjack table, continuing to win more of his dirty money. He caught me by surprise. I felt a hand slipping something into my jacket pocket. It was the DVD. I turned around. He was gone. Having no further need to be there, I cashed in the chips and drove back to the apartment.

I took his money out of my wallet and threw it on the table. I looked at it in disgust. Reaching for the disk in my pocket, I slotted it into the player. His business card was tucked inside the sleeve of the cover. I took it out - flipping the card between my fingers - and waited for the disk to load. For a start, just listening to the sinister music made me feel on edge. On edge, I watched the horrific scene, the shrieking cries of pain from the poor child turning my blood cold. And the sodomy… it was just all too much. I clutched hold of my stomach - the food in the pit of my gut surging up into my throat - then rushed towards the bathroom, wretching up the contents of his restaurant into the bowl. Leaning against the rim of the pan, I stretched my arm up and flushed the toilet.

"You disgust me, you sleazy bastard. How can anyone get any kind of sexual enjoyment out of torturing a child?"

Pulling myself up off the floor, I gazed at my reflection in the mirror. "I might be a lot of things, but one thing I'd never do is hurt a child like that. Raymond Cartwright, you have sealed your own fate."

The next night, I returned to the casino for a few hours. I saw him watching the roulette wheel. Standing behind him, my voice was barely audible. "You've got yourself a deal. I need a thousand copies. I'll be in touch with you in a few months time. I need to return to Scotland for a while."

He never turned round, nodding his head in agreement. I left him standing at the table, leaving the casino for what I thought was the last time.

****

The following day I returned to Edinburgh, cutting all contact with him. I needed to distance myself from the situation. I had to let the dust settle. One night after a busy day at the agency, I sat alone in my apartment looking at the blank sheet of paper. I lit a cigarette and picked up the pen, intent on writing down a plan of action. Instead, I started to draw him. It somehow managed to manifest itself into a distorted image of his face. Those evil eyes and that grin, snarling at some unknown tortured child. At that moment, I had an overwhelming desire to kill him - to seek revenge for all of his young victims. *Soon*, I thought to myself. *Very soon Raymond Cartwright.*

I tried to concentrate on writing my plan.

Several hours later, I had the list:

<u>Raymond Cartwright</u>
Evil, greedy, sleazy bastard (42)
Owner of the Diamond Life casino.
Distributor of child pornography.
Pimp to escorts and high-class hookers.
Sexual preference: prepubescent children and pubescent boys.
Background? Where does he live? Search for him online.

<u>Contact</u>
NO mobile phone contact.
Face to face contact ONLY.
NO more visits to the casino.
Take the train. Pay by cash. Slip in and out of London unoticed.

<u>Time scale</u>
Six months.
Three weekly visits every two months.
Base – my flat in London.

<u>Visit 1</u>
Stalking: follow him, get to know his background, who he talks to, who he meets and what he does on a daily basis?
Purchase clothing.
Contact him – informal discussion.

<u>Visit 2</u>
Continue to follow him.
Arrange a time and place to pick up the 'merchandise' ready for Visit 3.
Somewhere quiet – off the beaton track.
Get him on his own.

<u>Visit 3</u>
Showdown.
Slit his throat.
Minimal contact with the body.

    I read over it, feeling staisfied with the outcome. *I suppose all I can do is carry on as usual until I go back to London.* I checked the calendar on my phone. My diary was full of client meetings for the next four weeks. I pencilled in my trip to London for the second week in August. The next month was torturously slow. I became obsessed with him - going over and over the plan in my mind - feasting on my fantasies to end his life. The nervous excitement drove me to distraction. He was like a toxic drug, drawing me to him, knowing only too well that he could be lethal. I found it difficult not to contact him. I had to make sure there was no official record of our association. That meant staying away from him.

However, I kept a close eye on his activities through news feeds on the internet. He certainly knew how to manipulate the power of the media to emphasise the philanthropic nature of his manipulative yet generous character. I found information that stated he funded a children's charity. *What a joke!* On the one hand, this man supported the most vulnerable members in society through his charity work and on the other, he condoned the molestation of children to satisfy the sick fantasies of the paedophile community for greed, profit and money. There appeared to be no boundaries to his corrupt mentality. *Clever yet devious, very devious*, I thought to myself.

Finally… the day arrived to carry out the first phase of my plan.

Visit 1

I took a taxi into the city centre. I paid the driver then made made my way through the throng of travellers towards the ticket office, purchasing a first class return train ticket to London King's Cross. I found an empty booth then settled down for the five hour journey.

"Good afternoon. Can I get you some food or drink?" asked a young woman.

"Just a coffee, please. Espresso. Thanks."

"Nothing else?"

"I might have an early dinner. That's all for now."

She left, returning five minutes later. "Here you go. Just give me a shout if you need anything else."

"Thanks very much."

I took a sip of coffee then stared out of the window. *I wonder if he actually molests prepubescent boys or whether he's just a viewer and distributor of the vile material? Probably the latter. Both are equally as bad. It is people like him - through organised crime - that supplies the entire industry, fuelling the demand for it in the first place.* I knew this monster liked young boys. I saw his companion at the party. He must have been within the legal age limit to allow such a public display of his sexual preference. *Poor kid, but it's his choice to live his life in that way, unlike the young child in the video.*

To distract my mind, I went to the dining car. I ordered some food, read the newspaper for a while and caught up with some of my work. It was not long before I arrived at King's Cross station. I took a taxi to my flat and dumped the bags in the bedroom. It was stifling hot. I opened up the balcony doors to let in some fresh air then made myself a coffee. I drank it outside, lit a cigarette then scanned the information in my file.

He had been easy to find online. He was one of only a handful of Cartwright's in London, and one was of his age registered to a house in Greater London. Looking at the map in front of me, it appeared to be about a half hour drive from my apartment. I decided to follow him from his home in Richmond, assuming that he would be there, stalking him until the end of the week. I needed to pick up the rented car. As it was too late in the day, I left a message to say that I would go for it in the morning.

Stubbing out the cigarette in the ashtray, I lit another one, drawing the smoke deep into my lungs. As the sun started to set on the horizon, I watched a cruiser sail down the Thames, filled with eager tourists seeking the romance of the setting sunset with the added bonus of getting to see some of London's top attractions. A tiny part of me resented the laughter, music and besotted couples standing on the deck of the boat, eating canapes and drinking champagne, while I planned my next kill.

"This is the life you chose," I said, excitedly.

I picked everything up off the table, closed the the doors, went for a shower and climbed into bed. As I drifted off to sleep, I was conscious of the nervous energy tingling through my body, igniting one of the most lucid dreams I had ever experienced. Somehow, I was the one who was in control of the events, dictating my dreamscape environment, resulting in the gruesome death of Raymond Cartwright, not by my blade, but with an explosion of fire. I watched him burn to death - screaming in agony as the flames engulfed his body.

I woke up several times, checking the clock every few hours until a deep sleep took hold of my mind. Hearing the alarm in the morning, I stretched over to switch it off. Surprisingly, I felt quite refreshed despite my restless sleep. I got dressed into the tracksuit, put on my baseball cap, slung the rucksack across my shoulder and left to pick up the car.

Driving through the busy streets of London, I made my way towards Richmond. Not knowing the area, I had bought a more detailed map. I could have used the SatNav in the hired car, but did not want any digital record of my whereabouts in London. As I approached my destination, I thought to myself, *it's very suburban*! Somehow, it did not seem to fit with his character. I ended up following the signs to Richmond Park - one of the largest nature reserves in London - and passed his house. It was a detached family home. My brow pinched together, staring at it with a puzzled look on my face. *This is not what I expected at all!* There was a 4x4 parked in the driveway. The leafy suburbian street was busy at this time of the morning as families bundled their children into the back of cars for the school run. A woman came out of Raymond Cartwright's house with two teenage girls. *Well... well... well. How interesting! Is he a family man?*

I waited for the next three hours at the end of the road. During that time, the woman returned home, unloaded the shopping and carried it into the house. *He's clearly not here.* I headed back to London, dropping the car off at the flat. Since it was such a lovely day, I walked the two mile trip to the West End. Sitting down on the seat at an open air café, I blended into the crowd, watching the front entrance of the casino. I ordered some food, drank a coffee, then another and another. I also smoked a few cigarettes. After three hours, I was just about to give up and then, I noticed him passing in a car on the other side of the road. I looked twice. It was definitely him. He diverted down a side street towards the car park not far from the casino. I noted down the make, model and registration of the vehicle. He appeared on the main thoroughfare then bound up the stairs, disappearing through the grand entrance.

I felt satisfied with my snippets of information, I left the café, gazing into the shop windows. I needed to buy some clothes, ready for our meeting to pick up the DVD's in a few months time. Deciding on my usual attire, I bought some dark leisure wear, leather gloves, baseball cap and a pair of lightweight trainers. On the way back, I checked out the car park. It was a perfect place to keep an eye on his activities, situated away from the bustle of the main streets in Soho. Lighting a cigarette, I walked back to the flat, deciding to retire to bed early.

For the next three days, I established my routine. First, I drove to Richmond every morning. He was never there. Then, I loitered about the car park until lunchtime. His vehicle remained in the same spot throughout the day. And finally, I watched the entrance of the casino from the busy café. By the second day there was still no sign of him. On the third day, he emerged from the casino in the early hours of the evening. I waited until he turned the corner. I bolted off my seat in the café then made my way to the car park. Keeping my distance, I followed him as he drove out of the city towards Richmond. *A family visit, no doubt.* I watched him as he opened the front door and walked inside - never leaving the house for the rest of the evening.

When I arrived on the Thursday morning his car was still there. I waited for several hours. He appeared at noon then drove towards London. He parked in his usual spot, lingering about for at least half an hour. Then I saw someone approaching his vehicle. It was the dealer from the casino - Jake Driscoe. I tilted my head, staring at his lopsided features; the unsymmetrical shape of those close-knit eyes complementing the square shape of his jawline, set against thick neck muscles. His wide nose was squashed and slightly crooked, bending over to one side as if it had been broken at some point in time, but never had the chance to heal properly. This defect gave him a unique appearance that amplified his twisted smile.

Raymond got out of the car. I saw him slip a brown envelope into his dealer's hand. Driscoe then drove away while Cartwright made his way towards the casino.

Payment for the DVD's perhaps?

I had some lunch at the café then returned to the flat. I decided to break my own rules. I had an overpowering urge to meet him face to face. I waited until later in the day, got changed and took the underground to Leicester Square, walking the short distance to the casino in Soho. Striding through the entrance, I had one thing on my mind and one thing only - to discuss our transaction.

I played blackjack for a few hours, deliberately losing to avoid suspiscion of card counting. I felt a presence behind me. He laid his hand on my shoulder. "Not so lucky tonight, I see."

"Not really. Good to see you again, Raymond."

"Let me buy you a whisky," he said.

I followed him to the restaurant away from the prying eyes of the casino cameras. He ordered me a drink and got himself a beer.

"When can we finalise the deal? I need to put in the production order for the DVD's. It may take a couple of months to turn it around. Is that okay?"

Perfect timing! "Finalise it now," I told him.

I need a deposit upfront. As a down payment. That's how I operate, in case you pull out of the deal."

"I won't pull out. I can get it to you by tomorrow. How much?"

"Ten thousand. Meet me in the car park just around the corner from here at twelve."

"Sure."

He received a call on his mobile phone. "I need to go," he said, getting up to leave.

Having no more need to hang around, I left, returning the next day at noon. He arrived bang on time. I got out of the car. Taking the envelope out of my pocket filled with his own dirty money, I handed it to him. "Here you go."

"Get in touch with me soon. We can arrange for you to pick up the merchandise."

On that note, he got into his vehicle and left.

Visit 2

Based on his two month deadline to produce the digital discs, I brought the next visit forward by a month. I left Jessica in charge of the Edinburgh agency, knowing she was more than capable of running the business. This time, I intended to follow his every move over a period of four days, meeting him on the last day to arrange the details of the rendezvous.

I hired a car and followed the same routine as the previous month. Raymond Cartwright was never at his family home in Richmond. *Obviously they led separate lives. You're better off without him anyway*, I thought to myself. He always seemed to be in the casino. On the third day of my surveillance, I watched him get into his car and drive out of London, heading south from the city. I followed him for nearly an hour. He stopped at a petrol station, filled up the car then continued on his journey.

"Where the hell is the bastard going?" I mumbled to myself.

He deviated off the motorway onto a minor road, following it for at least two miles. It soon became clear that Raymond was driving east. The smell of the sea air became more apparent as we headed towards the coast. At least four cars behind, I swerved out slightly, watching him as he indicated right then drove towards the gates of a solitary warehouse shaped like an aircraft hangar. He got out, unlocked the padlock holding the chains together across the wire mesh, pushed them open and drove inside. I parked the car in a layby up the road, lit a cigarette, watching him as he parked outside the building and went inside. *What's in there?* I thought to msyelf.

I waited.

Daylight faded as darkness crept over the dreary sky. Just then, artificial light flooded from the entrance of the the hangar as he pushed open the steel doors. I watched a truck make its way down the track towards the open gates, driving into the space inside the warehouse. There was only one thing to do: go and take a look. I crossed the road, made my way down the path, sticking close to the bushes lining the side of the track. Sneaking through the gates, I went round the back of the building emerging at the far side, facing away from the main road. I peeked around the corner. The door was slightly ajar. My heart was pounding in my chest as I crept up to entrance.

At first, I just listened.

I recognised Raymond Cartwright's voice. "No problems then?"

"Nope, none at all, mate. My cargo was only checked in France for illegal immigrants. There were no problems getting through at this end."

"Did you manage to get my merchandise?"

"Yep, it's all there. The truck's been packed to get easy access to your cargo. It's right at the back. Hop on!"

I heard the screeching noise of the taillift at the back of the truck then the sound of the doors creaking open. The voices became muffled as they went inside the truck. All I could hear was the dragging noise of crates being forced across the floor accompanied by heavy breathing, gasps and grunts.

It was the truck driver's voice I heard next. "Here, hold onto the top of the box for as long as you can. I'll operate the button. When it's low enough, I'll jump down then you can take over so I can balance the crate on the ledge until it reaches ground level."

Raymond panted to catch his breath. "Phew! That sounds good."

I heard them doing this five or six times. I lost count to be honest. Then, there was a sound of splintering wood. Someone was forcing open a lid. I dared to peer through the opening in the door. They were both standing with their backs to me. Raymond was inspecting the DVDs.

"Perfect," he said. "And what about my other cargo?"

"Take a look for yourself."

The truck driver opened the lids to the other four boxes.

Raymond reached inside, grabbing hold of something. "My real merchandise," he declared, with a huge grin on his face.

I noticed the vent holes.

Oh my God!

He pulled out a young child who was bound across the mouth, arms and legs. Looking nervously around him, his dark eyes were wide with fear. The boy must have been about nine years old. Dressed in a t-shirt and shorts, he was shaking uncontrollably and then, I noticed a pool of urine spreading onto the floor around his bare feet.

"You dirty little bastard," Raymond shouted, slapping the boy across the face with the back of his hand.

"Calm down, mate. He's just scared," said the truck driver.

"Whatever! Can you untie him? I'll get the rest of them out of the crates."

"I'd rather not. Sorry…"

"Fuckin' hell. I'll do it myself then."

He finished about ten minutes later. Four prepubescent boys from who knows where in the world, huddled together, shivering in fear. Gasping, I turned away, trying to catch my breath without making too much noise.

How much worse can this get?

Just then, his mobile phone went off. "Driscoe where the hell are you? Why are you always late?"

Silence.

"You're two minutes away? Hurry up! We need to shift the cargo, now!"

Silence.

"She's with you?"

Silence.

"Okay... see you soon."

I saw the headlights from the dealer's van at the top of the road. I had to make a split-second decision. Scuttling around the side of the building, I ran to the back of the hangar. *What have I got myself into?*

I heard Driscoe's voice. "Perfect! Four more little fuckers to add to our sordid community," he cried.

"Keep your voice down!" said Raymond.

There was also a faint sound of a woman telling the boys to get into the back of the van. She also spoke in various different languages - none of which I recognised. To be honest, I switched off until the scratching noise of a solitary bird on the metal roof snapped me back to reality. I eventually stood up then crept towards the front of the hangar, daring to peer round the corner. They had gone. I slid down the wall, lit a cigarette and felt a sense of sadness that I had ordered the DVD's – all in the name of revenge.

I asked myself this: "The order I placed. Did it add to the abduction of those children?"

I pondered over this for a moment, then replied to my own question: "The trade in child trafficking for the sex industry is a global phenomenon. There's a huge demand. I suspect an extra thousand copies isn't going to make a significant difference..."

Feeling better that I had somehow managed to justify it in my mind, I walked towards the gate. I shook it with both hands. It was locked. Grabbing hold of the mesh, I heaved my body up over the fence. I unlocked the car then drove back to London in a daze.

I never slept at all that night. I just kept mulling over and over in my mind the events of the evening. When it was time to leave, I drove to the city for our meeting on the fourth day.

"Good to see you again," he said, slapping me on the back. "Fuckin' hell, you look a bit rough? Did you have a good night?"

"Just a bit!"

He nudged me on the arm. "Hey... you're a bit of a ladies man!"

"That's me," I laughed. *And you're a bloody child trafficker!* "Where can I pick up the merchandise? I need to leave tomorrow morning. I'll be back in London next month. "Does that suit you?"

"That's fine."

"Were shall we meet?"

He handed me a piece of paper with a drawing of a map. It led straight to the warehouse. "That's where I do all of my deals of this nature. Four weeks today, I'll see you there at nine o'clock. Don't be late."

Forcing a smile on my face, my mouth twitched. "I won't. See you then!"

He left me standing in the car park.

When I returned to the flat, I started to undress as I walked through the front door and then, passed out in my bed.

Visit 3

I checked the time. I decided to give myself two hours to get there. For the last time, I drove the rented car towards the coast. The late autumn light faded beyond the horizon. I watched as the glow of the setting sun radiated tinges of red light, breaking through the clouds in the sky. I felt its energising spirit, stirring my emotions, fuelling the passion deep inside me for revenge against one of the most vile people who had ever crossed my path. I could feel the tension rising through my body, the muscles in my neck stiffening as I gripped onto the steering wheel.

I stopped the car in a layby about fifteen minutes before the meeting place. I lit a cigarette. It was my first one in nearly a month. I took a short, sharp inhalation of smoke, blowing it quickly out of my mouth. Then, I sucked in a long drag, feeling it wrap around my lungs like a tight caress before letting out a huge breath of air. My head started to spin - making me feel dizzy - but I enjoyed the sensation. As I continued to draw in the smoke, the short-term fix of nicotine started to calm my nerves. I thought about the night ahead. *I really don't have any control over the unpredictable events of the evening. My modus operandi is about the element of surprise. How will I cope with this kind of prearranged situation? I need to think on my feet. Just stay calm!*

Taking in a deep breath, I drove to the warheouse. The gate was open - inviting me into his sordid life. As I approached the front of the hangar, I saw thin spears of light radiating through the slit in the doors and then, a blinding flash escaped from the hangar as he pushed them open. I turned my head, shielding my eyes from the flouorescent light then drove the car inside.

I watched him in the mirror as he dragged a box across the floor, stopping at the back of the vehicle. *My merchandise, no doubt.*

I got out of the car.

He stretched out his arm, shook my hand and said, "Good to see you again."

"And you. Is that the DVDs?"

A smug look passed across his face. "One thousand copies just as you ordered."

As I bent down to take a look inside the box, he placed his foot on the lid. "No... no... no. Money first."

I grabbed a large envelope off the passenger seat and handed it to him. "Here you go. Thirty thousand. Now... can I take a look?"

He moved his foot off the crate. "Go ahead."

I bent down, carefully lifting off the lid, watching his every move. Sure enough, it was filled with rows of plastic cases. I opened one, staring at the shiny disc inside. Looking over at him, his fingers were greedily counting the money.

"It's all there, Raymond."

He laughed. "I'm just fuckin' checking."

I smirked back at him. "Can you give me a hand to lift the box into the car."

"No problem," he said, placing the envelope on top of another crate.

I opened the boot. He helped to heave it inside. My hands reached up to grab the rim of the door then slammed it shut. "Thanks," I said, "it's been a pleasure doing business with you, Raymond Cartwright. I hope it's just the start of a more permanent business deal."

"I'm sure it is." He stretched out his arm to shake my hand. "Stay in touch."

"I better go. It's a long drive back."

He slapped me on the back. "See you soon."

He turned round to leave.

It was the perfect opportunity. My hand reached into the sheath. I gripped hold of the handle and whipped out the sharp blade. Placing one hand on his shoulder, the other reached for his neck, but before I had time to slash it across his throat, I felt his elbow hitting me on the side of the face.

"What the fuck," he shouted, spinning around on his feet.

His wide eyes glared at me, taking in the severity of the situation, looking at the blade in my hand. Shifting my chin from side to side, I stretched the muscles around my jawline. Through my half-closed eyes, I saw him lift his arm up towards his body as the back of his hand came swinging towards my face. I ducked down, my head butting into his stomach like a battering ram, pushing him away. He staggered back onto the ground. I took the opportunity to gain some distance between us. Raymond got up off his feet, reached into his pocket and produced a gun.

I'm a dead man!

He pointed it in my direction. "What's going on you fuckin' maniac?"

"What do you think? You're the maniac, Raymond. Who do you think you are?"

"What are you talking about?"

I nodded my head towards the boot of the car. "That! The paedophile porn! And you... you're a filthy human trafficker of children!"

He stammered. "How... do you know... about that?"

"I followed you last month to this warehouse. You're disgusting."

"You did what?" His eyes squinted, the lines on his forehead wrinkling together as a puzzled look passed across his face. He gasped. "You followed me... here?"

He was at least eight feet away and started walking in my direction, his eyes watching my every move. I crouched down - my hands on the ground supporting my body weight - as he pointed the gun out in front of him, his finger twitching on the trigger. I felt nothing but fear - waiting for the shot that would end my life.

I lifted up my head.

Our eyes locked together.

My killer instinct took over. The need for survival was the only thought on my mind. I made a split-second decision. At that moment, my life depended on one insane move. I had to take the risk. It was still in my hand. As quick as a flash, I hurled the knife. I watched the blade find its target, driving it through his heart with deadly accuracy. With a look of shock on his face, he dropped the gun, his hands instinctively reaching towards the wound in his chest.

He stared at me in disbelief. "AAAaaawww for fuck sake! This is not good."

Without any hesitation, I ran forward, picking up the firearm off the ground. Raymond's legs gave way beneath him, his body crumpling to the floor. I stood over him. He started laughing hysterically, trying to pull out the knife.

"I thought there wasn't something quite right about you. Who do you think you are, Mr. Vigilante Scott?"

"I'm your fucking worst nightmare come true, you sleazy bastard."

He laughed again, curling his body up into a tight ball, preparing to die.

His mobile phone went off. Reaching into his pocket, he looked at me and croaked, "That's Driscoe. He must be on his way here. That fuckin' maniac is always late!"

I grabbed it out of his hand. Sliding the bar along to answer it, I heard his familiar voice on the speaker phone, "Raymond... sorry I'm late. I'll be there soon, mate. Is the deal done?"

He somehow managed to summon an inner strength and cried, "HELP ME! FOR FUCK SAKE... HELP ME, DRISCOE!"

"Are you okay? What the hell is going on?"

I disconnected the call and waited.

I saw him peering out of the window of his van as he drove into the warehouse, registering the situation in his mind, watching his boss dying in a pool of blood. The silly bastard got out and ran towards me. I gave the dealer no time to react and shot him once in the body. He faltered and then, I open-fired again. As he slumped to the ground, I pulled the trigger, shooting him at point blank range in the head with a final bullet - finishing him off. I glanced over at Raymond. I pulled the ring off his dealer's finger, staring at the gold etchings. Taking in a deep breath into my lungs, nothing could beat the euphoric feeling surging through my body. In contrast, a look of horror passed across his face as I walked towards him. Leaning over, I watched Raymond Cartwright dying, noticing his face turn a dirty shade of white as he struggled to cling onto life.

A nervous laugh escaped from the back of my throat, staring at the chaos in the hangar. *Jesus Christ! I wonder what the police will think of this crime scene. Good luck, working it out!* I thought to myself. Careful not to step on any blood, I pulled my knife from his dying body and placed the gun in his hand before forcing the signature ring away from his finger. I stood over him. He was still alive, but only just. Thinking about my dream, I went to the dealer's van, found a spare can in the back of the vehicle and doused the entire crime scene in petrol, over the crates, bodies and vehicles. I picked up the envelope with the money in it on my way to the car. I took a lighter out of my trouser pocket, bent down and lit a trail of petrol. I watched the flames burst into life. As it reached his body, I heard his last dying screams as the flames engulfed his putrid soul. I put the blade into my rucksack, threw the box of DVDs from the boot of my car onto the ground and then, drove away from the scene of the crime.

I heard an almighty explosion, but never looked back.

10

THE CONFESSION

"If a person doesn't think that there is a God to be accountable to, then what's the point of trying to modify your behaviour to keep it within acceptable ranges? That's how I thought anyway... and I've since come to believe that the Lord Jesus Christ is truly God, and I believe that I, as well as everyone else, will be accountable to Him."
(Jeffrey Dahmer)

Thank God.

That awful night, two years ago at the warehouse is the last time I killed anyone - albeit two of them in one insane act of violence. Do not be misled, I have been tempted to do it again, but that incident was enough to put me off for the last two years of my life. It was on the front page of the news for weeks on end until it died down and then, eventually tapered off. It did not take the police long to figure out there was a third party involved. Over the weeks, months and years, they failed to solve the mystery. The headlines in the newspapers went into overdrive, unravelling every aspect of his sordid, double life:

"Diamond Life's Deadly Duo"

"Child Pornography Seized in Warehouse Wrap"

"Double Homicide: Mayhem, Money and Murder"

"Organised Crime: Paedophile Bust"

"Child Trafficking Ring Rumbled in Central London."

And so it continued. I felt satisfied that the police had uncovered the child trafficking ring in London, the sight of the young child's fearful eyes haunts me to this very day. I remember those poor children shivering in fear - aware yet unaware of the gruesome fate that awaited them.

The Metropolitan Police were convinced it was some kind of

gangland warfare. I left them to it, distancing myself from the headline news, returning to Scotland. And now, I have Kristina Cooper. *No more killing*, I think to myself, *it's time for a fresh start. Finally, I've found what I'm looking for. She's the promise of light in my dark, twisted world.*

It has been three weeks since I watched her plane heading off into the sky. And now, as I prepare to pack my bag to visit my mother and Charles for Christmas, I find it hard to contain my excitement. It is only four days until I pick her up from the airport then head back to the village to celebrate New Year.

I check the time. It is nearly ten o'clock at night.

I put the last of my clothes into the bag, have a shower, wrap a towel around the lower half of my body and lie on top of the bed. Once settled, I turn on the laptop, clicking on the Skype icon. It rings. It is not long until she connects, her pretty face lighting up my screen. Although I have not been to her flat yet, the décor in her bedroom is now familiar to me. She is lying on top of the black and gold jacquard bedspread.

"Good evening. How's my favourite criminologist?"

Her head flicks back, laughing at my comment. "I'm fine." She leans forward peering at my image. "Are you naked?"

"I've got on a towel. I'm just out of the shower. I've missed you."

"We only spoke to each other last night!"

"True! I still miss you."

"I miss you too, Jayden. Are you all set to go to your mother's tomorrow?"

"I've just finished packing. And you?"

"I'm looking forward to going home as well."

"Good. I'll pick you up at the airport on Monday at two o'clock. It's going to be great being together at New Year."

"I'm looking forward to it. I can't wait to see you," she says. "And... I love spending time with your mother and Charles."

"I'm glad they have each other. Fate has a strange way of bringing people together."

She brushes a hand through her wet hair. "It does."

"Are you just out of the shower?"

"The bath..."

I stare for longer than necessary. Kristina's beautiful green eyes

lock onto my penetrating gaze, wandering over the upper half of my body, the bottom half hidden from sight. She is wearing a silky bathrobe, looking at me, waiting for a response.
"Take it off."
She laughs. "Take what off?"
"Your robe. Stand up and take it off. Let me see your body."
She hesitates.
"Do it now... *please.*"
Repositioning the laptop, Kristina gets up off the bed, unties the belt, and opens it up, sliding the silky fabric from her shoulders, the garment falling to the ground.
Becoming aroused, I stare at her beautiful curves. "Touch your body," I say, letting her see me stroking my erection.
She picks up the bathrobe and puts it back on. "Jayden... stop it!" We'll see each other soon."
Burrowing my head into the pillow, I mumble, "This is torture. I want you so much!"
Kristina leans forward and kisses the screen. "Four days! It's not that much longer."
"I can't wait that long. I want you now!"
"Well... you can't have me now. There's no point in teasing yourself. Please, put it away!"
I start to calm down, put on a pair of jogging trousers, behaving myself for the rest of the conversation. It is hard though. I notice every single little nuance; her numerous facial expressions, the way she twirls her hair in her fingers, and how she flicks her head to the side when she laughs.
"I'm heading off to bed. It's nearly midnight," she says.
"Can I come with you?"
"Jayden... "
"I really can't help myself! Sleep well."
She blows me a kiss. "You too."
I disconnect the call.
I immediately send her a message.

> I'll be dreaming of your beautiful body. Actually, it's not just your body I want Kristina. I want all of you. Until next week, pretty lady x

I find my cigarettes on the table in the sitting room and look at the weather outside. It is cold, wet and miserable. *I'm not going out there. Not a chance!* Instead, I turn the fan on in the kitchen and light up, the soothing smoke filling my lungs. I decide on a small whisky to celebrate the fact that it is now Christmas Eve. My text alert goes off.

See you next week, lover boy Kxx

I chuckle away to myself. *Bloody tease!*

I finish my cigarette then gulp down the whisky. I wander into the sitting room, looking at the presents under the tree. There is one for Charles, two for my mother and five for Kristina. I want to give them to her when we are alone together - to share the intimacy of the moment. I turn off the lights, climb into bed and think about the image of her naked body. My desire is all-consuming. My heart rate increases as my imagination gears up into overdrive, fuelling wonderfully intense, erotic dreams as I drift off to sleep.

****

I put the money in the meter, watch the barrier rising up into the air and drive through the airport. The plane is due to land in fifteen minutes time. I roll down the window, light a cigarette, thinking about the time with my mother and Charles over Christmas. He gave a heart-warming speech at the midnight service on Christmas Eve for the villagers. The Reverend's church is truly a haven of joy - just like him. He talked about the birth of Christ, outlining his role in one of the world's most influential religions, ending the ceremony with a thought-provoking speech about sin and forgiveness.

Jesus Christ *is* the son of God. He lived, suffered and died for the sins of *all* men. As the New Year approaches, I think it's important to acknowledge our own misdemeanours. John the Baptist tells us that: "If we say we have no sins, we decide ourselves, and the truth is not in us." (John 1: 8). Therefore, do not fool yourself that man is free from sin. Seek forgiveness in Him. "Repent ye therefore, and be converted, that your sins may be blotted out, when the times of refreshing shall come from the presence of the Lord" (Acts 3: 19). So… this is not just a time to celebrate the birth of Christ, it is a time for reflection. He died for our sins, so repent, and humanity can live a more peaceful life.

It was very touching. It made me think about my own situation. Perhaps, I would be able to find peace if I at least acknowledged my sins to the Reverend's God? When I was alone in the church after the service, I decided there and then that I would, at some point in time on this break, seek resolution for my 'misdemeanours'. Despite my lack of remorse, I know deep within my soul that it would help to draw a line under my own past, allowing me to move onto a new chapter in my life with Kristina Cooper. Lighting a candle, I said to his Lord: "If Jesus Christ *is* the son of God, then she *is* the reason for my existence."

On Christmas Day, we ate too much, drank too much, played a lot of chess and sneaked off for a few whiskies as well as a fly smoke in his study on more than one occasion - much to the annoyance of my mother. I missed Kristina as we exchanged our presents. She gave me a woollen sweater, soft and luxurious to the touch. Charles loved his box of hand-rolled cigars. My mother was delighted with the perfume and candles. They both gave me a simple wooden cross along with a message inside the box.

"In the name of Christ's sacrifice. For His love to *all* men."

It took me by surprise, but gave me hope for the future. *I wish Kristina had been there to share it all with me,* I think to myself. *Definitely next year.*

I check the time. The plane should be arriving just about now. I finish the cigarette then blow the air out of my lungs, panting to try and get rid of the smell. I pop a few mints into my mouth. She knows I smoke, but does not really mind. However, I like to keep it to a minimum out of respect for a non-smoker. A nervous feeling of excitement develops in the pit of my stomach as I enter the airport. I make my way to the business lounge, my heart skipping a beat every time someone walks through the flight doors. I wait and wait and wait for more than half an hour. The plane has definitely landed - it clearly states it on the screen. I check my phone. There are no messages. *Where is she?* Just then, I see Kristina walking towards me with a huge grin on her face.

"Sorry, it took so long. There was a delay in getting the bags."

She looks gorgeous dressed in a sweater, tailored trousers and ankle boots with wild hair adding to her dishevelled beauty. I grab hold of the case and lead her out of the airport. I point the key at the Noble, open it and throw in the luggage.

"What's wrong?" she says with concern.

I slam the door shut and then, look at her with my intense brown eyes. I push Kristina against the back of the car, my mouth greedily kissing her lips. I lose myself in the moment, pressing myself into her body. My hands begin to wander over the contours of her body, wanting to make love, right at that very moment.

The persistent noise of a car horn disrupts the moment as a male voice shouts over to us, "Get a bloody room!"

I laugh, sticking my middle finger up in the air.

Winking, he flicks up his thumb.

She chuckles. "What a welcome!"

I let out a huge sigh. "You're too much! Get in the car."

On the journey back, we talk about our time over Christmas in more detail. She spent it with her parents and brother along with his family in a small town about fifteen miles from Lincoln. Kristina seems to love her childhood home just as much as our village. Her father moved there to take up a new job in one of the RAF bases. They have lived there ever since. She now has an apartment close to the marina near the university.

"You need to come and see my family soon. My parents can't wait to meet you again. I'll take you to Lincoln Cathedral. You'd love it there. It's so beautiful. I've got so many places I want to share with you."

"We can arrange something in the New Year."

"Are you not busy at the agency?"

"I'm the boss! I can do what I want. Besides, I have Jessica and Richard to run the agencies when I'm not there. I'd love to spend some time with you. I'll arrange it to coincide with a business meeting in London. I can spend a few days with you first."

"That would mean a lot to me, Jayden."

"I know."

We pass through several coastal towns. She gazes out of the window across at the sea for a while."

"You okay?"

She nods. "It's overwhelming coming back to the village. I have so many lovely memories."

I squeeze her hand.

She gives me a reassuring smile.

I approach the centre of the village. Driving up towards the house, I say, "We're home! You go to the house. I'll get the bags. It's too cold to hang around outside."

I hear the bell. My mother screams in delight as she embraces Kristina, pulling her by the hand into the house. I light a cigarette while I take our belongings out the car. We have seven days together this time. I want to spend four days here and three days in Edinburgh. *I can't wait to get to know her better.*

"Jayden, hurry up. It's freezing out there," he bellows.

"I'm just coming." I flick the cigarette into a bush. *Oops! I shouldn't have done that.* "Sorry," I whisper.

I pop a few mints in my mouth and walk into the house. I take the luggage upstairs. The heat in the room from the fire is warm and inviting. I pile on a few more logs, watching them catch fire. I wait for Kristina, but end up going down to rescue her from my mother. She is in the kitchen drinking a cup of tea.

"There you are!" I say. "Are you ready to unpack?"

"I'll just finish my drink first."

"Kristina's just been showing me some photographs on her phone. We must invite the Coopers here at some point in time. We'd both love to see them again."

"We certainly would," says the Reverend.

"I'll be contacting my parents at New Year," declares Kristina. "You can speak to them if you like."

"It'll be good to catch up with your family," replies my mother. "I look forward to that. Off you go. We'll give you both a shout when dinner is ready."

I grab a bottle of wine out of the fridge and two glasses from the cupboard.

"Don't drink too much," warns my mother.

"We won't!" I reply.

I walk behind Kristina on the way up the stairs admiring her curves.

She opens the door. "I just love this bedroom."

At last... I close it, turning the key in the lock.

I sit on the chair by the fire, watching her kick off her boots. I unscrew the top on the wine bottle and pour us both a glass. She pulls off a pair of woollen socks. "That's much better," she says, wriggling her toes.

"Come over here."

Kristina sits on the floor between my legs, resting her elbow on my knee, staring into the flames. Taking a sip of wine, she says, "This is lovely. I love being here with you."

My fingers run through her locks of hair. "Likewise."

It is a peaceful moment. We drink our wine, enjoying the silence. I continue to play with her curls while she stares at the burning flames.

"Refill," I ask.

She nods, turns round onto her knees, holding out the glass. I fill it up, staring into those beautiful green eyes. It feels like I am sinking into the depths of the ocean, drowning in her intoxicating beauty. I can never lose her now. This woman means the world to me. I remember Kristina is going to be working with Superintendent Marcus Hunter, so out of curiosity, I ask her about it. "Tell me a little more about your work. Have you got anything interesting under way?"

She thinks about it. "I'm just getting ready for my teaching next semester on the criminal justice system. However, my specialism focuses on bringing together both psychology and criminology, to understand the deviant behaviour of people in society, not just criminals, but also leaders in a position of power."

"It sounds very interesting. You said in your keynote speech that you liaise with the Metropolitan Police. That must be challenging."

"All I do is work with the evidence, to develop a description of an offender on personality and behavioural traits, ethnicity, gender, age, level of education and sometimes occupation as well as residential area."

"You must be good at what you do."

"I am. I gave the police an accurate description of a serial rapist terrorising young women in and around the London area only last year. From the point of access, I can also determine the area in which the perpetrator lives, which I estimated to the distance of two miles."

"Really."

She laughs. "Really. I've got an interesting case to work on when I go back. I've not received the information yet. It sounds very challenging."

"And what's that?"

"It's confidential, so I can't reveal too much. I'm going to be working with Superintendent Hunter from Police Scotland. You know, the officer at my keynote speech, the DCI who sent your family a letter of apology. That's all I can say at the moment. It's an unsolved case... spanning just over seven years. She was killed in the street apparently with a knife and there were no witnesses."

Bloody hell! It must be Annabel Taylor! I hold my nerve. "I have no doubt that you'll do a fantastic job." I pick up the bottle of wine. "Refill?"

"I'm fine. You have one if you want. I'm just going to the toilet."

"Okay."

As soon as she leaves the room, I take a large swig from the bottle, then another and another, pacing back and forth across the room. *Stay calm. It could be anyone. Don't ask any more questions. If it is, then you'll just have to deal with the situation when the time is right. This is not good. She'll find out everything - the connection between my father and his mistress. One thing for sure, I'll never let anything or anyone come between us, not now.*

I take in a few deep breaths, trying to calm down before she returns. The bedroom door opens. I retrieve the presents from my bag. When I turn round, she is sitting cross-legged on the bed, pulling the sleeves of the jumper over her hands, playing with the cuffs of the fabric.

"Are those for me?" she says, excitedly.

I look around the room. "Well... there's no one else here!"

She laughs.

Dismissing the profiling conversation from my mind, I sit on the bed, watching her tear off the paper to the first present. "It's your new brand of perfume." Spraying a small amount onto her wrists, she smells it and declares, "That *is* me, Jayden." Kristina opens the rest of the gifts which includes a cashmere jumper, candles and a bottle of champagne. "You shouldn't have bought me so much. It must have cost you a fortune!"

"There's just one more," I announce.

"Where?!"

I unclench my hand, spreading out my fingers to reveal a green velvet box. "Here!"

Her eyes light up. "What is it?"

"Open it and find out!"

I take a large mouthful of wine, watching Kristina take off the lid.

She gasps. "It's beautiful."

Mesmerised, she stares at the platinum ring. The oval shaped emerald is surrounded by a stunning collection of small-cut diamonds, the ice cold structure shimmering from deep within the jewel, exposing the minute fissures embedded within the dark green gemstone.

"I decided against silver or gold. I know you don't wear it. Your mother told me your size." *I hope it fits!* "Let me put it on for you."

I take hold of her wrist, slipping it over the third digit on her left hand.

"I love it. It's beautiful."

Throwing her arms around my neck, she pulls me down, smothering me with happy kisses. "Did you like your sweater?" she says, sheepishly.

"Of course I do. I wore it on Christmas Day. I'm wearing it again at New Year."

"That's good. I'm glad!"

"Right Miss Cooper, you take the wine glasses. I'll run us a bath. Then we can get ready for dinner."

She follows me, splaying out her fingers, enthralled by the enchanting ring.

"I know it's all happening so fast, but I do adore you Kristina."

"I know you do."

As we enter the bathroom, I kiss her lips then close the door.

****

Despite the shocking revelation of her work, we have an enjoyable couple of days; eating, sleeping, talking, walking, making love and before we know it, New Year's Eve arrives. I wake up first, watching her intently as she sleeps. I have a surprise planned for Kristina later in the evening. We are going to the theatre in my old university town after dinner, and then we can head back to the village later in the evening. Charles wants to have a small private service in the church before midnight - just the four of us - before we celebrate New Year.

I move closer, kissing her on the back of the neck.

"Good morning, Jayden."

"How are you today, Lady Cooper...?"

"What are talking about?"

"I want to invite you to the theatre tonight to see *Macbeth*. Shall my Lady accompany me?"

She nods her head in agreement. "Of course, my Lord."

My head disappears under the covers. "Something wicked this way comes."

She laughs.

I try to part her legs, my evil tongue wanting to find its pot of pleasure, but she refuses to comply. Placing lots of kisses up her body, my head emerges from the covers. I wink and say, "Fair is foul and foul is fair."

"You're so childish!"

A wicked smile passes across my face. "Let not light see my dark and deep desires."

"Stop talking in riddles. I suspect it's from *Macbeth*. I've read most of his other plays but surprisingly, I never got around to reading that one. I like to read more sinister books about the criminal mind."

"It's very sinister. *Macbeth* is full of murder, mystery and intrigue. He has such a dark criminal mind spurred on by Lady Macbeth. It's one of Shakespeare's deadliest tragedies. I'll see if Charles has a copy in the library. Let's just cuddle up for the rest of the day. I'll make us some breakfast first."

"That would be lovely."

I get out of bed, put on some clothes and head down the stairs. The house is quiet. It is just after twelve. *They've probably gone out*, I think to myself. My fingers follow the lines of books in his study, finding it on the bottom shelf. I make some herbal tea, scramble the eggs and add the thin strips of salmon, prepare the toast then place everything on the tray.

"Can you open the door?"

She is wearing an oversized sweater. Kristina takes the tray from me, bends over and places it on the bedside table, turns around and catches me staring at her naked bottom. She pulls down the jumper, shakes her head and warns me off. "No, no, no! Breakfast, Mr. Scott!" She changes the subject. "You've found the play. I'm intrigued now!"

"I have indeed."

There are still a few embers alight in the fire. I place on some kindling, watching the flames burst into life then top it up with some logs. We eat our breakfast on top of the bed. Briefly, I explain the story. It is one of my favourite tragedies. "The opening scene is dramatic, set against the backdrop of thunder and lightning as three witches plan to meet with Macbeth. He is a soldier, fighting in a great battle. When it's over, they tell him he will become Thane of Cawdor and eventually, King of Scotland. The old hags tell his friend Banquo that his descendants will also become royalty. Soon after, the witches' prophecy comes true as King Duncan announces that Macbeth is to become Thane of Cawdor for his bravery on the battlefield. He visits Macbeth's castle. Consumed by ambition, driven by delusions of grandeur, Macbeth murders King Duncan with his dagger, taking control of the throne. The drama unfolds, taking Macbeth and Lady Macbeth on a journey into a world of utter chaos and paranoia. Despite this madness, his reign of terror persists - killing his close friend Banquo as well as the Thane of Fife's (Macduff) wife and children. To exact revenge, Macduff returns to Scotland persuading Malcolm - the dead King's elder son - that the tyrannical ruler of Scotland killed his father. The bloodthirsty battle that occurs through a civil war, eventually leads to his downfall and the death of Macbeth in a breathtaking finale."

"How exciting, Jayden. I can't believe I've never read it before."

We stay in bed for the rest of the day, pondering over the meaning of Shakespeare's characters' dialogue. It is an intimate yet perfect way to spend our time together. I throw the book across the bed when we are finished. Becoming aware of her naked body underneath the sweater, my hands wander across her curves. Kristina pushes me away as she gets out of bed and announces, "Fair is foul and foul is fair. I'm getting up! Is that fair?"

I pull her back onto the bed. "It's definitely not fair!"

She struggles to free herself from my grasp. I brush my lips across her mouth, teasing with my tongue. Laughing, she shakes her head back and forth. I grip both her wrists with one hand as the other pulls at my jogging trousers, trying to kick them off with my feet. I find that the more she resists, the more aroused I become. My erection is solid. I gradually release my grip. She succumbs, wrapping her arms around my neck, submitting to the sensual touch of my kisses. Kristina's hand reaches for my shaft, pulling the folds of skin up and down over the swollen head of my penis.

Just then, I hear the front door slam.

She stares at me.

We stop dead in our tracks.

"Jayden, we're back from the farmer's market. Are you in?" shouts my mother.

"Perfect bloody timing!" I groan.

"JAYDEN!"

"Yes! I hear you."

"Come down. Help me with the dinner."

I look at Kristina. She pulls a silly face.

The moment has gone.

"Foul not fair!" I declare.

I pull her off the bed then we shower, get dressed and make our way down the stairs. The worktop is packed with fresh produce from the farmer's market.

"Have you both had a good day? What have you been up to?" asks my mother.

Trying not to laugh, I look at Kristina out of the corner of my eye. "We've just been reading *Macbeth*. We're going to the theatre tonight to see it."

"We saw it a few weeks ago. It's a fabulous production by the Royal Shakespeare Company. I'm sure you'll enjoy it. Can you both peel the vegetables for the stir fry? Cut them very thin, so they cook quickly."

I rifle about in the drawer for the peeler. "Where's Charles?"

"He's in the study preparing his service for tonight. It's important to him. He seems more nervous with just the four of us than he would be with an entire congregation."

"I'll just go and see if he's okay. I'll be back in a minute."

Seizing my opportunity, I bound up the stairs to get my cigarettes then knock on the door to the study. "Charles, are you there?"

His voice appears to be mellow. "Come in."

He is sitting at the bureau smoking a cigar, his hand resting on his forehead, contemplating the written words in front of him. "Jayden... sit down, my boy."

I light a cigarette, inhaling a deep breath into my lungs. *God that feels good*, I think to myself. I exhale the smoke out into the air. "Are you okay?"

"I just want it all to be perfect tonight. You all mean so much to me."

"It will be." It is not often that I see him in this state. He is a strong-willed man that likes to be in control, to take charge of his flock, leading them in the right direction. This man of God is normally a pillar of strength, but today he looks troubled. "Charles, please stop worrying about it."

"How I phrase these words tonight, especially as it's a start of a New Year, means everything to me. Your mother means everything to me."

"She knows that."

"If your father walked through that door right now. Who would she choose? I think we both know the answer to this question."

"That will never happen," I tell him.

"How do you know? His shadow follows me about, threatening to return, looming over me on a daily basis. I dread his arrival more than death itself."

"Charles, I need to tell you something."

"What is it?"

"I.... He... Please don't think badly of me."

He reverts to his confident self, holding his breath. "Tell me, boy. What is it?"

"Well... in the last seven years you've been more like a father to me than he ever was... that's what I wanted to say." *I can't believe I was about to tell him!*

He lets out a sigh of relief. "And you are like a son to me. Let's have a whisky. We can leave the girls to it."

I smile. "Whatever you say tonight, we know in here..." I say pounding on my chest, "that what you say, you will say from your heart."

"That's true. Thanks."

He fills up the whisky glasses. We indulge in another smoke.

My mother pops her head around the door, waving her hand in the air, coughing as she comes into the room. "That smoke is like a thick blanket of fog in here!" she declares, marching across to the window. "It's disgusting." She opens it wide. A blast of cold air gushes through the opening. "That's better. Dinner is in five minutes."

He takes hold of her fingers as she passes then kisses the back of her hand.

She smiles, shaking her head. "Don't be late!"

"We better go and help," he chortles, "before we get into serious trouble!"

The meal is delicious. It is a pleasant evening. The time arrives to get ready to go the theatre. We excuse ourselves from the dinner table. I decide to put on my suit. Kristina is wearing a green dress. The bodice tucks into her waist, grips hold of her legs then splays out at the bottom. It complements the subtle makeup, enhances her eyes and matches the emerald ring.

As we go down the stairs, she asks, "You don't think it's over the top do you? Is it too much?"

"It's perfect. Come here."

She steps forward.

I kiss her on the corner of the mouth.

"Right you two, that's enough of that!" he bellows.

He seems back in control, I think to myself.

She puts on a winter coat, wrapping it around her shoulders. We take the coastal road to my old university town and Charles drops us off outside the theatre. Taking hold of her hand, we walk through the door. I notice the sideward glances as we make our way towards the busy reception for some pre-theatre drinks, so I slide my arm around her waist, claiming my territory.

We drink our champagne.

"You look ravishing tonight," I say, kissing her soft skin.

"Thank you. And so do you!" she says, fixing my tie. "Why do you always wear a matching tie to go with my outfit?"

"To show everyone that you're mine."

"Stop being silly. I am yours… you know that."

"You don't notice do you?"

"Notice what?"

"All these predatory men eyeing you up!"

"Don't be silly!"

"If you say so. Finish up your drink. Let's go to our seats. I booked us the best in the house."

She rolls her eyes. "What a surprise!"

We settle down, waiting for the production to start. The lights dim and then, the theatre turns pitch black. There is a deafening silence that seems to go on forever. The curtain rolls up. The noise of thunder bellows out around the auditorium as streaks of lightening momentarily light up the stage, revealing the silhouettes of three old witches kneeling on the ground. One after the other, they sit up, those haggard faces looking around the audience. The cackling voices echo around the theatre.

First witch
When shall we three meet again
In thunder, lightning or rain?

Second witch
When the hurlyburly's done,
When the battle lost and won.

Third witch
That will be ere the set of sun.

First witch
Where the place?

Second witch
Upon the heath.

Third witch
There to meet with Macbeth.

"Are they away to meet him after the battle?" she whispers.
"Yes!"
"How exciting."
"King Duncan hears that his generals Macbeth and Banquo have defeated two invading armies. Then the witches meet them on the heath. That's where they tell him of his fate… that he will one day become King of Scotland. The story will all come together."
She watches intently throughout each scene; the camp scene where King Duncan learns of Macbeth and Banquo's victory, the witches on the moor and the prophecies, Lady Macbeth's obsession to kill King Duncan, his death by Macbeth's blade, King Duncan's sons (Malcom and Donaldain) fleeing from Scotland in fear of their lives, the demise of Banquo, the death of Lady Macbeth, the warning from the witches about the Scottish nobleman Macduff, the slaughter of his family, the civil war and the final moments of his life as

Out Of The Dark

Macduff returns to the stage with Macbeth's head in his hands.

Turning towards me she gasps, "You never told me that bit."

"I didn't want to ruin the ending!"

The cast address King Duncan's son Malcolm on the stage and shout, "**HAIL, KING OF SCOTLAND!**"

The curtain goes down and the lights go up.

"It was fantastic. That is what happens with serial killers. Events just spiral out of control into a spree of frenzied attacks. Don't you agree? I can certainly use *Macbeth* as an anecdote in my lectures."

She is right.

I think about my own situation. *First, I killed my father then Annabel Taylor, that embezzler, the Brazilian and finally, Raymond Cartwright along with his sidekick dealer. Where does it all end? I'm desperate for it all to end now. However... there's Inspector Canmore stirring up trouble, reopening the case, brandishing my father's ring at the memorial, waiting for me to crack. He is a modern-day Macduff. I need to watch myself. He will hunt me down if I'm not careful. I must kill him before my nemesis ruins this new phase of my life with Kristina... just one more. But wait... there's also Superintendent Hunter relying on Kristina's profile of Annabel Taylor's killer...*

"Are you listening?"

"Sorry... it's a great example to use."

"Thank you for bringing me here. Your mother is right. It *was* an amazing production." She kisses me on the lips. "Are you okay?"

I snap out of my reverie. "I'm fine." I check the time. It is ten o'clock. "We can just get a taxi back home. Charles and my mother will be waiting. You know he wants to have a private service, just the four of us before the bells. Do you want to leave now or have another drink first?"

"Let's just make our way back. I need to slip into something more comfortable!" She clutches her stomach, breathes in and says, "This dress is a bit tight!"

"I like it that way."

As the theatre empties, I kiss her on the lips, my hands wandering over the silky fabric of her dress. She gets to me every time, no matter where we are, teasing me with that beautiful body. "Let's get you home, Lady Cooper. I don't want to be too late. Tonight is important to Charles."

The taxis are lined up outside the theatre. It only takes us twenty minutes to reach the village. I help her out of the car and pay the driver.

"We're back," I shout, as we walk through the front door.

They both emerge from the sitting room.

"Did you enjoy it, Kristina?" asks my mother, excitedly.

"It was fantastic. I loved it. I'll speak to you about it once I get changed."

"Remember, we're going over to the church first and then we can hear all about it," he announces. "Half an hour?"

"That's fine," I reassure him.

We make our way up the stairs. As we enter the room, I pull her towards me. "We have some unfinished business from this afternoon to attend to first."

"Later, Jayden."

"No... *now* Lady Cooper."

The room is dark apart from the glow of the fire. I turn her round, unzipping the back of the dress. It falls to the floor. She steps out of the gown. I pick it up, placing it on the bed. She is standing before me in a black strapless bra and panties, the high heels adding to the length of her legs.

She bends down to take them off.

"Keep your shoes on."

At that moment, I feel myself reverting back to my old habits, stirring up feelings inside me that I have tried to contain for the last two years. That bloody play has rekindled memories buried deep within the recess of my mind, igniting my desire to plan, hunt and kill as well as the thrill of releasing myself inside a woman's body. I turn her around, placing her hands on the door. I unclip the bra then pull down her panties. She steps out of them. I take off my clothes then rub my body against her naked frame, spreading her legs further apart. I enter from behind. She feels tight around my cock. Grabbing hold of her hips, I thrust into Kristina's beautiful body... **pounding, pounding, pounding**. An overpowering urge takes hold of me, needing to release myself as quickly as possible.

I hear a voice, but do not hear her words. "Jayden, stop," she whispers. "I don't like this."

The words do not register in my mind.

"Please stop... JAYDEN! STOP!" she cries.

Something snaps me out of my trance. "What is it?" I say, releasing myself from her body.

She turns around, looking deep into my eyes. "I don't like that. I'm not a whore, so stop fucking me like one!"

"I'm sorry. I just got carried away."

She's right. What am I doing? To her, of all people!

I am full of remorse. She sits on the edge of the bed, with an angry look on her face, kicking off the high heeled shoes. Seeing the tears welling up in those beautiful green eyes, I take hold of her fingers, kissing the back of her hand. *Why did I ever treat her like that? Never do that again you fucking idiot*, I tell myself.

She is quiet.

"Are you okay?"

"You're such an intense lover, Jayden. Were you like that with…"

"Don't go there, Kristina. What matters is here and now. Okay?"

"Okay… "

I try to relieve the severity of the situation. "I'm sorry."

She looks at me straight in the eye. "Please, don't EVER do that again."

"I won't. I promise. Am I forgiven?"

"I suppose so."

"I adore you so much. So, so much," I declare.

"I know you do. Let's just forget about it."

"Jayden, are you both coming down," bellows the Reverend.

"We're just coming. We better hurry up. They'll be waiting on us."

We hear someone coming up the stairs.

Kristina bolts off the bed, grabbing her underwear, fumbling about trying to get them over her legs. "Bloody hell," she declares. "Pass my jogging trousers and a t-shirt… *QUICK*!"

I laugh at the scene before me.

"It's not funny! We better go and join them."

"We need take a shower first."

I grab her hand as we run across the landing to the bathroom. I turn on the shower. Five minutes later we are out and dress into some casual clothes. I wear the grey sweater she bought. "Do you like it?" I ask.

"It really suits you," she says, brushing her fingers across the woollen fabric. I love the feel of it." Kristina looks at the emerald ring. "Sorry, I didn't get you anything else."

"You're more than enough," I say, pecking her on the cheek.

Her hair is tied back, but some of it has come loose. To lighten the mood, I say, "Quick... fix your hair out. You look like you've just been fucked!"

"She forces a smile, pinning it back in place.

"Ready?"

"Yes... ready."

****

I hear the familiar tone of his classical music flowing from the sitting room. As we enter, they are both sitting in front of the fire having a drink. "A quick one for the road?" he says.

"That would be nice. I'll have a small whisky, Charles."

"Kristina?"

"A glass of white wine, please."

He heads off to the kitchen.

"How is he?" I ask my mother.

"He's fine. This is our first New Year together. He just wants it to be perfect."

The Reverend returns with a bottle of chilled wine in his hand and two glasses in the other. He pours the drinks. "Here you go. We can leave the clinking of the glasses until the bells. We can head off to the church soon. I need to go and get the key. It's in my study."

"He still seems a bit uptight," I say to my mother.

"Maybe a little."

I polish the whisky off in one go. "I'll be back in a minute." The door to the study is ajar. "Can I come in?"

"Of course."

He is puffing on a cigar with one hand, the metal key in the other. I light a cigarette. The after-sex-smoke fills me with pleasure as I inhale it deep into my lungs. I quickly dismiss the thought of our sexual encounter. It is inappropriate at this moment in time. "Are you not taking your written speech?"

"No, you're right. I need to say what I want to say from my heart." I smile. "You will find the right words."

"I will."

The grandfather clock in the hallway strikes out eleven chimes.

He takes in a sharp breath. "Finish your cigarette. It's time to go."

We get the girls then make the short trip to the church. He turns the key in the lock, pushing open the heavy door. The vestibule is dark. Kristina slips her hand into mine. I hear him shuffling through to the entrance that leads to the back door and then, the sound of a clicking noise as he presses down on the switch.

"We have light," he bellows.

Charles leads us through the doors into his domain. He must have been in here earlier, preparing for our arrival. The lights are low in this part of the building. Leading up to the altar, candles burn in each of the archways. It feels very surreal... almost heavenly. There are also four candles alight on the table next to the bible.

"I want us to gather next to the communion table and my holy book."

We sit on the front pew. I sit on the right, then my mother in the middle and Kristina on the other side. He lifts over a wooden chair, sitting down in front of us. Charles leans forward, stretching out his hands. We take hold of them, huddled together, waiting for his words.

"I am blessed - blessed to have you all here. God has answered my prayers. Until you became part of my life Carolyn, the love I felt deep inside my soul was... how shall I put it? Yes... vacuous, devoid of any kind of meaning. My love for Him will never change. My love for you blossoms inside my heart, growing that little bit more every day. Jayden, you are like a son to me, you know that. I am so proud of you, for the man you have become... considering your past. And our beautiful Kristina, you have brought so much joy into our lives, into Jayden's life. You both deserve happiness. It is such an elusive thing to find. It comes from deep within our hearts and that - that is where we experience true happiness. You bring that into my life. All of you, every moment of every day."

He lets go of our hands, leaning back on the chair. My mother gets up, kneeling down in front of him. Tears trickle down her cheeks. She gasps. "Charles, we love you dearly. That was beautiful."

I turn to look at Kristina. She tries to hold back the tears. My hand reaches into my pocket. I place my mobile phone on the wooden bench and give her the handkerchief.

"Charles, we'll see you back at the house." I tell him. "Are you okay? That was very sincere, extremely heartfelt. You're a good man," I say, squeezing his shoulder.

"I'm fine, my boy."

I take hold of Kristina's hand. "We'll see you soon."

As we are walking back to the house, she stifles back the tears. "That man has a way with words that reaches out and touches your very soul!"

"What a speech. He means every word of it. Every… single… word. Are you okay?"

"I'm fine. I need to get a grip of myself."

Trying to lighten the moment, I say, "You can take a grip of me later!"

"Behave yourself! Why does everything always end up in the gutter in your mind?"

"Because I'm riding on the tail of a sewer rat. I'm a filthy, ravenous rodent, seeking out a furry friend to satisfy my dirty habits."

She laughs. "A furry friend… you have such a way with words!"

I swing her around before planting a huge kiss on her lips. "Are you feeling a bit better?"

"Yes. Thanks for snapping me out of it, you dirty rat!"

Once we are in the house, I pour us both a drink. "It's not long before the start of the New Year, just another half an hour to go."

She takes a sip of wine. "It's so exciting. I'm going to text a few people just now. The messages just get jammed after twelve o'clock. I don't mean to be rude."

"I think I'll do the same." I reach into my pocket. "Damn! I've left my phone in the church. I'll be back in a minute."

I sprint down the gravel path, passing my mother and Charles walking hand in hand towards the house. "I've left my phone. I'll be back in a minute!"

"I've locked the front door. Go in the side entrance. It's open," he says.

I am out of breath as I reach the back of the church. Pushing the door open, I peer inside. It is very dark. My hands run along the side of the wall, my fingers resting on the switch. I push it down. Light floods into the tiny corridor. On entering, the candles have been extinguished. As I walk down the aisle, shadows loom out from the deepest, darkest recesses of the church. Feeling uneasy, my sole purpose is to retrieve my mobile phone and leave. It is still there. I pick it up off the wooden bench. A faint flicker of light still glows from one of the candles on the communion table. As I take a deep breath to blow it out, my eyes rest upon his bible. It is a combination of the Old and New Testament, outlining the years before and after Christ. Thinking about my mother that day in the church, my fingers reach towards the leather cover. *What she was reading? I suppose I'll never know.* I flick it open. My eyes wander over the text. It is the King James Version - written in much the same way as a Shakespearian play, and there, right there it says:

"And the man that committeth adultery with another man's wife, even he that committeth adultery with his neighbour's wife, the adulterer and the adulteress shall surely be put to death."

(Leviticus 20:10)

I catch my breath, thinking about my father. I take out the wooden cross in my pocket, stroking the smooth surface, pondering over these words.

"There," I cry out, looking up at the ceiling, "you say it in your bible. My father committed the sinful act of adultery all of his life on numerous occasions. He was even guilty of it with his neighbour's wife - with Rachel Fleming - cheating on my mother, tearing at her heart, breaking her will and torturing her soul. I hated him! In your own words, you tell me he shall surely be put to death. Well... he died by my very own hand. I do not want forgiveness for my sinful life. What I am searching for is resolution so I may find happiness and peace with Kristina Cooper. That is what I seek. Through your words, I believe that is a sign. Is it a sign? Tell me!" I drop to my knees in the middle of the aisle and mutter, "Redemption. That's all I want."

I wait for some kind of response.

The deafening silence is unbearable.

And it comes.

The sputtering candle flickers then teeters out, the black tendrils of smoke drifting up into the air. It is like my father's dark soul is being consumed by the Reverend's God.

A feeling of jubilation passes through my body. "Thank you," I whisper.

Just then, I hear a faint tinkling noise, like a piece of metal, falling onto the stone floor of the church.

"Who's there," I shout.

Silence.

Becoming paranoid, I turn this way, then the other, swirling around staring into the shadows.

Silence.

I get up off my knees and walk down the aisle, push open the doors and follow the corridor to the back entrance. I flick off the switch. It is five minutes to midnight. I run up the path then go into the house. Out of breath, I shout, "Sorry, it's taken me so long."

My mother appears at the sitting room door. "Hurry up! We've only got a few minutes. She hands me a glass of whisky. "Where's Charles?"

"Why are you asking me? "He went down to the church to get you. Did you not see him?"

For fuck sake! "I never saw him." *But I heard him.*

"Where is he?" she sighs.

Just then, the first four chimes of the bell blasts out from the grandfather clock in the hallway.

DONG… DONG… DONG… DONG…

The front door slams shut.

DONG… DONG… DONG…

I hear his footsteps on the stone floor.

DONG… DONG… DONG…

"Hurry up, Charles, before the last bell goes off," shouts my mother.

DONG…

The door opens to the sitting room.

DONG!

ABOUT THE AUTHOR

Marshall Hughes is a marketing lecturer in Edinburgh. Areas of expertise include how the work environment enhances or constrains creativity/innovation within the advertising sector as well as a fascination with the tantalising, creative minds that generate and produce inspirational ideas, products, services and media campaigns. Academic life aside, the author was brought up in a beautiful town with its gorgeous beaches and tranquil setting situated on the east coast of Scotland. The inspiration and motivation behind the compelling story transpires from the experiences, psychological challenges of life and somewhat morbid fascination with some of the most notorious serial killers the world has ever seen.

Made in the USA
Charleston, SC
10 March 2016